Dear Logan,

When I see you, it's all I can do not to melt into a puddle of desire. I want to know how it feels to have your hands on me. And to know how it feels to touch you, as well. All over. With you, I yearn to let go of all my fears and inhibitions and just do what my body urges me to. You are my dream, my fantasy. And with each passing day I wonder more and more if it can ever come true. I only hope and pray I can somehow find the courage to tell you who I am. Soon. Before it's too late.

Your Secret Admirer

By Toni Blake

TONI BLAKE

WILLOW SPRINGS

A DESTINY NOVEL

AVON

An Imprint of HarperCollinsPublishers

This is a work of fiction. Names, characters, places, and incidents are products of the author's imagination or are used fictitiously and are not to be construed as real. Any resemblance to actual events, locales, organizations, or persons, living or dead, is entirely coincidental.

AVON BOOKS
An Imprint of HarperCollins*Publishers*
10 East 53rd Street
New York, New York 10022–5299

Copyright © 2012 by Toni Herzog
ISBN 978–0–06–202461–9
www.avonromance.com

First Avon Books mass market printing: July 2012

Avon Trademark Reg. U.S. Pat. Off. and in Other Countries, Marca Registrada, Hecho en U.S.A.
HarperCollins® is a registered trademark of HarperCollins Publishers.

Printed in the U.S.A.

10 9 8 7 6 5 4 3 2 1

*To every girl who ever felt
plain, overlooked, or underappreciated,
this book is for you.*

Acknowledgments

$\mathcal{M}$y sincere and heartfelt thanks, as usual, go to Lindsey Faber, for her brainstorming help and story discussions, and to Renee Norris, for her feedback as my "first reader." Thanks to Renee, as well, for her helpful insights on the fire-related scenes.

Additionally, thank you to my editor, May Chen, and everyone at Avon, and to my agents, Meg Ruley and Christina Hogrebe, for all your support and enthusiasm for the Destiny series.

And finally, thank you to the Boone County Arboretum, aka Central Park, in northern Kentucky, where the bulk of this book was written, for providing such a peaceful, relaxing outdoor spot where I found an enormous amount of inspiration for Amy and Logan's story.

"You will be an old maid! And that's so dreadful!"

Jane Austen, from *Emma*

Prologue

"Meow."

Amy Bright stood next to the trunk of the old maple tree in her mother's front yard peering up into the branches, heavy and green with spring foliage. She could just barely make out the gray-and-white cat's tail peeking from between the leaves far above.

"Knightley, you come down from there right now," she said, head tilted back, her tone more encouraging than harsh. As frustrating as it was to have her cat stuck up a tree, she knew Mr. Knightley—named for the Jane Austen character—was probably frightened. And she hoped the sound of her voice might at once calm him and persuade him to make his way down.

But in response, her beloved kitty only let out another desperate-sounding "Meow."

Amy sighed, knowing what had to be done, much as

she didn't want to do it. She'd been trying to lure the cat down for over half an hour, after all, and he hadn't budged. And he was on a branch way too high for her reach, even if she dared to climb.

So she pulled out her cell phone, cast a last annoyed glance up at the furry tail dangling overhead, and dialed her old friend Logan Whitaker, who happened to be a fireman. And who she also knew was on duty at the Destiny firehouse today.

"What's up, freckles?" he answered cheerfully, clearly having seen that it was her. But he probably wouldn't stay so cheerful when he heard the reason why.

"Well . . . it's Mr. Knightley. He's stuck in my mom's maple tree."

Silence met her on the other end of the line before Logan finally replied in a dry voice. "You're kidding me, right?"

Because they'd had this conversation before. This wasn't the first cat rescue call she'd had to make to the Destiny Fire Department. Generally, Mr. Knightley was an indoor cat—and as a result, when he ended up outside for any reason, trouble often ensued. And she knew Logan disliked using town resources and taxpayer money to get her cat out of a tree, which she completely understood. But she still had to get Mr. Knightley down somehow, and if you couldn't call on one of your closest friends in the world for help, who could you call on? And it was a really tall tree.

"Mom was on cat-sitting duty this weekend while I went to Cincinnati with Rachel and Tessa." Both of her best girlfriends were getting married this summer and they'd gone on an overnight shopping trip, which had included a gown fitting for Rachel. And though Tessa's wedding would be a smaller affair than Rachel's, yesterday she'd succeeded in finding a simple lace dress that fit her slightly-Bohemian-yet-feminine fashion sense. "When I came by to pick him up," Amy went on, "he ran up the tree."

Now it was Logan who sighed, even as he said, "We're on our way. But one of these days, I'm buying you a leash for that cat."

"Thanks, Logan," she said with heartfelt sincerity before disconnecting. And though she had, of course, thought about a leash for Mr. Knightley's outdoor excursions, she just didn't like the idea. Life could hold you captive in so many ways—so she didn't like the notion of adding one more, even for her kitty.

As she waited for Logan then, an inexplicable sense of melancholy came washing over her. *Because your cat's up a tree? Because you were embarrassed to call the fire department?*

But no, it wasn't either of those things. It was . . . life. The sense that it was passing her by.

She was thirty-four years old, after all, and other than a few trips to the city with her friends, she'd barely set foot outside Destiny. And now her friends were getting married, starting romantic new lives that would demote her to fifth wheel status. And as for romance of her own . . . well, it had been painfully hard to come by and she had no reason to think that would change anytime soon.

Ugh. Stop this. It's not who you are. Amy was usually happy, upbeat, good at finding the sunny side of any situation. She'd always been that way—thankful for the blessings life had brought her, content and comfortable with her small town Destiny existence. Joy came naturally to her. So at a moment like this, when sadness crept in, it left her disoriented and at a loss for how to deal with it.

Fortunately, though, her spirits were lifted when, a few minutes later, she looked up to see a red fire engine rumbling around the bend on Meadowview Highway where her mother's house was located. Logan's mom still lived in the small cottage next door—and though the home of Logan's best friend, Mike Romo, sat up the road just a football field's length away, the two small houses where Logan and Amy had grown up were located side by side, a stone's throw apart.

"Meow," Mr. Knightley said from above.

"Help's on the way," she called up into the leaves.

For both of them, she thought. Because seeing Logan would surely distract her from her weird mood and lift her spirits. *Everything will be fine.* She was sincerely happy for her girlfriends, after all. As the unofficial town matchmaker, Amy delighted in seeing other people find romance even if she herself had not.

A couple of the other local firemen lifted their hands in waves to her, but as Logan stepped off the truck in his firefighting gear, it was *his* smile that warmed her heart. He was a lot like her—a generally amiable guy who always looked on the bright side—so no wonder they had such a solid, long-standing friendship.

A moment later, Amy pointed out the cat tail high up in the tree. And as Logan moved back toward the fire engine, ready to extend the attached ladder, he said playfully over his shoulder, "Gonna owe me a piece of pie for this, freckles."

That was how they traditionally paid off favors to each other, with pie at Dolly's Main Street Café. "You got it," she told him.

Then she watched as Logan worked his magic—
maneuvering the long ladder into the tree, toward the
highest branches, soon disappearing up into the foliage
himself, only his legs visible . . . until he emerged with
Mr. Knightley tucked securely in his arms.

Something about the sight sent a gentle pang of profound gratitude stretching through Amy's whole being.
She knew she really had no reason to be feeling down,
but getting her kitty safely back, delivered by the good,
capable man she'd felt close to for her whole life, seemed
. . . well, like the most wonderful gift life could give her
at the moment. Sometimes it was the little things.

As Logan transferred the cat from his grasp into hers,
their hands brushed together and she caught his musky
male scent. "Thank you," she told him, meeting his blue
eyes with her gaze and hoping it relayed the depth of her
appreciation.

He tilted his head, offering up a half grin. "For you,
freckles, anything." Then he pointed chidingly down at
Mr. Knightley. "And you, stay out of trees."

Just then, the two-way radio attached to Logan's hip
buzzed and, shifting immediately into work mode, he
snatched it up and spoke into it to dispatch. "What's happening, Jeanie?"

"House fire on Whisper Falls Road," Jeanie said, the
words masked just slightly with static. "Last house in the
valley before you reach the bridge."

"Shit," Logan murmured to himself. "That's the
Knight house." Everyone in Destiny knew the Knight
family, and Logan's reaction reminded Amy that the
Knights had been especially close with Logan's family
back when she and Logan were kids.

"It's a bad one," Jeanie added then. "Better hurry."

As Logan rushed back to the engine, his concern evident in his stride, Amy called, "Thanks! And be careful!" behind him.

Maybe someday I'll be lucky enough to end up with . . . a man that good. Maybe.

Although guys like Logan were few and far between, and as the red fire engine roared away a few seconds later, siren wailing, Amy knew in her heart that her chances for finding true love in Destiny were growing bleaker by the day.

A few minutes were sufficient for making her acquainted with her own heart.

Jane Austen, from *Emma*

One

As Amy pulled into the driveway next to the little green cottage that faced Blue Valley Lake, she noticed the fading yellow tulips beneath one window and thought they were the only bright thing about the small home right now. Even the willow trees—one next to the water, the other closer to the house—seemed more droopy than usual. It was as if the home itself had joined in Logan's mood.

It had been a month since the fire at the Knight place had burned the house to the ground. A month since Ken and Doreen Knight had died there. Both had been suffering from spring allergies and had taken a nap together in their upstairs bedroom that tragic evening. The community still reeled from the loss, and poor Christy Knight—their only child who'd been away at college at the time—had been left parentless.

It had been no one's fault. Old wiring had started the fire in the kitchen, and flames had quickly engulfed the home with the help of a spring breeze whipping through the valley below Whisper Falls. Turned out that Amy's friend Tessa, who lived near the falls, had been the one to spot the fire and call 9–1–1.

But Logan had taken the deaths unusually hard. He hadn't worked since then. He'd barely left the usually cheerful cottage, in fact. Despite having been trained to deal with this kind of loss, the deaths of his old family friends had thrown him into a deep, dark depression unlike any Amy had ever seen.

So she wasn't particularly happy to be here. But someone had to feed the dog and make sure Logan was still alive in there. She and Mike Romo had been taking turns, yet Mike's patience—which was not his strong suit to begin with—was reaching its end.

The cottage lay quiet as death as she ascended the small front porch and knocked.

Inside, Cocoa, Logan's chocolate lab, barked in response. But when no one came to the door, she knocked again, harder. And she *kept* knocking. *Her* patience was wearing pretty thin, too.

When finally the door opened, the guy on the other side looked more like a homeless derelict than her good, dependable friend. His dark blond hair, usually neat and attractive, needed a serious trim and pointed in all directions. And though he'd been known to sometimes go a few days without shaving, at the moment his handsome face lay hidden beneath a scraggly beard that left him almost unrecognizable—except for his pretty blue eyes.

"You look awful," she said.

"Thanks," he replied. "Go away."

At any other time in their relationship, Amy might have been offended, but this was how Logan greeted anyone who came by these days. So instead, she just opened the screen door and shoved her way inside, picking up the odor of beer that wafted from him as she passed by.

"How much have you had to drink today?"

"Don't know," he replied, his tone implying that he also didn't care. Up until the last several weeks, Logan had only drunk socially—with friends at the local watering hole, the Dew Drop Inn, or after a summer softball game at Creekside Park. But unfortunately, he'd had a large stockpile of beer left over from a party at his place a couple of months ago—and Amy only hoped it would run out soon.

After greeting Cocoa, who was clearly starved for attention, she set her purse on the coffee table and took in her surroundings. Like Logan himself, the place was a mess—with dirty dishes, empty beer cans, and take-out bags left behind from the fast food Mike had been dropping off. At first, Amy had been happy to pitch in and clean up after Logan, but at this point she was beginning to feel like an enabler, so she decided to focus on the one positive she saw. Looking him up and down, she said, "You changed clothes." The gray tee and blue jeans he now wore were a switch from her previous couple of visits.

As he plopped back on the couch where, as far as she could tell, he spent most of his time sleeping or staring mindlessly at the TV, he only shrugged. "Others stank."

"Did you take a shower, too?" she asked hopefully.

Another shrug from the couch. "Couple days ago. No energy."

He looked so sad, empty, that it almost made Amy

want to cry. While it was getting easy to be fed up with him, easy to demand he snap out of this once and for all, at the same time it broke her heart to peer into his once vibrant blue eyes and see that, quite simply, the light had gone out of them.

Rather than let herself get weepy, though, she decided to do something more practical. Mike had just delivered a large bag of dog food last week, so she filled Cocoa's bowl, then ran fresh water in the water dish and returned it to its spot on the floor. But as the chocolate lab— usually Logan's pride and joy ever since he'd gotten her as a puppy last year—rushed to gobble down the food, it only made Amy mad all over again. Clearly the dog hadn't been fed since she'd last done it two days ago. And while she'd tried to be nice to Logan through these past weeks, it was time for a little tough love.

As she approached the couch, taking a seat next to him, she said, "I didn't bring you anything to eat."

When this produced only another shrug, however— and the truth was, he didn't seem nearly as concerned with food as Cocoa did—she added, "And don't be expecting any more hamburgers from Mike, either. He's tired of babysitting you, Logan. And you know your mother can't do it, either." Mrs. Whitaker was getting older, and arthritis had her moving a lot slower these days. In fact, Mike and Amy had both done their best to keep the severity of Logan's condition from her lately.

"So it comes down to this," Amy went on. "I'm really all you've got left. And I'm afraid that if I keep coming over here, helping you out, it's not doing you any favors."

"I never *asked* anyone to come over," he reminded her glumly. "I always tell you to go away, remember?"

Darn it, he had her there. "True. But Logan . . ."

Exasperation gripped her as she motioned to where Cocoa still wolfed down her food, visible through the wide doorway that led to the kitchen. "You're not only neglecting yourself—you're neglecting your dog, too. And none of this is her fault. And—" She stopped, sighed, her frustration reaching an all-time high. "And I'm really worried about you. I don't know what exactly happened to you at that fire, because you won't tell me or anyone else, but the one thing I do know is that you've got to snap out of this. *Now.* You've got to wake up, *clean* up, and start living your life again. Once and for all. Got it?"

Next to her, though, Logan just sat there, looking as depleted as he had for the past month. The only thing different was that this time he turned to look her in the eye. And her heart crumbled in her chest all over again at what she saw on his face. One lone tear rolled down his cheek.

"It was awful," he told her in a raspy whisper. "I can't get it out of my head."

And it wasn't so much what he'd said that affected her as much as the starkly haunted look in his eyes. She even heard a short gasp escape her before she hurried to say, "But you did everything you could. And now you have to let it go."

Yet that quickly, she could tell Logan didn't see her anymore—he was clearly seeing something much worse in his mind. "Can't," he said absently. "Just can't."

And all Amy could do was let out a long, heartsick sigh. She couldn't imagine what he'd gone through that night, and despite herself, in that moment she thought that if he needed her to take care of him forever because of this, she would. She cared for him that much. "Oh

Logan," she finally breathed. They were the only words she could find, however useless.

And as another tear made a wet line down his opposite cheek, she followed the instinct to pull him into a hug. She didn't care if he was messy and unshowered. She didn't care if he smelled like beer. She only knew the compulsion to comfort him somehow.

When Logan's muscular arms closed warmly around her, she knew he needed the hug as badly as she'd needed to give it to him. And she wondered then—had anyone hugged Logan lately? Or was everyone just leaving him alone, getting fed up with him? It made her embrace him a little tighter, move her palms reassuringly across his back through his T-shirt. He held her tighter, too, and they stayed like that for a long moment—until finally she murmured in his ear, "Wish I could make you feel better."

He pulled back just slightly, just enough so that he could whisper in her ear, "I know."

And she felt the bond between them deepen, felt all the years of their friendship stretching between them; and she knew he was glad she was there, glad he'd made her understand the nightmare he was living in right now.

"It'll get better, Logan, I promise," she told him, their cheeks touching. And she became strangely aware that she wanted to just stay that way. For as long as she could.

That was when she felt his mouth, his lips. Just in front of her ear. He'd pressed a kiss there.

It threw her a little, made her suck in her breath. Because she felt the kiss . . . well, in places she didn't usually feel things in response to Logan. Like in her breasts. And her inner thighs.

But then again, Logan had never kissed her before.

Not even like this, on the cheek. As warm and long-lasting as their friendship was, their hugs were the short kind you exchange at a Christmas gathering or . . . she thought he'd probably given her one of those little hugs at her high school graduation, a year after his. Even at his father's funeral seven years ago, the hug had been solid but . . . brief.

Still, surely this kiss he'd just given her was . . . like a small hug. A way of expressing their closeness, a way of saying he appreciated her comfort.

And she might have gone her whole life easily believing that—if he hadn't then kissed her again, just above where the last one had landed. And then a third time, higher up on her cheek. And that one tingled all through her like the last glimmering bits of light from Fourth of July fireworks wafting through the sky. It had been far too long since she'd been kissed.

It made her turn her head to look at him, meet his gaze. But she wasn't sure their eyes, faces, had ever been that close before, and something about it was . . . shockingly intense. It made her lower her gaze—to his mouth.

And that was when he kissed her once more, this time on the lips. She hadn't seen it coming—firm, almost hard, and lingering—but this one felt more like the actual fireworks themselves, right at the moment they exploded in a starburst of little glowing, colored flames.

She didn't kiss him back really—either because she'd practically forgotten how or because she was so stunned and confused by this turn of events. But when he kissed her yet again, just as firmly yet longer this time, she found herself sinking into it, letting herself soak it up, and soon she even began to respond. It wasn't a conscious decision—she could barely think at the moment, after all—but her mouth began moving against his, just a little, trying it on for size, trying to find the rhythm of his kiss.

The next thing she knew, Logan was leaning against her, his chest to her breasts, lying her back onto the couch until they were stretched out there, his body angled over hers, still kissing the whole while. And the longer he kissed her, the less weird it began to feel, and the more . . . wonderful. Consuming. Almost overwhelming. In a good way.

She couldn't have cared less that he tasted like beer. She no longer even noticed how unkempt he was. Because this was Logan, her friend for her whole life, and that was what made this so . . . oddly easy even at the same time as it was strange. This was Logan, and with him everything was okay, always. Even kissing, it turned out.

Though that was when he suddenly stopped, pulled back, looked at her.

Shock overtook his expression.

Until finally he sat abruptly up and said, "Jesus, Amy, I'm sorry. I'm so damn sorry."

Amy just lay there, stunned all over again, this time for a different reason. A minute ago it had made no sense that Logan was kissing her, and now . . . well, now it made no sense that he'd quit. And that his eyes appeared almost horror-filled.

She swallowed nervously, embarrassed. Was it that awful to have kissed her?

Yet . . . maybe that was part of why it had caught her so off guard in the first place. As close as they were, Amy just wasn't the kind of girl Logan kissed. Logan dated girls who were prettier than her, sexier than her, all around hotter than her. And she dated . . . no one.

"It's . . . it's all right," she said softly. Mainly just to say something, fill the dead air, try to bring this weirdness to a close somehow.

"I . . . don't know what I was thinking. Didn't know what I was doing. I guess I just . . . got confused and thought you were somebody else. I'm kinda drunk," he added at the end.

Oh good. She was only kissable if he thought she was somebody else. And when he was drunk. And even then, he regretted it afterward. She let out a sigh.

But don't look at it that way. He's apologizing because you're friends. Purely platonic friends, always. And because it was *a weird thing for him to do. He's apologizing because he cares about you.* And apparently hadn't noticed that she'd been completely into it, too.

But she decided not to think about it that deeply right now. Right now, the important thing was to get out of this situation with their friendship intact. So it seemed like a good time to sit up, as well. "It's okay," she assured him once more after she was upright. She adjusted her top slightly and brushed her palms down over the thighs of her khaki capris as if to straighten them. "It's no big deal. We'll just . . . sort of forget it happened."

He cocked a surprisingly endearing half grin in her direction. "Shouldn't be a problem—since I forget a lot of stuff lately."

She pointed to the nearest beer can, trying to keep things light. "Drunk people often do."

Yet his smile faded. "I gotta stop that, don't I?"

She nodded. "Yes. Please."

"I'm really sorry, Amy," he told her again. And her chest tightened at how sad that made her. She couldn't believe how much she didn't *want* him to be sorry.

But what was she thinking? Of course he was sorry.

Of course it was crazy for them to be kissing. Of course it was some bizarre aberration brought on by alcohol and depression and comfort. And she would forget how good those kisses had felt soon enough. She would *make* herself forget. Because it was the only practical move here.

"I should go," she said, pushing to her feet.

"Okay," he said. And despite herself, she couldn't help thinking how nice it would have been if he'd tried to stop her, if he'd wanted her to stay. Clearly, they both thought it was a good idea to put this particular encounter behind them quickly.

"In the meantime, promise me you'll make yourself take a shower before the day is through. Maybe take a walk outside, or down to the dock. It's nice out. You should get out, get some fresh air."

"Get sobered up," he added.

And she nodded.

"Okay, freckles, I'll try."

"Don't just try. Promise, Logan. For me."

"All right, I promise. For you."

"I'll call you tomorrow. And you'll answer the phone, right?" Another thing Logan had stopped doing lately.

He gave her a solemn nod even though he still looked drained and sad. "I'll answer. And I'll try to be better, *do* better. I know you're right, I know I gotta shake this."

And it occurred to her then that, in a way, it was as if he himself had been perishing in the flames—in his mind—ever since that fire, albeit in a whole different way than Ken and Doreen Knight. And she almost wanted to hug him again—but that just seemed like a bad idea. So she simply said, "Yes, you do. And spend some time petting your dog. She misses you. We all do."

"You, too?" he asked. And something in her heart fluttered—just for a fraction of a second.

Even though she knew the question really meant nothing.

"Of course," she said. "Me, too."

Amy's commute to work every day was a short one. She needed only to exit the second floor apartment over Under the Covers—the bookstore she owned right across from the Destiny town square—walk down the steps, and unlock the front door.

Only today, she felt weird. Like she didn't particularly want to be around people for some reason. And Amy was a born people person, so what was going on here?

Ever since leaving Logan's house last night, her emotions were all over the place. She shifted from worrying about him to feeling terrible about what he'd endured. She flip-flopped from being embarrassed about the kissing to feeling almost . . . well, strangely giddy about it. *Because it's been a long time since you've been kissed, that's all.* And a girl *needed* to be kissed every now and then.

But her giddiness had nothing to do with . . . well, with Logan himself. Right? Even if he *had* stayed on her mind constantly since the moment she'd left his place. She was pretty sure she'd even thought about him while she'd slept. Not that she'd slept *much*.

Shoving the key in the lock on the front door, she gave her head a brisk shake. This was going to be a long day. A long, *weird* day.

No sooner had she stepped inside than she had a pretty little tabby cat twining around her ankles, mewing like there was no tomorrow. "Yes, good morning to you, too, Austen. I'll be happy to get you some Meow Mix if you'll stop trying to trip me, okay?"

The bookstore had become the unofficial drop-off center for unwanted cats over the last few years, but Amy didn't mind—not only did she love cats, but she'd been successful in finding good homes for every stray that had made its way through Under the Covers' front door. Austen was a relatively new arrival, showing up only a week ago—she'd heard the caterwauling outside one night while re-watching *Sense and Sensibility* for probably the hundredth time. And since only a cat—or maybe a kiss—would have a strong enough impact to make her pause *S&S* or any other Jane Austen classic, she'd decided Austen was a fitting name for the female kitty. "You're very needy, though," she criticized the cat now as it wove figure eights around her feet.

Not that she really minded a little neediness. Be it cats or people, she understood that the world could be a scary, lonely place sometimes, and she was happy to do what she could to alleviate that.

What had started out as a pretty May morning in the heart of Destiny soon turned gloomy and drizzly outside, keeping most customers away. And though normally a day this slow might bum her out a little, she found that today it suited her just fine. Since she hadn't particularly felt like being her usual social, chatty self anyway.

On the other hand, though, she realized she must feel like chatting at least a little when she found herself curled up with Austen in one of the easy chairs near the front door, trying to talk out her confusion. "What's going on with me?" she asked the cat. "It's like I feel . . . wonderful and awful at the same time when I think about Logan. Which suddenly seems to be . . . nonstop. And how can I feel good *at all* given everything he's dealing with? Is that terrible? For me to get all tingly every time I remember that kiss? And oh my God, Austen—this is Logan! My buddy, my pal! And I'm feeling tingly about him? That's crazy. Isn't it?"

Of course, Austen couldn't answer, so that kept the conversation short. But Amy still felt just as out of sorts when Tessa walked in to start her noon shift, carrying a pretty flowered umbrella. Tessa was in the midst of building a thriving interior decorating business, but she'd worked at the bookstore with Amy since returning to Destiny several years ago, and she continued to help her out a few days a week. "What's wrong?" Tessa asked instantly.

"Wrong? Why do you think something's wrong?" Amy had had no idea it was that obvious.

Tessa tilted her head first one way, then the other, clearly assessing her own observation. "You're not smiling. In fact, you even look sad. And that's not like you."

Amy hadn't considered whether or not to share the Logan incident with anyone, but if she picked any of her friends to tell, it would be Tessa, who she'd grown particularly close to these past years. Still, she felt ill-prepared for such a conversation, so she decided to keep it to herself for now. "Must be the rainy day bringing me down a little, that's all." Then she pasted on a smile, realizing even as she did so how easy it was. To pretend everything was fine. And it made her wonder: How long had she been doing that? How long had things maybe really *not* been fine deep down inside her? And what was it that really wasn't fine? "So . . . do you still love your dress?" Suddenly, wedding talk seemed the easiest route.

And as had been Amy's intent, the question sent a big smile unfurling across Tessa's face. "More than love it. It's perfect!" Tessa and her fiancé—big, bad, sexy biker dude Lucky Romo—were planning a small ceremony on the deck of her cabin, and Amy thought the wooded setting a beautiful, intimate place for their "I do"s.

"And I still think the plan we worked out on the drive back from Cincinnati is perfect, don't you?" Tessa went on. "You'll be my maid of honor, I'll be Rachel's, and Rachel will be yours when the time comes."

With the three girls being equally close friends, the maid of honor situation had seemed tricky at best, and something they'd toiled over after Rachel, and then Tessa, had gotten engaged. And yeah, sure, this had sounded like a fine way to deal with it when they'd talked about it a month ago, but now, suddenly, the solution made Amy feel . . . like a loser. And she was pretty sure her face had just reshaped itself into a big, fat grimace. Right before she blurted out, "Except that Rachel's getting a rotten deal. Because I'll *never* get married!" And then she slumped in her chair, feeling doomed to spinsterhood in Destiny in a way she never had before.

Above her, Tessa just blinked in astonishment. "What are you talking about? Of course you'll get married!"

But Amy just gave her a look and said, "Come on, Tessa—you don't have to be nice and pretend. We all know I don't date. I haven't dated anyone since Carl, after high school." Carl had been her only boyfriend ever, from Crestview, the next town over. And he'd been nice, and they'd been semi-serious for a year or so, but then things had fizzled—and though a guy or two had asked Amy out after that, she just hadn't felt that *zing,* that charge of chemistry she knew had to be there, and she'd turned them down. And been dateless ever since.

"Well, so what?" Tessa said hopefully anyway, clearly being a good, supportive, encouraging friend. "There are plenty of fish in the sea and you'll find the right fish one of these days."

Amy tried to smile at Tessa's hope—but it was hard. Mostly, she chose not to think about the lack of romance in her life. She tried to project her romantic tendencies on others—fixing them up, pointing out the obvious matches that they didn't always see. And the rest of the time, she let herself get swept away by the romantic stories of Jane Austen, where the endings were always happy, even if fictional. It was easier to focus on other people's happy endings than on her own loneliness.

Finally, after a long moment, she said something so honest to Tessa that it was the first time she'd ever realized how true it was. "I used to think that. But I'm just not sure I believe it anymore. I'm not sure I'm meant to have that kind of happiness."

Tessa's face fell as she instantly knelt next to Amy's chair. "Of course you are, Ames. Everyone is. I went through a long drought myself if you recall, and felt pretty undateable. But then Lucky came along and all that changed in the blink of an eye." Then she shook her head, obviously befuddled by Amy's attitude. "What on earth brought this on?"

Amy tried to swallow back all the emotion that rushed through her in response to the question even as she heard herself admit, "Something happened."

"Something happened?" Tessa asked.

"With Logan," Amy told her.

Tessa's eyebrows shot up as she moved smoothly into

the overstuffed chair across from Amy's and leaned forward, her gaze wide. "Start talking."

So Amy took a deep breath, and then she talked. She told Tessa the whole story of how Logan had kissed her but then afterward acted like she had the plague or something. Only Tessa didn't seem to hear the part about the plague. Instead, she seemed . . . unaccountably overjoyed. "Oh my God, this is so great! I mean, could it be any greater?"

Now it was Amy who blinked her astonishment. "Um, yes. Yes, it could be."

"Because you and Logan know each other so well! You've already got all of that behind you! You know each other's families and backgrounds, you know who the other is deep inside, you know the kind of life each other has lived and wants to live in the future. I mean, Lucky and I had problems with some of that stuff—and it counts for a lot. All you and Logan have to do is get past the awkward friends-to-lovers transition and then you'll have it made."

Amy just stared at her friend, feeling like they'd done a role reversal. It was usually Amy who saw everyone's relationships through rose-colored glasses, refusing to acknowledge the difficult parts. But now she was viewing things from the other side. "Except for one fairly important thing," she told Tessa. "He doesn't want to go from friends to lovers. Because he doesn't see me as a lover—only as a friend."

"But he didn't kiss you like a friend, right?"

"No." He'd kissed her like . . . like she'd always dreamed of being kissed. "But he also said he must have thought I was someone else. I think he sees me as . . . more of a sister."

At this, however, Tessa just made a face. "I think he said that just to cover up because it caught him off guard. And I'm sure you're exaggerating the part about him acting like you had the plague." Then she gave her head an inquisitive tilt. "But before we go any further, let's back up a minute and answer the most important question here. How do *you* feel about *him?*"

Amy expelled a sigh and let everything she'd thought and felt since that kiss play back through her head. Reliving it quickly made her heart beat too hard and her palms sweaty. Her skin got hotter, too, and she soon noticed that, at the moment, it wasn't particularly easy to breathe. And she still suffered that same mix of happy-sad-confused that had been making her feel a little crazy ever since the kiss. And she realized that even though she knew he didn't want her, would surely *never* want her, and that this whole thing was very likely going to ruin their lifelong friendship, she still felt weirdly happy and giddy inside when she pictured his handsome face in her mind.

And then, *then,* she had no choice but to face the truth, the truth which she suddenly understood had probably been festering inside her for a while now but she'd just been too in denial to admit to herself. It seemed useless to *keep on* denying it now, though, so she finally said to Tessa, "I think I'm in love with him."

There is no charm equal to tenderness of heart.

Jane Austen, from *Emma*

Two

ate that afternoon, Amy sat in her apartment, trying to get Austen and Mr. Knightley to be friends. She wasn't sure why—most of the time she left the strays down in the store—but she felt a little more attached to Austen already. And she liked the idea of Mr. Knightley having a playmate. Not that he seemed to want one. Right now he sat at one end of the couch staring down Austen, who was perched delicately at the other. And every now and then he even hissed.

"Is that how we welcome a guest into our home?" she reprimanded him. But when he just gave her a look, she answered herself. "I guess it is."

Next, she took a deep breath and picked up the phone. She'd told Logan she would check in on him today. But it wasn't as easy now, knowing what she knew. About her own feelings. Tessa had been even more overjoyed after Amy announced she was in love with Logan, but for her, it was a sobering realization. Now she'd been forced to add "horrified" to the growing list of emotions she was experiencing over this. Because this meant there was no going back, that things would never be the same between them. And though she could barely allow herself to think about it, deep inside she harbored a terrible fear—that she'd never be truly happy again.

In fact, the longer she'd talked with Tessa, the more even Tessa began to admit that Amy might have a problem here. And that maybe Logan *wouldn't* come around and suddenly decide he was crazy about her.

And even if by some miracle he did, the truth was, as much as Amy had always loved Logan as a friend, his track record with women wasn't great. He suffered from commitment issues—he never wanted anything serious. And Amy knew he'd hurt a lot of girls with that attitude—he was such a nice guy otherwise that each thought she'd be the one to change him only to find out, via a broken heart, that she was wrong. And Amy had, more than once, fixed him up with someone only to have to admit defeat later when it didn't work out.

God, what was I thinking—all these years I've spent trying to fix him up with other girls when I should have been trying to fix him up with me!

But even as that notion struck her, the cold hard fact hit home once more. She wasn't his type—she was too plain, too simple, too innocent. Then she rolled her eyes at her own thought. Too innocent by far. But she wasn't going to think about that—she suddenly had enough problems here without bringing that particular zinger into the mix.

When she put together all the many reasons why

Logan would never desire her, why they would never work as a couple, she was left with only one conclusion. *You have to do what you told him yesterday—forget it ever happened. And if you can't do that, at least act like you forgot.*

So quit beating around the bush and call him already.

After three rings, Logan said, "Hi freckles." And while it wasn't the most cheerful "Hi freckles" she'd ever gotten from him, she'd take it.

"You answered."

"Promised I would." One more great thing about Logan—even in the depths of depression, he was the sort of man who kept his promises.

"What are you doing right now?" she asked.

"Watching TV."

"Did you feed Cocoa today?"

"Yep. It was dumb of me when I didn't. Sorry about that."

"Well, you were obviously past the point of being able to make yourself do things—but now you're not, so this is great. I'm proud of you. You should go outside."

"It's raining," he pointed out.

And okay, she'd sort of forgotten that, but . . . "You should do it anyway. Just feel the rain on your skin, you know? It'll be good for you."

On the other end of the line, he let out a short chuckle and said, "I love ya, freckles, but that's goofy."

I love ya. He'd probably said that to her fifty times before, but this time she felt it in her gut. And, Lord, why did it almost hurt?

Because he means it in an entirely different way than you want him to now.

She held in the sigh she wanted to emit and suffered

the pain of unrequited affection settling deep in her stomach, but just said, "Do it anyway. Amy knows best."

This earned another little laugh—yet then he got more serious. "Thanks, freckles. For putting up with me."

"You're worth it," she told him, and hoped it hadn't come out sounding too breathy.

"About yesterday," he began then, and she cringed. *Why are we going there?* "Are we good? Cool? Whole thing's forgotten."

Her stomach went hollow for a brief second—and then she pulled herself back together. "I don't even know what you're talking about," she teased.

And he laughed again. And it felt good to make him laugh—but it also broke her heart, too. *I suddenly want to make him happy in other ways, ways I never can, and all this feels so weird.*

"I'm . . . gonna go," she said, having the urge to escape the conversation, or maybe just the memory of where she'd been approximately twenty-four hours ago. *You were under him. Under his hard male body. Being kissed as if you were the most desirable creature on the planet.* What a difference a day made.

"Okay, freckles. Talk to ya soon."

"Tomorrow," she specified. "I'm gonna keep checking in on you every day to monitor your progress."

"Fair enough. And thanks. You're the best."

Three days later, Logan sat in a lawn chair on the little dock in front of the cottage he rented, Cocoa by his side. The sun was shining, the lake was blue, and his feet were bare. He peered out over the water and tried his damnedest to think of good things. And slowly, life was beginning to get a little better.

He no longer saw Ken Knight's face during his every waking moment now—mostly only at certain times of day, like when he was trying to fall asleep at night. More than anything, what remained was a heavy lethargy—something both physical and in his head—that made it hard to want to move very much. It was as if his arms and legs were made of lead, as if he pulled around an anvil with every step he took. And as for his emotions—in a way he was almost numb, but also . . . frozen in place. Just like that night. He couldn't seem to move forward, or back. He was just stuck.

Still, though, at least he'd dragged his ass out here as he'd promised Amy he would. He'd sat out here for a while yesterday, too, and had to admit it had been worth the effort. It had been hard to muster the energy to come outside, but once he'd made it here after the rain had ended, he'd discovered it was a nice distraction from the grim darkness of his house.

Reaching down, he detached Cocoa's favorite tennis ball from between her teeth and tossed it in the lake. Not far, not as far as he used to throw it, but the dog didn't seem picky—she went merrily bounding into the water after it, clearly happy for the fun and exercise. And it made him feel good just to do this one normal thing, this little thing that his dog enjoyed.

He'd even picked up the mess around the house some, too, and this morning he'd gone so far as to call Mike— who'd been as stunned to hear from him as he'd expected.

"Hell, dude," Mike had said, "this is a surprise. A good one. What's up?"

"Just wanted to let you know I'm ready to take care of my best man duties, so don't go replacing me or anything."

"Wouldn't dream of it. And that's good to hear. But, uh . . . sorry I haven't been around much the last week or so."

Yet Logan didn't hold it against him. "Nah, was probably the best thing you could have done for me. I'm getting tired of eating cereal and I'm about out of milk anyway, so I'm gonna have to actually put on shoes and go to the store."

"Well, I'm glad to hear that, too. And thanks for being cool about it, man. You want some company or anything, just let me know."

"Soon," Logan said. "You can bring over your fishing pole and we'll sit on the dock and pretend we might catch something."

They had a long fishing history together that had started with Logan's dad taking them as boys, and which now was a lot more about just hanging out than catching fish.

Now, as he looked back on his conversation with Mike, he remembered something he'd perhaps forgotten for a little while: that everyone had problems, everyone had it rough. And up to now, Logan's life had actually been pretty easy. Other than the loss of his dad to a heart attack seven years ago, he simply hadn't known much loss. Whereas Mike, on the other hand, had experienced loss young.

His little sister, Anna, had disappeared at the age of five when they were kids. And his brother, Lucky, had run away from home as a teenager, only to return a couple of years ago. Mike had suffered for most of his life, not only from the uncertainty of that kind of tragedy but also from guilt—he'd been in charge of watching Anna on the day she vanished.

Logan had never really known much guilt before, and now that he did, he empathized with his best friend even more. *Damn, no wonder the guy is so gruff.* He'd always put up with Mike's often-less-than-genial attitude because they were best friends, but now he really got where it came from, in a gut-deep way.

Ken Knight had bounced Logan on his knee when he was only a toddler. Doreen had always made him chocolate cupcakes when his family was invited over because she knew they were his favorite. Hell, she'd even made the same cupcakes—chocolate with chocolate icing, sprinkles on top—for his thirty-fifth birthday a few months ago and dropped them off at the firehouse while he was on duty. He could still see her smile, still feel the small hug she'd given him, and it was still just so damn hard to believe . . .

He didn't finish the thought—couldn't. Because that invisible anvil he felt like he'd been dragging around now seemed to rest on his chest, squeezing the air out. *Stop. Just stop. Look at the lake. The dog.* Cocoa was back at his side now, ball in mouth, waiting for it to be thrown again. How long had she been sitting there? He didn't know, but he scratched lightly behind one of the dog's now-wet ears, took the saturated yellow ball from her mouth, and threw it again.

You have to stop thinking, stop remembering, somehow. You have to quit seeing the fire over and over again in your head. He'd been trained to deal with this sort of thing, after all. It shouldn't be that hard. Only . . . he'd never been trained on how to deal with a fire taking someone you knew, someone you'd known your whole life. And the truth was, the only other time someone had died in a blaze he'd been called to was a few years ago when the DFD had responded as backup to the Crest-view Fire Department after a row of condos had been struck by lightning and ignited. A middle-aged man he hadn't known had perished, and he'd never seen him while on the scene.

This was much, much worse—in so many ways. And it wasn't that he didn't want to tell anyone what had happened that evening at the Knight house—it was that he couldn't. He couldn't find the words. All he had were the horrific images in his head that wouldn't go away. It was policy that after this kind of incident a fireman had to see a counselor and complete a psych evaluation before returning to work, but he'd never made the appointment.

Still, though, you gotta find a way to put the pieces of your life back together and press on. He didn't know exactly how—every time he thought about returning to work as a firefighter he felt a little sick to his stomach— but he knew he had to start taking baby steps in that direction.

And he knew he had Amy to thank for pushing him. Pushing him out to this dock, pushing him to begin taking those steps. Mike was his best friend, yeah, but freckles, she was right up there, too.

When Cocoa returned, he took the wet ball and chucked it back toward the water, this time finally getting a little more distance on it. A second later, the chocolate lab was splashing her way eagerly toward it, and as Logan watched, paying closer attention now, her every energetic stride somehow made him begin to feel, deep down in his muscles, his bones, just a little bit more alive.

I need more of that, but I'm not sure where to get it. Maybe I need something . . . new.

That was when he remembered kissing Amy on his couch the other day. He cringed at the recollection and felt like some he-man brute. Or as if he'd treated her like some girl in a bar who was looking for action.

The truth was, kissing her hadn't been awful or anything. Maybe it had even been nice. Possibly even more than nice. But he sure as hell couldn't do it again. Amy was his buddy, after all. And he counted himself damn lucky that she was still even speaking to him after that, let alone continuing to help him see his way through this murky depression he'd sunk into.

So whatever the new thing was that he needed . . . well, it wasn't Amy. He treasured their friendship, and any more behavior like that could ruin it for good. If he wanted to make out with somebody, he could drag himself over to Bleachers, the sports bar in Crestview where he'd been known to find a willing woman or two over the years. Or—he looked skyward—maybe if what he really needed in his life was a woman, then God would make it easy and be kind enough to just politely drop one down for him in the middle of Destiny.

He wasn't completely on speaking terms with God at the moment—still struggling with why two good people had died on his watch—but if God wanted to make it up to him some way, maybe that would begin to change his feelings. Logan was the sort of guy who generally believed things happened for a reason, but this one was a toughie.

Just then, he heard a car and looked over his shoulder to see none other than Amy herself pulling into his driveway across the road. He lifted his hand in a wave, aware only afterward that it didn't require quite as much effort as he might have expected, and he knew she would be glad to see him outside soaking up some sun and playing with the dog.

"Well, look at you, Mr. Up and At 'Em," she said a minute later as she joined him on the dock. When he glanced up at her, the sun was positioned right behind her head, giving her shoulder-length strawberry blond curls a golden glow, like she was some kind of angel sent to watch over him. "You even look . . . normal," she went on. "Like a guy who takes care of himself."

He rewarded her with a soft grin. "Tryin'," he said. "Thanks to you."

"It's nice to see my efforts paying off," she told him as she leaned down to pet the wet dog who now stood eagerly greeting her. "Think you owe me a piece of pie in return."

And to his surprise, he realized that he was actually kind of glad to see her. He wasn't sure he was going to be the best company, but . . . well, maybe being alone was overrated. "Take a load off," he told her, and in response, she shed her sandals and sat down on the edge of the dock where she could dangle her toes in the water.

Amy was almost relieved to end up with her back facing Logan. She was thrilled to see him outside, look-ing and acting a lot more like his regular self even if he didn't seem exactly . . . energetic just yet. But she knew that part would come—she felt him bouncing back, thank goodness. On the other hand, though, seeing him just amped up the whole happy-sad-horrified thing going on inside her, and she feared she'd even blushed the first time they made eye contact. She knew he hadn't noticed, given that he wasn't at the top of his game yet— but *she* noticed, and the last thing she wanted to do was act weird around him.

After that, though, they made small talk—about the new cat at the bookstore, about the gorgeous weather, and she was pleased to hear he'd actually called Mike this morning—and she began to realize she could do this. She could act normal around Logan even while being in love with him.

And that will be my cross to bear in life. To be in love with my best friend without ever letting him know. Which sounded pretty tragic now that she thought about it, but she knew she could handle it with the same grace and aplomb of any Jane Austen heroine.

"Tessa minding the store?" he asked.

In front of him, she gave a nod. And didn't bother mentioning that Tessa had thought Amy driving out to see Logan was a fantastic idea—or why.

"That top looks nice on you," he said then from behind her. "Is it new?"

Hmm. She dared peek over her shoulder—just briefly. "Thanks. And yeah, it is. Rachel helped me pick it out." Rachel was Destiny's fashion maven—she kept up with style and knew what looked good on different body types. And perhaps Amy had worn it purposely today because it was slightly formfitting and made her feel a little more feminine than most of her clothes. But the most noteworthy thing at the moment was that Logan had never noticed that sort of thing—at least not with her. In fact, she wasn't sure he'd *ever* complimented something she'd worn.

"You should get more stuff like that," he said.

And she replied, "Maybe I will."

After a little more chatting and some time spent just sitting quietly together, Amy extracted her toes from the cool water and swiveled to face him, wrapping her arms around her bent knees. "You know, sitting on your dock with the dog is great and all, but you need to take the next step. We're going to town."

And when he immediately started to protest, she cut him off. "Look, it won't kill you to take a walk around town square, maybe see a few people. And besides, I know you need some groceries, so we'll stop at the store before we come back. We'll kill two birds with one stone, and you'll be glad afterward, I promise."

When Logan finally relented, and Amy stood to slip her shoes back on, Logan glanced down and said, "You have nice feet. I never noticed that before. I like that color."

Of toenail polish, she knew he meant. Sassy Salmon, and Tessa's choice—she'd insisted Amy try something brighter than usual when they'd decided to do home pedicures last week.

"Um, thanks." And she had no idea why a mere compliment to her toes made her tingle a little, or why her words almost definitely came out sounding too soft and breathy—but she decided not to overthink it. Not just yet anyway.

Don't jump to conclusions. It's a couple of compliments. And he's been cut off from society for more than a month; maybe he'd notice these things on anyone, any female who crossed his path.

But on the other hand, they were compliments he could only pay a female. Which meant . . . he knew she *was* a female. And maybe that part felt as new as the compliments themselves.

But do. Not. Over. Think. It. It probably means nothing.

Amy drove, more conscious than normal of having Logan in the seat next to her. Her toes and torso still felt the effects of being noticed by him. And now she was forced to look at him more, which, weirdly, still took some getting used to. Because she simply saw him in a whole new way now.

His eyes were so darn blue. As blue as Blue Valley Lake itself on a spring day like today. And they were so pretty, too—so much that she found it almost difficult to concentrate on what he was saying when she looked into them. His sandy hair still needed a trim and was a little messy, but she suddenly didn't mind it that way—it gave the impression that he'd just gotten up. From bed. What did Logan look like in bed? What did he *wear* to bed? She sucked in her breath, wondering, and he said, "Eyes on the road, freckles!"

"Sorry," she managed as she focused back out the windshield just in time to make one of the sharper curves on Blue Valley Road. But she still saw his face in her mind. He'd clearly shaved a couple of days ago but not recently, leaving that stubbly look she liked. What was it like to touch that stubble? *I should have touched it while I was kissing him, darn it.* But who could think clearly while being kissed like that? *Will I ever get another chance?*

Just a few hours ago, she'd have said a definitive no to that question. But now, somehow, she was beginning to let herself wonder, speculate, think, just a little . . . that maybe she was wrong. He was clearly noticing her in new ways, after all. And she couldn't deny feeling especially close to him right now. And as Tessa had repeatedly pointed out, he hadn't kissed her like a friend.

So while it still seemed dangerous—to her heart—to even begin thinking such a thing was possible, deep down inside, she was cautiously beginning to wonder . . . if maybe it was. Maybe.

It was late afternoon when they parked near Under the Covers, and Amy exited the car without any sort of pep talk to Logan. Besides the fact that she thought the time for coddling him was over, she suddenly had other, bigger things on her mind.

Like the crazy idea that had just entered her head.

Should she find a way to tell him? How she felt? Or maybe at least hint at it?

Maybe—given all he'd just been through—the timing was right. Maybe he *was* noticing her in new ways, thinking of her differently. Maybe having endured a tragedy had changed something inside him, regarding her, regarding relationships in general. Maybe he was ready to settle down. Dare she think with the sweet, small town girl next door?

But what are you thinking? Telling him would be crazy! A disaster! An utter humiliation of epic proportions!

So just be cool. Cool but . . . open. To the possibilities. He'd never tell Mike Romo *he* had nice feet, after all. It had to mean something.

Maybe it meant . . . a new beginning. A wonderful new beginning she never could have anticipated with the one and only guy in the universe who really was her perfect match.

So as they settled together on a park bench facing the white, latticed gazebo in the center of the green, shrubbery-laden square, she felt . . . hopeful. And even . . . ready. Like this could really happen. She could have a boyfriend. A lover. And it could be Logan.

"Can we talk about something?" he surprised her by asking then.

"Sure," she said a bit too quickly. Was this it? Was he

going to tell her his feelings for her had changed, deepened? Her heartbeat sped up.

"I don't think I want to be a firefighter anymore."

At this, Amy's heart sank. And not only because it wasn't the admission of love she'd been fantasizing about—but because it was just so . . . wrong. "What else would you be?" she asked. Because Logan was the kind of man whose job ran through his blood. He cared about it, he lived and breathed it—heck, it was practically part of his DNA. His father had been a Destiny fireman before him, and his grandfather had started the first Destiny Fire Department as a volunteer organization back in the fifties. "I mean, being a fireman is all you've ever wanted from the time we were little."

He didn't meet her eyes as he replied, but he sounded . . . resolute. "Sometimes things change. And things are changing in me right now. I don't know what I want to do—it might take some time to find a new path—but the more I mull it over, the more I realize that's one thing that's been keeping me inside that house. I don't want to go back to work at the fire station."

"Wow," Amy murmured, all the more stunned.

"And Mike mentioned that he heard Anita Garey needs a bartender at the Dew Drop. So I figure I'll look into that—it'll pay the bills for a while until I figure out my next step."

Amy simply gaped at him, mouth hanging open. Logan wanted to leave the DFD to serve drinks at the Dew Drop Inn? It made no sense.

And she was sitting there trying to think of how to tell him how absolutely wrong for him this was—because she'd never been more sure of anything in her life— when a 1965 candy-apple red Mustang rolled into a parking spot across the town square from them, attracting their attention.

"Don't see many of those these days," Logan said, clearly admiring the classic car. And Amy could understand why—even not being a big car person, this one drew the eye. And almost made you curious to find out who drove it.

But she had to get back to business here, had to find a way to make Logan understand that he couldn't give up his life's work over one incident—no matter how deeply it had affected him.

Yet then the car's door slammed and Amy felt them both looking at the girl who'd just gotten out. Arrestingly beautiful, with long, dark, straight hair that hung to her waist and shone in the sun, she walked in their general direction, crossing over the square. And the closer she got, the more Amy was struck by the strange, gut-jarring sensation that she looked . . . exactly like a grown-up version of the long-missing Anna Romo.

" . . . my astonishment is much beyond anything I can express . . ."

Jane Austen, from *Emma*

Three

Amy just stared, blinked. And so did Logan.

She knew it didn't make any sense—it made no more sense to think this could possibly be Anna Romo than it made for Logan to announce he no longer intended to be a fireman. And yet her heart beat harder for an entirely different reason now. Well, more than one. Logan openly gaped at this gorgeous girl, clearly mesmerized. And the closer she got to them, the more Amy couldn't stop feeling that strange pinch, the idea that maybe, just maybe . . .

And, oh God, the girl even had the same mole near her mouth as Anna. She'd seen too many pictures of little Anna over the years to forget it, and now, there it was.

The girl was tall and wore stylish platform wedges that only emphasized her lean, sexy body all the more.

Skinny jeans and a bright red top that hugged her shape made Amy sizzle with something she seldom experienced: jealousy. And yet jealousy seemed no less than insane at this moment. Because what if . . . ? Could it possibly be?

Both she and Logan stayed silent until the dark-haired girl sashayed past them, seeming as if she was headed toward town hall.

And then, finally, the two of them turned to look at each other—and she knew she wasn't crazy; she wasn't the only one thinking what she was thinking. The same stunned look resided in Logan's blue gaze and it was about more than how pretty the girl was.

Amy watched him swallow visibly, his Adam's apple shifting, before he quietly said, "Am I losing it, or did that girl look like . . ."

All Amy could offer was a numb sort of nod. But then she found her voice to say, "Except . . . that can't be, right? I mean, it couldn't be. It couldn't."

"Of course it couldn't," Logan said. Yet then he let out a breath and added, "Only . . . what if it is?"

As they watched her get closer to the front doors of the town hall, Logan suddenly grabbed Amy's hand, pulling them both to their feet, and began dragging her with him as he chased after the dark-haired girl. And she definitely liked having her hand in his, but somehow this wasn't how she'd imagined it. The whole situation was beginning to feel surreal.

"Excuse me," Logan said to the girl when they caught up with her a few seconds later.

And when she stopped and turned to look at them, Amy knew. She just knew. Without a doubt. It was her eyes. She had Romo eyes. She had *Anna* Romo's eyes.

"I . . . don't mean to be forward," Logan said, "but . . ."

And Amy realized he hadn't figured out what he was going to say to her—which was understandable given the bizarre circumstances—so when his voice trailed off, she automatically filled the gap. "You just . . . look like someone we know. Or . . . used to know."

The gorgeous brown-eyed girl blinked in such a way that Amy knew, too, that she knew who she was, and that was why she was here. But she just said, "Who?"

And though they both hesitated a second more—because it was all too strange, all too utterly impossible—Logan then said her name, as soft and tentative as a delicate prayer. "Anna Romo."

Even when her lips parted to form an "O," her eyes lighting with surprise, Anna Romo was beyond beautiful. "Yes," she said then, "that's . . . me. Even though . . ." She shook her head, her long, sleek hair falling around her face like a wild mane. "It's hard to get used to. I . . . didn't know that was my last name until recently." And when she looked a little embarrassed, befuddled, Amy couldn't help feeling sorry for her. My God, what had happened to Anna? What had she been through? She'd been missing for well over twenty years, after all, so it was almost too much to even contemplate.

"I . . . I was told I might have family here," she went on.

And Amy and Logan simply looked at each other. Boy, did she have family. But Amy knew it wasn't only the largest clan in Destiny that she and Logan were both thinking of. It was Mike. And Lucky. And their parents. It was a family who'd been torn apart by her disappearance. It was a man—Mike—who'd spent his whole life missing her, wallowing in guilt, and still hoping against hope that one day she would come home. Even though he and everyone else in Destiny knew that was impossible.

And yet . . . suddenly it wasn't impossible. Suddenly it was unfathomably real. A fact which kept Logan and Amy just standing there gawking at her like some figment of their imagination come to life.

"Yeah," Amy finally managed. "You have family here. Two brothers. Your parents live in Florida now, but . . ." At a loss for what else to say, how much to bombard her with, this time it was Amy who trailed off, looking to Logan for help.

"Your brother is my best friend," he supplied, peering back at Anna. "And he's gonna be *so* damn happy to see you, Anna." Then he dug his cell phone from his pocket, saying, "I have to call him."

Mike had just kissed Rachel goodbye, then started the cruiser, ready for the night shift. He generally preferred working days, since nights spent patrolling quiet Destiny streets could be long and uneventful, but he also appreciated the time it gave him to think.

And as he pulled out onto Meadowview Highway in the direction of town, he thought about the fact that he was getting married soon. And that, though he'd never much thought of himself as the marrying kind, he'd never been happier. At least not in his adult life. Rachel was the glue that held him together—even if, before she'd come along—he'd never been particularly aware that he was coming apart. But he had been. And she'd helped him see that life could be good even when you had troubles, even when you were filled with hard questions that had no answers. She'd made him almost begin to move on.

That part was the toughest, and that was why it was an "almost." When she'd entered his world, he'd still been obsessed with his own guilt over Anna. He'd still been harboring the insane hope that she'd come back, any day now. And the truth was, living like that for so long had worn on him; it had turned him into a stern, snarly guy not too many people wanted to be around. And he supposed he was probably still that same stern guy, but he was making efforts to change.

And the most important thing he supposed he'd achieved was . . . well, beginning to accept the idea that Anna would never come home, and they would probably never find out what happened to her. For him, that was a hard pill to swallow, but after all these years, he had to face the facts. He had to begin to let it go. And he was still working on that—but he was slowly taking steps in that direction.

He'd finally started putting away some of the pictures of Anna that had filled the house he now shared with Rachel. Not all of them, but some. And he still carried one in his wallet, but he didn't look at it as much anymore. Not that he needed to look in order to see it—he could see every single detail in his mind. But . . . baby steps. They were all baby steps. Which were a hell of a lot better than nothing.

As he drove out of the dead zone near his home where there was no cell reception, he saw he'd just missed a call—from Logan. Hmm, hearing from him again already? Seemed like a good sign. He punched the button to redial his best friend, still relieved to know he was finally coming out of the funk he'd been in since that house fire.

"Mike," Logan said pointedly as he answered. He sounded agitated.

"What is it? What's wrong?"

"Nothing's wrong. But something's right."

"What are you talking about?" *And why do you sound so intense?* But Mike decided to keep that part to himself until he found out what was going on here.

"Listen, are you sitting down?"

"Driving," Mike replied. "Why?"

"Pull over," Logan instructed him. "Anywhere."

"Why?" Mike asked again. Damn it, what was Logan's deal here?

"Just do it," Logan said sharply. So sharply that normally it might have pissed Mike off, but given what Logan had been going through, he let it slide. After easing into a gravel pull-off in front of an old red barn, he put the cruiser in park and said, "Okay, I stopped. What the hell is going on?"

And now Logan hesitated. And Mike felt himself getting more aggravated by the second, until Logan finally said, "Okay, here's the thing, buddy. You won't believe this—I mean you really won't fucking believe it—but . . . are you ready for this?"

"For Christ's sake, I'm ready already. Spit it out, dude, before I blow a gasket."

"Okay. I'm standing in front of town hall right now . . . with Anna. Your sister. Your sister, Anna."

Mike stayed silent as he tried to process what Logan had just said. Was this some kind of cruel joke? Had Logan completely lost his mind? He couldn't quite make sense of it, but he knew it couldn't be true. After a long pause, his stomach churning painfully at the very notion, he eventually replied with, "What the fuck?"

"I know it sounds crazy," Logan said. "I know it sounds impossible. But she's here. I don't know yet where she's been or what the story is or what brought her back, but she's here with me, looking for her family. Looking for you."

"You're serious," Mike said, feeling a little numb inside, afraid to believe.

"As a heart attack," Logan said.

"Are . . . are you sure? I mean, really sure? Because . . ."

"I'm sure, Mike," he said. "I wouldn't lay this on you if I wasn't sure."

Again, Mike just sat there, stunned into silence. And truthfully, he still wasn't quite certain he believed it. This was the moment he'd been waiting for all his life, but suddenly, the reality of it didn't make sense. Suddenly, he saw for the first time, with real clarity, how nonsensical it was to believe she'd come back.

And yet Logan was telling him the impossible had finally happened.

"I'm . . . on my way," he said after he managed to catch his breath and stop feeling like the twelve-year-old boy who'd lost her that day so long ago.

And then Mike did something he *never* did—he abused his power as a cop by turning on the blue lights and even the siren as he put the car back in drive and sped toward town.

Anna tried to be cool in all aspects of life. Especially lately. It was easier that way, if you could just act confident, cool, and like you had it all together. And she was usually good at it—because until recently, she mostly *had* been someone who was confident and had it all together. Life had made her a pretty tough cookie in ways, and she'd learned that a little confidence could be a girl's best friend.

But then her mother had gotten sick a few months ago.

And on her deathbed she'd confessed to Anna that she wasn't really her mother. And as shocking as it had been, there had been some small part of Anna that wasn't completely surprised, that had somehow always known there were parts of her life she wasn't really aware of, vague memories that didn't fit with who she was. And she'd maybe always known in the back of her mind that she should dig deeper into that, ask more questions, but . . . well, it had seemed crazy, and like the kind of thought that was easier to just push aside whenever it entered her head.

And so at the moment, it didn't matter how good she looked or how cool she wanted to be—she was nervous as hell. Because this was big. Bigger than big. And even if she hadn't rolled into the town of Destiny entirely discreetly—could she help it if she drove a fabulous car?—she'd thought she'd have time before she'd be confronted with her real family. In fact, she'd thought she'd be the one doing the confronting. She'd planned to go into town hall and quietly inquire about the Romo family. Maybe see if she could get a phone number, an address. And then she'd gather the next bit of courage she needed to contact them.

Yet instead, somehow, these people had miraculously recognized her—something she'd never even imagined happening. And now—now a police car was barreling around a corner and screeching to a halt in the middle of the street, siren blaring and lights blazing, and the guy she'd been talking to was saying, "It's Mike." And given that she thought she had vague, fond memories of someone named Mike from when she was very young, she now began to feel overwhelmed, bordering on terrified.

"Okay," was all she could manage, wondering if her fear showed on her face.

That was when the nice girl with the guy said, "Don't worry. I'm sure this isn't how you envisioned this, but Mike loves you more than anything."

Okay, so it showed. And Mike loved her more than anything. And that should be reassuring—yet it also felt pretty weird, considering that she didn't even know him.

And then, there he was, this large, dark-haired man in a beige police uniform rushing toward her, stopping in front of her, looking her over the same way the other two had—but after a few seconds, that began to matter much less than the fact that she could see, clear as day, that this was her brother. He looked like her. Uncannily. And then their eyes met—his eerily familiar, like staring in a mirror—and he said "Anna?"

All she could do was nod.

He appeared utterly in awe for a minute, like she was amazing, and then he said, "My God. Can I hug you?"

And somehow, the look in his eyes made that feel okay. So she gave another short nod.

And then his arms were around her in an embrace that was at first shockingly gentle—more gentle than she might have suspected this particular man could hug—but then it grew more fierce. Though she didn't mind that either, because as strange as it all was, she was beginning to feel, deep down inside, down in her very core, exactly what she'd hoped to by coming here: that she'd really, truly come home.

After that, there were obvious questions. "Where have you been all this time?" "How did you find us?" And she began the story as best she could, even when a small crowd slowly began to gather, at first probably in response to the siren, but she soon realized that apparently everyone in this town remembered her early life here, clearly far better than she did.

"I was raised in Indianapolis," she told them all, but really only Mike, keeping her eyes on him the whole time, "as Anna Karras. That was my mother's name. My mother, the woman who raised me," she said, shaking her head at the total strangeness of it, something that still hadn't worn off. And that strangeness then made her say, more softly, "Is there somewhere we could go . . . more private?"

That was when her newfound brother looked around and seemed to notice for the first time that they weren't alone. "Of course. Come with me." Then he took her hand and began to lead her away.

A few seconds later, she found herself following him into the police station, situated conveniently next door to town hall, more people staring, and she felt a little like a criminal until they reached an open office door, and Mike said very pointedly to the older, mustached man at the desk inside, "Chief, this is my sister—Anna. Could we possibly borrow your office?"

The chief clearly knew the magnitude of this meeting, too, as shown by the stunned look on his face as he pushed to his feet. "Good Lord. Of course. Take as long as you need."

He shut the door on the way out and they took seats in the two chairs sitting across from the desk. And their eyes met again. And rather than let herself fall prey to the odd emotions that threatened to overtake her, she told him what she knew he was waiting to hear—the horrifying truth.

"My mother, Claudia Karras, died three weeks ago,

from cervical cancer. And on her deathbed, she told me that . . . that she wasn't really my mom. And that she'd . . . taken me, when I was little, from a state park, because she couldn't have children, and the waiting list was so long she'd thought she'd never be able to adopt." She stopped, swallowed, because these were such horrific things to say. But then she pushed on. "I had a relatively normal childhood except for the fact that . . . well, my mom had some problems. There were a couple of times when I was a teenager that she was briefly admitted to a psych ward. And that was tough."

"No father? She wasn't married?" her brand new brother asked.

She shook her head. "No, it was just the two of us. No relatives, either—she was alone in the world before me, and I guess that made it easier to suddenly have a daughter. She worked in the records department of a hospital in Cincinnati at the time, and she forged a birth certificate. And then she quit her job and we moved to Indy where no one would know I was a new addition. She was . . . a little crazy, but smart, too—at least about how to pull something like this off. She explained it all to me on the night before she died."

Across from her, Mike looked like he was having trouble catching his breath but trying to hide it as he said, "How did you know about us, your real family? How did you find us?"

"She told me that part, too. Apparently she followed the story in the news after she abducted me. She found out who she'd taken me from and where you lived. She said she'd been eaten alive by guilt all these years, but that she couldn't face all the ramifications of telling the truth until she had nothing left to lose. And so . . . here I am. Feeling pretty damn weird. And just, I guess, trying to figure out who I really am."

"You're my little sister," he said simply then. "You're my little sister and you're finally home. That's all that matters."

Amy and Logan sat in a booth at Dolly's Main Street Café—he was buying her that piece of pie he owed her. But like everything else today, it wasn't going exactly the way she'd envisioned. For one thing, Logan seemed . . . totally back to his old self. Which was great, but weird—as in sudden. "You seem . . . in much better spirits," she pointed out as she forked a bite of cherry pie into her mouth.

"Well, not completely, but . . . I guess a miracle like this is enough to snap me out of it. I mean, that's what it is, you know? A miracle!"

Amy couldn't deny that. Her mind still whirled from what had to have been the most shocking—and fantastic—turn of events to take place in Destiny in . . . maybe forever. "I know. I still can't believe it."

Logan shook his head at the wonder of it all as he cut into his slice of pie. "It's incredible! And the fact that you and I were sitting there when she pulled up, and that we actually recognized her . . ." Another incredulous head shake. "I guess maybe it . . . restores my faith or something. That there's something bigger than us orchestrating things, you know. I mean, I realize she'd have found Mike anyway, without us, but since I went through all that with him when we were kids, and for our whole lives really—well, it just means something to me to be the one who called him and let him know."

Amy nodded—it was an unbelievably special thing.

And if it brought Logan back to the land of the living—well, the rest of the way back—all the better.

And the truth was, she was still trying to come down from the shock of it herself. As soon as Mike and Anna had departed, both she and Logan had called all their friends—including Tessa, so that she could tell Anna's other brother, Lucky—and it still felt . . . unreal.

"And damn, did you see how beautiful she is?" Logan asked then. "How amazing she looked?"

Hmm. Amy was beyond happy for Anna to be home, to rediscover her family after being gone for most of her life, but she could have lived without this part. Which was awful of her, she knew. It wasn't Anna's fault she was breathtakingly gorgeous. And it wasn't Logan's fault for noticing. But at the moment, it made her stomach sink, even as she felt obligated to say, "Yes, she's very pretty."

"Why'd you stop eating?" Logan asked her a minute later.

I just lost my appetite. She gave her head a short shake and tried to look unaffected. "Just taking a break, that's all."

Across from her, Logan appeared uncharacteristically introspective. "You know, maybe this happened for a reason, freckles. Not just for Mike and the rest of the family, but . . . for me, too."

"What do you mean?" she asked—even as she was struck with the nagging feeling that maybe she didn't really want to know.

"Did you know that when Anna was little, she followed me around all the time? And everyone said she had a crush on me?"

Amy sucked in her breath. "No, I didn't realize that."

And she understood they were talking about something cute that had taken place a gazillion years ago and had no bearing on today, but still . . . ugh.

"And even though I was older than her, our families always joked that we'd end up getting married someday."

Amy began to feel a little sick as she forced herself to lift her gaze from Logan's T-shirt to his face. "You don't say."

"And . . ." He stopped, laughed, cheerful as ever, cheerful as if the last month hadn't even happened. "It's not like I want to get married anytime soon or anything, but the thing is, just a few hours ago I was sort of thinking . . ."

Oh Lord. Could this get any worse? "Thinking what?"

"That maybe I needed a new woman in my life. Some romance, you know? And how nice it would be if God just dropped the right woman into my lap. So . . ." He ate another bite of pie. "Just kind of interesting timing. For Anna Romo to suddenly reappear. And to be incredible looking. And she seemed sweet, too, don't you think? I mean, I can only imagine how strange this is for her, everything she's going through, but she still seemed sweet as hell."

Okay, if Amy had felt a little sick a minute ago, now she pretty much wanted to throw up. Though in an odd, twisted way, it all made perfect sense.

Well, just thank God she hadn't been dumb enough to tell him how she felt about him. Because at almost the precise moment in time that she'd fallen in love with Logan, Logan had clearly fallen for Anna Romo.

Never had she felt so agitated, so mortified, grieved, at any circumstance in her life.

Jane Austen, from *Emma*

Four

Okay, maybe it wasn't love. Yet. But he was very clearly smitten. And not with *her* as Amy had so foolishly begun to let herself hope earlier.

And he was right—the timing was downright uncanny, in so many ways. And Anna was flawlessly gorgeous. Heck, Amy couldn't blame him for thinking fate had brought her to him even as it brought her to Mike and the rest of the Romos. If she were Logan, she'd draw the exact same conclusion.

Maybe it was meant to be, Logan and Anna. They'd make a lovely couple, in fact. And everyone in Destiny would think it was a perfect fairytale ending to Anna's long absence. And Amy would end up exactly where she'd always feared: alone forever. Only now, now that she'd realized how she felt about Logan, she'd be alone and brokenhearted. Wow.

"Aren't you gonna eat the rest of your pie?" Logan asked as he finished his.

"Um, I don't think so. Suddenly I'm not feeling well."

It didn't surprise her when he looked troubled on her behalf. He cared about her, after all. Just not in the way she wanted him to now. "Well, that sucks, freckles. This is too good a day for you to feel bad. Hopefully you'll feel better soon."

"We'll see," she said. But it didn't seem likely.

The final bridesmaid gown fitting for Rachel and Mike's wedding took place the next day at the Daisy Dress Shop, just around the corner from Under the Covers. It was another beautiful May day in Destiny—the sun was shining and flowers were blooming—and the fact that Anna Romo had miraculously returned home only made the gathering of girlfriends that much more festive.

"Oh, that's perfect for you," Rachel was saying to another of their old friends, Jenny Brody. "I'm so glad we put you in the lilac." Rachel, who was definitely the boldest of their group of girlfriends, had chosen to go with rich hues of blues and lavenders for her wedding, which would take place at the Destiny Church of Christ in just a few weeks. "And Sue Ann, the aqua is so working for you."

Sue Ann Simpkins swished her hips playfully back and forth in the princess style gown, her expression the sexy pout of a runway model, and Amy couldn't help joining in soft laughter with the other girls. Sue Ann had gone through a terrible divorce just last year, but after she'd started seeing Adam Becker at Christmastime, she'd bounced back to her usual, fun-loving self. And it was good to see that someone could endure heartbreak and go on to be happy. That someone could lose the relationship they valued the most but still smile.

Of course, Amy didn't have an Adam Becker, a backup Prince Charming. Heck, she'd only figured out who her first Prince Charming was the other day, and the notion was still more than a little jarring.

What if he's the only one for me? What if Logan is the only man I can ever love?

"Cheer up, girlfriend," Sue Ann said to her then, and Amy realized her smile had somehow transformed into a frown. "The sun is shining, it's wedding season in Destiny, and Anna Romo is home!"

Standing on the round pedestal in front of the large three-way mirror a few feet away, Tessa turned to face them, the skirt of her periwinkle dress rustling. She looked positively awestruck as she said, "It gives me chills every time I think about it. I mean, how amazing is this? And just in time for both Mike's and Lucky's weddings!" Since Tessa was marrying Lucky, Anna's other brother, she definitely had a vested interest in Anna's return. And really, they *all* did. The disappearance of Anna Romo was part of the fabric of the community, of their lives, and in a place like Destiny, you cared about your neighbor, so getting Anna back was like . . . bringing home a family member for *everyone.*

"I can't even envision Mike's reaction," Jenny said to Rachel then, who broke out into a huge smile.

"Oh, he's just beside himself. He barely slept last night, too keyed up, too happy. I've never seen him like this."

"Have you met her yet?" Sue Ann asked, bright-eyed.

Rachel, the only one of them in regular clothes since her bridal gown was coming from Cincinnati, nodded. "Mike brought her home for dinner last night, and she's staying with us for now. His parents are flying up from Florida today, and tonight we'll have a bigger family dinner so she can see them and Lucky."

"Can you imagine?" Jenny said. "Being Mr. and Mrs. Romo? Getting that phone call yesterday?"

Rachel continued beaming. "At first they had trouble believing it, of course, but then it was . . . total joy. It was just like when Lucky came home—except maybe even better because this means they have *all* their children back. It's just mind-blowing! And wonderful!"

That was when Tessa apparently noticed that Amy's smile still wasn't quite making it to her eyes. Which made her feel like a horrible, hideous person even as Tessa stepped quietly down from the platform and made her way over to Amy while the rest of the group continued chatting about Anna's homecoming.

"What's wrong?" her friend asked quietly. "You look a little less than thrilled about this."

Amy could only sigh. She'd never felt anything that seemed so . . . uncharitable. Downright shameful, in fact. She tried to explain by saying under her breath, "I *am* thrilled. For her. And them." Then she blinked and told Tessa the rest. "Just . . . not so much for me. Because when Logan saw her . . . it was like his dream girl had just walked into Destiny. He even pretty much told me that—that he'd been thinking maybe he needed someone new in his life and that she was obviously it. He seemed to think it was divine intervention or something. And so . . . I'm an awful person. Because I'm actually jealous of her. Which seems insane. Not to mention insensitive and monstrous."

In response, Tessa's face twisted into a troubled grimace. "Damn, she's that gorgeous?" And Amy was relieved to understand, without Tessa having to say it, that she saw the dilemma and didn't think Amy was the scum of the earth.

Amy simply nodded. "And I just can't compete with

that. I mean, I'm really *so* glad for everyone involved that she's home, but does she have to look like a movie star?" Of course, maybe it only stood to reason. After all, the two Romo brothers were unaccountably hot, so it made sense that the third Romo child would be amazingly attractive, too.

However, rather than answer, Tessa instead stood back and gave Amy a long once-over.

And she still had no idea why when Rachel stepped up and said, "The cobalt blue so works on you, Ames. Really highlights your pretty hair color. It brings out both the auburn and the gold, don't you guys think?"

All eyes turned her way, and everyone agreed—as Amy blushed. She'd always thought of her strawberry blond curls as generally untamable and the color a little left of center. She'd envied Rachel being a straight blond. And sure, her mom had always complimented her hair color, but that was *her mom*.

"What do you keep staring at?" she finally asked Tessa.

And in response, Tessa moved behind her and pulled the fabric around her waist snugger. "This," Tessa said, peeking around to where they could both see her in one side of the three-way mirror. "Your dress could definitely be taken in more and look a lot better."

"Wow, check you out," Rachel said, her eyes widening as she studied the results of Tessa's handiwork. "Who knew you had such a cute shape? Where on earth have you been hiding that?"

Amy just blinked. She thought they were exaggerating and that the dress was too tight the way Tessa held it—certainly far tighter than the formfitting top Rachel had picked out for her. "I . . . don't know. But—"

"You hide it under a lot of loose clothes, that's where," Tessa said.

"They're not *that* loose," Amy argued.

And then Tessa leaned up and whispered in Amy's ear, "They're too loose if you want to catch a hot man."

Amy just blinked at herself in the mirror, mildly alarmed by Tessa's words. Because she just didn't think like that. About *catching* a man. Let alone a hot one. Or about showing off her body to do it.

Since the rest of the girls were already busy talking amongst themselves again, she turned to Tessa and said with quiet doubt, through lightly clenched teeth, "You think tight clothes and cleavage are going to make Logan fall in love with me?"

"No," she replied. "But I think it could make him notice you in a whole new way. And *then* he might fall in love with you."

Hmm. Amy had to think about that for a minute.

She wasn't a naturally sexy person, and she'd never aspired to be something she wasn't.

But Anna Romo was back in town and Logan was smitten with her. And even though Amy herself had never done it before, she didn't think there was anything wrong with women dressing to show off their best assets.

And the longer she stood there, the more she saw the effect Tessa was talking about—her waist looked much more slender and her breasts stood out. And it really wasn't all that uncomfortable now that she was getting used to it.

So she finally said to Tessa, "Okay, we'll take it in at the waist."

"Hooray," Tessa said. "I'll go get Mary Ann and tell her she has one more alteration."

Of course, Amy knew it was going to take more than a fitted dress for Logan to really see her the way she wanted him to. And she still wouldn't hold a candle to Anna Romo. And the very idea of trying to be sexy, sexual, felt very foreign to her, even despite the urges of her body.

But she figured, on the other hand, that it couldn't hurt.

Anna sat in Mike and Rachel's living room on the sofa, one leg crossed over the other, hands resting easily on her knee, trying to be calm. And cool. And confident. That was how she'd dealt with her mother's mental illness. By just trying to be . . . above it all. It was like a wall, a barrier, that allowed her to feel some control. Except her mother wasn't her mother anymore. Tonight she was meeting her real mother. And she was scared shitless.

She supposed, deep inside, she'd felt that way ever since she'd realized she had no idea who she was. Anna Romo. Who came from a place she didn't remember. From a family she didn't know. The name still felt foreign on her tongue. *Romo. Ro-mo.* She'd learned it was Italian. In fact, last night Rachel had told her the story of how Anna's real grandfather had come to America from Italy in the fifties and had a romance with Rachel's grandma. It was a fascinating story. About people she didn't know.

When the doorbell rang, she flinched. She watched as Rachel came from the kitchen, an apron covering her stylish capris and sleek, silky leopard-print top, and something about the sight made her smile. Rachel didn't fit here anymore than she did—and yet . . . she'd learned how. She made it work. And she seemed incredibly happy. "That'll be Lucky and Tessa," she said. "And

I just got a text from Mike—he and your parents should be here in a few minutes."

"Great," she said, hoping it sounded more sincere than sarcastic. Since it *was* sincere. Except that maybe being scared shitless added just a *tinge* of sarcasm. They were all so happy to have her here—had anyone stopped at any point to realize how difficult this was from her end, how hard it had been to come driving into Destiny, opening up a whole new-yet-old life she knew nothing about? Yes, she wanted to be here, she wanted to know these people—but it was turning out to be more overwhelming than she'd ever stopped to envision.

"Oops, wrong," Rachel said as she opened the door. "It's Logan."

It had been Anna who had tossed out the idea of inviting him. Because something about him had made her immediately comfortable. She'd felt drawn to him. And he was cute and nice, two things she valued in a guy.

"Hey," he said, lifting his hand in a wave across the room.

Anna returned it. Though her smile felt manufactured, nervous. But she was glad to see him anyway.

"I need to get back to the kitchen," Rachel told them both as the tangy scent of lasagna wafted over the counter that separated the two rooms.

"Need any help?" Logan asked.

Crap. I should have offered to help. But it honestly hadn't crossed Anna's mind—too much else occupied it right now.

"No, I've got everything taken care of," Rachel replied.

"Gotcha," Logan said, then walked over to join Anna on the couch. Sitting down, he quietly asked, "So . . . you doin' okay?"

She tossed him a nervous sideways glance in reply. "Does it show that I'm not?"

His soft chuckle relaxed her a little, seeming to trickle down her spine like a warm touch. "It's a lot to deal with, I'm sure."

She nodded and didn't even weigh her words as she said, "I'm glad you're here."

Did his smile hold a hint of flirtation or was that only wishful thinking? "Why's that?"

"Because you'll be the only person here whose last name isn't Romo—or won't soon be." Then she got even more honest. "And because I like you." She'd never been shy.

When the doorbell rang again, this time it *was* Lucky and Tessa—Anna recognized them from pictures Mike had shown her last night. As she peered over from the couch, her heart rose to her throat.

And then—oh God—she heard Mike's voice, and then an older woman's, and realized Mike and her birth-parents were here already, too. She sucked in her breath.

That was when Logan reached out to touch her arm. "It's okay. They're great people and this is where you belong."

The words did something to calm her, strengthen her, just as they were intended to. And so Anna steeled her-self, pushed to her feet, and knew it was time to meet the rest of her family. This was what she'd come here for, after all. Even if it seemed utterly surreal.

As she made her way to the door, her mother and father walked through it. Everyone else was there, too—Mike, Lucky, their fiancées—but at the moment John and Nancy Romo were really all she could see.

Like her brothers, they looked like her, especially John. Clearly, the Romo genes ran deep. *And that's who*

I am now. It's actually who I've always *been. A Romo.*
Both of her parents appeared as emotional as she might
have expected, their eyes glassy, expressions drawn.

"Oh," her mother breathed. Her new mother. "Mike
said you were beautiful, but . . ." She stepped forward,
reached out—yet then stopped. "Is it okay? For me to
hug you?"

A lump had risen to Anna's throat, seizing her voice,
so she only nodded. And then Nancy Romo's arms fell
around her in a huge, crushing embrace—more crushing than she'd have thought the small woman capable of.
And Anna hugged her back and soon felt her new father
join the embrace as well.

Both of them were crying, her new parents, and for
Anna, it was one more unreal moment in a long string
of them that had begun the night her mother died, the
night her mother had said the words she could still hear
echoing through her brain. *You're not who you think.
You're not really mine.* And now she felt bad because
the people holding her were in tears, and they loved her,
and they'd missed her for so incredibly long, and she
couldn't return the love they felt because she didn't even
know them. Walls. She was so used to putting up walls
to protect herself.

But still she stood between them, soaking up their
emotions for her, and she realized that it didn't feel odd
to have these two strangers hugging her. It didn't feel
weird at all. And she began to understand that deep
down inside, she did feel a connection to them. Already.
Or maybe . . . always?

And without quite knowing what was happening, tears
began to roll down her cheeks, too. For the lost life with
these people that she would never know, never recover,
never get back. For all the years and love she'd missed.

For all the pain they'd suffered because of her. And though this wasn't going to be easy, maybe Logan was right—maybe she belonged here.

After that came the slightly awkward moment of separating, and reaching for tissues, and the slightly embarrassed laughter that somehow put her at ease to be standing around crying and wiping her eyes with people she didn't know even though they'd given birth to her.

But it wasn't over yet—because that was when she made eye contact with the largest guy in the room, whose eyes yet looked unaccountably gentle. It was her other brother, Lucky. His hair was long and his arms covered with tattoos, and she knew from Mike that, though he was now settling down and getting married, he'd once been in an outlaw biker gang in California. And so he should have maybe scared her a little. But the truth was, she felt immediately drawn to him, immediately safe with him, and . . . and as if somehow she maybe almost remembered him. "Lucky," she said softly when he looked too shy to speak.

He nodded, swallowed visibly, and said, "Yeah." And this time, on gut instinct, she was the one to initiate the hug, surprised once more to discover how right and pure it felt to be in his burly embrace.

And after a long, warm moment, he whispered in her ear, "I'm so glad you're home now. I have your name on my chest."

And it struck her as an awkward thing to say, and yet the earnestness in his voice negated that, along with finding out that this man holding her now had tattooed the memory of her onto his skin, that she'd been that important to him. As more tears threatened, she pulled back to say, "Can I see?"

And though he looked a bit sheepish doing it, Lucky reached down to peel the black T-shirt he wore upward over a well-muscled stomach and chest until she saw two names tattooed in dark script across his flesh: Tessa's and her own. And for some reason, seeing it there made her cry a little more. And more tissues were handed around, and more nervous laughter resonated until finally Mike said, "Lasagna's done, so let's eat."

The meal, to her surprise, was easier. Being an only child of a working single parent, Anna had spent her fair share of time at friends' houses, with their families, and this felt like *that*. It was easy to sit and listen to them talk, and she found she liked drinking in the cadence of their voices, hearing how they interacted with each other. Sometimes they asked *her* questions, but thankfully it was simple stuff.

"Anna," her new mother said, "I haven't even asked—where do you work? What do you do?"

"I have a degree in hotel management," she explained, "and I've been with the Hyatt chain since before I was out of college. But I'm taking some time off right now." The truth was, she'd resigned. Her mother's death had brought her a surprising inheritance, passed down from Claudia Karras's parents and saved for Anna—it was way more than enough to buy her dream car and to take some time away from work. Not that she'd ever expected that she'd want or need so much time away. But her mother's deathbed confession had turned her world upside down. And the car indulgence . . . well, she could blame that on temporary insanity, but the fact was, she didn't regret it—she loved her Mustang.

"That sounds like a fun job," Rachel told her. "Were you at the Hyatt downtown in Indy? My ad firm, before I moved back to Destiny, was just around the corner from there."

It had been nice to discover Rachel had lived in Indianapolis for most of her adult life. "Yes, I was," Anna replied.

"And where did you go to school, dear?" her new mom asked.

"The University of Indiana. It allowed me to live at home and take care of—" Okay, maybe these questions weren't so easy after all.

But her new dad—not that she'd ever had an old one—immediately put her at ease, even reaching to touch her hand where it absently held her fork near the edge of her plate. "It's all right, Anna. Really."

Yet she'd accidentally brought up an unpleasant subject. "Well, it allowed me to take care of . . . my mom. My other mom." God, her stomach pinched saying it—no matter how you sliced it, it was still awkward.

"She . . . wasn't well?" her father asked.

And then Anna did her best to explain. About the nervous breakdowns and the occasional psychotic breaks. She didn't like discussing it; she didn't like remembering how it had forced her to be the grown-up in the house long before she should have had to take on that role—but . . . "I hope maybe that can help you all to . . . forgive her, just a little. Or at least understand. I've struggled with that myself since her death, and I still harbor a lot of anger, but . . . she raised me, and she loved me, and she never meant to hurt anyone."

Everyone stayed silent after that, and she realized it was far, far too soon to be asking anything like forgiveness of them and she wished she hadn't gone there. And she found she wasn't quite able to meet anyone's eyes in that exact moment—well, except for Logan's, who sat across the table from her. Her gaze stopped there and, like before, she felt she had a friend in him.

And maybe something more.

"Well, the lasagna was great, Rachel," Logan said with a big smile.

Which spurred happy conversation and thankfully ended the awkwardness Anna had created. "From Grandma Romo's recipe," Rachel said.

Anna's new mother told her, "You've really got it down, Rachel. It took me years to make it just like hers."

And while that was going on, Anna kept her eyes on Logan and mouthed the words, *Thank you.*

Once dinner was over, everyone gathered in the living room to look at family pictures. Which all seemed good and easy and fine until they began showing her the ones of her as a little girl. She'd never seen herself so young. "My mother told me all my baby pictures were lost in a fire," she said softly as she reached down, running her fingertips over one of the photos of her in a white Easter dress. Maybe she was trying to connect with it that way, feel it, remember it. God, she looked so happy.

And then she turned the page of the photo album in her lap to find snapshots of her with her two older brothers, both of them looking so protective of her—and she gasped. Because . . . "I think I remember."

"What do you remember?" Mike asked. He sat by her side, almost hovering, the way he had ever since they'd met yesterday. He hadn't even really wanted to leave to go meet their parents this afternoon.

She met his gaze, so close—and again, so much like her own—and swallowed back the lump in her throat before she said, "You. And Lucky. Just a little."

She'd had the vague notion of recollection about them both before, but this was more. She stared off before her without really seeing anything in the room for a moment, trying to go back in time, trying to recall. "I think . . . I used to ask my mother about you both. I think I called you Mikey and Lucky."

"You're kind of how I ended up with the nickname," Lucky told her from where he sat perched on the arm of the couch. "Mike called me 'lucky' one night because I kept beating him at board games, and it stuck with you for some reason. You called me that over and over until everybody else did, too."

She smiled, liking that idea—that in her short time with this family she'd given them one small thing that had lasted besides heartache and pain—but then she went back into the memory to say, "She told me you were imaginary friends. Imaginary," she repeated—and then she burst into fresh tears of anger she couldn't push down. "But you weren't imaginary at all. You were real, and you were here all the time, and she took me from you."

And then Mike was hugging her, and she was letting him, even turning her face inward against his shoulder, suddenly ready to let him protect her again—just a bit, even if he did like to hover.

By the end of the evening, Anna was exhausted. And the truth was, she didn't quite know how to feel. Warmly welcomed—or, again, overwhelmed. She'd been told there were lots more Romo relatives who would want to see her soon, and someone suggested having a big party to welcome her home to Destiny. Which sounded very nice . . . but also intimidating. Who wanted that kind of attention? It'd be different if she'd done something great—won an award, written a book, saved a child—but who wanted to be the center of attention for being abducted twenty-five years ago? "I'm . . . not sure I'd be up for that," she admitted.

Despite the fact that Mike and Rachel had plenty of bedrooms—they lived in the same family house where Anna had lived, too, when she was little—their parents had decided to stay in a motel in Crestview, the next town over and the closest place with accommodations, probably because they didn't want to crowd Anna too much, which she appreciated. But that meant very long goodnight hugs at the door and a few more emotions and tears. And before they even left, Anna excused herself to go to the bathroom. She didn't really need to go—she just needed a quiet moment to wrap her head around all that had taken place tonight.

As she glanced in the mirror, though, she felt still more tears gathering behind her eyes. And she crushed them shut, but—damn it—it was too late. Grabbing for a tissue, she blotted away the wetness, tried to pull herself back together.

She was leaning against a wall in the hallway a minute later, just out of view, still dabbing gingerly at the corners of her eyes, when she looked up to find Logan.

"Hey, you okay?" he asked.

She let out a sigh, bummed to be caught looking weepy again, yet gave him a nod. "Yeah. I guess. Just . . . kind of overwhelmed, I suppose. Needed a minute."

And she could tell he had indeed noticed the tissue in her hand and knew it meant she'd been crying. "I can imagine," he replied, his voice soothing. "I just wanted to check on you when I saw you head in this direction, but I'll leave you to yourself."

Though when he turned to go, she reached out, latched onto his wrist. Despite everything else going on, she'd stayed aware of him all night, and of the strange comfort his presence continued to bring her. So now it just seemed natural to say, "Thank you for being here. I realize I barely know you, but it helps."

"Glad to," he told her, his blue eyes sparkling on her. Then he tilted his head. "Hey, any chance you remember *me* from when you were little?"

She tried to think back, but the memories were so few, and so very hazy. Though it made her kind of sad to shake her head and say, "No. I'm afraid I don't. Wish I did."

He shrugged. "I just wondered because you used to follow me around. You liked me a lot back then," he added on a laugh.

She didn't hesitate to say, "I like you a lot *now,* too." And then she followed one more instinct—to reach up and give him a hug.

His body was sturdy and warm against hers, and . . . mmm, it felt far different than the hugs she got from Lucky or Mike. Just as she'd known it would.

And maybe she even would have gone so far as to give him a kiss—but that was when she realized she'd stepped out of her little hiding place to hug him and that they now stood in a doorway, visible to the whole family, gathered near the front door.

And her new mother smiled as she quipped, "We always said you two would end up together someday," and everyone chuckled, and Anna knew it was a joke, but also maybe not *completely* a joke. And she looked up into Logan's eyes and hoped he saw in her gaze the message she was trying to send: *I think I want you.*

* * *

Amy stood behind the counter ringing up a murder mystery novel for Rachel's grandma, Edna Farris. Edna lived at the apple orchard just outside town, which Rachel and Mike helped her operate. "Now that Bret Michaels isn't on TV anymore, need something to keep me awake 'til my bedtime," she said of the novel, making both Amy and Tessa laugh.

Though lately, when Amy laughed or smiled, it was only on the outside. Inside, she remained filled with heartache. It was the strangest feeling, being in love. One part of her wished it had never happened, or that she'd never figured it out, because she'd been a much merrier, even-keeled person up to now. But another part of her couldn't imagine not knowing this amazingly overwhelming emotion, the way her heart—her whole body—somehow just felt filled to overflowing every time she thought of Logan. Which was constantly now.

She woke up with him on her mind and she fell asleep thinking about him. She dreamed of him at night and she fantasized about him during the day.

Some of the fantasies were simple, pure things. She saw them holding hands as they walked across the town square. She envisioned cheering for him at softball games, him coming off the field and giving her a kiss afterward just because she was his girl. She planned imaginary dinners with him at her mother's house, or at his mom's—or heck, anywhere at all.

But some of the fantasies were . . . sexier. They were about kissing the way they had at his cottage that day, but not stopping. They were about clothes coming off, touches being exchanged. They were about their bodies being connected, moving together. How would that feel? To be that close to Logan, to share that with him?

She stayed lost in thought while Edna and Tessa indulged in wedding talk. Rachel and Mike's post-wedding party was taking place in the orchard's barn, and Tessa's expertise in interior design was being put to work to turn the red barn into a suitable reception hall. But when the bookshop's door closed behind Edna, the little bell up above tinkling at her departure, Tessa looked over at Amy from where she stood stocking a display of summer-themed books and said, "What's wrong? You look weird. What are you thinking about?"

"Cats," Amy lied, her gaze landing on Austen, who lay curled in the wide windowsill next to the counter.

"Cats? Really? Because cats usually make you happy."

"I've been trying to get Austen and Mr. Knightley to play together and make friends, but it's just not working. And it's bumming me out because I've gotten attached to Austen, more than the other past strays for some reason, and I guess I was thinking I might actually keep her if she and Knightley could work out their differences. But so far, no go." And all that was true—though of course it wasn't what she'd really been thinking about.

"Well, you never know—keep at it and maybe they'll mend their fences. Now," Tessa went on, her look turning more knowing, "what *really* has you so depressed?"

And Amy just sighed. She'd never had much reason to lie and apparently she wasn't very good at it. So now she simply shot Tessa a pointed glance and said, "Okay, think about it."

It took only a second for the light of understanding to click on in Tessa's eyes. "Oh. Him. You're thinking about Logan."

"It's all I do these days," Amy replied on a sad sigh.

"Any happy thoughts, or only sad ones?" Tessa asked.

Amy gave her head a glum tilt. "All of them. The good, the bad, and the ugly. And I'm already very tired of feeling so down all the time. Unrequited love is exhausting."

Just then, the bell above the door rang and they both looked up to see Logan himself.

"Speak of the . . ." Tessa murmured, but let her words trail off.

"I hope you weren't about to call me the devil," Logan said with a cheerful smile that trickled down through Amy all the way to her toes. Then he looked playfully back and forth between them. "Were you two talking about me?"

Amy and Tessa exchanged glances, and Amy's said, *Do something.* Under normal circumstances, she was usually pretty good at fudging an answer, but these weren't normal circumstances.

Fortunately, Tessa came up with an easy reply. "We were just talking about how glad we are to see you acting like your old self lately. And I was saying how lucky you are to have someone like Amy to stick by you through rough times."

As designed, the words caused Logan to shift his gaze her way. Their eyes met, and his were all sparkly and blue, and she wanted to melt. Just from that. How weird. They'd looked at each other thousands of times in their lives, but now his eyes suddenly got her all hot and tingly. And somehow it was both torture and ecstasy all at once.

"Tessa's right about that—I'm a lucky guy to have someone as sweet as you looking out for me. I'm not sure I've really thanked you enough for that, freckles."

And then—oh God—he actually reached out and squeezed her hand where it rested on the counter. And just like his gaze, the touch rippled all through her—only worse. It ran up her arm and down through her breasts, and—oh my—she even felt it in her panties. She bit her lip, praying her reaction, or how nervous it made her, didn't show on her face.

"Well," she said, then stopped to clear her throat because something suddenly seemed to be clogging it, "I'm just glad that, you know, I could, um, help." Oh good Lord, it was as if she'd lost the ability to form sentences around him. This was insane. She'd never dreamed something as simple as love could fog up her brain so badly.

But then again, love, it turned out, wasn't so simple at all. She'd watched all her friends go through the trials and tribulations of falling in love, and she'd somehow convinced herself that their dramas and troubles were romantic and exciting—yet now, for the first time, she truly understood the pain they'd been experiencing and she sympathized in a whole new way.

And sadly, she didn't even *have* any drama with Logan. Her troubles were . . . nonevents. Her troubles were secretly loving a guy who didn't love her back. How boring compared to all her friends' romances. *Figures. I'm always the boring one, the simple one, the nice one. Nothing ever happens to me—ever.*

Not that she really wanted drama like she'd seen Rachel and Tessa go through before ending up with the men of their dreams. Or Jenny and Sue Ann, either. But somehow, just now, she felt so incredibly . . . dull. Like her life was suddenly empty. She'd always thought she was happy here in Destiny, running her little store, living with her cat, finding romance for other people even though she never found any of her own. But it was just hitting her in a brand new, horrible way that . . . she'd been living her life through other people. Her friends, her customers, the couples she tried to fix up for better or worse. And that . . . it wasn't really living at all. Other than Carl, back when she'd been young, the greatest romance of her life had been with . . . Mr. Knightley in Jane Austen's *Emma*. Oh God—how pathetic was that? And she'd even named her cat after him! Was she insane?

Maybe. And if not insane, then pathetic definitely fit. *You're thirty-four years old and you've lived your whole life in this little town, seeing the same people and doing the same things every single day, all the while waiting for something interesting to happen to you.* And it wasn't happening. Nothing was happening. And it probably never would.

"What's wrong, freckles?" Logan asked then, still wearing the sexy grin she now loved in a whole new way. "You look like you just ate something bad."

"I, um, just . . ." Crap. Why couldn't she act normal anymore?

Thankfully, Tessa spoke up. "I think Amy's just getting worn out from bridesmaid duties. Two weddings so close together—and she's being such a big help to both Rachel and me. We're probably exhausting her."

What a good friend Tessa was—Amy made a mental note to thank her later. Once she pulled herself back together. *If* she pulled herself back together.

"Well," Logan said, his smile fading, "I came in to ask a favor, but maybe it's not the best time."

Logan needed something from her? At the moment, it felt as if he'd just breathed fresh life into her perishing body. *For you, anything.* "No, it's fine. What do you need?"

Yet he still looked doubtful. "You sure? Because it can wait."

"Absolutely. Fire away. What's up?" Suddenly she could speak normally again.

"Well, you know how you've spent our entire adult lives trying to fix me up with different women?"

Oh my. What was this about? Where was it going? Her heartbeat kicked up, but she still managed to respond. "Only to have it fail miserably each and every time," she reminded him, hoping she didn't appear too happy about that.

A soft chuckle erupted from his throat, and—oh God—he was so, so cute. When had he gotten this cute? "I know, and I'm sorry about that. But, uh, something's kinda changed."

Now her chest tightened. Because she wanted to believe this was going to be a *good* change—like him announcing, "Freckles, I'm in love with you and I have to have you!"—but deep inside she knew it was going to be a bad one. In fact, she felt the words in the pit of her stomach before he even spoke them.

"I want you to fix me up with Anna."

"If I loved you less, I might be able to talk about it more."

Jane Austen, from *Emma*

Five

Amy tried to keep her jaw from dropping but wasn't sure she succeeded. *Of course* Logan would ask her to fix him up with Anna—heck, he was probably surprised she hadn't already thought of it herself. After all, she *was* the town matchmaker who usually couldn't be stopped the second she sensed even the most miniscule hint of romance in the air. And God knew she'd sensed it between *those* two. A shame the very suggestion ripped her heart out.

"Oh, I think Amy's plate is a little too full for matchmaking duties right now," Tessa chimed in, still trying to help. "And besides, don't you think Anna's probably got more than enough going on, too?"

"I would," Logan replied, switching his glance to Tessa, "but you saw us together the other night at Mike's. I think she's interested, but I figure a nudge from our little matchmaker here couldn't hurt, you know? Amy's the expert at this sort of thing, so I figure why not let her work her magic."

Amy darted her gaze from Logan to her friend. What had Tessa seen at Mike's? And why hadn't she told Amy? Tessa's slightly guilty expression confirmed that she had indeed held something back about Anna's homecoming dinner, and the notion made Amy's stomach churn harder than it already was.

Yet when Logan looked expectantly back at her, waiting for an answer, she said the only thing she really could. "Sure. Of course."

Thankfully, he didn't see Tessa's eyes go wide since his gaze remained focused on Amy. The town matchmaker. Never before had that title sounded so horrible to her. "Thanks, freckles," he said easily. "I knew I could count on you."

"Always," she said. Though it came out sounding more whispery than she'd intended. "Though . . . it may not be right away. I mean, it's not like I really know her yet. You two already know her way better than I do." Maybe this would get her out of it somehow since, already, she regretted agreeing to do it.

Yet Logan had a ready reply. "Yeah, but you'll get to know her in no time, just like you do when anyone new comes to town."

Darn it, she did always reach out to newcomers, trying to make them welcome. And if Logan wasn't already so into Anna, Amy probably *would* be making a point of befriending her. *Why do I have to be so darn nice?*

"And the couples' shower is coming," he said, "so that'll be a great time to chat her up a little."

Once again, Tessa intervened. "Um, Amy's running

the shower, you know. She's gonna have her hands full."

But Logan just tossed Amy a grin. "If I know my freckles, she'll be wanting to get to know Anna anyway, right?"

Amy swallowed back the lump in her throat. "Right," she managed.

"Thanks again, freckles. I know you'll weave your magic spell over Anna just like you do everyone else, and then I'll be golden. Gotta go."

"Where are you off to?" she asked.

"Gonna stop by the Dew Drop and see about that bartending job," he said easily.

And now it was Amy whose eyes widened. "You're still doing that? Because I just figured, now that you were feeling all revived and everything, that—"

"Nope," Logan cut her off. "Still needing that new direction, so for now, as long as Anita will have me, the Dew Drop Inn it is."

"Well, I still think that's a rotten idea," Amy informed him, "but for what it's worth, I just saw Anita walk by a little while ago. So she might still be somewhere in town."

"Great—I'll see if I can find her. Catch you two later." And he was out the door, exiting almost as unexpectedly as he'd arrived.

After the bell rang and the door fell shut, Amy and Tessa just looked at each other.

"What the hell is he going to the Dew Drop for?" Tessa asked at the precise moment Amy said, "What did you see at the Romo family dinner that you didn't tell me?"

They both stayed silent for a moment until Amy decided to rush through an answer so they could move on to what felt more important at the moment—the unknown. "Logan has this cockamamie idea that he's giving up firefighting. And while he's figuring out what else he wants to do, he's going to apply for the open position at the bar. Now what did you see?"

Tessa sighed, met Amy's gaze, and looked more troubled than Amy liked. "Well, they just . . . seemed chummy, looked cozy. At the end of the night, they were hugging. But not like hugging goodbye—more like hugging across the room when they didn't realize anyone saw them."

Amy's stomach dropped. It could have been worse and maybe she'd even been expecting something more awful, but the picture in her head stung.

Anna was beautiful and could surely have any guy she wanted. Why did she have to want Logan? And why on earth did Logan even think he needed her help anyway? He'd gotten further with Anna in a couple of hours than Amy ever hoped to get with Logan again. And sure, there'd been the kissing incident on the couch, but given that he hadn't been fully aware it was her he'd been kissing, that just didn't seem to count for much. Except in her mind. And her body. Both of which craved more.

"I'm an awful person," Amy announced then.

Tessa looked skeptical. "Since when?"

"Since I have the nerve to be jealous of Anna Romo. After all she's been through. I should be happy to fix her up with Logan if that's what they both want. I should want them both to be happy."

Though, in response, Tessa's eyes narrowed and she said, "Are you crazy?"

Amy shrugged. "Lately I can't really rule that out."

Facing Amy, Tessa planted her hands on her hips and appeared almost angry. "Look, sympathizing with Anna for what she's endured is one thing. But fixing her up with Logan is another. You have nothing to feel bad about at all. You've known Logan your whole life and you have big, new feelings for him, and of course you can't want him to hook up with someone else, no matter who she is. Anna's going through a difficult time right now, but that doesn't mean you have to surrender Logan to her. And I can't believe you agreed to fix them up!"

"Well, what else could I say? I mean, unless I want to confess my feelings, I have no reason to refuse. And surrender has nothing to do with this. You can't surrender something you never had."

Tessa shrugged. "Maybe not, but you can fight to have it."

Amy just sighed. She appreciated Tessa's support, but . . . "Seriously, Tessa, have you seen Anna? Have you noticed that she's the most gorgeous thing to ever grace the Destiny town square? And has it occurred to you that if Logan was going to start having romantic feelings for me that it probably would not be at the very moment the most beautiful girl this town has ever produced is putting the moves on him?"

All of this actually quieted Tessa for a second and Amy felt she'd made some pretty irrefutable arguments. So it surprised her when Tessa finally walked over to the counter, standing across it from Amy, and said, "I'm not sure any of that matters, Ames."

"What do you mean?"

"Do you remember when I was first falling for Lucky? How I felt so desperate to just . . . live a little, to just somehow experience life before it passed me by?"

"Yes. And you got a tattoo. But I don't think a tattoo is going to help me much. And I'm not sure I could pull it off anyway."

Tessa just cocked her head at an annoyed angle. "If you'll recall, the tattoo was only one way I chose to express myself and throw caution to the wind a little."

Okay, true enough—Tessa had gone through an interesting transformation back then. And in fact, Amy thought her friend had really blossomed, come into her own, when all that happened. She'd discovered and indulged more of who she really was with no regrets, and the fact was, nothing but good had come from Tessa's daring. Still . . . "What's your point?"

"You're at a crossroads right now, Amy, a big one."

"How do you know?"

"Because I can feel it. You're just not yourself lately—you want something more, just like I did. And I'm telling you, you have to be bold enough to just go for it."

Amy blinked nervously. In honesty, she thought—feared—that Tessa was right; she was at a crossroads. She was suddenly dissatisfied with a life she'd always loved. She felt adrift, lost, abandoned—by something she couldn't even name—and bored. Yet . . . "What is it I'm supposed to be going for, and how do I go for it?"

"The thing you're going for is Logan, of course," Tessa said. "But the how part is something only you can decide."

Amy just gave her a helpless look. "I hate to tell you this since I know you're trying to come to my aid, but . . . I have no idea what to do with that advice."

"All I'm saying is . . . you have to do *something*. Right now. To change the way this is going. To change your life. You have to at least try. Because if you don't, well . . . I just have a feeling you'll always regret it."

Those were pretty horrible, serious words and they sank into Amy's bones. And then a hideous idea—

complete with images—entered her head. That the next wedding in Destiny after the two already planned this summer would be Logan and Anna's. And the whole town would rejoice at how perfect it all was. And Amy would be forced to stand there and watch them take vows that would join them together forever—and heck, knowing her, she'd probably be the one to pin on Logan's boutonniere and hand out punch at the reception. And that . . . oh Lord, that would be the final nail in the coffin of her happiness. She'd just be *done* after that, *finished*—she couldn't imagine ever feeling hopeful again if Logan married Anna.

Of course, she was being overly dramatic here, and getting way ahead of herself, but still . . . maybe Tessa was right. Maybe she needed to do something, make some sort of brave and dramatic move. "Okay," she finally said.

And Tessa looked happily stunned. "Really?"

"Yes," Amy said, trying to get used to the idea.

"What are you doing to do?" Tessa asked.

"I don't know yet," Amy said.

Only then, seized by just the beginning spark of inspiration, Amy stepped out from behind the counter and walked to the wide window near the easy chairs and looked out. Logan's Grand Prix still sat parked along the curb outside. And as she leaned to glance farther down the street, she spotted Logan and Anita Garey, owner of the Dew Drop Inn, walking toward Dolly's Main Street Café together. Logan had obviously found her and was using the opportunity to approach her about the job.

Then, as the notion in her head started to take more shape, she turned to face Tessa again. "What if . . . what if I wrote him a letter? From . . . a secret admirer."

She waited for Tessa to be awed by the idea—only to hear her friend say, "Weak at best. But better than nothing if it's all you've got."

Half an hour later, Amy stood at the counter reading over the letter she'd painstakingly written on a sheet of scented blue stationery she kept under the bookstore counter for letters she occasionally wrote to her grandma. Though this was more of a note than a letter. The important part, she figured, was that it would let Logan know that someone else besides just Anna was interested in him. He would at least be curious—and maybe even intrigued. And between the options of this and simply blurting out a proclamation of love for him, this seemed much more manageable until she could figure out a Step 2.

Dear Logan,

> *To me, you are amazing. You are everything a woman could ever want in a man: kind, generous, loyal, loving. I wish I could tell you this in person, but I'm too shy. So for now, please just know that there is someone nearby who thinks you're incredible and who dreams you might somehow feel the same way about her.*

> *Your Secret Admirer*

Then, fairly impressed with her work, she passed it across the counter to Tessa. Who sneered slightly. "Sounds kind of typical," she said. "And you didn't say anything about how attractive he is. Men want to know that sort of thing. They have huge egos."

Amy hadn't realized that, but . . . "I'm not sure I'm ready to go there, to say something like that. It sounds corny to me."

Tessa simply gave her a look that said, *Do I have to do everything here?* "Corny or not, you have to include something like that. Men also want sex. You want him to think there's a hot girl on the other end of this note, after all." She waved the letter in the air as if to emphasize her point.

"But, um, there's not," Amy reminded her.

Which shifted Tessa's look from annoyed to more . . . empathetic. "Of course there is," she said softly.

Still, Amy knew the truth about herself. And it didn't even bother her. Or . . . it hadn't before now anyway. "Tessa, no one has ever thought I was hot in my entire life."

"What about Carl?" Tessa countered. "Back when you and he—"

"No," Amy cut her off, not wanting to go down that road. "I'm sure he found me . . . attractive *enough,* but I've never ventured anywhere even remotely near hot."

At this, Tessa set the note back on the counter between them and pursed her lips, her expression set and determined. "Well, you at least know you're cute, don't you?"

Cute? Hmm. Maybe on her good days. "Okay, I guess I can go with cute." In fact, it made her feel good to think cute was still worth something in this day and age when hot and sexy were all you ever heard about.

"Well, cute is good, and it's a lot to work with. And you could easily go from cute to totally hot if you tried."

"I could?" That sounded like a leap to her.

"And besides," Tessa went on, "hot is as much a matter

of attitude and enthusiasm as anything else. Trust me on this."

Says one of my totally hot friends. But Amy held that inside and tried to think of what else she could say in her note to Logan. Something sexual. Yikes. She just didn't know how to do that. "I'm new at this part of it," she said to Tessa as she stared back down at the letter. "Oh heck, I'm new at *all* of it. I don't know how to do any of this."

"Well, if you don't hurry, Logan will come back to his car and it'll be too late." And, of course, Amy knew she'd see Logan's car sometime again soon, but this suddenly felt urgent, and she'd come too far now, worked up her courage too much—she didn't want to wait; she wanted to get this over with, in fact.

But as she looked to the letter in front of her again, her thoughts froze. She just didn't know how to tell a man she found him insanely perfect and sexy in every way. She felt . . . embarrassingly inept.

And that was when Tessa yanked both the letter and pen away from her, laid the sheet of stationery back on the counter facing in her direction, and began adding something to the bottom. Oh boy. Apparently, this felt urgent to Tessa now, too.

A minute later, she finished, saying, "Okay, this is much better now. Where's the envelope?"

But Amy only replied by snatching up the piece of paper and looking toward the bottom. Thankfully, Tessa had mimicked her handwriting pretty well. And then she read the new part.

P.S. You have the most beautiful blue eyes I've ever seen. And I fall asleep at night dreaming of your kisses.

Whoa. Had Tessa read her mind? Because if she could
have thought of it—and had been brave enough—that
might be exactly what she would have written. Because
it wasn't *too* over-the-top sexual. And it was so, so true.

Still, though, the idea of giving this to Logan—well,
somehow this upped the stakes. Because if the time ever
truly came to admit she'd written it, he'd know. That
she wanted to . . . do things with him, things like kiss
him. And she knew that was normal—she knew it pretty
much went hand in hand with the other things the letter
said—yet this stuff was just so much more difficult for
her than for other people.

"Don't just stand there," Tessa said. "Put it in the envelope and get it out on his car."

Okay. You can do this. Even though it meant there was
no turning back.

Well, okay, technically, she guessed she *could* turn
back afterward—by never letting Logan know it had
come from her. Yet even so, taking the step of putting
this on his car seemed monumental.

Under Tessa's prodding gaze, she folded the blue sheet
of stationery and slid it into a matching envelope, then
simply wrote Logan's initials on the outside: *LW.* And
without further ado, they both walked to the door and
stepped out onto the sidewalk, Amy's heart beating like
a drum.

One or two people meandered along the opposite side
of the square, but no one seemed to be paying attention
to Amy and Tessa. "Do it," Tessa said. "I'm watching
Dolly's front door. Do it now. Before it's too late."

So with her palms as sweaty as any twelve-year-old
sending her first love note, Amy walked up to Logan's
car and slipped the envelope under the windshield

wiper on the driver's side. Then she gave a panicky look around, thankful to find no eyes upon her, and scurried back inside the bookstore like a mouse.

A second later, Tessa ducked in behind her, appearing a little alarmed. "That was close," she said. "He just came out."

"*What?* Are you serious?"

"Don't worry—he was still talking to Anita and he didn't see a thing." Then she let out a big breath. "But it was close."

They stood frozen a few seconds longer, both a little spooked by the timing, until Amy said, "We should try to look normal. He's going to pass by the window any second now."

So Tessa speedily went back to stocking the summer display, and Amy—seeking a little comfort, she supposed—bent down to scoop Austen into her arms from where the tabby had situated herself in one of the easy chairs. Then, with the kitty in her grasp, she eased down into the chair herself, realizing she suddenly felt a little unsteady.

"This is all gonna turn out great, Ames, you'll see," Tessa said from behind her then, perhaps sensing her unease now that the deed was done. And Amy only wished she could be so sure. For the second time already since falling for her old friend, she kind of wanted to throw up.

And when she saw Logan go striding past the shop's big window, a shiver rippled through her. He was about to find it, read it. Her words of love. Passion. Things that were so foreign to her. It felt beyond strange to be sharing them. And so soon. And especially like this. Even if he didn't know they'd come from her.

When the door opened a few minutes later, the bell jangling, she flinched, and her stomach practically shriveled when she saw who it was. "Logan," she murmured, her heart in her throat. She sensed Tessa darting her head around from where she stood working behind her.

"Hey, did you guys see anyone near my car?" he asked, his brow knit.

"No," Amy answered quickly.

"Why?" Tessa asked much more easily. "Something wrong with it?"

"No," he said uncertainly. "Just wondering." But then he stood there looking understandably perplexed and Amy wished she could read his thoughts. Was he intrigued, as she hoped? Or did he think it was juvenile? Or worse, creepy. She hadn't really taken the time to consider all his possible responses.

"Did Anita give you a job?" she asked then, feeling the need to take his mind off the letter for at least as long as he was in her presence—since she still felt a little sick.

It worked—he grinned. "Um, yeah. She did. I start in a couple days."

"Well, I still think you belong back in the firehouse— but for now, I'm glad for you."

"It has to be this way, Ames. Gotta do something else." He sounded completely resolute.

And it hit her then how so many people in her world were suddenly undergoing big transitions: Tessa and Rachel getting married, Mike and Lucky not only getting married but having Anna return home. And Logan, of course. And Anna Romo herself. And . . . her.

And maybe her own transition seemed like the smallest of the lot, but it was actually the most significant of her entire life.

She'd never been in love before, after all.

And so she'd certainly never been in love with one of her lifelong best friends.

And she'd also never wanted to *kiss* one of her best friends, or . . . do more than that with one of them, either.

And if by some truly amazing miracle Logan ever wanted her in the same way . . . well, then the time would come when she'd have to face doing something else she'd never done before. Something she feared deeply. Something she secretly craved with all her heart. And something she'd begun to think she might never get to do.

And who knew—if Logan ended up with Anna Romo, maybe she never would. She let out a sigh, sad about it in a whole new way now.

No one knew Amy's deepest, darkest secret.

Not even Tessa or Rachel.

Which meant Tessa didn't even completely realize all that was at stake here.

The sad truth was that, at thirty-four, Amy was still a virgin.

. . . and communicate all that need be told by letter . . .

Jane Austen, from *Emma*

Six

Amy buzzed around Edna Farris's yard, just outside the little white farmhouse, like the busy bees currently enjoying the white clover dotting the late springtime grass beneath her feet. Edna had volunteered her place for the joint couples shower Amy was throwing for Rachel and Tessa, and since the weather was nice, the lush orchard was the perfect setting.

The tables Mike had transported in his pickup truck from town hall filled the space between the house and little red barn, some designated especially for gifts or food, the rest vacant for seating, and all were laden with fresh flowers, some cut from Amy's mother's yard, some from Edna's. Fortunately, both yards possessed such a proliferation that even using so many left plenty to spare.

"Does everything look pretty?" Amy asked Edna, who stood glancing around, fists planted on her hips.

"Reckon it does," Rachel's grandma said. "You done good, Amy."

Amy smiled at the simple praise, feeling almost like her old self for a change. She'd always enjoyed doing things for others and making people happy. Though she still suffered from the recent realization that she also wanted something more. And that she didn't quite know how to go about getting it.

"And don't you worry none. Your day'll come soon enough, too," Edna said.

Amy tried to hold in her sigh. *Thanks for reminding me, Edna, that I have Destiny's worst case of always-a-bridesmaid syndrome. And that people probably feel as sorry for me as I'm feeling for myself lately at having my two best friends get married in the same summer.* But she knew Edna meant well, so she only said, "Thanks, Edna. I just hope Rachel and Tessa enjoy the afternoon."

They both looked up to see a couple of cars crossing the old stone bridge that spanned Sugar Creek and led into the orchard. A third could be seen turning in next to the Farris-Romo Family Orchard sign out by the road.

"Looks like the party's startin'," Edna said. And over the next twenty minutes, nearly all the guests arrived, which meant most of Destiny's population. As luck had it, even Mike and Lucky's parents were still in town, allowing them to come, too.

And so Amy did what she did best—she continued buzzing about, greeting people, serving up punch, setting out food. The more she buzzed around, after all, the less time she had to think about everything weighing on her. Like her virginity.

Sometimes she didn't think about it at all. Sometimes she almost pretended to herself that she was like all the other girls, that she had a sexual past. She knew her friends thought she'd done it with Carl back in the day. At the time, they'd assumed it had happened—and for some reason she'd let them. And as years had begun to pass, she'd been glad she hadn't dispelled the notion. Because the older she got, the more horrifying her virginity became.

Yet she just didn't know how to get rid of it. She supposed some women in her position would go into the city with friends, go dancing, clubbing, find a man looking for a good time and let him have it. But she wasn't "some women." She didn't *go* clubbing. And she wouldn't know how to send those kinds of signals to a man anyway. And as badly as Amy wanted to lose her virginity—as desperately as her body sometimes ached for that—she just couldn't imagine doing it with someone she didn't know or care about. Ever. But especially not the first time.

And so she kept the unpleasant and secret distinction of being Destiny's oldest virgin, and she felt like a loser every time she thought about it.

Which had, unfortunately, been a lot lately. And maybe that was what had driven her to make a move, like Tessa had said, to just *do something*.

Not that she really thought she had a prayer of ever getting a guy as hot as Logan to fall for her the way she'd officially fallen for him. But the idea of just delivering him, practically gift-wrapped with a bow around his waist, to another woman, made her feel . . . desperate beyond measure. Hence the note. And the plan. To do something else soon. She just didn't know *what* yet. Or what, realistically, she expected to come from this. Besides maybe utter humiliation and despair. She didn't *like* this business of feeling desperate, yet she wasn't sure how to get rid of *that* any more than she knew how to get rid of her virginity.

She held back the long sigh that wanted to escape her as she passed a cup of punch to Mrs. Sheridan, Tessa's mother. "You always do such a nice job on things like this, Amy," the other woman said.

"Thanks, Mrs. Sheridan."

"And I'm sure one day soon we'll be having a shower for you, too."

She simply nodded. One more person who meant well but somehow made her feel more pathetic than she already did.

"Need help with anything, freckles?"

When she looked up to see Logan at her side, as handsome and gorgeous as ever in khaki cargo shorts and a bright polo shirt, her chest tightened—along with a few other key body parts. A week ago, the idea of wanting him had been so new that she hadn't quite been comfortable with even her own thoughts about it, but now . . . well, now it would be far too easy to just melt into his well-muscled arms.

"Um, no—I'm good, thanks." *In ways, that is. In other ways, I'm a mess. And I want you so much I can barely stand it.* Yep, apparently she was getting used to thinking of Logan like this.

"As always, you've got it all under control," he said with a sexy grin.

No, not all of it. Even so, she tried her best to smile and act normal.

"Hey, there's Anna," he said, his eyes lighting up.

And inside, Amy emitted a low growl. It was the kind of reaction she didn't even know she had inside her. Until now. And—oh no—it was directed at a perfectly nice woman who'd been abducted as a child, for God's sake, and was surely going through some serious turmoil as she tried to get to know her family. Amy felt like scum.

And even more so when she saw how stunning Anna looked in a long, flowy skirt with an exotic-looking print and a lacy top that accentuated what appeared to be an absolutely perfect pair of breasts.

"Don't forget to try to talk to her today, okay?" Logan reminded her.

As if she could forget the request. "In all my spare time," Amy replied, trying to sound teasing, and then she added, "I'll do my best," thinking that with any luck she really wouldn't have the opportunity. "Tessa was right—I'm pretty busy."

He just shrugged in his easy, amiable Logan way. That was one more thing she loved about him—he was so easygoing, so understanding. And it was nice to have the old Logan back. "Well, you know whatever you can do will be appreciated."

Just then, Anna spotted him and lifted her hand in a wave. And—blegh—she looked as happy to see him as he was to see her.

"Looks like you might not need my help anyway," she heard herself say, hoping it didn't come out too bitter.

"Maybe not," he answered, suddenly sounding confident. Which bugged her just as much.

And that must have been what prompted the next words out of her mouth. "On the other hand, you never know. Without my magic involvement, it might not work out."

Logan just looked at her. And she immediately understood why. When it came to matters of romance and matchmaking, she was always the picture of optimism. Always. She was, after all, upbeat, cheerful Amy, who constantly built people up, expected the best for everyone, and assured them that love was on the way. So she added a hasty, "Just kidding," to try to cover the weird blunder.

After which the object of her desire tossed her a quick smile that she actually felt in her panties, even under these particularly horrible circumstances, and said, "Well, I'm gonna go talk to her."

"Okeydoke," she said, then looked back to the punch bowl as if it was in dire need of her attention.

Only a second later, though, she glanced up. Because she couldn't stop herself. And she watched as Anna Romo greeted Logan with a hug. A hug that made her heart crumble.

Oh God, I want to hug him that way. Why can't it be me? Just this once. With just this one guy. Why can't I have the same kind of romantic fun, the same kind of love, the rest of the world seems to have?

"Well, just standin' there starin' at 'em ain't gonna fix anything."

She whipped her head around to find Edna at her elbow, a punch cup in her hand—and gasped. Edna knew! "How did you know?"

"Got eyes in my head, don't I?"

Oh no, was her new affection for Logan that obvious? But Edna clearly read her mind on that, too, since she went on to say, "Don't worry—nobody else can tell. I'm just a keen observer is all."

"Please don't tell anybody, Edna."

Rachel's grandma drew back, appearing almost offended. "Do I look like I got loose lips? No need to fret—your secret's safe with me. But I wouldn't take it to the grave or anything if I was you. Nope—if it was me, I'd do somethin'."

Just like Tessa had told her. *Do something.* But they both made it sound so easy. "Have you seen her, Edna?" Amy asked pointedly. "She's beautiful."

It surprised her when Edna merely shrugged. "Men'll go for that sorta thing, sure. But there's more important stuff about a woman and most of the good ones eventually smarten up enough to figure that out."

"So what do you think I should do?" She was just beginning to remember that Edna had a wily wisdom about her that she'd always envied and admired.

"Not sure," Edna said, disappointing her. "Only you know what's in your heart, what kinda move you're ready to make. But I'm just sayin' I wouldn't lay low for too long 'cause he's got that look in his eye."

Amy cringed. "What look?"

"The look of a man tryin' to find somethin'. Somethin' important in life—somethin' he can sink his teeth into, if ya know what I mean. And ya don't wanna let him start thinkin' that somethin' is her just because she was in the right place at the right time."

And with that, Edna moved off, leaving Amy to her thoughts.

She feared it was already too late to stop Logan from thinking Anna was exactly what he needed right now. Heck, *she* almost wondered if Anna was what he needed. Fate *had* dropped her smack in the middle of Destiny right after Logan had decided he wanted someone new in his life. Add that to Anna being so . . . Anna, and it was hard for Amy to believe she had a chance in hell.

Watching them together was almost more than her

heart could stand. It made her want to cry. And she didn't think she'd ever felt so alone in her entire life, even standing there hosting a party with all of her closest friends around her.

The big question was: What next?

And the only answer she could come up with was, sadly, another love note from Logan's secret admirer.

Of course, there was no blue stationery handy today. But time really did seem to be of the essence here, so she'd just have to improvise. As people milled about, she made her way into Edna's house through the back door, suddenly glad to be alone, away from everyone. Because she was starting to cry a little, and this would give her a chance to get it under control.

Making her way into Edna's little bathroom with the claw-foot tub and old-fashioned pedestal sink, she looked in the mirror and barely recognized herself. She wasn't used to seeing herself cry—her eyes glassy, a tear sneaking out to roll down her cheek before she could stop it. Reaching for a tissue, she dabbed at the wetness, hoping to keep her makeup intact. Not that she wore a lot of makeup—that just wasn't who she was.

Still looking, she took in the small lines beginning to form near her mouth, the tiny wrinkles developing around her eyes. She was getting older and she couldn't stop the march of time. Not even the freckles sprinkling her cheeks could hide it. *I'm going to be alone forever.*

And why, why, why do I suddenly care so much? Why does it suddenly feel like life is slipping away, out of my grasp? Why don't I care about the things I used to? Where did all my blind contentment go?

Love, she had discovered quickly, was something that

filled you up so much, so full, that even when it was unrequited, you couldn't not want it. You couldn't will yourself to go back in time and not feel it anymore. It was too consuming. And yet . . . right now, she wished she could. She hated the way she felt. Undesirable. Unnoticed. Underappreciated. Unlovable. All because Logan had kissed her and then gone back to acting the same way he always had before. While nothing in *her* world would ever be quite the same.

Part of her wanted to just run away. Just get in her car and leave the shower, leave Destiny, and drive . . . someplace. But besides being an unrealistic non-solution, she couldn't leave Tessa and Rachel right now anyway. Her friends meant everything to her and they were always there for her, and the way things were looking, them and the cat might be all she had to cling to as life went on.

So, when she eliminated the idea of running away from everything, that left only two options.

Accept your life as it is—accept that you're going to stay in this town, running the bookstore, being the smiling-on-the-outside-while-you're-crying-on-the-inside matchmaker for the rest of your days.

Or seriously fight to win the man you love.

Even if fighting, at this moment, meant only being brave enough to send him another missive from his secret admirer.

Letting out the breath she hadn't quite realized she was holding, she swallowed back her tears and forced herself to toughen up. Because that was how it had to be. She had a letter to write. And then she had to walk back out of this house and straight into the party she was hosting, head held high.

Passing back through Edna's front parlor, she spied an

old rolltop desk, the top open. And it took only a slight pull on one drawer to locate a stack of small folded note cards, the corners adorned with an antique-looking rose design. She knew Edna would gladly donate one to the cause.

As she seated herself in the wooden chair before the desk, it occurred to her that this particular note card seemed made for sweet, shy, flowery sentiments of burgeoning affection. However, at the moment, she felt far too desperate—and even daring—for that. Now was the time to be more outgoing, like Tessa had prodded her to before. And she didn't have time to sit around analyzing this—so she just wrote.

Dear Logan,

When I see you, it's all I can do not to melt into a puddle of desire. I want to know how it feels to have your hands on me. And to know how it feels to touch you, as well. All over. With you, I yearn to let go of all my fears and inhibitions and just do what my body urges me to. You are my dream, my fantasy. And with each passing day, I wonder more and more if it can ever come true. I only hope and pray I can somehow find the courage to tell you who I am. Soon. Before it's too late.

Your Secret Admirer _

When she was done, she read back over it. A puddle of desire? Yikes, where had that come from? And *all over? What my body urges me to?* Good Lord, who was she?

Well, she was a woman driven to desperate measures, obviously. Which was what desperate times called for. And as she rose from the desk and walked into the kitchen, stopping to peer out the window, the first people she caught sight of were Anna and Logan—she touched his arm now as she leaned in to tell him something private—and the sight reminded Amy that these were definitely desperate times.

Taking a deep breath, she put on a smile and walked out the door, doing her best to keep the note card hidden. Though even if anyone noticed it, they'd think it just belonged on a shower gift.

She'd taken only a few steps when Tessa looked up from a conversation with Lettie Hart and Old Mrs. Lampley to meet her gaze knowingly, as if she could tell something was up. So Amy wasted no time casting a speedy glance toward Logan and Anna—ugh, they were laughing now—then quickly flashed the card in her hand. Tessa winked, and Amy knew her friend got the message.

"Hey, freckles."

Crap. *Now, Logan? Really?* She looked up to see him walking toward her and re-hid the card behind her back.

"Logan!" Tessa called, and hurriedly broke away from the other ladies to make her way over. And before he even reached Amy, Tessa grabbed onto his arm and said, "We need you over here for a big bridesmaid-and-groomsmen discussion about Rachel and Mike's wedding."

As she began to drag him away, he pointed toward Amy and said, "Well, *she's* in the wedding, too," but thankfully, Tessa just kept talking, something about who was escorting who down the aisle, and she also kept dragging Logan deeper into the clumps of people milling about. Which gave Amy the chance to finally sneak away.

Fortunately, no one else noticed or called after her as she made a beeline toward the many cars parked neatly beneath the first few rows of apple trees growing along Sugar Creek. As she grew closer, she felt as if the foliage made her all the more inconspicuous.

Though as she neared Logan's car, she spotted Duke Dawson coming in the opposite direction. Duke was Lucky Romo's best friend and owned the biker bar, Gravediggers, over in Crestview. He wore a trim, dark goatee, sported a few tattoos, and generally made Amy a little nervous. She'd heard a motorcycle in the vicinity a minute ago, so it must have been his.

"Hi," she said simply as they prepared to pass one another in the cool shade the trees provided. They'd only met a couple of times in passing, at Lucky's place, next to Tessa's on Whisper Falls Road.

"You're Tessa's cute little friend, right?" he asked.

Huh. So maybe she *was* cute. Only—wait, *Duke* thought she was cute? She wasn't sure whether to be flattered or frightened.

"Um, right," she managed, picking up her pace a little as she moved past him.

He stopped, gave his head a tilt. "Where ya runnin' off to, cutie?"

Oh dear. "I . . . just need to get something from my car."

"Need help?"

Sheesh—Lucky's intimidating biker buddy had to pick now to be chivalrous? Why did guys keep offering to help her *today* when—of all times *ever*—she really needed to be left alone?

"No—I'm good, thanks." She pointed toward the party. "Lucky and Tessa are over there."

"Okay then," he said, looking amused, as if he thought he made her nervous. And on a normal day, yes, *of course* he would have been making her nervous. But today—nope, she already had enough to be uncomfortable about for one little comment from Duke Dawson to add to it.

Finally, Duke went on his way, so Amy did, too, and just when she'd reached Logan's car, she heard Rachel call out, "Tessa said to hurry up, that she can't keep Logan occupied all day—whatever that means."

And Amy nearly leaped out of her skin. Spinning, she spouted, "Oh my gosh, where did you come from? Quit sneaking up on me like that."

"Sorry," Rachel said as she approached, looking as summer chic as ever in a sleek, silky dress and strappy platform shoes. "But what are you hurrying to do, and what is she occupying Logan for?"

"For crying out loud," Amy murmured. She might have to kill Tessa now—if Tessa weren't busy being such a good friend. And for the moment, all she could reply to Rachel was, "It's a long story. Just please act like you don't know anything for now."

"That'll be easy since I don't. But I want to." Her eyes dropped to the note card in Amy's hand. "Like what that says and what you're about to do with it."

Sheesh. "Just walk away, Rachel," she said quietly.

Rachel drew back, clearly stunned, since Amy never bossed anyone around—unless it had to do with matchmaking—and she certainly never did so while sounding as stressed as she surely did right now.

"I'm sorry, Rach," she said then, working hard to

sound nicer, more normal. "And I promise I'll explain
the next time I see you, okay? Right now I'm just . . . on
a mission. And it's important. And I don't have time to
tell you the whole long, pathetic story. Fair enough?"

Rachel still wore an odd expression, like she was
wondering what slightly crazy person had invaded
Amy's body. Amy was actually beginning to wonder
that herself, too. But finally Rachel said, "Sure. Fair
enough. Good luck on your mission." Then, when Amy
least expected it, a small smile turned up the corners
of Rachel's mouth. "I must admit, Amy, you have me
intrigued. And that might be a first. I like it."

Amy watched as Rachel turned and sashayed back
across the orchard to where the party was still going on
without her, and when finally—at last—she was convinced she was alone, she sidled up alongside Logan's
car and slipped the rose-laden note card beneath the
windshield wiper, just like before.

Okay, there. It was done. Step 2. Note 2. It upped the
stakes. At least if Logan ever found out it was from her.
And . . . well, if nothing else, she supposed it—again—
let him know there was someone else out there who
wanted him besides Anna Romo.

And as she headed back toward the wedding shower,
she realized she was sweating like crazy and her heart
was beating as fast as if she'd just run a race.

God, this being-in-love business was grueling.

After lunch but before gifts and cake, Logan found himself sitting beneath a shade tree with Anna in a couple of
white Adirondack chairs. If it was possible, he thought
maybe she looked even more striking today than the
other times he'd seen her. For a woman going through so

much, he admired how comfortable she appeared in her own skin. Especially when she began to tell him more about the troubles plaguing her.

"It's so amazing to find out I have this big, wonderful, loving family, but . . . it's a lot to take in. It's what I came here for, sure, but Mike . . ." Then she stopped, shook her head.

And Logan couldn't help feeling a little troubled—on Mike's behalf. "What about him?" he asked cautiously.

"Well, he hovers," she said. "In fact, he's watching me right now, from over by the barn. See?"

Logan looked, and sure enough, even as Mike chatted with shower guests, his glance kept shifting in their direction.

"Here we are, at *his* wedding shower, and all he can think about is me?"

Logan couldn't help taking up for his buddy. "It's not really too surprising if you think about it. I mean, he's literally been looking for you since he was twelve. He's gonna hover for a while, Anna. Just be patient." The fact was—it would be hard for Anna to know what Mike had gone through, the guilt and self-torture he'd suffered. But Logan didn't figure Anna needed more of those reminders heaped on her right now.

"I get that. But I'm kind of . . . an independent woman, you know? I'm used to doing my own thing, my own way. I've had to. Because I grew up kind of fast—because of my mom's problems."

"You guys will work it out," he promised her. And he meant it. He wanted her to feel reassured.

Yet she only shrugged. "I hope so. But I'm actually . . . well, not the most patient person in the world."

And when he caught the look she was giving him

then—something flirtatious and expectant in her dark eyes—he wondered if she was talking about Mike now, or him. Was she waiting to be asked out? Kissed?

And hell—maybe he *should* be asking her out. And in fact, he wasn't sure why he hadn't yet.

Maybe because of Mike, because dating his best friend's just-returned-home-after-all-these-years little sister might get a little weird? Or maybe he wasn't sure he was great dating material at the moment—after what he'd just come through, and given that he'd just left an admirable career for a job some people might consider less than a lateral move. And it wasn't like he was really over the Knight fire anyway—the truth was, it still bothered him, every day; he'd just gotten better at hiding it. Or . . . maybe there was some *other* reason he wasn't asking her out, one he couldn't quite put his finger on.

Just then, he found his gaze drifting over to Amy, where she stood talking to Jenny and Mick Brody next to the punch bowl. She looked pretty today in a spring green dress that brought out the green in her eyes. Yet she'd seemed . . . a little off, too. Though it was a big party—he supposed she did have a lot to handle here.

And even now . . . well, not just anybody would be able to spot this, but he could have sworn he saw something sad behind her smile. It didn't quite reach her eyes, and that wasn't like Amy at all. He'd have to check in with her later, make sure everything was all right. He hated the idea of anything making his freckles sad—and he knew he'd been too caught up in his own drama lately and that it was time to get back to paying attention to the people who mattered.

Seeming to follow his gaze just then, Anna said, "Like it?"

He blinked, looked at her. "Like what?"

"My Mustang, silly."

Oh. Her car was parked in the distance, directly behind where Amy stood. "Uh, yeah, it's great." And it really was. Right now, the red exterior gleamed in the sun. The top was down and the mint-condition classic convertible looked made for fun.

"Want me to take you for a ride sometime?" she asked.

"I was very foolishly tempted to say and do many things . . ."

Jane Austen, from *Emma*

Seven

Logan's groin tightened, just a little. Because he was pretty sure he heard something sexual in the invitation. Not just the way the words could be interpreted, but it was in her voice, too, and definitely—again—in her seductive brown eyes.

"Um, sounds good," he said. After all, if beautiful Anna Romo wanted to take him for a ride, who was he to say no? Whatever was holding him back . . . well, if she was asking him out, it must be God's way of telling him to get over it and get on with things. Right?

"Free tomorrow night?" she asked with a hopeful, confident smile.

Yeah, he was. But . . . aw hell, despite himself, something continued to hold him back a little. "Not sure," he heard himself say.

And she flashed a look that told him she'd been around the block a time or two and sensed he might not be telling the whole truth. But she was still smiling, and he realized Anna wasn't overly sensitive or too emotional—she clearly knew how to do the casual-dating thing with some finesse. "Well, you let me know if you want to get together," she said.

And he thought, *Of course I do.*

Or do I?

Damn. Why did he feel so torn inside, for God's sake?

Then she said, "Oh brother, here comes Mike."

And Logan instinctively said, "Go easy on him, okay?"

"Anna, I want you to meet some people," Mike called as he grew nearer, motioning her over.

And as she got up to go, she peered down into Logan's eyes to say, "Don't go anywhere, all right? So far, you're definitely one of the best things I've found in Destiny." And she concluded with another one of those come-hither looks that seemed to spill from her so naturally with him. And which made it a little hard for him to draw a deep breath.

But . . . what the hell was the deal? Why wasn't he thrilled out of his mind? After all, she was great. Pretty. Funny. Outgoing and confident. And ridiculously sexy without even trying.

He usually *liked* women who let you know what they wanted.

But this was different. This was Mike's long lost little sister.

And . . . why did he get the idea Amy wasn't crazy about fixing them up? Because if Amy thought there was something not right about it . . . well, that mattered to him. She had good instincts, and he knew she cared about him—a lot. She'd been so damn good to him lately, and it dawned on him all over again that he wasn't sure he'd let her know how much he appreciated that.

"Okay, everybody, I need the happy couples up here with me," Amy called out then over the general din of the crowd. "We'll cut the cake and let them start digging in to all these presents."

That was when two things struck him at once: He realized he'd forgotten his shower gifts in the car, and he flashed back to the strange moment when he'd kissed Amy on his couch.

And as he made his way from the party out into the orchard . . . hell, his groin began tightening again. Huh. Over Amy? Groin tightening? Really? Not that there was anything wrong with her—she was cute and funny and probably the sweetest person he'd ever known. But he'd just never thought of her that way. Ever.

Oh well, don't overthink it. You've got a lot of crap in your head right now—the old job, the new job, Anna coming home, Anna asking him out, and apparently those kisses with Amy were still lingering there, too. And of course, just because he was walking around acting normal and had gotten his shit together, that *still* didn't mean he was over what had happened to the Knights.

In fact, his heart clenched just now, just from letting his thoughts go there. And he felt a little dizzy, unsteady. *Keep walking, just keep walking. Don't think about it anymore. Don't see it anymore. Block it back out.* That was pretty much the only way he *managed* the walking-around-acting-normal thing, by just blotting out the rec-ollections he'd begun to fear would haunt him the rest of his life.

Given his current state, the cool air beneath the trees—lightly scented with the last spring apple blossoms—was more than a little refreshing on a day that had grown hot. *Think about Anna,* he commanded himself. Because she put a lot more pleasant visions in his head than that damn fire did. *Think about Anna, who showed up exactly when you needed someone, so it must be meant to be.*

He'd just reached his car and was headed past it toward the trunk when—damn—he caught sight of a note on his windshield. Another one. Wow.

Though the first one had freaked him out a little, he'd almost forgotten about it now. After all, he'd heard or seen nothing unusual since then, and maybe he'd decided it was just kids playing a prank or something. But if there was another one . . . well, that changed things.

And things *really* changed after he read it. Because the woman who'd written it wanted to touch him now. And be touched *by* him. All over. Whoa.

Who the hell could be sending these things?

Okay, stop. Think. He tried to mentally sort through all the single females at the shower today, but most of Destiny was there, making it pretty impossible to narrow it down. And hell—for all he knew, it could be . . . some smitten ten-year-old girl. Though this was starting to sound like a pretty advanced ten-year-old if that was the case. It could really be anyone, he supposed. Someone shy maybe, as the note indicated. Or . . . someone with something to hide, some reason she couldn't be up-front with him.

His ponderings got him nowhere, but they left him curious to say the least. Who the hell could his secret admirer be?

Oh well, no matter how he sliced it, it was one more distraction from unpleasant thoughts of the fire, so if someone wanted to send him secret love notes, he supposed that was fine with him.

After the cake was eaten and all the presents opened, a few people left the party, but most stuck around, nibbling at more food and catching up with friends. Mike had just finished talking with his mom—telling her he'd invited Anna to stay with him and Rachel for as long as she wanted—when he saw Logan standing by himself near an old hay wagon.

"What's up, bud?" he asked, approaching.

"Just enjoying the day."

Mike simply nodded, though he could see some trouble still lurking in his best friend's gaze. "Sure you're doing okay?"

Logan shrugged. "Hell of a lot better than I was a few weeks ago. That's about as much as I can ask for right now. Just taking it one day at a time."

"Well, you know if you need anything, I'm here."

Now his old friend tilted his head accusingly. "Sure, you say that now, but you bailed on Cocoa and me in the end."

Mike knew he was only kidding, though. "For your own good and you know it," he replied with a smile.

"Yeah, I can't believe I let myself get down so low."

"Well, just glad you're back," Mike said. Then a short laugh escaped him. "And glad Anna's back. You know, man, sometimes I still can't believe it." Then he shook his head. He'd spent so many years hoping, praying, not giving up deep down inside, no matter how crazy it seemed. And now, here his baby sister was, back in his arms! And sure, he was still pissed as hell about the whole thing, but he was working through that, and he just kept reminding himself that the important thing was knowing she'd been with someone who loved her and that she was happy, healthy, and here with him now.

"Speaking of Anna," Logan said, appearing a little uncertain, "I, uh, figure I should tell you she kinda asked me out earlier. For tomorrow night."

Mike tried not to react, yet his chest tightened and the muscles in his shoulders tensed. He knew Anna was an adult and all, but . . . damn, he couldn't help it—after everything his family had been through, the urge to be protective flowed through his veins like hot lava.

"I won't go if you don't want me to," Logan said, clearly sensing the reaction anyway.

And Mike felt kind of like an idiot, even as he let out a sigh. "Hell, I don't know the answer," he admitted at a loss. "You're my best friend. And a damn good guy most of the time. Maybe you'd be the best person in the world for her to date." Only then his chest clenched all over again. "But on the other hand, you're my best friend and I know everything you've ever done and every girl you've ever done it with. And if you ever hurt her . . ."

"Geez, would you relax, dude? You're getting way ahead of yourself here."

Mike blew out a long breath. "You're right. I get that. But . . . the idea of you even touching her . . ."

Logan looked him in the eye in the way very few people seemed able to—since most backed off or left him alone when he acted this gruff. "Mike, don't slug me or anything, but you know she's thirty years old, right? Thirty? Not twelve. Or sixteen. Or even twenty. But thirty."

Another long, deep breath left him. "Yeah, I know. But it's hard for me. In a way, to me, she's still five." He knew that sounded a little crazy, but he could say that to Logan. Logan would understand. Logan had been there when Anna *was* five. And ever since.

Still, his best friend simply said, "You can't go back."

Yeah, he realized that. And he hated it. "I don't like the fact that she grew up without me to . . . to . . ."

Logan narrowed his gaze. "Make her into exactly what you think your little sister should be."

He just shrugged. "Something like that, maybe. Not that there's anything wrong with her—she's amazing. Except . . . I think I intimidate her."

"I think you do, too," Logan said. No hesitation. Shit, that sealed the deal—he officially made his little sister uncomfortable. Great.

"It's just that I care so much. That's all."

"I don't think you want me to go out with her," Logan concluded.

And Mike knew that, deep down, that was probably true. Right now, *no one* would be good enough for Anna. And even as perfect as his parents thought the two of them were together—and it was true that when they were all kids, everyone had joked that Logan and Anna would get married someday—it just seemed weird for her to date his best friend. Too much could go wrong. He felt too much loyalty—and love—for both of them.

And still, he knew he couldn't stand in the way of something like that. Anna would end up hating him. And Logan probably wouldn't—but he might have every right to. So finally he said, "Tell ya what, how about you come over to dinner tomorrow instead. We'll invite Lucky and Tessa, too, and we'll all hang out. Play horseshoes afterward in the yard. How would that be?"

And, true to him as the day was long, Logan agreeably said, "Whatever you want, man."

"Baby steps," Mike told him. "I'll do this in baby steps and before long, I'll do better with it. And hey, dude, thanks. For asking. And for being cool about it."

"This is Anna we're talking about," Logan said. And that was all he had to say. They both understood how deep that loss—and this brand new rediscovery—ran.

Only a few people milled about now, the last few saying their goodbyes to Edna as Logan, Adam, and Duke helped load gifts into Mike's pickup and Lucky's Jeep. Amy looked around at the mess—but she didn't mind that it would take a while to clean up. Any distraction was a good one these days. And she was happy that Anna had left a little while ago, by herself, with plans to meet her parents for dinner at Dolly's before they headed back to Florida in the morning.

As for Logan, she was pretty sure he'd already found her note. He'd had to go to his car for gifts after she'd stuck it there. And—oh God—she still couldn't believe she'd turned into some mad secret note writer. That was so not like her. Then again, she still couldn't believe she loved Logan, either. And how horribly painful it continued to be even as it lifted her very soul every time he came to mind.

Just then, J. Geils' "Love Stinks" filled the air and she spun to see that Logan had just pulled his car up near the house. The windows were down and Destiny's only tunable radio station—which played retro music—blared out. Love stinks? Yeah, she had to pretty much agree that it did.

She was shoving used paper plates into an already-packed garbage bag when Logan turned off the car, killing the music, then got out and came over to her.

"What's up?" she asked, trying her best to sound cheerful, normal. Ugh. That was getting harder all the time.

Logan gave his head a pointed tilt, his expression sweet. "You okay, freckles? 'Cause I thought you looked a little sad at times today."

Oh boy. Even when she was able to hide it with other people, Logan could see. Double ugh. "I'm fine," she lied. "Just tired, I guess. The party and all."

"Want me to stick around, help clean up?"

Her first thought was to say no—she didn't like to impose on people, and she didn't mind hard work. But just as quickly, it dawned on her that Tessa would tell her to say yes, that she should be trying to spend more time with him. And she still didn't really believe she could ever win Logan's heart, but even so, spending time with him was . . . a different experience now. Each smile he gave her was sweeter. Each word he said resonated with her more deeply.

So she said, "Um, yeah—sure. Thanks."

And then she held open the garbage bag while he stuffed more trash inside. Which occasionally meant incidental touching, his hands brushing over hers, their arms grazing. And things got even better when it came to breaking down the tables to be returned to town hall. Unlocking the table legs to press them flat required some strength, and Logan kept telling her to stop, then shoving his way into her space to take over. She kept purposely having trouble with them.

"That's a great dress, by the way," he told her at one point.

And she blushed like a schoolgirl. "Thanks. I spotted it at the Daisy Dress Shop during our last fitting for Rachel's wedding."

"It's nice. You look really pretty today."

And that—oh my—she even felt fluttering down through her chest and tummy. "Thanks." Yet still, somehow it embarrassed her a little. She wasn't used to that, looking pretty. So she heard herself adding, unplanned, "Probably a mess now, though." Then she blew a few wayward strands of hair out of her face.

After which he just grinned and said, "No, still pretty, freckles."

Then he even lifted his hand to brush back the out-of-place hair. And he looked into her eyes as he did it. And for a few seconds, she forgot to breathe. And she thought about kissing him some more. Oh God, how she wanted that. With her whole being. And she suddenly knew with her entire heart that she'd never be fully complete if she didn't someday get to kiss Logan again, the way she wanted to. With utter abandon. Full-on passion. The full-on passion she'd never quite known was hiding inside her until that day on his couch.

Only then he began telling her how Anna had asked him out. *Swell.* And everything that had been feeling so wonderful there for a few minutes turned decidedly less so. But apparently Mike then put the kibosh on it. *Thank you, Mike!* Except then Mike had invited him over for dinner with them instead. She let out a sigh. Before she knew it, he'd be tooling around Destiny in Anna's Mustang with her. And probably doing other things with her, too. Her stomach sank.

"I guess you didn't get a chance to talk to her," he said, "about fixing us up."

"Um, no," she said, adding a very small and not very heartfelt, "Sorry."

"No problem—I know you had a lot to take care of today. And if it doesn't happen, well, like you said, maybe it's not necessary. But still, if you get a chance, like you *also* said, maybe it wouldn't hurt if you put in a good word—just give the relationship the magic Amy touch."

"Um . . . yeah, sure," she said. "Of course."

And by the time they were finished, Amy felt completely conflicted. In fact, she almost wished she'd let him leave. In one sense, spending time with him was now heart-stoppingly special. But in another, hearing about another girl . . . not so special after all.

"Well, looks like everything's back to normal," he said cheerfully when all that remained were some full trash bags next to Edna's back door and a stack of tables Mike would return the next day.

But for Amy, nothing was back to normal at all.

And that was when it hit her, hard, like a punch in the gut. That it really never would be.

No matter what happens now, my life will never be the same.

Amy stood in Under the Covers, saying goodbye to Rose Marie Keckley, who held her enormous cat, Milo, in her arms. Milo was a Maine Coon who weighed twenty pounds and nearly dwarfed Rose Marie.

"Sorry it didn't work out," Amy said earnestly. She clutched Mr. Knightley firmly in her grasp, but he continued hissing at the visiting long-haired cat.

"Yes—me, too. It seemed like a good idea, didn't it?" Just then, Milo took another light swipe at Mr. K. and both women took an additional step backward.

"Best laid plans," Amy said. And this seemed like just one more thing out of her control lately. When Rose Marie had mentioned at the shower that she thought Milo needed some interaction with other cats, Amy had thought of Mr. Knightley, deciding he could use some socialization, too. She'd thought if Mr. Knightley got used to being around some different felines that maybe he'd learn to get along with Austen, as well. She'd even gone so far as to envision playdates with all the cats in town, for both Knightley *and* Austen. But as it turned out, he and Milo had begun hissing and screeching and swiping at each other the moment Rose Marie had brought her big, handsome cat through the door. Mr. Knightley had even ended up scratching Amy, for heaven's sake.

"Well, that was a weird idea," Tessa said after Rose Marie left.

Amy just flashed a look across the room. "What was wrong with it?"

"Well, if the goal is to get Knightley to be friendly to Austen, shouldn't you be putting *them* together, as opposed to sticking him with other cats?"

Okay, Amy supposed that made sense. She'd just thought . . . "He was so mean to Austen before. I kind of didn't want to put her through that again until I thought he'd be nicer."

"All right, I guess I can understand that—you're trying to protect the innocent. But sometimes you have to go through some unpleasantness to get troubles worked out, you know? I really think it makes more sense for you to keep pushing them together if that's what you really want."

Amy nodded, because she knew Tessa made sense. But she just held such a soft spot for the little black-striped kitty—who currently hid somewhere in the bookshelves to escape all the catfighting going on at the front of the store. She wasn't sure why since she loved *all* cats, but something about Austen made her feel overprotective. Maybe Amy just sympathized with feeling unloved more than ever right now, so much that it was carrying over to the bookstore's current stray.

"Well, either way, Mr. Knightley's in too much of a mood for me to try making them play together again today, so I'm taking him back up to the apartment," she told Tessa. "Then we can shelve the new romances." Even if the very idea of romance shredded Amy's heart every time she thought about it lately.

By the time she returned to the bookstore five minutes later, Rachel had shown up. And Amy had no sooner walked in the door than Rachel said, "Okay, out with it. Start talking, girlfriend."

Oh crap. She'd almost forgotten. That she'd been forced into promising Rachel she'd explain what she was doing skulking around the parked cars at the shower, and why Tessa had been keeping Logan occupied. She'd even forgotten to yell at Tessa for letting Rachel know something was up. She supposed her thoughts had been all over the place the last couple of days—like on Logan, and cats. And Logan, and Anna. And Logan, and the fact that she'd watched all six hours of the Colin Firth version of *Pride and Prejudice* last night, while draining a tub of strawberry ice cream, just to distract herself a little.

"Don't you have more pressing things on your mind?" she asked Rachel. "Like your wedding in less than two weeks? Or your honeymoon?" She and Mike were going to Italy to rediscover his roots, and though everything was completely planned, she knew there were plenty of last minute things to be done.

"Yes, that's why it took me an entire two days to track you down and find out what's going on. What are you keeping a secret from Logan?" she asked, eyes wide with wonder.

And Amy simply sighed. She didn't look forward to going through this again so soon after having just shared it with Tessa. So she cut to the chase. "I'm in love with him."

Rachel gasped.

"But he's all into Anna."

"Oh," Rachel said glumly.

"And the whole thing is very weird right now, that's all. So it's not my favorite topic."

"But what were you doing at his car?" Rachel asked, her voice a little softer now.

Another sigh left her. And her stomach churned. She felt so childish about this part. "I don't have the guts to tell him how I feel, since I know he doesn't feel the same way. But Tessa felt I should do *something,* so the something I'm doing is . . . sending him letters from a secret admirer."

"Wow," Rachel said. "This is far bigger than anything I could have imagined was going on. You and Logan? I guess, actually, it makes perfect sense in a way—I just never thought about it before."

"But the thing is—there *is* no me and Logan. There's Logan and Anna. And then there's me by myself. Like always."

"Oh Amy," Rachel said, looking profoundly sad for her and sort of making her want to cry. Especially when she moved in for a hug. It was sweet and all—in fact, it was exactly the way *she* would normally respond to something like this, always ready to comfort a friend—but what she'd just learned was that when someone was feeling down, this kind of reaction could be almost enough to push them over the edge.

So she struggled to hold herself together as—oh God—now Tessa joined the hug, too, making it into a group experience, and that was when a few tears snuck free. Amy simply couldn't stop them. Because she did feel alone. Because everyone was getting married, everyone else had love in their lives, the true, deep, lasting kind she craved. It was still hard to fathom that she'd gone from being her normal, generally happy self to feeling so empty inside.

And yet . . . as she stood there hugging her friends, finally letting out her tears, she realized that maybe this had been coming for a long time and that she'd just gotten pretty good at hiding it, even from herself. She'd *always* wanted love, but figuring out who she wanted it from had just pushed all these yearnings, all this emptiness, to the surface in a way nothing else had before.

And as awful as it felt to stand there and cry, she supposed she needed to get it out, and she was thankful to have such good, caring girlfriends to do it with.

Almost the second the tears waned, though, as they pulled back and reached for tissues for Amy, Rachel said, "There's really only one thing to be done here, Ames."

Amy blinked, surprised that Rachel was coming at her with a plan that quickly. "There is?"

Rachel gave a succinct nod and said, "You have to seduce him."

Oh brother. Some plan. "I can't do that," she said simply.

"Why not?" Rachel argued. "Look, I know that's not your usual mode of operation, and it will take you out of your comfort zone, but it'll be worth it. And not that I want to scare you or make things feel any more dire here, but . . . it might be a matter of beating Anna to the punch. Because don't get me wrong—she's great, and she's going to be my sister-in-law, but she . . . isn't shy with him. So you have to not be shy with him, too, now. If you really want him, Amy, you have to just go for it."

Amy couldn't hold in her sigh. The advice sounded so much like Tessa's in a way, like everything was on the line here if she didn't make a bolder move. And she even believed that was true. But she didn't have a bolder move to make. "Look, it's not that I don't want to, and believe me, I see the urgency, it's just . . ."

"Just what?" Rachel asked. "Because even if it's been awhile, it's only sex, you know? You're both adults, you've both done it before, and you know him really well, so . . . what's the problem?"

Only sex. Rachel *would* look at it that way. She had no idea, no idea at all, what she was actually suggesting here or how impossible it was.

And as much as Amy had never wished to share this particular tidbit of information, now she suddenly heard herself blurting it out, because there seemed to be no other way to make Rachel understand why she couldn't seduce Logan. "The problem is—both of us *haven't* done it, okay?"

Amy felt the weight of her words as they left her. God—it was even worse saying it out loud. She felt . . . so left out, so undesirable, so utterly childish as she watched both their expressions transform into pure shock.

And when they said nothing, just stood there gaping

at her as if she were the two-headed goat they'd once seen together as teenagers at the summer carnival, she said, "You guys have to swear you'll take this to the grave. And Rachel, you absolutely cannot tell Mike! I'd be even *more* humiliated. And he would probably tell Logan, too."

"But I have this honesty thing going with him, remember? Because I'm marrying him." Honesty between Mike and Rachel had been an issue a few times since they'd met.

"Well, not about this you don't! This doesn't affect him, so he doesn't need to know. Got it?"

Rachel blinked, still clearly stunned—apparently by Amy's laying-down-the-law attitude as much as anything else. "You're seriously not yourself these days, are you?"

"No, it just so happens that I'm not. Got a problem with that?"

Rachel gave her head a speculative tilt and said, "No. In fact, like I said before, I actually kinda like it."

"So you're not telling Mike any of this, right?" she felt the need to confirm.

"Okay, yes, correct. I won't. Because you're right—it doesn't affect him." Yet then her expression became pinched. "But . . . oh my God, Amy—you never did it with Carl back when you dated him for so long?"

She could only sigh at the sad reminder. "No."

"Well, why not? He was cute, kind of."

At this, Amy let out a huff. "Unlike you, when I was younger it took more than someone being cute, kind of, for me to have sex with them."

"Wow, you really *aren't* yourself," Rachel said, visibly taken aback.

And Amy realized what she'd just said. "I'm sorry. That was uncalled for. I didn't mean to criticize."

Yet Rachel merely held her hands up in front of her as if it were no biggie and replied, "No—I really, really *like* this side of you. It's like . . . you're human or something. You have flaws like the rest of us."

Wow. She'd never thought about that, that having these kinds of flaws might actually make her friends relate to her more. It was heartening under all the weird circumstances. Yet it also reminded her . . . she *was* flawed. In huge ways that made her feel bad. "You don't think I'm awful for being jealous of Anna?"

"Not about Logan, no. You've known Logan your whole life—to me, that means you're . . . entitled to be a little jealous."

Yet something about that answer made Amy's stomach churn anew. It meant she wasn't imagining any of this, that there was definitely something to be jealous of. "Do you think I should worry? About them, together?"

And now it was Rachel who sighed, looking lost for an answer. Which was rare. And which told Amy all she needed to know. Yes, she needed to worry. And if Rachel had found herself in this position, she had what it took to make a big move—Rachel had always been confident, outgoing, sexy. But Amy had none of that. Amy was just . . . Amy.

And so when Rachel finally said, "Don't worry—this will all work out," Amy knew they were only pretty words, all Rachel could come up with.

And she felt more certain than ever that it wouldn't work out the way she wanted at all.

What blindness, what madness had led her on!

Jane Austen, from *Emma*

Eight

Anna sat at the bar in the little hole-in-the-wall gathering place outside town, the Dew Drop Inn. As bars went, it wasn't much, but like every place in Destiny, everyone there was friendly. And the beer was cold. And Logan was behind the bar. That was the best part, of course.

Except . . . she was beginning to wonder if he liked her as much as she'd first thought. He seemed to enjoy her company, but he hadn't made a move on her, or even tried to kiss her, even though she thought she'd made it pretty clear she was into him.

Of course, they were hardly ever alone, so when would he kiss her? Every time she saw him, they ended up in a crowd—even if that crowd was only her brothers and their fiancées.

And even as much as she hoped they might end up

leaving the bar together later, she knew it was doubtful. Tonight was Rachel's bachelorette party—she was waiting for Rachel and her friends to show up now—and she just knew something would happen before the end of the night to blow her plans for Logan.

As she sat sipping from a beer bottle, she watched him tend bar.

"Fuzzy navel, coming up," he told the short blonde, an older woman, who'd just ordered it. Then added, a bit sheepishly, "As soon as I figure out what that is."

The woman and Anna both spoke at the same time. "Peach Schnapps and vodka," and it made Anna let out a good-natured laugh. She'd been observing him for nearly an hour now and this wasn't the first drink he hadn't known how to make. How on earth had he become a bartender, for heaven's sake? After she'd first met Logan, Mike had mentioned he'd recently left his longtime job at the Destiny Fire Department, but he hadn't said why and she hadn't felt at liberty to ask.

"Uh, how much of each?" he asked then, looking back and forth between the two women.

"Between you and me, darlin'," the blonde said, "you might need to go back to bartendin' school."

"You can tell I'm new on the job, can't ya?" he asked with a disarming grin that clearly won the lady over. But even so, Anna couldn't help thinking he seemed as out of place behind that bar as she felt at moments in this town.

Oh, she liked the people well enough. And she felt a real bond with the family that had embraced her. No one here had been anything but kind to her. And she'd had flashes, early on, when she'd really thought the place—and the people—could begin to feel like home.

But she was a city girl at heart, and even as quaint as it was, Destiny was no city. And the people here . . . they were almost *too* nice. She knew herself well enough to realize she had certain sharp edges about her—she went after what she wanted, she generally said what she meant, she dressed boldly and wasn't afraid to show off her shape—and the longer she spent here, the more she began to feel like a fish out of water.

She had the most in common with Rachel, which was fortunate since she was staying with her and Mike— but she couldn't help feeling she was intruding on their happy home. And she couldn't live there forever, even if she knew Mike would make it hard for her to leave.

And that was another thing—Mike. She cared for him already—she truly did—and she understood what he'd gone through when she'd been taken. But if he hovered any more, he'd be on top of her. She'd been relieved to have a reason to get out of the house tonight without him, thankful when Rachel had pointed out that it was a girls-only event.

"Shit," Logan muttered behind the bar, and she looked up to see that he'd managed to spray himself with water from the soda gun.

She couldn't stifle her laugh and he met her gaze with another cute grin. "You're jealous of how good I am at this, right?" he asked her.

"You read my mind," she playfully replied.

Blotting at his button-down shirt with a rag, then wiping up the mess he'd made, he resumed working on another concoction, telling her with a confident side-ways glance, "I'll get better at it."

She responded with another smile—since even if he was a bad bartender, he was cute at being bad. And when he came back down to where she sat a minute later, she gave him one more smile and said, "I have a feeling you'd make a better fireman than a bartender."

He responded with a tilt of his dark blond head. "Someone told you about that, huh?"

She nodded. "Mike mentioned it when I first got to town. Why'd you give it up? Don't you know girls think firemen are sexy?"

He smiled at the last part, but didn't exactly answer the first. "Eh, it was just time for a change. And I can still be perfectly sexy without all the fire gear, promise," he told her with a wink.

"Oh, no worries there," she assured him. "You're sexy as hell no matter *what* you do."

"Good to know," he informed her as he started wiping down some glasses. But then he paused in his work and gave her a slow, speculative look. "Um, this might sound like a weird question, but . . . you haven't been sending me . . . little messages, have you?"

She wasn't exactly sure what he meant—maybe this was some small town way of asking if she was coming on to him? So finally she said, "Um, yeah, sure I have."

But now he gave her a funny look, as if perhaps *he* wasn't sure she knew what he was asking, either. And it began to feel a little awkward, so she decided to just move on. "So . . . doing anything after you get off work tonight?"

Logan just replied with a laugh and said, "Sleeping. We're open 'til two, and then I have to clean up. Makes for a pretty late night."

And Anna merely nodded, getting the message loud and clear. After which she made an even bolder decision, to simply lay it on the line and be blunt. "You know, I've been starting to wonder if maybe . . . you're just not into me."

She appreciated it when his eyes went wide. "Why would you think that?"

She pursed her lips slightly, tried to look teasingly aloof. "Well, I pretty much asked you out, but you haven't taken me up on it. You seem to like hanging out with me, but . . . only in a crowd."

"Well, the reason for that is . . . complicated."

She leaned her head to one side, not sure she liked the sound of this. With a guy, complicated was never good. "Complicated how?"

He hesitated a few seconds, now wiping down the bar, before saying, "Mike's my best friend. And so . . . it only seemed right for me to sort of . . . get his blessing before getting involved with you."

Okay, now she was starting to *really* not like the sound of this. "And . . . ?"

"He had some mixed feelings, and basically kinda wanted me to . . . take it slow, you know? So that's what I'm doing. Out of respect for him and our friendship."

"I see," she said as her blood boiled. And she was trying not to let it show, because she didn't want to seem crazy, or unreasonable, or as if she was so nuts about Logan that it was maddening. But the maddening part— the part that made her absolutely livid—was that her brother thought it was okay to dictate her dating life. After they'd known each other less than two weeks. And for God's sake, she was thirty freaking years old!

"It's only because he cares about you so much, you know? And he thought it might be weird if . . . if things didn't work out between us or something, I guess."

"Ah," she said shortly. So Mike already had things

"not working out" between her and Logan. And he'd felt free to put this idea in Logan's head. "That's just great."

"Don't be pissed at him," Logan said with a sweet smile, and she realized her efforts at hiding her emotions clearly weren't working.

So she got honest again. "I think Mike needs to understand that I'm an adult. He might not have seen me since I was five, but I'm completely grown up and capable of deciding who I socialize with." At this point, it was all she could do to keep sitting on her bar stool without completely exploding in anger. She was learning to love her brother, but already she wanted to kill him.

Just then, the door to the Dew Drop Inn opened, admitting Rachel and all of her friends. Anna had gotten to know Tessa some already, and she remembered Amy from the moment she'd first arrived in Destiny. The other two she'd met at the wedding shower—what were their names? Jenny and Sue Ann? So many names to try to retain since her return.

And Anna truly liked Rachel's group of companions, but like everything else here, she didn't feel she was a part of them. Of course, how could she—they were life-long friends and she'd just arrived. So even if everyone kept telling her how much she belonged here, she still felt—more and more—like she was on the outside looking in.

Rachel wore a feathery silver tiara on her head that said *BRIDE,* with a small veil of white netting hanging from the back, which looked completely ridiculous with her otherwise smart, stylish appearance—but she was laughing, smiling, and Anna could feel how deep her sister-in-law-to-be's joy really ran.

"If you'd told me a few years ago that I'd be having my

bachelorette party here," she was saying merrily to the other girls, "I'd have thought you were crazy!" None of them had noticed Anna yet.

"You'd have thought we were crazy to even say you were getting married," Tessa pointed out. "And living in Destiny."

"True," she said, settling at a table with all her girlfriends—who also happened to be her bridesmaids. "And look at me now—happier than ever. Crazy, huh?"

But maybe what was crazy was Anna thinking *she* could ever really be happy here. She was trying, but Mike was making it difficult. *Lots* of things were making it difficult. She might have been born here, but she wasn't sure she was cut out for small town life in Destiny.

Just then, she realized Amy was looking at her, so she lifted her hand in a wave.

Amy returned it, but appeared a little awkward, maybe even sad.

That was when Rachel spotted her, too. "Anna!" she said. "Come join us."

The truth was, as it had been since her arrival, that she felt more comfortable with Logan and honestly would have preferred staying at the bar near him—and of course she liked being near him for other reasons, too, even if Mike was doing his best to thwart her efforts. But she had a feeling that when in Destiny, it was best to do as the Destiny-ites did—and who knew, maybe before the night was over she'd feel a little more like one of the girls.

Amy watched as Anna, looking utterly sleek and gorgeous even wearing just a fitted silky red T-shirt, jeans, and more of the high-heeled strappy shoes she seemed to favor, climbed down from her stool at the bar and made her way over. How long had she been here? She'd obviously come early to spend time with Logan. And even that tiny tidbit of knowledge was enough to make Amy's stomach ache.

"Hi, everybody," Anna said, her smile bright and pretty and enviable. And, as usual, Amy hated herself for envying it—but she just couldn't seem to control her emotions regarding Anna Romo.

"Hi Anna," Amy said, joining in the other girls' greetings and hoping like heck that it came off sounding natural.

After that, small talk ensued—Anna was nice enough to ask lots of questions about Rachel's wedding next weekend, and talk turned to all the remaining little tasks that had to be accomplished between now and then, many of which Amy had volunteered to do. She even pulled out the list in her purse. "I'll check on the cake and flowers Thursday. And I'll be working on birdseed packets all week." She was tying handfuls of it into pastel netting to be thrown instead of rice.

"If you need any help with that, I have plenty of time on my hands," Anna offered.

And—wow—it was a nice offer. And Amy could use the help. And any normal, nice person would take her up on it, maybe even make a point of including her in activities so she could feel like a part of things. But Amy was beginning to fear she just wasn't a normal, nice person anymore. Because she simply couldn't face the idea of hanging out with Anna in her apartment working on wedding tasks. She froze in place, unable to answer.

"Actually, you won't have time for that," Rachel said to Anna, "because I was planning to enlist you for table decoration duty."

And as Anna readily agreed, Rachel and Amy exchanged quick glances that allowed Amy to send an unspoken *thank you* with her eyes. Thank God for her friends or she'd never get through this. Even if she'd felt a bit of fresh embarrassment—as if she were wearing a big red "V" on her forehead—when she picked up Rachel and Tessa tonight, they were still there for her in every way.

"We need drinks," Sue Ann said, playfully pounding her fist on the table.

"Maybe we can get Logan to wait on us," Anna suggested.

To which Jenny cheerfully replied, "I'm sure he will if *you* ask him, Anna—I saw the way he kept looking at you at the shower."

No, no, no, Jenny—stop. But of course Jenny wasn't a mind reader, so she had no idea of the turmoil Amy was currently going through.

And as Sue Ann added, "From what I hear, he might make a better waitress than a bartender," Tessa chimed in to say, "No, he looks too busy already—one of us should just go to the bar and order. Amy, Miss Designated Driver, will you do it?"

"Okay," she said without hesitation. "What does everybody want?"

After taking drink orders from everyone but Anna, who already had a beer, she made her way over to Logan behind the bar.

"Hey there, freckles, what's shakin'?"

Somehow that seemed like a loaded question just now, so she simply replied, "I'm playing waitress for the bachelorette party," and ordered the drinks. Thankfully, they were all simple, since news that Logan was a terrible bartender had made its way around town like wildfire. And all of Destiny remained completely perplexed as to why he was doing *this* rather than resuming his position at the fire department.

As Logan assembled the beverages, Amy said, "I hear Mike's bachelor party is tomorrow. You don't have any-thing . . . bad planned, do you?"

He cast her a mischievous look. "Who, me?" Then said, "Nah, keeping it on the straight and narrow. Bunch of us are swimming and grilling out at my place tomor-row, then we'll head over to Bleachers tomorrow night." Bleachers was a sports bar in Crestview where the guys had hung out for years.

"Sounds fun," Amy said.

"And, uh, hey, not to beat a dead horse, but if you get a chance to talk to Anna tonight . . ."

And Amy could only sigh. And then the following words left her mouth without planning. "I don't think you need my help with Anna. I think you've got her exactly where you want her."

Logan flinched and—oh God—she knew it had come out too sharply. "Well . . . okay. You don't have to snap at me about it."

She sucked in her breath, blinked, tried to look natu-ral. "I'm sorry," she said. "I'm just . . . stressed." Com-pletely true.

"Rachel and Tessa both have you doing a lot for the weddings, don't they?"

"Yes." And though not the source of her stress, also completely true.

"Sorry I've asked about this Anna thing so many times—don't worry about it." Then he reached out and pressed his hand over hers where it rested on the bar.

And as usual with Logan lately, the simple friendly touch shot straight up her arm and then seemed to explode through the rest of her body like a starburst. She just swallowed, hard, trying to quell any reaction that might show on her face.

"Um, okay," she managed. But darn it, her voice came out softer than intended. "And . . . sorry I snapped, Logan."

"No worries, freckles," he said warmly, his blue eyes shining on her, giving her that wonderful, melty feeling. Or, well, it would *be* wonderful if he ever thought about her as a girl, a woman.

And then a brainstorm hit her. And she didn't even stop to consider it—she just rolled with it. "I need to get out more."

"Huh?" he said.

Take a deep breath. Keep rolling. "I was just thinking I need to get out more. Do you know any nice guys you could fix me up with?"

"Fix you up with?" he asked, sounding a little astonished. Which maybe made sense given that they hadn't really talked about Amy's love life since her break up with Carl a million years ago. And also since, realistically, she knew all of Logan's friends.

But she just said, "Yeah, fix me up with," anyway, like it was a perfectly normal, typical request from her. "I need to have more fun."

"Huh," he said again, still appearing dumbfounded. "I don't know. I mean, you know pretty much everyone I do."

But that was okay. Because this wasn't about actually trying to make him jealous. It was only about . . . reminding him. That she was a female. Who liked guys. Who was capable of going on dates. In case he'd forgotten. And the look on his handsome face pretty much made her think he had. So . . . mission accomplished. Small mission though it was.

"Yeah, guess that's true," she said, watching as he finished the drinks and began loading them onto a round tray. "But if you think of anybody . . ."

He squinted at her. "Mind if I ask what brought this on? I mean, the truth is, freckles, I don't even know what kind of guy you'd . . . you know . . . be looking for."

Amy gave it a moment's thought and told him, "Just someone who could maybe . . . broaden my horizons," she said. Which wouldn't take much, given that her horizons stretched only to the edge of Destiny. And she thought that sounded . . . adventurous. And being adventurous was an idea that suddenly appealed. "And as for what brought it on . . . who knows? Maybe it has to do with Rachel and Tessa getting married. Or maybe it's about Anna coming back to town. I'm just realizing that . . . life changes and I have to change *with* it. There's a world beyond the four walls of Under the Covers and maybe I want to explore it."

"Huh," he said yet one more time. Just that.

And as she picked up the tray to walk away, she realized how good all that had sounded, and how confident she suddenly felt, inside and out.

Maybe it's true. Maybe I can change, be bolder, step outside the usual borders of my life.

Only . . . what that meant right now, she knew in her heart, was finding the way to do what Tessa kept telling her she had to: admitting the truth to Logan. And that still sounded unthinkable, but . . . maybe it was a teeny tiny little smidge more thinkable in this moment than it had been an hour ago. Maybe.

"Drinks," she said, lowering the tray to the table and feeling a bit more festive than when she'd departed.

"How much?" Tessa asked, reaching for her purse. "First round's on me."

Which is when Amy realized, "Oh—I don't know. He forgot to charge me."

"Boy, Anita's got herself a great bartender there," Rachel quipped, shaking her head. "We'll remind him next round."

Amy took her seat next to Tessa and reached for the Coke Logan had poured for her while everyone else claimed glasses of wine or mixed drinks. Meanwhile, Sue Ann asked Anna, "Are you getting used to Destiny yet?"

Though Anna smiled, Amy thought it looked slightly forced. "Slowly but surely."

And Rachel added, "The tougher part, I'm guessing, is getting used to Mike. Trust me, I know." Both being strongheaded, Rachel and Mike had had quite a difficult time getting along early in their relationship.

Even as everyone laughed, however, Amy still thought Anna's reaction didn't seem completely sincere. Although she smiled as she said, "You could say that."

And apparently Rachel could see through it, too—and had gotten to know Anna well enough to be up front about it. "All right—you don't look happy. So what has the big lout done now that I don't know about?"

At this, Anna let out a sigh, fiddled with her beer bottle, and said, "Well, the truth is, I just discovered that when he found out Logan and I were attracted to each other, he asked Logan to take it slow. As in, apparently, not even being alone with me."

It was difficult for Amy to hide her elation as she sent

up a silent, *Thank you, Mike!,* same as she had once before.

"And it's freaking ridiculous," Anna went on, picking up steam. "I mean, I'm a grown woman! And I've gotten by just fine without him up to now! And I wanted to come here and find my family and all—and everyone's been great, don't get me wrong—but for him to think it's okay to try to run my love life in any way whatsoever . . . um, no. That's majorly out of bounds."

"Oh my God, what a jerk!" Sue Ann said, never shy about expressing an opinion. But then she apparently remembered where she was and tossed Rachel a sheepish glance. "Sorry, Rach. Normally, I love Mike."

But Rachel just swiped a hand down through the air. "No need to apologize. He *can* be a jerk. And Anna, I'm so sorry he's being so heavy-handed with you. You're right—it's completely over the line. But . . . I hope you can understand that it's only because he loves you so much."

It surprised Amy when Anna only let out another forlorn sigh. "That's what Logan said, too, but it's too much."

"Um," Tessa began uncertainly, "what was Logan's reaction to Mike's request? If you don't mind my asking."

Anna pursed her lips, looking unhappy. "Well, he was a lot more understanding about it than I am."

"That's Logan," Jenny chimed in. "Loyal as a guy can be."

"So you kinda gotta respect that," Tessa added, "even if it's unreasonable. Right?"

And the unchanged look on Anna's face told Amy that maybe this hadn't yet crossed her mind. "Oh. Hmm. I don't know. Maybe."

"They *are* best friends," Sue Ann added, unknowingly helping Amy's cause. "You don't want to do anything to come between best friends, you know? Even if Mike *is* being a big buttinski."

Anna dropped her gaze to the table for a moment before raising her eyes again. "I guess that's true."

"And it's not like he's . . . forbidden you to see him or something," Tessa pointed out. "He just said take it slow. And slow can be nice sometimes."

Anna didn't look like she particularly believed that part, but she still offered up a grudging nod.

Just then, the first note of Katy Perry's "Teenage Dream" blared from the jukebox and Rachel said, "I want to dance!"

And Jenny asked "Here?" No one danced at the Dew Drop Inn.

Yet Rachel looked aghast. "Look, this is my bachelorette party—my proverbial last night of freedom before I attach myself to the old ball and chain. If I say we dance, we dance! Now come on, girls—we're dancing."

Since Rachel was clearly in the mood to rule with an iron fist, everyone at the table started getting to their feet—except for Amy, who grabbed Tessa's wrist and yanked her back down as well. When Rachel gave her a pointed look, Amy told her, "We'll be there in a minute," and when Rachel's expression softened, she knew her friend realized this probably had something to do with her current dilemma.

"What is it?" Tessa asked as everyone else walked away.

"Something awful just hit me."

"What's that?"

"What happens after the wedding?"

"What are you talking about?"

"Mike and Rachel's wedding is next Saturday night," Amy explained. "And then they're going to Italy. And even that night, they'll be leaving the reception before everyone else anyway to go have wedding night sex. And so who's to stop Anna from having her way with Logan after the wedding? I mean, if I were her I'd totally be putting the moves on him the second Mike walks out the door. Wouldn't you?"

When Tessa cast a light scowl in response, Amy knew she agreed.

Which prompted her to add, "What am I gonna do? How am I gonna stop that?"

Tessa's look came half speculative, half scolding. "You could take a chance and tell him how you feel."

But Amy just let out a long, tired breath. Yes, she knew about that option already and thought it was clear she was choosing to bypass it. Even if it was beginning to seem more in the realm of possibility, more like a thing that, deep down, Amy knew had to happen eventually, one way or the other—she wasn't ready to do it *yet*. She had to work up to it, over time. She had to find the right way, the right moment. It would be a very delicate, well-thought-out, well-planned operation. So she simply told Tessa, "Not on the table for right now."

Tessa offered up a thoughtful sigh. "Then all you've got is your love notes. Which means you should write one right now."

At which Amy gasped. "Here? Now? With such a limited number of females here tonight, most of whom he'd be able to rule out?"

Tessa shrugged. "Sure. Anyone could have stopped by the parking lot and put it on his car."

Okay, that was true.

"And get serious this time. About what you want. About sex," Tessa insisted.

"I did that in the last one," she explained.

But Tessa appeared skeptical. "Well, whatever you wrote, make it more this time. Sexier, naughtier."

Amy swallowed. "Naughtier?"

Tessa just tilted her head. "You think Anna wouldn't go for naughty with him? The Anna threat is getting serious and you have to play hardball here—it's the only way. I mean, if all you've got are these love letters, you have to make them really count."

After lamenting that she didn't have any paper, Amy watched as Tessa reached in her purse and neatly tore a small pink note sheet from a pad. Passing her a pen along with it, she said, "Do me proud."

So, at a loss, Amy began.

Dear Logan,

I want you more every day. I want you day and night. I want your kisses, your touches—I want it all. I want you . . .

She stopped writing then, out of ideas. Which was when Tessa, looking over her shoulder, said, "Inside me."

"What?" Amy drew back to look at her, aghast.

"Write it," Tessa demanded.

"You seriously think I should go that far?"

"I seriously do." Her tone was downright commanding—Amy wasn't even sure she'd ever seen Tessa this way.

So she took a deep breath—or tried to anyway, because

it didn't come easily at the moment. And then, stomach churning, she forced herself to pen the two words that felt so stunningly intimate that she couldn't believe she was really doing it. Even if what she was writing happened to be profoundly true and she fantasized about it all the time now.

"And one more thing," Tessa said. "Tell him you'll reveal your identity to him at the wedding reception."

Amy darted her head around to glare at Tessa once more.

"You don't really have to do it," Tessa explained, calming her down. "Just make him *think* you will. It will keep his focus off Anna—at least a little—and hopefully keep him from leaving with her if he's waiting for the mystery woman to appear. It's worth a try anyway."

"Oh. Yeah. You're right. That's good," Amy said, bending over the page to add that part.

No envelope this time, so when she was done, she simply handed Tessa her pen back and folded the little pink sheet in half.

"Okay," Tessa said. "Now I'm going to walk behind the bar, turn Logan around to face away from the door, and take as long as I can paying for that round of drinks. While I'm doing that, go put that on his car as fast as you can. Got it?"

"Got it," Amy said. Then waited as Tessa put the plan into action.

As usual when engaging in this particular activity, her heart beat a mile a minute until Logan's back was turned, then she padded quickly toward the bar's front door. But this time it was almost worse, because the chances of being caught seemed greater. Even more than at the wedding shower, because then he'd been all wrapped up in Anna.

A burst of cool spring evening air hit her as she rushed to Logan's car and slid the note under the wiper. *I want you inside me.* Could she ever tell him her identity after *that? Well, you can't worry about that now. Right now, all you can worry about is getting back inside before Logan looks up and sees you walking through the door.*

As she re-entered the Dew Drop, Logan was—thank God—still talking with Tessa. And Amy headed straight for the makeshift dance floor, where the girls now moved to Lady Gaga's "Bad Romance." She stepped instantly into the circle of her friends, so relieved that she almost didn't even mind that Anna was a part of it.

When Tessa joined them a minute later, she gave Amy a quick wink that, again, made her beyond grateful for her friends.

And as she continued to dance, she tried her best to get lost in the moment. Rachel seemed so happy, and Amy thought she'd never seen her look more carefree— and this was one of those girlfriend moments, the ones where you were supposed to just disconnect from everything else for a little while and do nothing but soak up the fun and camaraderie.

But her eyes—and thoughts—kept being unwittingly drawn back to Anna, who, of course, moved like liquid rhythm on the dance floor, even in those huge heels, and looked like every guy's perfect fantasy girl come to life with her perfect body and perfect face and perfect hair.

I don't want to be jealous of you, I really don't. I know how much you've lost, and I can't imagine being in your shoes right now, impossibly high-heeled or not. And yet, despite all you've lost, in other ways you have so much more than I'll ever have. I'll never know what it's like to be beautiful. I'll never know what it's like to be so utterly cool and confident. I'll never know what it's like to walk into a room knowing every man there will want me. I'll never have all the choices you do, all the options—with men, with sex, with what to wear, how to be.

I'm just me, and it doesn't matter what anyone says or tries to convince me of, I'll never be pretty. I'll never be sexy. And I'm pretty sure Logan is going to be the only guy I'll ever love. So please don't take him away from me. Please, please pick someone else. Anyone else in the world.

And yet, even as she danced on, a plastic smile pasted on her face, she felt the flaw in her silent plea, and she had no choice but to ask herself a painful question: Who would be to blame if Anna did take him, win him, and Amy had never even let him know she was in the game?

Nobody who has not been in the interior of a family can say what the difficulties of any individual of that family may be.

Jane Austen, from *Emma*

Nine

*M*ike sat in a small room in the basement of the Destiny Church of Christ. He wore a tux. He was getting married in less than an hour. He heard the echo of Rachel's laughter from another room somewhere above him on the main floor.

It was one of those moments in life that made a man stop and reflect. His life had changed so much in the past couple of years. He had a woman he loved, and knowing he was going to spend the rest of his life with her made him feel damn fortunate. He had good friends, and a loving family. His wayward brother, Lucky, had come home and they'd mended their relationship. And now his baby sister had miraculously returned, too. For the last year or two, he'd been trying hard to quit believing that would ever happen, trying to finally let her go, give himself some closure. But he'd never completely gotten there—and he supposed there'd been a reason why. Somehow, all along, he'd known—just known—that she couldn't really be gone forever.

So he was a man who had it all. Everything. And he wasn't even sure he really deserved it all, but he wasn't complaining. It should be a crime to have so much good fortune in one life.

He looked up when Anna walked in, as stunning as ever in a low cut red dress. And, well, maybe it was a little too low cut for his liking, actually. He wished she were a little more modest—she was a beautiful girl and didn't need to show off her body to get male attention.

"Rachel sent me down with the boutonnieres," she said, holding out a clear plastic box containing small cream-colored rosebuds.

"Thanks," he told her. "For everything." She'd been a big help in little ways this past week, and especially today, passing on messages and running small errands to help make sure all the details were in place while the bride and groom avoided seeing each other. Unfortunately, though, his gaze stuck on the V of his sister's dress because—he couldn't help it—the sight made everything inside him clench up.

"Let me guess," she said then. "You don't like my dress." Her dry tone accompanied the roll of her eyes. Damn, he hadn't realized he was so obvious.

"Well, it's not that I don't like it." In fact, on another woman—probably *any* other woman—he would think it was great. But Anna wasn't any other woman. Far from it. "It's just that . . . well, you wear a lot of clothes that . . . show off your body. And you don't need to."

Uh-oh. He could tell just from her eyes, the set of her mouth, that he'd said the wrong thing. She'd seemed a little irritated or something with him this past week—but this, he knew instantly, went beyond that. "I'm a big girl, Mike. I can wear what I want."

Shit. "I know, I know," he said, trying to calm her down. "Don't get mad. It's just that . . . you don't want to send the wrong message, do you?"

That was when her eyes bolted open wide, in anger, and he knew he'd screwed up further while he'd been trying to make the situation better.

"What if I do? What business is it of yours what message I send? And for your information, the only message I happen to be sending is that I'm a confident woman who feels good about the way she looks. I'm not a slut, Mike. But I'm also not a saint. So get over it."

Mike simply sat there, dumbfounded. "Anna—I never said you were . . ." God, the very idea that he could even think of her that way tore at his stomach.

"And another thing," she said. "You have absolutely no right to keep me from seeing Logan. I've been trying to hold back on all this because your wedding was coming, but . . . I'm sorry, I can't stand by and let you try to run my life for a minute more!"

Mike pushed to his feet out of sheer frustration. "I'm not trying to run your life, Anna—it's just that I care about you. For God's sake, how can I not care?"

At this, she merely let out an exasperated sigh, like he was the most unreasonable guy on the planet. "I'm not asking you not to care! I'm asking you not to interfere where you shouldn't."

"But I'm your brother. Any big brother who loves his little sister is gonna look out for her that way."

"Mike," she said tensely, her tone quieter but still sharp, "you haven't been my brother for the last twenty-five years. You barely know me. We're not much more than strangers to each other. How I dress or who I see is, frankly, just none of your business."

It was like a blow to the gut, like having the wind knocked out of him—he couldn't remember a time in his life when he'd ever been so . . . wounded. And he immediately knew why—it was because only Anna, only his baby sister, could ever have that power over him.

And if she only knew. He had indeed been her loving brother for each and every day of the last twenty-five years. He'd been *ripping his heart out over losing her* for the last twenty-five years. He'd let the loss consume his whole life—at least until Rachel had come along. And the hurt washing over him now . . . God. He could barely even process it. He needed to be alone. So he simply broke eye contact and walked numbly past her, out of the room.

"Mike," she said, halting him in his tracks just outside the doorway. He drew a deep breath, turned back to face her. His chest still burned.

"I really don't mean to upset you on your wedding day, so I'm sorry for that. But . . . when you come home from your honeymoon, I'll be back in Indianapolis. I . . ." She shook her head. "I can't stay here. You and this whole place are suffocating me."

Jesus. He stared at her blankly, speechless. Because he had no idea what to say.

And so he said nothing and instead simply turned back around and walked away.

He couldn't believe it. After all these years, he'd finally gotten her back—only to lose her again so quickly, just in a different way this time.

* * *

All the girls had gotten ready at Edna's house, then had photos taken outside in the orchard, and some in front of the little red barn, which was all decked out for the reception tonight. It was a beautiful day in Destiny— one which most people would never have dreamed could happen. Rachel and Mike were laying to rest the old Farris-Romo family feud by bringing them all together under one roof at the Destiny Church of Christ—and then even forcing them to eat and dance together at the orchard that had caused the feud in the first place, back in the fifties when Edna had squabbled over ownership of the place with Mike's grandfather.

However, now that the bridal party was at the church, Amy had come under fire from Tessa, who insisted she wasn't wearing enough makeup.

"It's the same amount I always wear," she'd argued.

"That's the problem," Tessa told her. Amy had just never been a big makeup person—what difference did it make if she had on lipstick or eye shadow? She generally wore a little—but who had the energy to spend time worrying how you looked every day, especially when she knew no amount of it was ever suddenly going to make her beautiful?

And then Rachel—who absolutely glowed in her bridal gown—had even chimed in. "Tessa's right. You look as pale as a ghost, Ames. Let her put some more on you." Then she'd done a totally tricky thing—rather than be the usual this-is-how-it's-going-to-be Rachel, she'd turned the tables and been sweet! She'd tilted her head and said, "Pretty please? For me? It's my wedding day, after all."

So now Amy sat letting Tessa paint her face, and

though she only occasionally got a glimpse in the hand mirror all the girls were passing around, she thought it was just too much.

And—oh Lord—now Sue Ann had decided her *hair* was too plain, too! She was insisting on pulling it back from her face, up off her neck into some sort of up-do.

"Am I that hideous on a daily basis?" Amy groused.

"Oh, be quiet, of course not," Sue Ann said. "But today is a special day! Why not have fun with it like the rest of us and do something different?" And true enough, the rest of Rachel's bridesmaids had indeed gone all out and enjoyed the girly-girlness of the occasion to the max. So Amy finally chose to just shut up and roll with it and hope she didn't look completely ridiculous walking down the aisle. Though already she felt self-conscious about how close her blue dress fit her now, and the fact that it even gave her cleavage. She simply wasn't used to that.

After Sue Ann finished with a happy-sounding, "There!" and stepped away, Tessa came back at her with another makeup brush.

"Aren't you done yet?" Amy complained.

And just then, Logan stopped at the doorway of the little room they were in to say, "Five minutes, ladies," before going on his way.

He hadn't even seen her. But, Lord, had she ever seen *him*. Her heart did flip-flops in her chest. "Oh God," she whispered to Tessa, "did you see him in his tux? He looked so . . . yummy."

In reply, Tessa smiled down at her, her expression something like Rachel's a little while ago—almost sweet. "You know, I like you like this. All caught up in a guy. Despite you being a romantic, I'd actually worried at times that . . . that you maybe didn't have it in you to go that deep, to give your whole heart, your whole self, over to those kinds of emotions."

Amy let out a short sigh, feeling Tessa's words gut-deep. "Maybe I didn't for awhile. But then it finally hit me. And now . . . oh God, I hate it—it's awful."

"But it's also . . . wonderful, isn't it?" Tessa suggested, reminding Amy of the truth that constantly plagued her now. She'd never dreamed love was such a two-sided coin.

"Yes and no. I just wish I were more like you. Or Rachel. You guys have always been so confident—you know how to talk with guys, flirt with guys, how to just *be* with guys."

Yet Tessa only shrugged. "I was pretty off my game for a while. Even with Lucky at first. And honestly, what it all comes down to in the end is really just . . . being yourself. Or . . . the new self he brings out in you. And then you hope it all clicks."

Amy's shoulders slumped as that notion sank down inside her. "For me, I'm not sure it does."

"You should consider following through tonight," Tessa said to her.

"On what?"

"Revealing your identity."

And Amy gasped, totally aghast. "I couldn't. I can't. Not yet."

"Just a thought," Tessa said, offering another light shrug. "But you know, weddings can be . . . kind of magical. And not only for the bride and groom. Sometimes things *happen* at weddings. Big things. So just think about it." Then she stepped back, surveying her work. "Done." And she passed Amy the mirror.

Another move which made her gasp. But this time in . . . pure wonder. Because . . . who was this girl she saw in the glass right now? How could this be? How had it happened? It was that easy?

"What?" Tessa asked, sounding worried.

"I'm pretty," Amy said softly. "You made me pretty."

"You've always been pretty, dummy. You just hide it." Then Tessa leaned closer to say, "Now get out there and make Logan want you to be his secret admirer."

Anna felt like a heel. It had all needed to be said. It had reached a point where she couldn't contain it—apparently not even for one more minute. But her timing had plain sucked.

She did still feel like Mike was something of a stranger to her—along with everyone else in Destiny, too, except maybe for Logan—but she cared about him, enough that it had been selfish to explode on him that way right before his wedding.

She'd spent the last hour not only feeling crappy about the whole thing, but she'd also had a chat first with Tessa, and then Lucky, and had come up with a plan she hoped would smooth things over with her overbearing oldest brother.

When she approached the room where she'd argued with him, she heard him inside, now arguing with *other* people—namely, his groomsmen. "Where's the fucking minister?" he snapped.

"Dude," she heard Logan say, "calm down. The minister's here. And I hope you don't go to hell for calling him *that, here.*"

And as the rest of the guys chuckled softly, Anna noted how easily Logan dealt with Mike. You could tell

he'd been at this for a long time and was skilled at it.
One more reason to like him.

"Now," Logan said calmly, "it's time."

"Time?" Mike sounded a little alarmed.

"Time to go out. Time for you to go get married."

"Shit," he said. "Already? God damn it, I don't know
if . . ." She'd never heard Mike sound like this before—
almost . . . panicky. But then, she'd always heard that
even the most steady of men could have last minute jit-
ters right before they walked down the aisle.

Logan was clearly thinking the same thing. "Listen, I
know this is huge. But you love Rachel—she makes you
happy. This is what you want, man. You're just a little
nervous right now, that's all."

And Mike snapped, "Of course I love Rachel—that's
not the problem here. The problem is . . . I had a big fight
with Anna, and I think she hates me."

Oh. Oh God. It was *her* causing this? Their argument
had upset him that deeply? But then again, it only made
sense—she just kept forgetting, or maybe choosing to
forget, how much she'd affected Mike's life. And now
she felt like *worse* than a heel. She was the caked-on
dirt on the *bottom* of someone's heel. And she knew she
had to fix this *now,* that it couldn't wait until after the
ceremony.

"Mike, I'm sorry," she said, stepping into the room.
"I didn't mean to upset you so much. And on today of
all days—my timing stinks. All I ask is that . . . can you
please try to be a little more reasonable?"

He appeared at once shocked and relieved at her
arrival. Yet still he said, "I thought I *was* being reasonable."

At which she noticed Logan rolling his eyes and flashing Mike a look—which made her brother say, "Okay, okay—yes, I can try to be more reasonable."

"Listen," she told him, "when you come home, I'll still be in Destiny—just not at your house. It's too close, and as nice as Rachel has been about this, newlyweds don't need a houseguest. Tessa and Lucky have offered to let me stay at his place since he's mostly moved in to hers now anyway. And I think that will be best for everyone. So . . . how's that for a compromise?"

Mike sighed and she couldn't read his expression. "Well, I'd rather have you with me and Rachel . . . but at least you'll still be here in town. And that makes me happy."

She gave a short nod, then added, "And you have no say over who I date or what I do unless I ask for your opinion. Cool?"

She thought he looked like he was having a little difficulty breathing as he said, "Not really, but—"

"Dude, it's time," Logan said, tapping at his wrist impatiently. "Be nice and make up."

Mike let out a breath. "But . . . yeah. Whatever you say."

And though she still thought Mike was one of the most intolerant, narrow-minded, unreasonable men she'd ever met, she knew now was the time to let it go. She had a feeling their battles weren't over, but she'd won this first one, and she didn't want to cause him any more grief right now.

And she also realized in that moment that . . . well, maybe she'd grown to care about the big lug even more than she'd thought. Because she really wanted him to be happy. She really didn't like hurting him. And she looked forward to seeing him walk down the aisle and marry the woman of his dreams.

So without weighing it, she stepped up, rose on her tiptoes, and gave him a hug and a kiss on the cheek. And she said, "Despite all this, Mike, I'm still glad you're my big brother."

She watched then as he closed his eyes, and she knew—felt—how deeply the simple gesture had moved him, perhaps at a moment when he'd needed it most.

"Thank you," he said then, hugging her back. "You just gave me the best wedding gift in the world."

Logan's mind whirled. He stood next to Mike, serving as his best man, with Mike's brother Lucky on the other side of him, watching as Sue Ann's little girl, Sophie, made her way carefully up the aisle, dropping cream-colored rose petals from a basket with every delicate, nervous step she took. A version of Norah Jones's "Come Away With Me" played on a harp, Rachel and Mike having bypassed the traditional wedding march for something more modern. And his whole focus should be *here, now*—on the details of his best friend's wedding as it took place. Yet Anna sat in the front pew along with Mike's parents, distracting him in a rockin' hot dress, her lips glossy and red and kissable. And then there was that last mystery note, last week outside the Dew Drop, promising that his secret admirer would reveal herself— tonight!

But hell, do I even care who it is if I've got Anna Romo interested in me?

Yet . . . something niggled deep inside him, telling him he did. Logically, it was probably someone he'd never be into—the idea of some adolescent or high school girl seemed likely, and horrible—and still he couldn't deny that the mystery was titillating, and flattering, even if also a little nerve-wracking.

At the other end of the aisle now, Jenny Brody stepped onto the runner and made her way toward the altar as everyone turned to look.

And what if . . . what if whoever had written those notes was somebody amazing? Not that he could envision who that could be. After all, he knew everyone in town. But even so, his imagination roamed.

And of course he'd asked Anna about the notes last week at the Dew Drop—but even when she'd said yes, she'd said it so easily, so casually, that he'd decided she'd misinterpreted the question and thought that by messages he'd meant . . . signs, or hints or something.

Could it be her? But why would she be so cryptic when she didn't seem like a cryptic person at all? On the other hand, though, maybe she thought it was sexy, romantic, fun.

Well, tonight he'd find out, one way or the other.

Next came Sue Ann, who had definitely gotten back to being her perky self since starting a new relationship with his buddy Adam back in the winter. Adam stood two spots down from him in the line of groomsmen and Logan caught Sue Ann casting a smile in his direction. They made a perfect couple and he couldn't help thinking how odd it was that he'd never thought of them together before, even though they'd been lifelong friends.

Amy would be next in line, which took his thoughts back to Rachel's bachelorette party, to when Amy suggested he fix her up with someone. Since when did Amy date? Not that it was weird, but she just . . . didn't usually. Still, *of course* she would want to find a guy to go out with, just like anyone else. And yet . . . the idea of fixing up with somebody rankled a little. Because . . . who would be good enough for her? Guys could be dogs, after all. Who could he be sure would treat her right, the way she deserved?

He switched his gaze to the back of the church then to see Amy begin making her way down the aisle in a bold, cobalt blue dress and—wait. Holy shit. *Was* that Amy? He knew it was, but . . . he stood there dumbfounded, amazed. He'd never seen her look so gorgeous. He'd never known she . . . could.

He drank in the vibrant emerald of her eyes from where he stood, somehow drawn out by the hue of the dress. And they looked bigger, wider, than he'd ever realized before. Her lips appeared . . . downright lush, moist. And her freckles were paler than usual, covered by makeup he guessed, but . . . well, hell, who cared about freckles at a time like this?

He'd never before noticed her breasts, not in their whole lives really, but damn—he was noticing them now. Their pale upper ridges curved from the bodice of that dress which . . . God, did nice things to the rest of her body, too.

Really? This was his Amy? His freckles? He had to give his head a short, brisk shake to clear it and hope no one noticed. He couldn't believe that Amy, his Amy, had somehow become . . . a complete and total knockout.

" . . . she is loveliness itself . . ."

Jane Austen, from *Emma*

Ten

The ceremony at the church had been truly heartrending—Amy had seen in Rachel and Mike's eyes, and heard in their voices, how incredibly happy they were. Not a cross word had been spoken between any Romos and Farrises, and now—after all following Rachel and Mike here in his Grandpa Giovanni's turquoise Cadillac, in which the two had done a lot of their falling in love—everyone mingled about the orchard's barn like old friends.

With the help of sparkling mini lights and festive lanterns, the barn at Edna's place had been transformed into the perfect reception hall. Round tables draped with white cloths filled one end while a dance floor had been assembled at the other.

It was one of the largest weddings Destiny had seen, with over two hundred guests. And now Amy watched as Mike greeted his cousin Joe, and Joe's wife Trish, who'd come from Indiana for the occasion. And most of Rachel's family had traveled a variety of distances to be here, as well.

Amy stood with Tessa, admiring it all, when Rachel came rushing up, still the most vibrant bride Amy had ever seen, to give them both a hug. "I did it! I'm married! I'm Mike's wife! Can you believe it?"

Amy couldn't have been happier for her. Her friend who'd once left Destiny, determined to never look back, was now more content and joyous here at home than Amy had ever seen her.

I only hope I can be that happy one day.

But at the moment, it felt doubtful. As she caught sight of Logan across the barn talking to Anna, she realized just how weak and futile her attempts to keep the two apart had been. Notes from a secret admirer? That was all she had in her? She let out a huge sigh. Apparently so.

And maybe her attempts were even . . . selfish. What if God *had* delivered Anna to Destiny as much for Logan as for Mike? What if Amy was actually trying to stand in the way of something being orchestrated by fate?

As always, Anna looked stunning—and it was clear to see that the townsfolk of Destiny were still in awe that their missing princess had at last returned home. If you stood quietly in any corner of the barn, you could hear the happy whispers: how wonderful this was for Mike, and what perfect timing that she could be here for his wedding, and what an amazing happy ending to a story people thought had ended long ago. It was a miracle.

And it truly was. Amy knew that. Yet that ugly jealousy still burned inside her and she couldn't seem to will it away.

"Amy, you look fabulous tonight," Caroline Meeks approached to say just then.

Amy switched her gaze to the other woman, her smile sincere. "Thank you, Caroline."

"That shade of blue is definitely your color."

Then LeeAnn Turner chimed in, as well. "And you should wear your hair up more often. It really shows off your pretty eyes and those high cheekbones."

"I barely recognized you at the wedding," said Cara Collins, a sweet teenage girl Amy knew from the bookstore. Amy had fixed Cara up with her boyfriend, Tyler Fleet.

Amy graciously accepted the compliments and let them fill her heart with just a pinch of hope—for a minute or two. And it *was* truly gratifying to discover she could be pretty, and maybe she would try to fix herself up a little more from now on. But after the others drifted off, another glance across the way reminded her that . . . well, it didn't matter how good everyone else in town thought she looked if Logan didn't notice. And as far as she could tell, he still had eyes only for Anna.

"Go make him notice ya," Edna said behind her then, nearly making her leap out of her skin.

Amy turned toward Rachel's grandma. "Sheesh, Edna, you nearly scared the wits out of me."

But Edna ignored that and went on. "She don't own him, ya know. You can walk right up and start a conversation with the both of 'em without it lookin' the least bit pushy. So go remind him you're here. See what happens."

Amy appreciated Edna's encouraging spirit, yet . . . "I don't know, Edna. Aren't things supposed to happen naturally? Seems to me like if you have to work too hard for it that maybe it's just not meant to be."

Yet Edna merely shrugged. "Maybe yes, maybe no. Sometimes the best things in life are worth working for. It's God's way of makin' ya appreciate 'em more. Or maybe . . . showin' ya what you're capable of. Which is usually more than anybody thinks they are." And with that, Edna toddled off toward the table where Rachel's parents sat with Rachel's brother, all from out of town. And to leave Amy stewing in the mess that was her life. When she'd been helping Rachel plan all this a few months ago, she'd never dreamed she'd feel so forlorn tonight, so empty inside.

"Hey there, cutie—lookin' good."

She glanced up in time to see Duke Dawson toss a wink her way as he passed by heading to the portable bar near the dance floor, and the warmth of a blush climbed her cheeks. Hmm. Wow. Duke Dawson thought she looked good tonight, too. And was he . . . making a pass at her? Maybe she was reading it wrong, but it almost felt that way, same as it had at the wedding shower.

Still . . . Duke? Really? And could she ever be attracted to him? Duke was the kind of guy who often wore a knit hat over his dark hair, even in the summertime— though he'd made the good call of leaving it at home for the wedding—and sported a few tattoos on his muscular arms. A dark goatee and piercing eyes rounded out the picture, making him . . . well, an attractive enough guy, but more than a little intimidating. God only knew how many women he'd been with. And Amy knew from Tessa that he'd once been in an outlaw biker gang in California. But then again, so had Lucky, and that hadn't stopped Tessa from having a wonderful relationship with him, and Lucky was a great guy.

A little while later, dinner was served—in keeping

with the barn setting, Rachel and Mike had decided to go with a simple country menu: fried chicken, baked beans, potato salad, and baked cinnamon apples straight from the orchard. Though Amy seldom drank, when Logan moved up and down the long wedding party table pouring wine, she didn't stop him, since it was for toasting. And not only was she celebrating her friend's wedding—maybe she *needed* a drink. She'd been under so much emotional pressure lately, and tonight was the worst yet.

"I've known Mike since we were little kids and I've seen him go through a lot," Logan said, beginning his toast shortly thereafter, "and I can honestly say that it's not easy to be this man's friend." Soft laughter rippled through the crowd. "But I can also say that it's been much *easier* to be his friend since Rachel came back to Destiny. Don't get me wrong—he's still no picnic to be around most of the time. But Rachel softens Mike's hard edges, and she doesn't let him get away with any crap. I've never seen him happier than he's been since she came along, and if you add all that up, she's the perfect woman for him. To a long, happy life together, with Rachel keeping Mike on his toes the whole time."

Then it was Tessa's turn to stand up and toast the happy couple. "This orchard brought Rachel home," she said, "but it was Mike who made her stay, and I'm grateful to him for that each and every day. While this union ends a family feud, it's just one of many happy beginnings Rachel and Mike will share together. To Rachel and Mike and all their new beginnings."

"And to Anna," Logan added, chiming in again as he raised his glass in her direction, "for making this day even more perfect for Mike and the entire Romo family."

Oh brother—even this, even toasts to Mike and Rachel, end up being about Anna.

And as glasses clinked and the sounds of a few, "Here, here"s echoed through the barn, some people even clapped lightly at the part about Anna. And Amy lectured herself. *Stop this—stop being so evil. This isn't like you.* She took a big sip of her wine to help drown out her selfishness.

She drank the remainder of the glass with dinner—who cared if wine and fried chicken didn't necessarily go together?—and helped herself to a second glass when it was time to cut the cake. Amy could have pretty much predicted that Mike would end up with a faceful of it—the crowd would have been let down if Rachel didn't let him have it. And everyone laughed and applauded when it happened, one more part of a perfect Destiny event on a perfect Destiny summer night in June. *But if everything's so perfect, then why am I smiling on the outside and dying on the inside?*

Especially during Mike and Rachel's first dance, to one of their special songs—James Taylor's "Something in the Way She Moves"—because Logan and Anna were one of the couples who joined them as the song went on. Amy could almost feel her heart breaking in her chest as she watched from the bridal party table. If Logan was waiting for his secret admirer to identify herself tonight, it didn't show. He looked completely enmeshed in Anna Romo.

Amy's thoughts from earlier felt truer with each passing minute. *You're wasting your time here, pining for a guy who thinks of you like his little sister, trying to compete with the most beautiful girl in Destiny.*

And who knew—maybe if Duke Dawson was expressing an interest in her, it was a sign. From fate, or God, or the universe. It wasn't that Duke made her heart go *zing* or anything like that, but maybe it was a sign to . . . be bold, like Tessa and Rachel kept telling her—but . . . in a new way. With someone who had noticed her. With someone . . . unexpected and surprising.

Maybe it was time to show people in Destiny that she could surprise people, too.

So during the next slow song, Amy took a deep breath, followed by another swig of wine, and she crossed the barn floor to where Duke stood talking with Lucky. She walked right up to him without hesitation, making it clear she had something to say to him.

He broke his conversation with Lucky to glance down at her. "Hey, cutie, what's up?"

"Would you like to dance?"

He shrugged, the corners of his mouth turning up in a slight smile. "Sure," he said.

And to her surprise, and even amid the slight fear that plagued her, Amy felt positively . . . triumphant. *No matter what happens now, something or nothing, I'm living. I'm making changes. I'm changing my own landscape. I'm taking my life and making it . . . a journey, an adventure, no longer just this passive existence I've been drifting through.* All because she'd had the courage to ask a biker to dance with her.

Logan sat talking to Anna—but he suddenly found himself watching Amy. Because . . . was he seeing things, or was she seriously slow dancing with Duke Dawson? He saw it, but it didn't quite make sense to his eyes. Duke was a rough biker type, not suited to her at all—and the kind of person Amy would usually avoid.

And the fact was, ever since he'd seen her walk down

that aisle a couple of hours ago . . . well, his mind kept
drifting back to that day he'd kissed her. In the moment,
it had seemed right, natural—but then afterward, he'd
been so confused by it that . . . well, he'd been half drunk
and when he realized what he'd done, he'd assumed he'd
just kissed the nearest available girl. And he'd felt like
an ass, lucky she'd forgiven him. And then he'd put it out
of his mind, because it was Amy, his buddy Amy. But
now it was *back* in his mind.

Every time he remembered it now, his stomach fluttered. And he wished he could remember it even more.
Had he been aware of her breasts pressed against his
chest beneath him? They looked so damn pretty tonight,
after all—how could he have *not* been aware? Had her
kiss been gentle and pliable, or firmer? Or maybe a little
bit of both depending upon the moment? Had her lips
been as soft beneath his mouth as they looked right now?

"Well, what do you think?" Anna said, her voice cutting into his thoughts.

He flinched, drawing his gaze from Amy and Duke
down to Anna beside him. "Huh?"

A pretty laugh echoed from her throat. "Where's your
head at, silly?"

He just gave it a short shake. "Sorry. Something dis-
tracted me. What were you saying?"

But as Anna began telling him whatever she'd been
talking about, he still couldn't quite hear her, couldn't
quite concentrate, because . . . could he really be feeling
that way about Amy?

Surely not. It was just too . . . strange of an idea. Not
that anything about Amy was strange, but he'd just never
thought of her that way. Ever. Okay, except for the kissing day. But he wasn't sure that counted.

And besides, he had Anna. And also whoever was sending him those hot, seductive little notes.

Which led him to start looking around the barn—around the tables where people sat talking, then the dance floor, now full of couples swaying to the music. It could be anyone—anyone at all—and yet he saw no likely candidates, or at least he didn't see anyone giving him the eye. Well, other than Anna. Damn, maybe he needed to lay off drinking tonight—he'd only had a couple of glasses of wine, but everything was beginning to feel confusing.

Just then, a high-pitched trill of laughter drew his eyes back to Amy, who was giggling girlishly at something Duke had said. Were the two of them actually . . . flirting? What exactly was she smiling about? And Duke was really funny enough to make her laugh like that? They seemed to be chatting more now and . . . what on earth were they talking about? He couldn't imagine Amy having a conversation about motorcycles anymore than he could imagine Duke discussing books. Or cats. And why did watching them put a knot in his stomach that seemed to be growing by the minute?

Without weighing it, he said to Anna, "Excuse me—there's something I need to take care of."

He barely caught her dry tone as she murmured, "Sure, go ahead—you're not listening to me anyway."

Then he pushed to his feet, strode out onto the dance floor, and reached up to place a hand on Duke's shoulder. "Mind if I cut in?"

As the biker turned to make bold eye contact, he looked surprised and not particularly amused, and for the first time it occurred to Logan that maybe this wasn't the best guy to be messing with. But it was too late for that now, so he simply held his ground until Duke slowly said, "Uh, sure, dude," then moved aside, allowing Logan to take his place.

Stepping up to Amy, he slid his arms around her waist, letting them settle into the warm curve there, surprised all over again when the new nearness brought on a fresh heat he felt from his head to his toes. He couldn't help but wonder—was she feeling this, too? Or was it all him? He was almost embarrassed by it and hoped she'd never know.

"What on earth do you think you're doing?" she snapped. Okay, apparently it was all him.

"I could ask you the same question," he replied pointedly.

"I was having a perfectly pleasant dance with the first man who's shown an interest in me in longer than I can remember—and you break in like some kind of he-man?"

Logan just let out a breath. "First of all, I'm not acting like a he-man—I just cut in on a dance, that's all. And second, what are you thinking, freckles? Duke Dawson? The guy has some shady past we don't even know about. He's dangerous."

Even as she rolled her eyes, Logan remained aware of the fact that her palms curved over his shoulders. "Dangerous how? You're just stereotyping him. What do you know about him that's so dangerous? He's Lucky's best friend and Tessa likes him fine—heck, even Mike likes him."

Logan blew out an exasperated breath—mainly because she was right and he didn't have an answer. Other than . . . "He's just all wrong for you."

She blinked, looking incredulous. "How do you know what's right and wrong for me?"

For some reason, the fact that she was arguing with him made him tighten his grip on her thin waist a little more. He felt the strangest compulsion to just . . . take care of her. And maybe he'd *always* felt that, but he'd just never really acted on it—until now. "I know you, Amy," he told her. "I know you better than anybody does."

Yet even this brought a saucy reply that caught him off guard. "Do you, Logan? Really?" Something in her tone implied that maybe he didn't. And that made him feel a little panicky.

"What does *that* mean?"

"Maybe there are things about me you don't know. Maybe there are things about me that would shock the hell out of you!"

Hell? Amy never cussed. He leaned forward slightly as they danced. "Are you drunk or something?"

She just let out an irritated breath. "A little tipsy maybe, but not drunk. In fact, maybe I'm . . . more in my right mind than usual."

He let his eyes go even wider on her than they already were. "And what does *that* mean?"

"Never mind," she muttered, just as a new song began to play—the Rod Stewart classic, "You're In My Heart."

She started to pull away, end the dance—and the embrace—but he followed the urge to pull her back to him, not let her go. "By the way, you look great tonight."

And this was the first time since he'd started dancing with her that she seemed . . . like herself a little. Her expression relaxed, her eyes softened. "Really? Thank you."

"I barely recognized you coming down the aisle. I had no idea you were so . . ."

She peered up at him, into his eyes. "So what?"

For some reason, a slight lump rose in his throat then—maybe because they just didn't usually say things like this to each other—but he spoke around it. "Pretty, I guess. You're really pretty, Amy, in a way I just never noticed before."

She bit her lip, lowered her gaze bashfully—and he thought in that moment she looked even prettier than she had all night. "Thanks," she murmured, her voice little more than a whisper.

Amy could barely process what was happening. One minute she'd been dancing with Duke, and it had been . . . well, more entertaining than she'd expected. Because even if they had absolutely nothing in common, he made her feel good about herself, like he enjoyed her company, like he found her attractive. And that was something Amy hadn't experienced in a very long time. Maybe she hadn't realized until that minute how much it mattered, how much a girl needed to feel . . . appreciated. As a female, a woman.

And just when she'd been getting into that, wrapping her head around the idea that—nothing in common or not—something could happen here, between them, that she could maybe let go of her old shyness and embrace that idea, along had come Logan! Cutting in on her dance, and on her chance for romance . . . or well, at least for some much-needed male attention.

And even as mad as she'd been at him—for his pre-sumptuousness, for driving away Duke but not wanting her for himself—his hands on her had felt . . . so, so good.

And now, now he was telling her he'd noticed. That she was pretty. And the words tingled down through her as potent as any kiss or touch. And maybe she wasn't so mad anymore. Because maybe . . . just maybe . . . something was changing here, sparking to life. Maybe her dreams were beginning to come true.

She let herself get lost in the old Rod Stewart tune that suddenly struck her as the most deep-down romantic song she'd ever heard. It was about more than being in love—it was about being in someone's soul, forever, and that was really what she and Logan shared. They were in each other's souls—you couldn't *not* be with a relationship as long as theirs. And even if up to now it had been all about friendship, she believed—in her heart—that in this moment things were shifting.

"There's something I want to tell you, Amy," he said then.

And, oh Lord. It was happening—it was really happening. Warm and happy in his strong arms, she gazed up into his eyes, let her fingers curl slightly into his shoulders. "What is it, Logan?"

"Someone's been sending me notes—from a secret admirer. And I can't figure out who they're from, so it's driving me a little crazy at this point, you know?"

Oh. God. Same old Logan. Bringing his problems and questions and concerns to her. And until recently, that would have been totally fine—and she couldn't even be mad at him, because this was the nature of their relationship; she was his pal, his friend, the girl he talked to about all the *other* girls in his life. The only thing different was—now it tore her heart out.

She swallowed back her sadness and found the strength to push words past the tightness in her chest. "I can imagine."

"I mean, who could it be? And why don't they just tell me?"

Amy only nodded—no reply seemed necessary, and she couldn't summon one anyway.

"The only person I can think of is Anna. Not that she needs to let me know she's into me with notes—she's let me know well enough in person."

Oh no—he thought they were from Anna? That had never even occurred to her! Why hadn't she and Tessa thought of that? What a major flaw in their plan!

"So," Logan went on, his own frustration clearly building, "I think I'm just gonna ask Anna, flat out, right now, if they're from her. Because if they are, what am I waiting for? How come I'm not making a move?"

"Well, because of Mike," Amy answered, desperate to stop this train that suddenly felt as if it were speeding out of control. "I thought Mike wanted you to take things slow. Or that's what I heard anyway." Logan hadn't actually told her that—ironically, it had been Anna who had, at Rachel's bachelorette party.

"Sure, I don't want to piss Mike off—but just like Anna's told him, she's old enough to make her own decisions. And it's not like I'm a creep or something. So I'm just gonna ask her, as soon as this song ends."

And then the song ended.

But Amy didn't quite let go of him.

Because if she did—well, it didn't matter that Anna didn't write those notes. Once he asked her, one thing would lead to another. And it would be just as she feared—this wedding would turn out to be the perfect night for them to move things forward, have sex!

Logan peered down into her eyes. "Thanks for the dance, freckles. And . . . don't be pissed at me for cutting in, okay? It's only because I care about you, you know."

She nodded numbly. "I know." Then felt him pulling away.

And then he was walking toward the edge of the dance floor, and a whole new desperation clawed at her—*you're damned if you do and damned if you don't.*

And that left only one real choice. *Do something. Something bold. This is the moment of truth.*

Without quite having a plan, she followed after him, grabbed his arm tight.

He came to a quick halt, turning back to look at her.

"Wait, stop, don't ask her if she wrote the notes," she said.

Logan's eyes widened slightly. "Why not?"

Amy could barely breathe. "Because they're not from her."

"How do you know?"

"Because I know who they're from."

"Who?" he asked.

And she whispered, "Me."

Eleven

*Y*ou?" he said, and Amy wanted to die. She wanted the dance floor and the ground beneath it to open up and swallow her whole.

She said nothing—she couldn't. She didn't even nod. She simply stood there, frozen, her gaze locked with his, trying to swallow past the nervous lump in her throat. And she knew the look on her face surely said it all anyway.

"Really?" he finally asked, his voice soft, introspective. He was processing this, realizing, understanding. And oh Lord, surely remembering some of the most key lines from those notes. *I fall asleep at night dreaming of your kisses. I want to know how it feels to have your hands on me. I want you inside me.*

And so then the truth simply began spilling from her lips in a rush. "After that day you kissed me, I realized that . . . that I liked it, and that I . . . have feelings for you. Those kinds of feelings." Oh God, she couldn't breathe. "And I . . . I couldn't tell you because . . . because I couldn't face what you might think or how shocked you'd be or . . . the look on your face right now. But I wanted to let you know. Just in some little way. And I . . . I . . . just want to be with you, Logan. Like . . . that." The last part came out in a whisper, but still she'd said it, which she couldn't quite believe.

"Like you said in the notes," he murmured softly.

She managed a nod, but had no idea what he was thinking, what he was feeling. Pity? *Oh, please don't let it be pity.* And then she realized what was probably coming. He would tell her how much he cared about her and how sweet she was and how he'd always be her friend, but that he just didn't feel that way about her. And she'd be humiliated and their friendship would never really be the same, and she'd be stuck like this— loving but unloved, filled with passion but never experiencing it, full of desire but undesirable—for the rest of her sad, pathetic life.

She braced herself but dreaded what was coming, right down to the marrow of her bones. *Why? Don't I deserve some happiness? Finally?*

Yet Logan didn't speak. Instead, he took her arm and led her from the dance floor, unnoticed by the rest of the wedding guests.

And he pulled her into a small, isolated alcove beneath one of the haylofts, where tools were stored and the air was shadowy and smelled of old wood. She might have forgotten she was even at a wedding if the music and laughter beyond hadn't echoed in her ears.

Logan looked at her long and hard, and she met his

gorgeous blue gaze with a painful combination of want and terror, and when he leaned in to press his forehead lightly against hers, she ceased smelling the barn, her senses now filled only with the slightly musky, masculine scent of Logan himself. "Listen," he began, "the whole idea of this kinda freaks me out, freckles . . ."

She sucked in her breath, relished being so close to him, and prayed.

"But . . . but maybe . . ."

"Maybe . . . ?" She had to repeat it to ensure she'd heard him correctly. He was saying maybe? Really? Not no?

"Maybe I should just . . . do *this* and see what happens." And with that, he tilted his head and kissed her.

It was a short, soft kiss that trickled all through Amy, right down to the tips of her fingers and toes. And she'd just started catching her breath when he came back in for another, his mouth pressing to hers in a slightly deeper, more sensual kiss that caused her to tense at first—but then she relaxed into it, because it just felt too good and was sweeping her away. Now there was no music, no laughter, no wedding at all—only Logan.

When he ended the kiss, she felt suspended in space, time, standing there with her eyes shut, lips still parted. It had been possibly the best moment of her life. Because unlike the kisses on the couch, this time she knew she loved him and she had yearned for this, prayed for this, craved this, with her whole heart, ever since the moment she'd figured that out and started accepting it.

She drew in her breath as he leaned his forehead back against hers now, both of them silent. And Amy's heart had never beat faster. Because . . . she suddenly wanted to grab hold of this moment. In a way she'd never grabbed hold of any moment in her life before. She knew it with her entire being. And she feared that if she didn't do what she wanted to do right now, what her very soul was driving her to, that the opportunity might never come her way again. And that she'd always regret letting it pass her by. *Just say what's in your heart. Just say it.*

"Logan, I . . . I want you. Right now. More than I've . . . maybe ever wanted anything."

She heard the deep breath he expelled, and she was just about to wonder, worry, what it meant—when he took her hand and led her from the alcove, and then out the back of the barn until they emerged into the dark of night. He never said a word, just kept walking, leading her, hand in hand. Summer fragrances met her nose— honeysuckle and the wild roses she'd seen growing behind the barn on the day of the shower. And then they were stopping at his car and he was grabbing a picnic blanket from the trunk that she'd seen—even sat upon— many times before. Having known Logan his whole life, she knew it was the quilt, made by his mother, that had covered his bed as a boy.

Amy's heart was in her throat as Logan tucked the old quilt under one arm and proceeded to lead her back into the orchard. The sky above was clear and star-filled as they walked between billowing apple trees.

"Where are we going?" she asked softly.

"Just a place I know, from working here with Mike sometimes."

It didn't take long to get there, and when Logan drew them both to a halt, the moonlit night allowed her to see they'd arrived at a small clearing—a blanket of soft summer grass along burbling Sugar Creek stretched toward a tranquil pool of water, and the willow trees dipping over it from the creek's edge reminded her of the willows at Logan's cottage next to Blue Valley Lake.

"This is one of those spots that's nice and cool even on a hot summer day," Logan told her, "and Mike says there's a natural spring somewhere nearby." But his voice came deeper than usual, and she sensed he was ... excited. Aroused. Oh God, he wanted her, too. She'd realized what they were coming here for, of course, but he really, honestly, truly wanted her, too!

After he spread the blanket on the ground, though, he turned to face her—suddenly appearing a little doubtful—to say, "Are you sure, Amy? Because, I mean, this is kind of fast."

Unfortunately, however, she couldn't speak. Because despite that she *was* sure, she was also a little bit terrified, all things considered. Yet she knew she had to push the terror aside—that it was now or never. And yeah, maybe she'd be a little more comfortable with what was about to happen if she, say, *dated* Logan, if they worked up to this more slowly. But she'd waited long enough—thirty-four years to be exact. And she wasn't going to wait even one more night.

So she nodded, then bit her lower lip just slightly—just before Logan took her hand back into his and stepped up close for another kiss.

And then one turned into another—kisses that came soft and slow, lingering and intoxicating.

Amy didn't know a kiss could be like that, such a gentle meeting of mouths that could stretch so infinitely, powerfully through her. At first she thought such slow, tender affections shouldn't be moving her so deeply, making her tingle so much from head to toe. But then she remembered: This was Logan. Of course it was making her tingle. Heck, these days just a look from him accomplished that.

It took only seconds before she was lost in his tender kisses in a way she'd never truly been lost in anything before. Back when she'd been with Carl—yes, there'd been plenty of kissing, making out, touching, but she'd simply never felt for him as she did for Logan, and besides, that had been a lifetime ago. And she couldn't think of a time or a place that had ever felt more truly perfect to her than here, now.

She didn't know how long they'd kissed that way before Logan's hands closed warmly on her waist, his fingers beginning to knead, massage. Her breasts ached as she instinctively leaned into him, pressed them against his firm chest. The move caused him to deepen his kisses, and soon his tongue flirted with her lips and she immediately parted them further, welcoming him inside, letting her own tongue begin to play with his.

That one simple, new intimacy made the juncture of her thighs weep and want. Oh Lord, what a hunger to have never had fulfilled. And knowing that it soon *would* be, in the sweetest possible way by the most perfect man on earth, drove Amy's desire higher and higher, and any inhibitions she'd continued to suffer now melted away in the warmth of the Destiny summer night.

When Logan's hand rose smoothly to her breast, a soft gasp echoed from her throat—both from the shock of what it felt like to be touched there, and also the pleasure. It expanded outward as he brushed his thumb across her nipple through her dress and bra and she gave herself over completely to the sensations now rushing through her body as they never had before. What she'd experienced with Carl simply paled in comparison to this—in every way.

Now Amy kissed him back eagerly, fervently, no longer shy—her mouth and her body followed their natural urges as thick arousal pulsed through every inch of her being.

I love you, I love you, I love you. Those words threatened to come spilling out of her as that love raced through her veins and pounded in her chest—so it was probably a good thing her lips were too busy kissing him for that to happen. And maybe he already knew—maybe the notes and the things she'd said to him a little while ago pretty much made it clear—but she still didn't think this was the time to be telling him about it.

No, now was the time to just feel. And bask. And follow instincts. And drink in all the pleasure she'd never experienced before.

It surprised her when she was the one—without even making the decision—to take things to the next level, clutching at the front of Logan's tuxedo shirt, soon digging her fingers into the pleated placket, trying to undo the buttons and get to more of him.

He responded in kind, pulling the blue strap of her bridesmaid dress from her shoulder as he bent to kiss her neck. She instinctually leaned her head to one side to better soak in this new affection, and mmm . . . she'd forgotten just how much she'd once loved having her neck kissed. A soft moan even escaped her lips.

But she didn't care—she held nothing back now. And she could hear both of them breathing audibly, labored, as she finally succeeded in getting some buttons undone on his shirt. Only to—darn it!—find a T-shirt underneath, of course. A light sound of frustration left her and

Logan answered it by abandoning her just long enough
to rid himself of the bow tie still around his neck, then
the shirt itself. He ripped the T-shirt off over his head
then and—oh!—Amy sighed at the sight of him.

It wasn't that she'd never seen him shirtless before—it
was that she'd never seen him shirtless for her.

They resumed kissing, her palms pressed flat against his
chest, and soon she began to move them, explore, experiment with touching. *This is Logan. And I'm touching him.
Just the way I fantasized.* How amazing was that? She'd
actually, somehow, made her fantasy come true.

As his perfect kisses continued, he reached behind
her, found the top of the zipper on the back of her dress.
And then it loosened and Amy knew the moment of
truth had arrived. But then a less-than-perfect aspect of
this timing struck her. "I'm wearing a bunch of complicated undergarments," she heard herself telling him.

Yet it only caused a soft smile to light his face. "That's
okay—I don't mind if it takes a little while to get you out
of them. Builds the suspense."

*Oh, if you only knew just how high my suspense
already is, Logan.* But she kept that thought to herself
and simply smiled back as he gently tugged the dress
from her shoulders, and then a moment later, her hips.
It fell around her in a taffeta heap on the edge of the
quilt and she stepped out of her dyed-to-match shoes
at the same time to stand before him in a white strapless bra, more like a corset of sorts, that extended to her
waist, and a netted crinoline that had given the princess-
skirted dress the right amount of fluff.

Logan stood back and looked her over, his eyes filled
with both sex and amusement. "How do we get you out
of this stuff?"

"The crinoline's easy," she said, dropping her glance to it. "Drawstring in the back."

"Should I do the honors?" he asked.

And she whispered, "Yeah"—then waited patiently as he reached around behind her and pulled the string.

The crinoline relaxed around her waist immediately and fell to the ground atop her dress revealing a pair of white cotton bikini panties with little yellow happy faces on them.

"Cute," he said, stepping back to look.

And Amy managed a "Thanks," but it wasn't easy with Logan's eyes suddenly on her *there*.

"The bra thing? How does that come off?"

"There are hooks in the back. A lot of them," she warned.

He stepped around behind her, and seeing what she meant, said, "Good thing I'm a patient man."

Whereas Amy was now caught in a struggle between patience—as in fresh nervousness—and urgency. So she simply stood there, trying her best to breathe normally as Logan's fingers toiled with the row of hooks, the strapless bra loosening around her bit by bit.

Finally she could tell only a few hooks remained fastened, and then those were undone, too, and she knew Logan was still holding it around her with his hands, perhaps letting them both prepare for what came next.

As he released his hold on the boned fabric, Amy looked down, watched the bra fall away from her, watched her breasts be bared beneath the stars. A soft breeze blew past just then, causing her nipples to pucker even further than they already had beneath Logan's enticing touches. And then, his voice lower in timbre than she'd ever heard it before, he said, "Turn around, Amy. Let me see."

Despite the return of shyness, Amy made the move to face him in the moonlight. She heard the soft gurgling of Sugar Creek in the distance and the ragged sound of her own breathing. Logan's eyes burned on her.

"Don't take this the wrong way," he finally said, "but I couldn't have imagined how beautiful you would look like this. Undressed."

She sucked in her breath as her nipples grew still tighter beneath his gaze. "I don't take it the wrong way. I take it in a good way."

"Good. Because you are. Beautiful. And I . . . . just never knew."

"I wish I had on different panties," she heard herself admit.

But he only laughed and said, "I don't. These are perfect." Then he held out a hand to her and said, "Let me kiss you some more."

Feeling, for the first time in her life, as beautiful as he'd just said, Amy went willingly back into his arms. Only of course it was different this time because she was mostly naked. Her bare breasts met with the firm wall of his chest as his arms enclosed her.

As their kisses became even deeper, more filled with the desire that threatened to consume Amy now, Logan situated his body in such a way that—oh, oh God—the hardness between his legs pressed rigidly into the soft flesh of her belly, at the front of her panties. Mmm . . . ohhh . . . yes. And if the crux of her thighs had been hungry and achy before . . . well, now it was almost the greatest part of her. The need was colossal, overwhelming. She found herself moving against him, longing to feel that hardness a little lower, where she needed it most.

Their breathing came heavy again, audible, and Logan murmured, "Let's lie down."

Amy said nothing, only went willingly as they both eased onto the quilt until she lay on her back peering up into his eyes while light fingertips caressed her tummy. His kisses returned, but they touched her lips only briefly before drifting downward—first onto the tender skin of her neck, and then lower, lower. Her breath came in heated sighs as Logan kissed his way slowly down her chest and onto one sensitive breast.

Her hands curled into his hair as he raked his tongue delicately across the taut, pointed peak, and she could have sworn some invisible string stretched directly from there to the needy spot in her panties. She moaned as he closed his mouth over the beaded nipple; her eyes fell shut and she knew a near bliss she'd never experienced.

She had no idea how long he laved and kissed her breasts, moving back and forth between them, leaving whichever one was unattended to tingle beneath a breeze that grew slightly cooler as the night grew later. And as he finally began to kiss his way down onto her stomach, the muscles within contracted sharply, and he smiled up at her, clearly having felt it, too. "Try to relax, freckles," he told her.

"I am. Mostly." Though she wasn't sure if it was the truth or a lie. She'd begun to grow comfortable with him, with this, what they were doing—but some tension remained since she knew they were headed someplace she'd never been before. And besides, it was hard to relax when . . . "It just feels so nice," she confessed in a heated whisper.

"Good," he murmured. "I'm glad to hear that."

And then . . . oh Lord, as he rained delicate kisses across her torso, he eased his fingers into her panties and she bit her lip and held her breath until they sank into the moist crevices within, making her let out a soft cry of pleasure.

"That good?" he stopped to ask.

"Uh huh," she said. Only that. Maybe other girls he'd been with weren't quite as sensitive or responsive. Since, of course, other girls he'd been with weren't still virgins.

And as she moved against his touch, it occurred to her that it was so right for her to be sharing this with Logan. Logan who had known her forever. Logan who had always been there for her. Logan who cared about her. And even if nothing more ever came between them after this night, this was . . . perfect.

Amy shut her eyes, shut out the twinkling stars above, shut out the sounds of crickets in the trees, and simply gave herself over to the sensations Logan delivered. Her desire rose, higher and higher, until her finger-nails clawed at the quilt on either side of her, until she'd made fists around handfuls of old fabric, and until—oh God, yes!—she was sobbing her ecstasy as the orgasm washed over her. It covered her thick and hot, taking her to a place where nothing mattered but the release and the pleasure. And, well, Logan. Even now, she was deeply, fully aware that he was the one who'd taken her to such delicious and unfathomable heights.

When finally she came back to herself, she opened her eyes, found Logan hovering above her, peering back down at her. "You're pretty damn beautiful right now, Amy. And I'm glad this is happening. I'm glad you told me. Something about this is . . . easier than I ever could have predicted. Something about this just feels . . . right."

Right. Just as she'd been thinking herself. He felt it, too. She smiled up at him, then even curled her arms

around his neck and drew him down for another intoxicating kiss.

And then one kiss turned into another, and another,
and it struck her that being nearly naked with him
already felt natural now, almost miraculously so, and
when—mmm, yes—what lay between his legs hardened
further against her hip, she wanted more.

And she wasn't afraid any longer. She needed this
as badly as she needed to draw air into her lungs. And
this was Logan, and her dream was coming true, so
she didn't hesitate to tell him again what she'd told him
earlier. "I want you, Logan." After which she went one
better—without even remembering or weighing it, she
said the words she'd written in her last love note. "I want
you inside me."

I give myself joy of this.

Jane Austen, from *Emma*

#

Logan let out a hot breath at her words. She'd excited him by saying it. And she'd never imagined she could feel as truly sexy as she did right now.

He answered with another heated tongue kiss, this one firm and full of intention.

And he carried that intention further by beginning to ease down her panties.

She lifted to let him and felt them slipping away, felt the thrill of becoming even more naked for him, with him.

And then she followed the instinct to reach for his waistband—only then paused, whispering, "Oh God."

"What?" He sounded worried.

She lowered her gaze to say, "I guess I'm just . . . shy about this part. Undressing you."

He arched one eyebrow, his look playful. "You didn't seem shy about it a little while ago."

Which made her bite her lip, and unfortunately, get a little more specific. "Well . . . about undressing *this* part of you."

He flashed a conciliatory grin. "No worries, freckles. I'll handle it." Then he reached for his zipper, but stopped to glance back at her. "If you're sure you're ready."

So, so ready. But she only answered with a nod.

She tried not to seem intensely interested in watching him take off his pants, but her gaze drifted down into the shadows between them a few times without her consent. Her breath grew shallow as she waited, and she knew when the pants were gone, knew when he was putting on a condom, knew when there was nothing else to keep their bodies apart.

He said nothing more, just angled his body over hers to resume kissing her, caressing her. His warm hand moved over her breast, down across her stomach, onto her hip. At her other hip, his erection pushed insistently.

Without ever actually deciding to do so, she found herself parting her legs beneath him, sliding herself under him to draw him between her thighs. It wasn't about being consciously aggressive—she didn't know *how* to be aggressive—it was just about her body's instincts; it was about primal needs bubbling hotter and higher than she'd even known they could.

Silently, Logan positioned himself, using his hands to spread her thighs further, and she experienced the distinct power of opening herself to him, welcoming him, in a way she'd never opened herself to a man before. And nothing in her life had ever felt quite so amazingly right.

She pulled in a deep breath when the pressure began, her arms wrapped snugly around his broad shoulders as the scent of him, the nearness of him, permeated her senses. She shut her eyes, clenched her teeth slightly, and waited.

As he tried to penetrate her, a soft soreness spread there, and she heard his labored breath grow even more so—maybe with frustration. She could almost read his thoughts. *Why isn't this working more easily?* Suffering the sudden, momentary fear that he would give up, stop, she pushed herself against him.

Then he thrust inward—hard—and Amy suffered a short, jagged burst of pain, followed by an impossible tightness inside her. She hugged him with all the strength she possessed, clinging to him. Only she didn't dwell on the pain—because Logan had just set her free. Finally. And she'd never felt closer to him.

That was when he pulled back slightly to look into her eyes, his filled with uncertainty as he whispered, "Amy . . . are you a . . . ?"

She let out the breath she'd been holding, getting more comfortable with how he felt in her. "I . . . I was," she admitted. "But not anymore. Thank God!" Then she even let out a small laugh.

He just blinked, continuing to peer down at her, looking dumbfounded. "But . . . how? I mean, there was that one guy . . ."

Amy hadn't ever thought about this moment, about having to confirm and explain, but she just shook her head and whispered, "Never happened."

"So . . . I'm the first one?"

She thought they'd already established that, but she guessed he was still shocked. She simply gave a soft nod.

And he let out a breathy sort of, "Wow," that told her he wasn't wowing the amazing fact that she was still a virgin, but the fact that she'd chosen *him* to change that.

"It . . . it only makes sense that it's you," she said on a whisper. *Because we've known each other our whole lives and you've always been one of my very best friends.* That was the unspoken part she knew he heard anyway. *And because I love you.* That part, though, felt a little more secret.

"I wanna make this so special for you," he told her then.

And she bit her lip and spoke the simple truth. "You already are."

After that, he lowered his mouth to hers, and he began to slowly, cautiously move inside her—and all talking ceased.

She sensed him being careful, and she appreciated that because she needed it. One more reason why it was so perfect that this was Logan and not anyone else, not some arbitrary man she might have met or dated for a little while but who didn't really care about her in a deep way. Amy had always believed things happened for a reason, but she'd never understood why or thought it fair that she'd had to wait so long to be intimate with a guy. Yet now she knew God, or destiny, had been leading her, slowly but surely, to this one perfect moment in time.

Logan's soft drives into her newly-breached flesh hurt a little, but she knew he was being as gentle as he could, and even amid the discomfort, she took pleasure from the utter closeness she shared with him right now. She continued to cling to him, maybe too tightly, but she knew he understood.

As his kisses dropped to her neck, she peered up at the millions of stars overhead and experienced that feeling of being small—but in the good way, in the way of knowing there was nowhere else in the whole cosmos she'd rather be right now than where she was, in the Farris-Romo Family Apple Orchard, making love with Logan Whitaker.

Somewhere along the way her pain dissipated, giving way to at first a subtle, gentle pleasure, and then one that filled her deeper, more thoroughly, beginning to stretch all through her.

Oh! This . . . this was it. This, she understood already, was the good part. Though she was sure there were plenty of other good parts, too, this was the "wow" part that made Rachel and Tessa sigh in that lost-looking way when they talked about sex.

Out of pure happiness, as Amy absorbed Logan's every sexy thrust into her body, she held to him still more snugly. And then she began to thrust back. She heard both of them breathing harder, felt the connection with him deepen. Her legs wrapped around his without planning and a soft groan echoed from his throat as he planted his hands on her hips and plunged a little deeper, rougher.

Amy cried out at the power and heat he delivered and found herself kissing his cheek, pulling him close, and—oh, oh God—then she started to cry. It made her angry at herself, especially when he pulled back, appearing slightly alarmed, to say, "What? What's wrong?"

She could only shake her head as she tried to summon words. "Nothing. Not sad tears. Happy ones." *I just feel so close to you right now.* But she couldn't tell him that—it just seemed too . . . well, like she'd already done enough of that tonight, and despite the perfection of this moment, she didn't want to overdo that stuff. "Just can't believe this is finally happening," she told him, which was just as true. "I'd begun to think it never would."

"Aw, honey, I'm sorry you ever had to think that."
Then he flashed a soft, teasing grin. "You should've
come to me with this sooner."

Tears gone, the offer made her emit a light giggle, but
then she told him, "I didn't know until recently that I
wanted it to be you." Then she bit her lip, gazed up into
his pretty eyes, and felt the pure magic of the night rolling all through her again. "And I'm so *glad* it's you."

"Me, too," he whispered, brushing a few stray bangs
from her eyes. "I couldn't have imagined that before
tonight, but me, too." Then he tilted his head, peered
down at her. "So . . . it's okay? Doesn't hurt or anything?"

Another nod. "A little at first, but now . . ."

He raised his eyebrows. "Now?"

"I love it."

"Aw, baby," he murmured deeply, and fresh desire
flared in her at the very point where their bodies connected, and she automatically lifted her pelvis, thrusting
upward. Which made him let out a small growl. And
made her smile.

As they continued moving together, Amy shut her
eyes and sank back into it—without crying this time,
and just basking in the wonder of it. *I get it. I finally get
it. I finally get what's so incredible about this.*

And soon they were both moaning as Logan's plunges
into her body increased in intensity, and Amy thought
she could do this with him forever and ever—but that
was when he said, "Aw, honey, I'm gonna come." And
the next thing she knew, the hands at her hips gripped
her tighter, and his drives into her came harder, wilder,
and she loved knowing she'd taken him there.

Like earlier, upon going still, he touched his forehead
to hers—and then he kissed her.

And once more she suffered the heartwrenching urge to say *I love you,* but she literally bit her tongue to stop herself. Because this had all happened so fast—well, fast in ways—and she didn't know where it would lead or what would happen tomorrow, and again, she'd already put enough of her emotions out there tonight. And, of course, she longed for *him* to say those three little words, but when he didn't, it made up for it a lot when he instead told her, "You're so beautiful, Amy. And this was so special." She even lifted another kiss to his mouth in reply.

And she realized there would indeed be no promises, or talk of the future—that tonight, on this quilt next to Sugar Creek, it was just about dealing with the intimacy of the moment. And that was okay.

After he'd shed the condom, Logan flipped one side of the quilt over them since the night had finally started turning chilly. Amy rested her head on his chest and he held her in a loose embrace, and they lay silently that way a few minutes before he asked her, "When did you start . . . feeling this way?"

She wasn't dying to discuss all that, especially not knowing where they would stand in the morning, but she figured it was a fair question. And besides . . . maybe he would just love her back. Maybe it would be simple from this point forward. "After that day at your house last month, the day you kissed me."

He tipped his head back, clearly well aware it had happened—which was a relief. They'd never talked about it after she'd left, and he *had* been drinking at the time, so she hadn't been sure he'd clearly remember it. "I felt . . . so weird about that. Like I didn't give you any choice in the matter."

"You didn't really," she said with an understanding

shrug, "but it was you, so it was easy enough to forgive. Especially when I realized . . . that I didn't mind it so much."

He grinned down at her. "Why didn't you tell me you liked it?"

She rolled her eyes. *Let me count the reasons.* "Well, you acted like it was the most unthinkable thing that ever could have happened. So I didn't think *you* liked it much."

He leaned his head to one side on the quilt. "I liked it fine. I was just . . . freaked out. And, well, you know I wasn't exactly myself back then."

She spoke softer now, rising up, propped on one elbow, to peer down into his eyes. "About the, uh, fire . . . are you good now? Fine?"

Logan gazed up at Amy, his lifelong friend, now his lover, and the sweetest girl in the world. The truth was, he'd been doing everything in his power lately not to think about the reasons he'd been in such a funk after that fire. He supposed that over the last few weeks he'd gotten pretty good at finding distractions, things that kept his mood up, his thoughts occupied with better things. And hell, there'd been plenty going on in Destiny to help with that: Anna's return and their subsequent connection, Mike's wedding, love notes from a secret admirer—and tonight, finding out the notes had come from his freckles and the fact that no matter what happened now, it would pretty much change their relationship forever.

So yeah, he'd found plenty of easy walls to put up between him and that night, him and those awful memories. But now that Amy had brought it back with that one simple question, he had to ask himself: Was he really doing all that much better if he was only pushing it away every time it came to mind? He'd *thought* he was doing better—he'd *made himself* do better. But if it still gouged at his soul as sharply as he felt it right this minute, was he really doing all that well or was it just a head game he played with himself?

"You're not answering," she said then, her strawberry blond curls—a few of which had come loose from her fancy hairdo—tickling his chest. And she sounded worried.

His instant urge was to put her at ease—because that was his urge with *everybody* lately. He was embarrassed, even ashamed, of how low he'd gotten after the fire, and now he just wanted people to forget that and think everything was fine. And so he almost went into an explanation of just how fine he was, how that was all water under the bridge—but then he remembered: This was Amy. And he felt closer to her right now than ever, and if he could tell anyone the real truth, it was her.

"I guess it's . . . complicated," he said.

She lifted her head to peer down at him. "Complicated how?" And despite wishing he could ease her worries, he realized this moment was about just being real. Amy had been real with *him* tonight; he needed to be real with her, too.

If he could.

"I guess I still feel a lot of what I felt back then. I'm just . . . working harder not to let it show."

"Oh," she murmured, sounding sad. And he felt a little like he was letting her down, letting them both down. "I'm sorry to hear that. I thought things were better."

"Yeah," he mumbled. It seemed the only thing to say.

"If . . . you wanted to talk about it, about that night, I'm happy to listen," she offered.

Yet his chest tightened at the very idea. He didn't think words existed to describe that night. And even if they did, he wasn't sure he could say them. "Thanks," he said tightly. "But can't."

"I understand," she said. She still gazed down at him, sweet and caring in the moonlight, but he didn't meet her eyes now—he couldn't. Instead he stared upward at nothing, his gaze fixed on stars he didn't really see, and his chest grew tight as certain visions began to invade his memory more than usual.

For God's sake, didn't he have enough other stuff to think about? He'd just had sex with Amy, after all. Amy! And even if it had felt totally, shockingly good and right, it was still a damn big surprise. And then there was Anna. And his job situation. And even as confusing as all that stuff was, too, at least it didn't rip his guts out every time he thought about it.

"But maybe talking about it would be good," she suggested, and his chest ached further. Crap—she'd said she understood that he couldn't talk about it; he'd thought they were done with this topic. "Sometimes, putting something into words is . . . the thing that helps you deal with it, process it. Maybe talking about it would help you put it behind you."

Logan's jaw clenched. What she was saying made sense to him, logically. He just didn't know . . . if he could face going there again. So it caught him off guard when he heard himself force out one lone, solitary word. "Maybe."

Amy said nothing else for a while. She rested her head back on his chest and he lay there soaking up the night, soaking up the memory of what they'd just shared. And things began to feel easier, like before . . . except that the fire was lodged in the back of his brain now, creeping into the edge of his thoughts, whether he liked it or not.

And he knew if he lay there long enough trying to focus on other things, he'd get back to that almost comfortable place, that place where he was happy, upbeat Logan, or pretending to be anyway, and that he could probably go on this way for a very long time—who knew, maybe forever—and no one would be the wiser. No one but him.

Or he could do what Amy had said. He could talk about it. Just once. He could put it into words. And then he could hope and pray that maybe getting it off his chest would actually do what she'd said, help him move on.

The only thing was, if he told her, he had to tell her the whole truth, not just part of it. And if he told her the whole truth, that made it . . . feel more real. And it meant . . . someone else would know.

His stomach went hollow at the thought, and he heard himself whisper in a low rasp, "You might not want to hear all of this, freckles. It's not pretty."

"I didn't expect it to be. If it was pretty, you'd have already told me. I can take it, Logan."

Of course she could. She would. For him. No hesitation. Her reaction—so tough, so sure—made him spontaneously kiss her. "You're the best," he told her. "The absolute best person I know."

In response, she bit her lip, looking prettily bashful as she said, "Thank you. But . . ."

"But?"

"Wanting to help you through this isn't about me being a good person. It's about . . . how I feel about you. There's not much I wouldn't do for you, Logan."

And he'd pretty much already known that. But somehow, hearing it, feeling it, made him—again—*need* to tell her.

He needed to bare his soul to her.

He needed to tell her what he could tell no one else.

"I couldn't get to them," he blurted out, his throat catching on the words.

"What?" she whispered.

"Ken and Doreen. I couldn't help them."

She was perched back on one elbow, peering down at him again. "I know," she replied, sounding confused.

And he realized that what he'd just said sounded ridiculously obvious, but she couldn't see the images in his mind. He had to swallow, hard, before he tried to explain. "I . . . I was standing outside the bedroom door, so close to them, but a wall of flames and smoke separated us. I knew it was too much and that I had to get out of there before the floor collapsed." Another swallow as he stared blankly back up at the sky. "And then part of the bedroom floor did start to collapse. Ken . . . he was across the bedroom. He and Doreen both. The smoke was thick, but I could still see them, backed up against the far wall, and they were looking at me, and I called out through my respirator that it was me, thinking somehow that mattered, and . . ." Jesus God, he didn't want to remember this, he didn't want to keep hearing the sounds. "Ken was screaming for me to help them. Begging me."

Somewhere on the periphery of his brain, he heard Amy expel a soft breath of horror.

"Like I said, I already knew there was no hope. The floor between us was half gone, and the floor beneath *me* was about to give way. And it was some kind of miracle they hadn't succumbed to the smoke already. Yet still, there I was, so close to these two people I've known my whole life, and I just went . . . numb. I just stood there. Staring at them while Ken cried for help. In one way, I could barely hear him over the noise of the fire, but in another . . . he was all I *could* hear. I'll never forget that sound. I wake up sometimes at night—still—hearing it, seeing his face flickering between the flames and smoke that separated us, seeing the look in his eyes, the despair, when he realized I wasn't doing anything, wasn't *going* to do anything.

"I've never felt so fucking helpless, so fucking useless, in my entire life. I was just . . . frozen. I couldn't help them—but I couldn't leave, either. So I just stood there, the flames getting higher around us, the smoke getting thicker and more toxic by the second—I just fucking stood there like a helpless little kid."

"Oh Logan," she murmured, softly stroking his arm.

And he felt it, the comfort, her care, a little, but mostly he was lost in the memory now. "Finally, the chief was calling for me to get the hell out of there, and so . . . I just took one last look at them and said, 'I'm sorry'—which I know damn good and well they couldn't even begin to hear at that point, so I guess maybe I was saying it more to me than to them—and then I turned my back on them and left. Just left them there to die. Just left them there to suffer a horrible, awful death. I just left them there, Amy."

"You had no choice, Logan," she said. "Surely you know that."

He switched his gaze briefly to hers. And yeah, he knew she was right—he'd known that since the moment it had happened; he'd been *trained* to know these things—but . . . "It's different with friends, people you care about."

Above him, she only sighed, and he knew she got what he was saying. That this was about more than logic, that it went deeper than that.

"When it's someone you care about, you feel like . . . no matter what it takes, you should be in there trying to save them, even if you know you can't. You feel like you should have fought 'til the end, like . . . like . . ."

Amy blew out a breath. "Logan," she whispered, sounding as tense as he felt, "if . . . if you're saying you should have fought to save them until you died there with them, that's . . . crazy. Surely you know that."

Logan just lay there. Because, in fact, that was exactly what he was saying, exactly how he'd felt ever since that night. Like he'd let them die there alone when he should have found some way to save them, even if it meant his own death. "I'm a firefighter, Amy," he told her. "My job is to put my life on the line for people. And I've never backed away from that before—I never thought I'd let somebody die just to save myself."

"That's not what happened, not how it was!" she argued.

"Did you ever see the movie *The Poseidon Adventure,* the original, with Gene Hackman?" he asked.

"Yeah," she said. "But so what?"

"I watched it with my dad when I was little," he told her. "And do you remember the part where Gene Hackman used the last bit of his strength to turn that steel wheel, to open the hatch and save the rest of them, and then dropped to his death? Seeing that had an effect on me. I remember thinking—now that guy's a hero, a real hero. He was willing to give up his life to save others."

"But that's not how it was in this situation. You couldn't save them, you just told me that. And if you'd sacrificed your own life, it would have been . . . meaningless, and . . . a huge waste, Logan. And besides, you're talking about a movie, not real life. I don't think it's wise to hold yourself to the standards of someone who isn't real."

"I just worry," he softly went on, "that . . . my dad would have been disappointed in me."

Still looking skeptical, Amy tilted her head. "What do you think he'd have done in your place?"

"I'm not sure," Logan told her, shaking his head lightly against his old bedcover. "Maybe he'd have gotten to the second floor a little faster. Or seen some way to get them out that I didn't. But I think he'd have found a way to save his friends. He wouldn't have left them there like that."

Yet Amy shook her head, clearly unconvinced, her expression downright stalwart now. "You're wrong," she said. "I knew your dad. He was as heroic as they come, Logan, just like you, but he wasn't impractical, either. And it would have broken his heart, same as it's broken yours, but he would have done exactly what he had to do, what *you* had to do, what you *did*. He'd have saved himself. Because he'd have known one more death would only make it that much more of a tragedy, and—" Her voice broke then, and he realized she'd gotten almost as emotional as him. "And . . . my God, Logan. If you had died in that fire, needlessly . . . I would never get over it. And now *I'd* have a broken heart, too, but for a whole different reason."

And by then tears were streaming down her face, and Logan's heart felt like it was bending, stretching in his chest as she said, "Just think about what that would have done to me, and your mother, and Mike, and everyone else who knows you and cares about you. Just think about how much more empty our lives would be right now, Logan."

"Hey now, freckles, calm down," he said soothingly. "Everything's all right. I'm right here, honey, and I'm not going anywhere. Nothing to cry about." And as she sniffed back her tears, he didn't for a second fight the urge to slip his hand around her neck and pull her down for another slow, passionate kiss. Because he hated making her cry, and yet . . . it touched him to know how much she cared.

They kissed for a few long, pain-numbing minutes that brought Logan back to a better place. And when they were done, Amy said to him, "Do you see now? Do you see why you had to do what you did? That no good could have come from any other decision?"

Logan drew in a deep breath, thinking it through. He'd never thought ahead to how it would affect anyone else if he'd lost his life in that fire—he'd only thought of Ken and Doreen, and of what he thought it meant to be a real man, a *good* man. He'd thought only of the look on Ken's face, the feeling that he'd let them down in the biggest possible way you could fail someone. But she was right—it was pretty horrible to imagine putting his mother through something like that, and Amy, and everyone else, too. "Maybe," he finally said. "It's just hard . . . hard to know the last thing the Knights saw was me . . . leaving them to die."

"And that'll probably *always* be hard, Logan," she told him. A bitter pill, a hard thing to hear, yet it was true. "But you have to know nothing that happened that night was your fault. You did all you could. And I'm sure Ken and Doreen knew that as well as I do."

And it was then that something took place inside Logan

that never had before, or at least not since he'd reached adulthood. His eyes began to ache, and his throat went tight, and he grew aware that his cheeks were wet. And he realized that—shit—now he'd begun to cry, too.

And at first, he tried to suck back the tears. Because he was a guy—a fireman, for God's sake—and he didn't cry. But Amy was watching him, and she was whispering, "No, Logan, no. Just let it go. Let it go."

And without quite making the decision, not quite being able to hold it back any longer, that was what he did—he'd had enough, too much, and now he'd finally reached the breaking point. Tears flowed from the corners of his eyes, wetting his cheeks, his hairline, as he crushed his eyes shut and finally felt the wrenching release mixed with the relief of just giving in to this, just for a minute. And he held Amy tight as she wiped away the wetness and kissed his cheek, again and again, soft and sweet, blurring the pain until finally, slowly, it faded—and all he remained aware of were the sweet scents of the orchard at night and Amy making everything better.

As Amy and Logan made the walk back up through the orchard the next morning, shortly past dawn, she couldn't imagine what she must look like by now. She supposed this was technically the infamous "walk of shame" she'd heard people speak of.

But she didn't feel any shame—in fact, she only felt . . . happy. She had no idea what would happen between her and Logan now—she'd noticed, in fact, that neither of them were talking about it—but she knew that last night had been special, and right, and exactly what it should have been. To lose her virginity with Logan had been worth the wait, worth every blasted month and year of it. And the fact that he'd opened up to her about the fire . . . well, now she understood what he'd been going through, and she hoped sharing it had helped. And if not, well . . . at least he didn't have to go through it alone any longer because he'd have *her* if times got rough or he needed to talk some more.

Logan walked her to her car, parked out front near Edna's house, and kissed her goodbye, saying simply, "Last night was really special, freckles," and she knew he wasn't talking about the wedding.

"For me, too," she told him. "And . . . I hope that maybe talking about things . . . helped a little."

He nodded. "It did. Thank you for that." And then he kissed her again before turning to walk away, back toward his car parked behind the barn.

And as Amy opened her car door, she didn't miss the curtain being pulled back in the window on the side of Edna's house, nor Edna's face behind the glass giving her a wink and a smile.

. . . how very happy a summer must be before her!

Jane Austen, from *Emma*

Thirteen

That afternoon, Amy sat in one of the easy chairs at Under the Covers, trying once more to get Mr. Knightley and Austen to be friends. Her night with Logan had lifted her spirits so high that she felt inspired to try again with these two.

She'd put down a pie pan with some Meow Mix and a little milk—the pan being plenty wide enough that they could learn to share, but without quite being in each other's faces. Austen stepped up cautiously, after a nudge from Amy, to where Knightley already stood eating. At first, he gave a low hiss, so Amy scolded him. "Bad, Mr. Knightley, very bad indeed. Be nice and share with Austen. She wants to be your friend." Then she looked back to the more timid cat. "Go on, Austen, don't be afraid," she said, prodding her lightly again.

Austen kept her eye on Knightley, and it took her a

minute to get bold enough to actually eat, but once she started, Mr. K. didn't protest. And Amy smiled. "Maybe there's hope for you two yet."

And at the moment, she was starting to think she could accomplish just about anything.

First, she'd miraculously gotten prettier—and she'd even spent extra time on her makeup today upon seeing how much more her eyes and lips stood out with a little added effort.

Then she'd won Logan's affections and finally lost her virginity.

And now she'd even made peace between enemy cats!

Leaning back in the chair, she let out a happy sigh. She couldn't remember ever being so simply filled with joy. Thanks to Logan. And the way they had connected last night, in both body and soul. She bit her lip, still all atwitter at the memory.

And he'd even opened up to her about the fire afterward, too. And now she finally understood what had really been going on with him that first time he'd kissed her. Perhaps those kisses were the only good thing to come out of a tragedy that had stretched far beyond the Knight house. She hoped and prayed that she'd been some help to Logan last night—and she believed in her heart that she had. And though she hated his pain, she felt all the more connected to him because he'd shared it with her.

After that, she'd slept in his arms and she was pretty sure no sleep had ever been sweeter. Summer night scents and cool, blossom-scented air had surrounded them as they lay wrapped in the old quilt, the gentle cadence of crickets and the burble of Sugar Creek lulling them to sleep.

Once, she'd woken up, and upon realizing where she was, she'd simply lay there looking over at him, taking in all that male beauty, and let the same joy she still felt now permeate her from head to toe. He'd made everything about her first time so easy, so right. Her smile widened as she relived the moment in her mind.

Now, she felt almost like her old, happy self. But an even better, more experienced, more thrilled version of herself. She'd even found herself doing a little matchmaking this morning, something that hadn't held the same natural appeal for her as usual lately. But when Caroline Meeks had come in the store, Amy suggested she might consider pursuing Sue Ann's boss at Destiny Properties, Dan Lindley. Caroline had seemed fairly aghast at the idea, but Amy thought it a good one, and she'd resolved to work on it soon. She'd also found herself thinking about Chuck Whaley, the young guy who worked for Adam at Becker Landscaping. She didn't have anyone in mind for him yet, but she was going to keep an eye out for just the right girl.

Just then, the door opened with a jingle from the bell above, and Tessa came in. She wore a big smile, too. "Sooooo?" she said.

"So . . . what?" Amy asked.

"So you and Logan disappeared around the same time last night, that's so what. What happened?"

Amy hadn't quite realized it would be so obvious they were both gone, but she supposed it made sense that Tessa would notice. She cast her friend a happy, confiding look to softly say, "I told him."

Tessa's eyes flew wide, her expression hopeful. "And?"

Amy gave her lower lip a small, bashful nibble, remembering. "And . . . I am no longer the V-word."

At this, Tessa gasped with joy. "Really? Oh my God, Amy. And was it amazing?"

Amy's whole body tingled with the memory as she gave a soft nod. "It was perfect."

"I'm so happy for you! This is the best news!" She reached down to squeeze Amy's hand. "See? You told him and it was okay. Better than okay. It was perfect. And so . . . are you, like, together now? Like officially a couple?"

And Amy's heart took a brief dip down toward her stomach, but she didn't let it dampen her mood for more than a second or two. "The *sex* was perfect," she corrected herself. "The rest . . . we didn't talk about."

"Why not?" Tessa asked, looking bummed out.

Amy just sighed. "Well, I kind of thought I'd put enough weird pressure on him for one night. I mean, he was pretty shocked to discover how I felt. And it was a beautiful night . . . with no promises. And that's okay. Because how could I really ask him for more after dropping a bomb like that?"

As Tessa pursed her lips, Amy could tell her friend was seeing her point of view. "Okay, fair enough, you can only do so much in one night, but . . ."

"But what?"

"But now we have to figure out your next move. Because it's not like Anna Romo has suddenly just vanished, you know?"

Amy didn't answer, instead just quietly pulling in her breath. She'd been floating around on her dreamy little cloud of love ever since parting ways with Logan, and she hadn't let herself think ahead. She'd been trying to be all mature and patient about the whole thing. But she couldn't argue with Tessa's logic.

"In fact, she was pretty perplexed when he disappeared, and she wasn't shy about asking if people had seen him. I think she was disappointed, that she probably *was* hoping something would happen between them last night, and that makes me think . . . well, she might be even more aggressive with him now. Especially with Mike gone to Italy."

And now Amy's heart dropped further. She hated thinking of this as some kind of competition between her and Anna—but she supposed it was.

"So we need to talk strategy."

Ugh. "Strategy, Tessa? You make it sound so much . . . like a game."

But Tessa just shrugged. "Love *is* a game. One in which all is fair. Get my point?"

Amy let out a sigh. She didn't like it, but Tessa was right. One wonderful, romantic, sexy, exciting night with the man of her dreams didn't necessarily mean she could rest on her laurels. "Okay, yes, but . . . can't I just have a day or two to bask in the glory of last night? I mean, it was so special, so perfect, that I don't want to feel . . . conniving about it."

"No," Tessa said simply. "I'm sorry, but I think you need to take the bull by the horns here. You can't go soft now."

Amy actually admired Tessa's go-get-'em attitude— her bold daring was what had ultimately led to her relationship with Lucky—but she wasn't that good at it herself. "Well," she asked skeptically, "what is it exactly that you want me to do?"

Walking around to settle in one of the other chairs, Tessa thought for a minute, then said, "The summer carnival starts in a few days. And you *love* the summer carnival."

It was true—the annual carnival in Creekside Park

was one of Amy's favorite times of year. With midway rides, games, and cotton candy, it was a fun place to connect with friends and fellow Destiny residents every June. "Yes, I do," she said. "So what?"

"So you should ask Logan if he'd like to go with you. You know, make an official date."

But Amy cringed slightly. "Shouldn't I be leaving it to *him* to ask *me* on a date?"

Tessa just rolled her eyes. "I love you, Ames, but you are so twentieth century sometimes. It's entirely okay for you to suggest getting together with him—doesn't matter if the girl or the guy does it these days. So will you ask him?"

Amy drew in her breath and let out a less-than-excited sigh. "I don't know. I'm really more of an old-fashioned girl."

Yet Tessa didn't cut her any slack. "And that's gotten you really far in your dating life, hasn't it?"

"Ouch."

"I'm sorry, but it's like we've been saying all along— this is your time, the time for you to grab onto, the time for you to do something before it passes you by."

"But I did something. Something huge. And it worked. So I thought I could relax a little now."

Fortunately, that was the moment Tessa finally noticed the two kitties eating peacefully on the floor near Amy. "Oh," she said, her smile coming back. "What did you do to make them get along?"

Amy thought about it and said, "I guess it really just took a little patience, and letting them get used to each other."

And it was at that precise moment that the phone behind the counter trilled, which alarmed the cats and made Knightley suddenly strike out an angry paw, claws bared, at Austen's nose. Both Tessa and Amy gasped as Austen drew back, then went running for the bookshelves.

"Bad, Knightley!" Amy scolded, severely ashamed of her kitty, not to mention disappointed that what had been going so well had suddenly fallen apart, all over the ring of a phone. Meanwhile, Tessa went to answer it.

"Under the Covers," Amy heard her say as she busily lectured Mr. K, bending down to pick up bits of Meow Mix that had gotten flung out in the kerfluffle. She could tell from tidbits of conversation that whoever was on the phone was someone Tessa knew, someone who'd been at the wedding—but that could be about anyone in Destiny, so she wasn't paying much attention until Tessa said, "Amy—for you." And when Amy looked up to see Tessa eagerly holding out the receiver of the old push-button princess phone she'd once had in her room as a girl, Tessa mouthed: *Logan*.

Heat filled Amy's cheeks, even though she wasn't quite sure why, and her legs went a little numb as she stood to make her way to the phone. This was Logan, so there was nothing to be nervous about. But then again, this change in their relationship was so new, so different, and she felt so . . . giddy that somehow it almost embarrassed her.

She tried her level best not to *sound* giddy when she took the phone and said hello.

"Hey freckles, how are ya?"

"I'm . . . good," she said. "Really good."

She could almost feel his smile on the other end of the line—the warmth Logan gave off was that strong. "I'm glad. Guess I just wanted to, you know, call and check up on you, make sure you didn't have any regrets about last night."

She drew in her breath and found herself overanalyzing his every word. It was sweet to check on her, but . . . maybe when she'd found out it was him, she'd thought he was calling to ask her out, thought maybe life would be that good, that easy, that simple from here on out. So it was, weirdly, almost a disappointment that he was only being his usual sweet self instead. "No," she said, her voice coming out a little too breathy at the reminder of last night's intimacy. "None at all. It was . . . perfect."

She wasn't making eye contact with Tessa, yet even in her peripheral vision she could tell her friend was pleased with that little stroke of boldness.

"I'm really glad, honey. Just since . . . well, it happened so suddenly, I wasn't sure how you'd feel once it was over."

More boldness. *Try.* She swallowed back her usual shyness—because that had certainly turned out well last night—and said, "Could be that what was sudden for you was more of a . . . long time coming for me."

He chuckled lightly and said, "I guess so. And I'm honored. To be the one. And last night was . . . real nice, Amy."

Real nice, huh? She supposed she could live with that. But on the other hand, something like *spectacular* or *life-changing* might have been better. "For me, too," she reminded him easily. Because what else could she do? Be mad at him for saying it was nice? Oh God, this hyper-analyzing everything sucked. She had to stop it—now.

And yet . . . she was starting to think Tessa might be right. She'd won him for the night, but she hadn't won him. As in forever. Or even for this month or this week. The realization made her feel just a little sick—until she gathered her strength and said, "Um, I was thinking of going to the carnival Wednesday night."

"Oh, that's this week, isn't it? With the wedding and everything, I forgot."

Another rough swallow before she could get the next part out. "Would you like to go together?"

A few feet away, she sensed Tessa holding her breath in anticipation.

"Sure, that sounds fun," Logan said. And Amy started breathing again. And nodding at Tessa, who also breathed, and gave her a happy thumbs-up. But then he went on to tell her, "I have to work at ten, though, so maybe we can go early."

"Sure," she said.

"And I'll meet you there—if we both drive, that way you won't have to leave just because I do."

"Okay," she heard herself say. Even though she realized this made it much less of a date and much more like two pals meeting each other to hang out for a few hours. There would be no goodnight kiss at the door—or a goodnight anything else, for that matter. Which made her add, "Or would another night be better?"

"Nah, same schedule on Thursday, and I start my shift at six on Friday and Saturday. So Wednesday's good."

After that, they made plans for when and where to meet, and Amy said, "I'll be looking forward to it."

"Me too, freckles," he said, and then he hung up the phone, and Amy thought: *What just happened here?*

"Why do you look unhappy?" Tessa asked her.

"Because a few minutes ago I was on the top of the world. But now my cats are back to fighting, and I'm not

sure if I have a date or if Logan and I are already back
to being just friends."

The scents of funnel cakes and cotton candy filled the
air, and lights from booths and rides flickered all around
them, even though it was only dusk. Organ music echoing from the carousel took Amy back to when she was
a little girl. Maybe that was why she loved the carnival
so much—it reminded her of times when life had been
easy, with no responsibilities, and no grown-up worries like love or lust or whether she'd get the guy she
wanted.

"Do you remember coming here when we were kids?"
she asked Logan as they meandered through the light
crowd that circled around the midway.

"Yep. You and I used to ride the merry-go-round
together while our parents stood outside and took blurry
pictures of us going past."

The memory made her laugh because it was so true—
both their mothers had photo albums filled with carousel
blurs. "Those were such good, easy times," she mused.

He gave her a thoughtful grin. "Reminiscing a little
there, freckles?"

She nodded. "Being an adult is a lot more complicated. Life was easier when the biggest question was
which color horse to ride."

Now he looked wistful, too. "You can say that again."
Just then they walked past the funnel cake booth. "My
dad and I always used to share a funnel cake," he said.
"First thing after we got here, every summer. But I
haven't had one in years, probably since he died."

Amy pondered that for a moment and hoped it wouldn't
be out of line when she said, "I could share a funnel cake

with you. It sounds good, but I don't think I could eat a whole one."

He cast her a sweet look in the shadows of flashing lights. "All right, freckles, you're on. One funnel cake, coming up."

Logan stepped up to the booth that practically dripped with the delicious aroma of fried dough covered in powdered sugar, ordering one cake and two soft drinks to help wash it down. Together, they found a spot to sit side by side, on the narrow metal steps that led to something called The Crazy Shack, which wasn't quite up and running yet. It was a squeeze for both of them to share the same step, but Amy didn't mind—it was nice being close to him again—and their fingers mingled in the messy, sugary funnel cake as they tore off bits and pieces to eat.

"We're a mess," she announced laughingly as the plate grew emptier.

And then Logan looked at her for a few long, quiet seconds—in a way she felt in her chest—before lifting his hand and using two fingers to brush some powdered sugar from the corner of her mouth. "There," he said softly. "All better."

"Thanks," she whispered.

"By the way, forgot to tell you," he said, ending the slightly intense moment, "I ran into Anita before you got here, and turns out the schedule changed—she's manning the bar tonight, which means I'm off, after all. So now we don't have to rush."

And the news made Amy smile since . . . well, who knew where the evening would lead, and she was certainly enjoying it so far.

Just then, the carousel eased to a stop just beyond the Scrambler. As an idea blossomed inside her, she gave her lower lip a small bite and glanced hopefully at the man beside her. "Let's go ride the merry-go-round. Like when we were kids."

She couldn't read his look at first, and when he hesitated, she grew certain he was going to refuse—but that was when those gorgeous blue eyes widened dramatically, just before he said, "Race ya."

Ditching their plate and his empty cup in a trash can beside them, Logan took off—so Amy tossed the rest of her soda in, too, and dashed after him. She hadn't done a lot of running lately, so she arrived at the carousel's entry gate breathless, accidentally bumping into him from behind. He just laughed, steadying her, then bought two tickets from the ride operator.

Climbing on, they found horses side by side, Amy's white and Logan's gray. And as the carousel began to turn, Amy held on to the silver pole in front of her, her white steed bobbing up and down upon it, and felt . . . carefree. Like a child without a worry in the world. And yet also like a grown-up woman with all the rewards that held, as well. It was the best of both worlds, and Logan was giving it all to her in this moment.

She'd never liked to see herself—or any of her friends—as a woman who needed a man to make her happy, but she was learning that love complicated all your emotions. And she couldn't deny as the soft summer breeze whipped through her hair that being with Logan, with all these new feelings for him, made her . . . happier, fuller, more complete. And . . . maybe he'd *always* made her that way but she'd just been too blind to see it until now.

When the ride came to a stop, Logan dropped easily off his horse, then placed his hands on Amy's waist to lift her down, like it was the natural thing to do, and she loved having his hands on her, even for just for a few seconds, every bit as much as she'd loved everything they'd done together after Rachel's wedding.

"You looked lost in your own little world there for a while, freckles," he told her with a typical Logan grin.

"Just thinking it felt a little like being a kid again—but better," she confessed. "With you."

His eyes softened on her then, his palms resting lightly on her hips. "Ya know, I'm still trying to wrap my head around this change in our relationship," he told her, "but no matter how you slice it, I'm having fun with you tonight. I'm glad you suggested this."

Logan held her hand as they descended the few steps that led to the ground, and Amy thought: *This is what I missed, my whole life. This is the kind of wonderful, simple fun I should have been having with boys in high school, like all my friends.* But you couldn't live in the past—so she was just thankful for now.

"Hey Amy! Hi Logan!"

Amy looked up to see Cara Collins with boyfriend Tyler Fleet. Each lifted a hand in a casual wave as Amy said, "Hey, you two—how's it going?" She considered the teenagers one of her best matches ever.

And as she and Logan continued on their way, they began to see more people they knew, sharing hellos and smiles. When she spotted handsome Dan Lindley from Destiny Properties, looking as dapper and staid as usual, even at a carnival, she said to Logan, "What do you think about Dan Lindley and Caroline Meeks? As a couple?"

Logan just shrugged. "I don't know. I guess it would matter more how Dan and Caroline see it than how I do."

"Well, Caroline wasn't crazy about the idea, but I think it could work." And without further ado, Amy then boldly greeted Dan and before the conversation was over, she'd mentioned Caroline twice, making her sound wonderful.

It surprised her when, a few minutes later, they even encountered Miss Ellie, Destiny's eighty-something matriarch—given that she hadn't been able to get around very well in recent years. But looked like she was getting more mobile—she rode a four-wheeled scooter, with her daughter, Linda Sue, walking alongside her.

"Look at you, Miss Ellie—you've got wheels," Amy said in greeting, speaking loudly, since the older lady's hearing wasn't what it used to be and she was famous in town for mishearing what people said.

Logan began chatting with Linda Sue as Miss Ellie replied, "Was time for a new way to get around, so life wouldn't pass me by. Now, tell me, dear, what's new with you?"

Amy wasn't particularly close to Miss Ellie, and they'd never really discussed her personal life before, yet it seemed natural—and even fun—to tell her in a not-quite-as-loud voice, "Well, I'm sort of seeing Logan now," as she glanced over to where he stood talking.

"Well, of course I can see Logan," Miss Ellie said, "he's standing right there." Then the hard-of-hearing old woman gave her head a thoughtful tilt. "You two would make a nice couple. Ever think of that?"

Amy could only laugh as she said, "You know, that's a great idea, Miss Ellie."

After parting ways with Miss Ellie and her daughter, Amy spied the cotton candy trailer, and Logan bought her some—just before they came upon the dunking booth. Seeing it was currently manned by Johnny Fulks, head of the town council, Logan loudly declared that he couldn't pass up an opportunity like this. Johnny was a good-natured guy who Logan often joked around with, and Amy was more than happy to stand by watching as he paid for five softballs.

The two exchanged some ribbing and trash talk as Logan's first two throws just missed the little round target, and a small crowd of people they knew gathered to watch, including Jenny and her husband, Mick. Johnny yelled to Logan, "Maybe you need your buddy Mike to help you out. Too bad he's out of town." Mike was the pitcher on Logan's softball team. And apparently the comment inspired Logan, since his only reply was to throw the next ball, which hit the target dead-on and sent Johnny plummeting into the tank of water below.

Laughter and a little applause filled the air, along with more good-natured kidding between the men, until finally someone new came along to try their luck.

Jenny and Mick stuck around to talk with Logan and Amy for a minute, mentioning they were there with Tessa and Lucky. "And Anna, too," Jenny added innocently enough. "They got her all moved in to Lucky's place today."

Amy tried not to clench her jaw at the very mention of Anna's name, but her stomach knotted anyway. And as usual, she hated her jealousy of Anna. At moments it was hard to remember that she actually *liked* Anna, and her sense of dread over Anna was only heightened by how close she felt to Logan after their night in the orchard.

"So where are they?" Logan asked. Which of course

made Amy wonder if he was asking about the group in
general or if he really just wanted to know about Anna.

"Lucky and Tessa are on the Tilt-a-Whirl right now,"
Jenny said. "But I'm not sure where Anna is, now that
you mention it."

"Hmm," Mick pondered with an eye toward his wife,
"I remember that ride being good for making out when
I was young."

"Then maybe we should ride it, too," she said, casting
a flirtatious smile.

And Amy only wished she could be so bold with
Logan—since she was dying to kiss him. But she supposed one night of passion—no matter how natural it
had seemed—didn't mean they were instantly comfortable with the shift in their relationship. If it did, surely
they would have kissed by now.

*But sitting so close to him, our fingers touching when
we ate the funnel cake, was nice. And so was the way he
helped me down from the carousel horse, and then held
my hand for a minute after.* It was like . . . well, like their
courtship was coming *after* the sex, that was all. And
maybe that was fine. Maybe it was sweet that Logan
wasn't jumping her bones. Maybe now that she'd gotten
the proverbial scarlet V off her chest she should try to
slow down and enjoy the gentle progression of this.

*All that really matters is that he's here with you tonight,
and that you're both having a nice time.* And that thought
heartened her. She didn't need to wish for anyone else's
relationship—she and Logan would develop their own,
in their own time, and everything would be just fine.
In fact, everything would go smoothly now. And Anna
would no longer feel like such a threat.

They moved on from Jenny and Mick and soon

encountered a few of Logan's buddies, all of whom seemed glad to see him and told him they missed having him around the firehouse. "Place isn't the same without you, man," Donnie Dugan, a friendly guy in his late thirties said. Donnie and his wife and kids had moved to Destiny only last year, but Amy knew he and Logan had become fast friends.

"Surprised you guys are able to get along without me at all," Logan joked.

"Yeah, you're the only one who knows how to look like he's working when he's really goofing off," said a younger firefighter, Dave Leech. "I was hoping to learn from the master."

As they went on their way, still strolling the midway area, which was getting busier as dusk fell deeper over the park, Amy thought she caught a pensive expression on Logan's face.

"Do you miss it?" she asked him. She tore off a piece of cotton candy to eat after she spoke, trying not to look overly concerned. Even though she definitely still was.

"Do I miss hanging with the guys? Sure," he said without quite looking at her. "But there's a lot more to the job than that."

Amy took a moment to choose her next words carefully. "That's the part I meant, though. The job itself."

He just shrugged. "You know there aren't that many fires, Amy. I spent the bulk of my time keeping equipment clean and doing volunteer work around town."

"But what I'm asking," she said, a little frustrated that he was obviously avoiding the real question, "is if you miss being a fireman, Logan. The whole thing. Because . . . it was such a big part of who you are."

Now he spared her a glance, but only a quick one.

They'd strolled into a darker, quieter part of the midway now—over by the still-not-up-and-running Crazy Shack where they'd shared the funnel cake. "It doesn't matter because it's not right for me anymore. That part of my life is done."

"But that's so wrong, Logan. Because you *are* a firefighter. It's in your blood. It's what you're supposed to be doing."

He stopped and looked at her then, his eyes suddenly filled with more anger than she'd seen in them since he'd finally come out of his funk. "Damn it, Amy, I *told* you what happened that night. I *told* you. And I thought you understood."

"I did. I do. I just . . ."

"Want to butt into my business? Want to make my decisions for me? Just like you do with everyone?"

She sucked in her breath, stunned. "What?"

Logan let out a sigh she could hear even above the carnival sounds nearby. "I'm sorry, I shouldn't have said that."

She felt a little numb. "But you did. What did you mean?"

He shook his head. "You just always kind of . . . think you know what's best for people. You always think you know who belongs together in relationships. And you . . . well, you give a lot of advice, sometimes even when nobody's asking for it."

"Oh," she said, deflated. More than deflated—hurt. She'd had no idea anyone thought that about her. "Everyone feels this way?"

He released another sigh, looking tired and clearly sorry he'd blurted that out. "No, I'm sure they don't. Like I said, that came out wrong and I'm sorry."

"But *you* feel that way." She found herself unable to

meet his eyes, staring at the front of the T-shirt he wore, her words wooden and stiff.

"Only times like right now. And maybe every time you've ever wanted to fix me up with somebody. That's all. I promise. It was a mean thing to say and I shouldn't have. I'm just . . . done with firefighting and I don't want to talk about it anymore. Okay?"

It had started out sounding like an apology, but now he was back to seeming testy again.

"Sure, okay," she said, even though she still felt a little empty inside—in a whole different way than back when she was longing for him. And embarrassed, too. And a part of her was tempted to remind him he'd very recently asked her to fix him up with Anna—but she surely didn't want to bring *that* up.

Clearly realizing he'd hurt her feelings, Logan teasingly leaned down and bit off a big chunk of the pink cotton candy she held.

And when that failed to make her laugh or even smile, he put his arm around her, squeezed her shoulder tight, and said, "Come on, freckles, don't be mad. You know I love ya—I'm just still touchy about the whole fire thing. Okay?"

Just then, they emerged back into the light and the louder sounds of the carnival. The brightly illuminated ferris wheel stood nearby. "Okay," she whispered.

"Let's kiss and make up," he said.

And that sounded like the best idea Amy had heard in a while, and just what the doctor ordered. And as a warm ripple of desire ran through her, she whispered that maybe the ferris wheel would be a nice place to do that—and that was when Logan was yanked away from her.

"No line for the ferris wheel—come on!" Amy heard

Anna Romo say, and then realized she'd somehow come running up behind them and had grabbed his hand and pulled him away.

Logan and Anna stood a few feet from her now, Anna still tugging at him and laughing prettily—looking stunning and perfect as usual—and he glanced back toward Amy, saying to Anna, "I really can't, I'm—"

"Yes you can," she cut him off, and proceeded to drag him toward the ferris wheel. The very ferris wheel Amy had just been thinking it would be so romantic to ride with him.

Logan looked truly bereft as he glanced again in her direction to mouth the words: *Sorry. I'll be back*.

But that didn't mend the puncture wound to her heart. And as she watched Anna Romo still holding tight to his arm as they stepped onto the ride together, Amy felt completely alone, completely abandoned.

Seldom, very seldom, does complete truth belong to any human disclosure; seldom can it happen that something is not a little disguised, or a little mistaken.

Jane Austen, from *Emma*

Fourteen

Anna had come to the carnival feeling a mixture of dread and boredom. She'd let herself be talked into staying in Destiny, but at moments she wasn't sure why, and this had been one of those times. And then, from a distance, she'd seen Logan and everything had changed. Her boredom had turned into anticipation—and into the wild need to make something happen in this quiet little town before she completely lost her mind. She'd suddenly felt aggressive and take-charge in a way she couldn't have stopped if she'd wanted to—that was just how she was sometimes, how her upbringing had made her. She was in the mood to have some fun, and now she was going to have it—finally—with Logan Whitaker.

As soon as their ferris wheel car started upward, she

faced him, flashing her best coy smile. "So where'd you disappear to at the wedding? I'd been hoping we might get together afterward, and then suddenly—poof—you were gone." Still turned in his direction, she crossed her arms in mock anger. "You abandoned me."

Yet the sheepish expression he wore in reply completely surprised her—she'd never seen Logan react to anything that way before. "I, um . . . well, it's a long story, but I was with . . . a friend."

Hmm. She wasn't sure what that meant, or why he was being so vague, but her current mood kept her from caring very much. The truth was, it didn't matter where he'd gone after the wedding—that was old news and she was much more concerned with right now. And right now, once and for all, she wanted to kiss him. She'd been waiting for *him* to make that particular move, but she was *tired* of waiting.

So without further ado, she leaned over, placed her hands on his shoulders, and energetically pressed her lips to his.

She could tell it shocked him, though she wasn't quite sure why. Had he not known things were headed in this direction? Did things in Destiny move that slow?

Well, it didn't matter—stopping the kiss for a brief second, she met his gaze, only inches from hers, and then kissed him again. Her palms drifted lower, to his chest, and his closed lightly on her upper arms. She moved her mouth on his, sinking into the kiss, or attempting to anyway. She wasn't quite sure he was into it, but she kept trying, luring with her lips, attempting to get him where she wanted him.

That was when he drew back.

She bit her lip, dismayed, then let out a breath. And

since she wasn't in the mood to pull any punches, she said, "Um, why are we stopping?"

"Well . . . I'm kinda here with Amy."

Whoa. What? The ferris wheel came to a stop to let more people on or off below, parking Anna and Logan at the very top. Other than the glow of lights far beneath them, darkness surrounded them and Anna couldn't help but think how wrong this suddenly felt. This should be romantic, exciting, the moment when she and Logan were finally moving forward. Could she have truly read the whole situation so wrong?

"Amy? I didn't know you and she were . . ." She trailed off, though, remembering that, in fact, he *had* been walking with Amy when she'd first spotted him on the ground a few minutes ago. But everything she'd seen and heard, even from Logan himself, had led her to believe the two were just friends, so it had never even occurred to her that they were here *together. That* way.

"We weren't," he finally said. "It's . . . new. Something we're trying on for size."

Oh. Hmm. She didn't exactly know how to interpret that, but . . . well, it sounded pretty sketchy and undefined, and made her feel a lot less like a trespasser than she had a few seconds earlier. And though logic and good manners told her now was the time to back off, she'd suffered nothing but various frustrations since arriving in this tiny town, and she just wanted . . . what she wanted. And besides, she wasn't used to guys turning her down or not being interested, and having Logan say no compelled her to change his mind and make him say yes.

"Maybe you should try *me* on for size," she said— and then she kissed him again, deeply, passionately. She knew she hadn't misread all the signals he'd sent her these last few weeks—and she was determined to prove that to both of them.

And then finally—finally—she felt him relax a little, kiss her back more naturally, more like she'd expected in the first place, and a hot ping of desire danced through her body. *Yes! At last! Thank God.*

So it surprised her when he again ended the kiss, almost abruptly, pulling back, using his hands to push her slightly away. Wow. She'd never had any guy do that in her entire life and she couldn't deny that it felt, at this point, downright embarrassing.

She simply drew in her breath, let it back out. And as the ride began to move again, she just looked at him, waiting for him to explain. Maybe this really *was* about Amy—but whatever the reason, she needed to hear more. After all, they'd been spending time together, and it hadn't been purely platonic. If he wasn't going to kiss her, he needed to tell her why.

"It's not that I'm not into you, Anna," he said, "but like I said, I came with Amy tonight. So I feel pretty shitty about this—both for her sake and yours. And besides, maybe this doesn't feel right . . . because of Mike, too."

"Oh, for crying out loud!" she practically spat at him. "I'm so tired of hearing about Mike trying to protect me. I don't need protecting, Logan—I'm a big girl more than capable of handling my own affairs. He has no right whatsoever to just march into my life and try to tell me—or you—who I can see or what I can do. It's freaking ridiculous!"

"Technically, *you* marched into *his* life, and he loves you," he retorted. "Don't get me wrong, I totally see your point—but he's my best friend, Anna. When you disappeared, I went through that with him. And I've gone through everything with him ever since. So I can't just ignore his feelings on this."

She sat there, speechless, seething, as the ferris wheel turned, fast enough now that the breeze lifted her hair from her shoulders. She understood about Mike, how hard his life had been because of her, and she was truly, deeply sorry about that. In fact, it was a lot of weight to bear on top of everything else. But what happened wasn't her fault—she'd been one of the victims—and she didn't intend to spend the rest of her life paying for a crime she hadn't committed.

Logan went on. "It doesn't mean he'll be like this forever. It's only that having you back is new—he's going through a period of adjustment, and so are you. Things'll get easier. And so . . . even though I like you a lot, and even though I know at the wedding he said he'd back off, for now we just need to . . . stay in this holding pattern. I know that sucks, but try to be patient and remember it's because he cares so much. And because *I* care about *him*. He's not the easiest guy in the world to be with— trust me, I know—but it all comes from a good place, I promise."

She let out a sigh, almost annoyed that the stuff he was saying sounded so . . . reasonable. Patience was a virtue—just one she didn't necessarily possess right now.

She must have looked upset, because that was when Logan put his arm around her, as if to comfort her. "Look, this will all even itself out. Just give Mike a chance to work through his growing pains with you, okay?"

She hardly had words to answer with. Because she

still thought the whole issue was beyond silly. But since Logan was such a nice guy, she murmured, "Okay. Only . . ." And maybe she should shut up, but again, she'd never been shy, and she just needed to know. "What *are* we, Logan, you and me? Is anything going to come of this?"

He let out a breath she could hear as the ferris wheel carried them upward. And he looked just as confused as she felt at the moment when he said, "I don't know, Anna. I'm sorry, but I honestly don't know right now."

Logan felt like a jerk. To both Amy and Anna. Damn it, sometimes it was easier to let yourself be swept along by the tides of life—like when Anna had grabbed his hand and pulled him toward the ferris wheel and he hadn't wanted to embarrass her or hurt her feelings by breaking away. But then he'd looked back, seen the expression on Amy's face, and knew he'd made the wrong call—and by that time it had felt too late, like the deed was already done.

And then Anna had started kissing him. And he'd thought—*hell, I know I've screwed up tonight with Amy, and I've wanted Anna for awhile now, so maybe I should just go with the flow*—but that hadn't worked either. He didn't know why, but kissing her somehow . . . hadn't felt right. And he'd told her, and himself, that maybe it was about Amy, and that maybe it was about Mike—but it was more than that. It just hadn't been . . . like he'd thought it would, like he'd wanted it to be. And he had no idea why.

God, he was torn inside. About a lot of things.

In addition to this Anna situation, he was still trying to decipher his feelings for Amy. They were good friends. Now they were lovers. But could you really be both? He had no idea. And as much as he loved Amy, things were suddenly a hell of a lot more complex between them. He suddenly had to worry about hurting her feelings if he was with her and another girl came along—that was brand new, and a little hard to adjust to. And it had felt . . . different to him than before when she'd insisted he should return to his old job. What had previously felt like friendly advice now felt . . . more insistent. And he knew she meant well, but he also knew that being a firefighter just wasn't right for him anymore.

As the ferris wheel continued to turn, he tried to make more casual conversation with Anna, just to relax things, for both of them. "Clear night. Look at all the stars."

"Yeah," she said quietly. She still didn't sound happy, but she leaned her head back to look as their car again passed over the highest point in the rotation. "It's nice."

"Bet you see a lot more stars out here than when you lived in the city, huh?"

She nodded, admitting almost grudgingly, "I guess this place *does* have a few perks."

He laughed. "More than a few. You'll see. Things really will get better for you here, Anna."

"I hope so, Logan," she said, arms crossed, but at least it came with a small smile. Then her look grew more introspective. "You know, I never came here expecting to stay. Somehow that part just happened. And now I feel . . . like something invisible is holding me here, like I'm *supposed* to stay, even though I don't fit in and don't like being smothered by my family and my existence would surely be easier back in Indy where I have friends and a life. It's hard to explain. And even harder to deal with."

But Logan didn't answer—instead, he simply met

Anna's gaze with his own, letting her know he empathized.

And for a moment, he almost had the urge to tell Anna
. . . other things. Important things. About him. He'd
almost had the same urge on the night of Rachel's bachelorette party at the Dew Drop Inn—when Anna had
said he'd make a better fireman than a bartender. In one
way, he hadn't wanted to burden her with his troubles,
but as the night had gone on, he'd considered finding
some moment and maybe telling her . . . the reason he
couldn't be a firefighter anymore. The way he'd ended up
telling Amy after the wedding.

But just as quickly as the thought occurred to him, he
let it pass, same as he had that night at the bar. Because
it was kind of like that kiss. Maybe some time in the
future, it would feel right—but not tonight. Tonight was
weird enough already. Confiding in Amy had made
sense, and once he'd started, it had come . . . almost
naturally. But confiding in Anna, even right after she'd
confided something in him . . . well, for some reason, his
heart just wasn't in it.

The next time the ride carried them downward, their
car came to a halt at the loading ramp and the operator opened the door. And as they stepped off, reim-
mersed into the sights and sounds of the carnival, Logan
remained just as conflicted as when he'd stepped on.

Anna was easy to be with, fun. Other than the Mike
situation, she came with no real complications. No judg-
ment. No history between them. And that was usually
exactly the kind of relationship he enjoyed with a girl.

And yet . . . he was beginning to wonder if maybe he
really *did* have feelings for Amy, romantic ones. She was
harder to be with in ways—and the conversation about

him returning to work at the fire station still rankled. And yet . . . he was bummed when he got off the ferris wheel and didn't see her standing anywhere around.

Which was the precise moment it hit him: Had he really expected her to be? After he'd let Anna lead him away from her like that? It was still hard to grasp that what would have been fine between him and Amy a week ago wasn't anymore. And if he'd come off that ride thinking she'd be standing there waiting for him with open arms . . . damn, he was an idiot.

"I, uh, kinda gotta go," he told Anna.

"I, uh, kinda figured that," she said in a teasing way. But at least, again, she was smiling.

"I'm sorry about what happened on the ride, Anna. As the old saying goes, 'It's not you, it's me.' And in this case, it really *is* me."

In response, she gave her head a tilt, her look somehow light and sarcastic and judgmental all at the same time, and it clearly said: *You don't know what you're missing.* "Well, if you get over whatever *it* is, Logan," she said, "you let me know." Then she gave him a wink and walked away.

When he spotted Jenny and Mick at the nearest game booth, he approached. Mick threw baseballs at milk bottles, apparently trying to win Jenny a big, stuffed cat that he instantly knew Amy would love. "Have you seen Amy?" he asked Jenny.

"Yeah—I spotted her heading to the parking lot a minute ago. She looked pretty bummed out and didn't even say bye." Her eyebrows knit. "Is anything wrong?"

Damn. His stomach sank. Upsetting Amy suddenly felt a lot worse than upsetting Anna. "Pretty sure I hurt her feelings."

Jenny sneered lightly. "That's not like you, Logan. I hope you're gonna do something to make it up to her."

He glanced to the stuffed cats again. They were gray and white, just like Mr. K. And it just so happened that he was pretty good with a baseball, as he'd proved earlier at the dunking booth. "As soon as I win her a stuffed Mr. Knightley," he said, then got out his wallet and handed over a five-dollar bill to the young guy running the game.

If there was one way to Amy's heart, he knew it was a cat—stuffed, real, or otherwise. And that was when it hit him squarely in the face—he still didn't know where he and Amy were going, but in this moment, that was where he wanted to be: in Amy's heart.

Amy sat in the dark in the bookstore, curled up in the easy chair that faced the wide window, Austen snuggled in her lap. Running her hand through the fur on the kitty's back was comforting. Cats. They never hurt you. They might ignore you a little sometime, or even misbehave, but they were always there when you needed a friend.

She wore pajamas—well, a large nightshirt featuring a gray cartoon cat and the words *Cat Lady*, a birthday gift from Rachel one year. She'd only come down to the bookstore from her apartment above because she'd felt the need to be in the place she loved most, surrounded by the things she loved most—books. Another comfort. It was less lonely here than the apartment had suddenly felt. Especially since Knightley had been in a persnickety mood. "You could teach him a thing or two about being a good cat," she told Austen now. She loved Knightley with all her heart, but his unpredictable behavior lately had her feeling a little critical at the moment.

The glow from the streetlamps that lined town square threw shadows of light in the window, illuminating her feet, which she'd now lifted to the coffee table resting between the big chairs. She glanced at her perfectly painted pink toenails—Cotton Candy, selected especially for her date with Logan. "Ha, some date," she said then.

She still couldn't believe one minute he'd been ready to kiss her, and the next Anna Romo had dragged him away. "I could have made a stink, I could have pulled at his other arm," she told the cat in her lap, "but who wants to be in a tug of war over a guy, especially with Anna Romo at the other end." Even as desperate as she felt in moments, she wasn't *that* desperate, not desperate enough to lose her dignity. And she'd just had too much self-respect to stand waiting for him at the bottom of that stupid ferris wheel. After all, he'd let himself be dragged onto it. It had put him in an awkward position, sure, but he could have stopped it if Amy's feelings had been more important to him than Anna's.

So she'd left. And so it turned out that driving separately had been a blessing. And maybe Logan didn't even know this had been a date, and maybe that was the way it was meant to be—maybe that meant she could feel a little less humiliated by the whole thing.

"Maybe when all is said and done," she said thoughtfully to Austen, "I'm just destined to be alone. Maybe one night of happiness is all I get. Maybe that's . . . supposed to be enough, better than nothing. And at least I won't die a virgin, right?"

Though the last words had almost come with tears, because the truth was—better than nothing still didn't equal great. And even as cool and unruffled as she'd acted about it to Tessa the next day—still lost in the

dreamy afterglow—deep inside, that one night with
Logan had only made her want more. And maybe even
worse, it had made her believe there could *be* more, that
there *would* be more. She'd begun to believe he could
love her, that she could truly have her heart's desire,
that she could make her dreams come true. But now she
knew she'd only deluded herself. She'd let that one night
cloud her reality. And the reality was: She'd never be the
kind of girl who got a guy like Logan. Not for real. Not
for keeps.

When a loud knock came on the door, she nearly threw
the cat up in the air. Instead, though, she just flinched and
let out a small yelp that sent Austen scurrying anyway. It
was nearly midnight—who the heck would be knocking
on Under the Covers' door at this hour?

Getting up, she headed cautiously to the store's
entrance, conscious of her bare feet and nightshirt, then
peeked through the window to see Logan outside. Her
sigh of relief was accompanied by a churning stomach, though—she didn't know why he was here, but she
wasn't in the mood to see him. She felt stupid enough
already and would have preferred to keep licking her
wounds in private.

Even so, she supposed she couldn't just leave him
standing out there—even in moments like this, she was
just too darn polite—so she turned the lock and opened
the door. "How did you know I was in here?" she asked
by way of greeting.

"Saw you through the window. Well, your feet anyway,
on the coffee table." Darn streetlamps.

She just stood back to let him in. But she didn't bother
turning on any lights, especially considering how she
was dressed.

"I brought you something," he told her, and held out some sort of stuffed animal. Which—drat it all—kind of meant she *had* to turn on a light, to see it. So she chose the small antique Tiffany lamp on one side of the counter, as opposed to the ones overhead, illuminating the room only softly.

And she saw—oh wow! It was a big, stuffed Mr. Knightley. Crap. She loved it. She didn't *want* to love it, but she loved it and knew it was written all over her face. Cat love was a thing Amy just couldn't hide. "A stuffed Mr. K," she said, both happy and sad at once. "He's adorable."

"And he only cost me fifty bucks," Logan said with a slightly sheepish grin.

She raised her eyebrows. "Okay, it's adorable, but not that adorable."

"Once I started throwing balls at those milk bottles, I couldn't stop. Forgot you gotta hit the damn things just the right way. But I really wanted to win this for you. Because I knew you'd like it. And because I'm hoping maybe it'll somehow begin to make up for me being an ass earlier." He stopped, sighed, eyes somber. "I'm sorry, Amy."

Amy drew in her breath. She hadn't expected him to show up here. She hadn't really even expected him to know he'd done anything wrong exactly, since maybe he hadn't even realized they were on a date. Leaving things open-ended after they'd made love had sounded so mature and reasonable at the time, but the truth was that it had just made everything unclear, murky. "Thanks," she finally said, albeit too quietly for her own liking.

That was who she was, though—quiet, gentle, amiable Amy. So maybe it didn't really matter how she answered; Logan knew who she was at heart and surely wasn't surprised by it. There were just moments when . . . when she wished she were more like, say, Rachel. Or even Anna. Moments when she wished she were bolder, tougher, and could just lay things on the line.

She took the big, stuffed version of Mr. Knightley and, for now, set him in the chair nearest the picture window. Then she turned back to Logan in the shadows.

In one way, she wanted to kiss him. Because that was what her body had been aching for since she'd met him at the carnival hours earlier. And because that was what her body ached for *most* of the time these days—kissing, and much more, too.

But at the same time, she kind of wanted to smack him. For letting it come to this. For letting Anna drag him away when, apparently, he *had* realized they were on a date. It had technically been Anna's fault, but he'd let her mess up what had otherwise been a wonderful night. Well, other than their disagreement about Logan's recent career decision, but she couldn't help it—she just wouldn't hold her tongue on that because it was too important.

"I . . . I need to ask you something, Logan," she began, trying to summon, from somewhere inside herself, that bolder side.

Yet the question she wanted to ask was scary as hell. Because he might not give her the answer she sought.

"I need to ask you where we stand. And I know the idea of us is new and all, but . . . well, things are different between us now, and I'm not sure there's any going back, for better or worse. And what you did to me tonight was . . . well, it was just rude. And you've never been rude to me in my life—and it hurt." It had hurt worse than Amy had even known it could, but she decided to keep that last tidbit to herself. He already knew how she felt—no need to embarrass herself with it.

"I know," he said, "and I'm sorry. I should have broken away from her. I guess I just . . . think of her as fragile."

A burst of laughter shot from Amy's throat—she couldn't contain it. "Anna? That girl isn't fragile. That girl is as tough as nails."

He looked like he was taking that in, maybe thinking it over, yet only concluded, "Maybe."

"But you didn't answer my question." Lord, it was hard to ask it yet again. Because what if he broke her heart in two, right here and now? But she had to—she just had to. "Where do we stand, Logan?"

When he took on a sad, serious sort of look, Amy instantly feared the worst. *This is it. This is the end of everything that just started, and the end of our friendship, too. Why, oh why, did I have to fall in love with him?*

Yet then he held his hands out before him and said, "Honestly, freckles, I don't know. I wish I did, but it *is* new to me, like you said, and I'm feeling my way through it. All I can tell you for sure is that the other night, by the creek, was amazing, and really special. And what happened tonight . . . well, when I realized you'd left, I felt sick. And I knew things had changed between us in a way we can't go back from. And that it meant I have to get with the program, straighten up, and figure out how I feel about you, about us."

Amy bit her lip. All in all . . . well, it wasn't the miraculous declaration of love she might have been dreaming about. But he wasn't breaking her heart, either. In fact, he'd just said that sex with her was amazing. And given how long she'd waited to *have* sex—maybe hearing that did feel a little miraculous, after all.

"I . . . know you've gone through hell lately, Logan, and that the timing on this probably isn't great. And so . . . I'm willing to be patient. All I ask is that while you're figuring it all out, you treat me with the same consideration you would show any girl you cared about."

"Of course, Amy, and I'm so sorry I dropped the ball on that tonight." He stepped forward, reached out, and took her hand. "Can you forgive me?"

What is right to be done cannot be done too soon.

Jane Austen, from *Emma*

Fifteen

Amy accepted his hand, but what she really felt most in that moment was his eyes. Warming her from the inside out. She knew Logan hadn't abandoned her tonight on purpose. She knew he was confused, still recovering from what had happened to the Knights, and that he'd had a lot heaped on him lately. And when he'd asked God to drop a girl out of the sky for him, Anna Romo had landed on the town square. So yeah, she could forgive him. She didn't want to seem like some kind of doormat—she didn't think she could ever be that, no matter how much she loved him—but their history was long and deep, and she understood that he'd messed up tonight and had come here because he was sincerely apologetic.

So after a long, thoughtful moment, she finally said, "Yeah. I can forgive you, Logan."

His smile was small, and laced with a tinge of melancholy as he told her, "Thanks. I'm glad. Because . . ." He
stopped, sighed once more. "If I ever lost you, Amy . . .
hell, I don't know what I'd do. You're . . . you're the one
who's always been there. Always. Even longer than Mike."
She sometimes forgot that, but it was true. His friendship
with Mike had formed during their first few years of grade
school and little league, but Amy and Logan had played
together in the sandbox behind her house as toddlers. He
was one of her earliest memories. There'd never been a
time when Logan wasn't a part of her life.

"I . . ." Oh darn it, a lump rose to her throat—but she
spoke around it. "I don't know what I'd do if I lost you,
either, Logan."

Still holding her hand, he let out a sigh and said,
"These changes we're going through . . . they're hard,
but . . . they definitely have their upside."

This perked her up a little. "Oh?"

That was when his expression grew just a bit lascivi-
ous, and though never in her life had she realized she
might like that kind of attitude on a man, right now, she
did. "Well, it makes it okay," he informed her, "that I'm
getting turned on by the way you look in your pajamas."

Oh. Lord. Until that moment, Amy had almost forgotten what she was wearing, but now that she remembered,
she was almost embarrassed. And certainly confused.
"My *Cat Lady* shirt turns you on?"

"Not so much the shirt," he admitted. "More the way
your, uh, nipples, are showing through."

"Oh . . ." she breathed, glancing down. And sure
enough, there in the shadowy light, the peaks of her
breasts stood erect, jutting clearly through her otherwise
completely unseductive nightshirt.

He stepped slightly closer to her, his look bordering somewhere between romantic and aroused. "Would you slap me if I kissed you right now?"

In fact, she was still dying to be kissed. It was all she wanted in the world. Her body needed it. And her soul needed it. Because just a few minutes ago, she'd been sure she'd lost him forever—at least in the way she really wanted him now—and his being back felt . . . amazing. Yet her strong sense of self-esteem forced her to ask the question that maybe she didn't really want to know the answer to. "Did you kiss Anna tonight?"

And when he hesitated, her heart sank. "*She* kissed *me*," he finally said. "A couple of times. But I wasn't into it."

"Why not? After all, you've been crazy about her since she showed up here."

He let out a sigh, looking a bit guarded as he said, "I'm not sure. It didn't feel right. And I won't lie to ya—I *wanted* it to feel right, because I *have* been attracted to her. But it just didn't. I don't know why. Maybe it's . . . about you. Maybe it's because I was with you tonight. I *am* with you tonight. I . . . *wanna* be with you tonight, Amy."

Amy drew in her breath. There was a lot to consider here. Anna's lips had touched his tonight and she didn't like that—the very thought made her burn with jealousy.

But he hadn't liked it. And he did like kissing *her*. And he wanted to kiss her *now*.

So after weighing it, she reached a conclusion. One that made her body happy. "You can kiss me, Logan," she whispered.

The words caused Logan's eyes to narrow on her with

intent. She drew in her breath and almost felt her nipples tighten further.

And then he was stepping up close, so close the heat of his body practically radiated through her, and he lifted his hand to cup her cheek and delivered the most slow, tender, delicious kiss Amy could imagine.

She shut her eyes, let her lips move against his as her body absorbed every nuance of the moment. She couldn't have dreamed a little while ago that this night would end up a happy one for her, but this was starting to change her mind.

When the kiss ended, she drew in her breath, tried to come back to herself. But a kiss from Logan had the ability to truly sweep her away into what felt like another dimension. A dimension she'd waited her whole life to find—and mmm, it really did exist! *I love you, I love you, I love you.* The words ached to spill from her lips, but she held them in. *Be cool. Even if your notes pretty much told him how crazy you are about him, now is the time to act mature, and to just take this—this night, this moment—for what it's worth.*

"Kiss me again," she heard herself demand. But she wasn't even embarrassed, because she could feel his passion rising along with hers, and what had felt so completely new and tentative the other night now felt . . . more familiar, easier, more like passion between them was the norm.

Logan's next kiss was just as scintillating as the first, melting down through her like warm molasses. And whereas, before, kissing had felt so . . . almost new, foreign, like a brand new skill she was learning—now she forgot to even think as she kissed him. It just happened of its own volition—her mouth, her body, her whole self, simply followed natural urges. The urge to press against him, to run her fingertips through his hair, across the soft skin on his neck. The urge to lick ever-so-delicately at his mouth—not unlike a cat—and to then press her tongue inward until it met with his. The other night had been like . . . taking first, tentative steps, him guiding her, tutoring her in a way. But tonight she was becoming a woman of her own, exploring her desires, following her whims, letting her body take over.

As their kisses deepened, growing more heated and driven by pure instinct with each passing second, Logan's palms sank greedily to her bottom, pulling her torso tight to his. And mmm, God, yes, he was hard. And she'd learned already how much she loved that. She loved that she'd done that to him, made that part of him respond in such a primal way. She loved the automatic response—the yearning—it created in her. She loved the power she felt behind it—loved that she felt just a little intimidated by it and yet wholeheartedly wanted it at the same time.

"Oh God, you feel so good," she heard herself murmur without ever having quite decided to.

"Mmm, you too, honey," he said. And oh, she liked that as well. *Honey*. She loved being his freckles, yes, but this felt much sexier, especially right now.

And even as one minute he was massaging her rear, his fingers digging hotly into her flesh through her panties, the next he was reaching down inside them, his hands closing over bare flesh. And then—oh!—his fingers dipped lower, lower, until he was stroking between her legs.

She broke the kiss, sucking in her breath—she couldn't help it. And then she was moving against his touch, welcoming it, and soon found herself practically clawing at his chest.

The next thing she knew, Logan had pushed her panties to her thighs—after which they fell to her ankles. She slid her hands up under his shirt to run them over his stomach, chest. He withdrew his touch to rip the shirt off over his head—and then he took her hand again, this time silently drawing her toward the same easy chair where she'd sat moping when he'd arrived. Well, she certainly wasn't moping anymore.

She stepped free of the panties as she went, soon straddling his hips in the chair as naturally as if she sat in his lap like that every day. And oh, the crux of her thighs met with that wonderfully hard column within his pants again—and it pressed into her exactly where she desired it most. And now—oh God, she could hardly stand it—nothing but his khaki shorts separated those parts of their bodies. She moved against him—she couldn't not—and loved how raggedly he breathed as his touch moved up under her shirt to settle on her hips.

After a long, hot kiss, she found herself softly biting his earlobe, then dragging her teeth downward, making him shudder. She had no idea where that had come from, except clearly some bold, animalistic place inside her she couldn't have imagined until this very moment. And then she was murmuring, "I want you," against his neck.

"Aw, Amy baby, I want you, too," he said, his timbre deep, throaty, exciting her even more than she already was.

And then he was lifting them both up a little in order to reach behind him, into his back pocket—and as he extracted his wallet, and then a condom, Amy followed the raw, simple urge to reach for his belt. Undoing the buckle, then unzipping his shorts felt . . . almost surreal. At once natural but also . . . as if she were someone else. It was both easy yet mysteriously new, and it just drove home for her how right it was to be with Logan, how deeply she yearned to cement their connection again.

They both worked to push down his pants, underwear. But somehow the sight of him—his erection—caught her off guard and nearly took her breath away. It was a little lighter in here than it had been next to the creek. And she was in his lap—he was already so close to her. And she didn't fight the nearly primitive urge to wrap her fist warmly around the rigid shaft now standing between them.

A moan left his throat and their eyes met.

And she was honest, with nothing to hide. "I'm still trying to get used to this—to you *like* this."

He nodded slowly in agreement. "Me too, with you," he rasped. "I still kinda can't believe your hand is around my cock right now."

Amy drew in her breath. She wasn't used to hearing him talk like that. But she knew that was how guys thought, and she liked that he was being so open, natural with her about this. So she kept being honest. "I love it, though. I love being with you this way. I love that you want to be inside me right now as much as I want you there."

"Aw baby," he murmured, "I do. I really, really do."

The sentiment pushed her to take the condom he'd opened from between his fingertips into her own. She'd never done this before, but now seemed like a good time to learn.

She bit her lower lip in concentration as she balanced the thin rubber disk at the tip of his erection, then rolled it slowly down onto him, using the thumbs and forefingers of both hands. Part of her didn't like covering him up, putting even that one thin barrier between them—and yet if it had to be there, it made her feel just a little bit powerful to be the one making it happen.

When he was sheathed, she raised her gaze back to his in time to hear him say, "Ready for this, freckles?"

She simply nodded.

And he curled his hands back over her bottom and lifted her until the juncture of her thighs was poised just above him. And the rest, she realized, he was leaving to her.

And so she lowered herself until the tip of him jutted upward into the exact spot where she wanted it. And then she pressed her palms to his chest, clenched her teeth lightly in anticipation, and sank her body onto his.

The slow yet smooth descent was profound, leaving her to feel impossibly and deliciously full with him. She cried out softly when he was inside her completely. And the small groan he emitted at the same time pleased her deep inside.

Somehow, she'd never felt so close to him, not even the first time they'd made love the other night. Maybe it was about the position, about their faces being so close right now, their eyes connecting. Or maybe it was because the first time had been . . . almost like an experiment, this whole new thing for them, but the second time was . . . getting used to it, and liking it enough to have come back for more.

She never made the decision to begin moving on him, undulating—it just happened. Her body guided her and she knew a pleasure she'd never even dreamed of. Oh God, finally, *finally*. She bit her lip, drew in her breath.

Everything inside her seemed to shift and move in pre-
cisely the right ways, driving her onward, her pelvis
rotating in little circles that grew instinctively tighter
and tighter as the pleasure intensified.

She was going to come soon. And she thought it was
possibly the most amazing feeling in the world—to
know it was on the horizon but to still be moving toward
it, and to be sharing it with Logan, a pleasure so thick
and perfect and boundless.

Her breath grew thready, came faster. Logan's hands
firmly caressed her hips, her bottom, her thighs. "So, so
pretty," he whispered then, and whether he meant her
body or her face, she didn't even care—she just relished
Logan thinking she was pretty in any way whatsoever.

Soon he was lifting her nightshirt, and she knew he
wanted it off her. So she helped, holding her arms over
her head as he pushed it upward, without ever halting or
changing her rhythm on him. And as the fabric left her,
her body being bared in the soft light as she gyrated on
him, she felt *more* than pretty—she felt utterly beautiful.

When she saw Logan's eyes on her appearing almost
mesmerized, she glanced down to see herself in the
shadows as well. And she again knew that Tessa and her
other friends were right—she'd been hiding herself, or
not caring enough to show herself off a little. And maybe
all that had seemed silly to her—or like it would mean
she thought she was attractive, and how embarrassing
it would have been if she'd been wrong and she wasn't.
But no matter the reasons why, now she *wanted* to show
herself off—to Logan. She *wanted* to feel attractive, and
pretty, and sexy. And it wasn't silly—it wasn't silly at all.
It made her feel . . . alive.

Logan's gaze roamed her body, then rose back to her

face, and all the while she rode him, relishing the profound way he filled her, and the still-growing pleasure where her flesh met his just above where they were joined. Oh yeah—when it came to sex, now she definitely got what all the fuss was about.

And she got it maybe even a little more when his hands resumed roaming, too, when they found her breasts, kneading and caressing, his thumbs raking over her nipples, again . . . again. And ohhh . . . maybe she got it even still more when he licked one of the pink, beaded tips—because she felt that gentle flick of his tongue everywhere. She gasped softly, heard her own breath coming faster. And then he licked more, more, and the pleasure gathered deeper and fuller between her legs. And then he drew the same hardened nipple into his mouth and began to suck, deeply—and oh Lord, it pushed her over the edge.

The orgasm came on fast and furious, roaring through her wildly. She heard the sobs of release leaving her without quite being conscious of making them. Her body was rocked, jolted, as jagged pleasure ripped through her. *Oh wow. Oh wow, wow, wow.* She became vaguely aware of the sound of a cat skittering somewhere in the bookshelves and knew she'd scared Austen, but she was too overcome with joy to care. She didn't think she'd ever let her inhibitions go quite so completely, and *mmm*—it was high time she had!

She found herself slumping into his embrace to rest, her head dipping to his shoulder for a minute as she regained her strength. And she'd just raised her eyes to his, their faces no more than an inch apart, about to tell him how amazing that had been, when he said deeply, "I want you under me now."

"Huh?" The sound came from her breathlessly; she was barely able to think.

"I liked you on top, honey," he told her, "but now I want you underneath me." And with that, he planted his hands on her butt, stood up with her still in his arms and still inside her, and then he lay her across the wide, oak coffee table, right on top of the few magazines and newspaper already there.

She drew in her breath as the hard wood met her back, and as the warmth of his body met hers. And his eyes— Lord, how on earth had she stared into these same eyes for the last thirty-plus years without ever realizing how beautiful they were? Right now, they held her willingly captive as she tightened her hold around his broad shoulders.

As he began to move in her, she got his point; she liked him being on top, too, like he'd been by the creek. She liked peering up into his eyes. And whereas before, in the chair, she'd done most of the work, now he thrust into her in deep, slow strokes, going still inside her at the end of each, making her feel him at her very core. Soft moans echoed from her throat in rhythm with his drives. And she lay there feeling pretty sure life didn't get any better than this—until he began to pound into her harder, harder, making her cry out.

Above her, he clenched his teeth and she loved the passion etched on his handsome face. *All for me. It's all for me.* Just like after the wedding, she didn't think she'd ever been happier. And he filled her with that passion over and over again, until she could process nothing but sensation—and then finally he murmured, "God, honey, I'm gonna come. I'm gonna come in you."

It was Amy who then clenched her teeth as Logan

delivered those last ferocious drives—so ferocious they almost hurt a little, but she didn't mind. She loved the powerful way he thrust into her; she loved knowing she had taken him to such heights.

Afterward, it was *him* who collapsed gently on *her.* And she hugged him to her, soaking up every detail of the moment—the musky scent of him, the feel of his skin on hers, his breath on her ear. And then, without quite realizing, she let out a trill of laughter.

Still appearing spent, Logan pulled back slightly to look at her. "What?"

A little surprised at her own outburst, she gave her lower lip a sheepish nibble even as she smiled at him. "I'm just wondering if my butt is going to be tattooed with the ink from the front page of the *Destiny Gazette.*"

Logan gave her a grin she felt all the way to her soul. "If the front page is on your butt, that might make reading it a lot more fun."

She giggled in reply—at the same time realizing that she probably hadn't spent enough time in her life giggling—and then told Logan exactly what she was thinking. "Sex is great!"

And now it was he who laughed. "Yep, it is."

"And now that I finally know what this is like, I want more of it." She met his eyes for that part, hoping like crazy he would volunteer for the job of giving it to her.

And he did. "I'm, uh, good with that," he informed her.

And she smiled. "Nice to know."

"But maybe next time we'll . . . try a bed or something," he said on another laugh, finally easing up off her—and she resisted telling him how much she missed him when he was gone.

She sat up, surprised by how comfortable she felt with her nudity, even near the window—despite that Destiny was quiet as a ghost town at night, normally the very notion would have freaked her out. "I guess a bed would be okay," she said, "but I don't mind . . . you know, experimenting with other places."

He cast her a grin as he pulled up his pants. "You're a wild woman suddenly."

She smiled back, kinda liking that idea, even as foreign to her as it seemed. "Maybe. A little."

Logan couldn't help feeling tired—it had been a long night in ways. But also a good night—in other ways. Like just now, with Amy. He hadn't come here planning to seduce her—but now that he saw her in this new way . . . well, it had just happened. "If we were in a bed," he pointed out to her, "we could be snuggling right now." And in fact, he found himself wanting to do exactly that, just as they had by the creek.

She sat up, reaching for her nightshirt, which had landed on the floor. "You can come upstairs if you want."

To her bed, she clearly meant. And that idea definitely appealed. Except . . . "When Anita told me I had the night off, she also asked me to help her with some heavy lifting first thing in the morning. Early. So I should probably get some sleep—and if I lay down with you, not sure that'll happen."

She tilted her head, peering up at him, the nightshirt still in her grip and not yet on her body. "It's nice out tonight—maybe we could just sit outside together for a few minutes."

It was so strange to him to see Amy perched there naked on the coffee table in Under the Covers that for a moment, he could barely process it. And yet, at the same time, maybe he was starting to get just a little bit used to this—him and her. Maybe he was starting to get used to the fact that she was pretty, even sexy in her cute and quirky ways. And touching her, being intimate with her—hell, he couldn't deny that being with Amy that way was just special. There was no getting around it.

So now he said, "That sounds nice." Because even if he did have to get up early, he really wasn't quite ready to go yet. He really wanted to stay here with her a while, hold her, maybe kiss her some more. "But you better put something on or people will talk," he finished with a wink.

She just laughed, a sound he hadn't ever realized was quite so pretty until now, and finally slid that silly night-shirt over her head. Bending down, he scooped up the panties he'd just noticed on the floor next to him, passing them to her. They were pink, with the word *Meow* written in a fancy red script across the front—and noticing that was perhaps the first time he'd thought Amy's love of cats was downright sexy.

She didn't bother putting on shoes, even when he offered to go up to her apartment and get some for her—she said she liked the feel of cool green grass under her toes sometimes. "Reminds me of being a kid," she said, taking him back to their youth yet one more time tonight. When you lived in the country, it was pretty easy to find yourself going outside barefoot in the summer, and though he'd never thought about it before, at the moment, as he walked with Amy across the street and onto the grassy square, he suddenly even thought that was kind of sexy, too.

Maybe *everything* about her was suddenly a little sexy. Just because he could see that in her now. She was so natural. So real. Not a showy or pretentious bone in her pretty body. But after having had sex with her, having seen her take—and give—that kind of pleasure, even very simple things about her, like bare feet in cool grass, now held the power to turn him on.

Without ever discussing it, they bypassed the square's white gazebo and settled on a wooden park bench outside it. They sat close and Amy automatically angled her legs across his lap, which he liked. But at the same time, she didn't focus solely on him—instead she leaned back and looked up into the darkness. "Pretty night," she said, taking it all in. "Look how many."

She didn't even have to say stars, because that was how often the two of them had peered up at the night sky together in their lives. It had always been something they both appreciated. Just as he had on the ferris wheel. Where he knew he should have been with Amy. "Wish I'd ridden the ferris wheel with you tonight, freckles."

The sentiment drew her gaze from the blanket of stars above down to meet his eyes. He hoped she could see in them how much he truly regretted hurting her tonight. And also how much he felt for her in this moment. And she must have, because that was when she slid her arms around his neck and leaned in to kiss him.

There was something sweet and easy about kissing Amy on the quiet square in the middle of the night. He couldn't have imagined this a week ago, but with each passing minute it made more and more sense to him. And though at first, she'd been nervous about kissing him, now it felt as if they'd been kissing each other for years.

After a few minutes of kissing, they just enjoyed the night air in companionable silence, and Logan drank in the scent of the rosebushes near the gazebo. And the moment continued to feel easy—maybe easier than any he'd had in a long time—until he noticed Amy peering across the way to the firehouse. It sat next to the police station, just across the square from the bookstore.

"Are you feeling any better about . . . you know, the fire? After talking about it?"

Logan's chest tightened. But not a lot. Which was an improvement. And he thought talking probably *had* helped. The last few days had begun to feel . . . less heavy, more normal. "A little. Maybe a little better each day. Thanks for that," he said, then gave her another lingering kiss.

"Well, I'm not sure I had much to do with it," she informed him afterward.

"You made me talk about it, and . . . maybe the weight really feels lighter now."

When she reached up to cup his cheek in her palm, the touch vibrated through him stronger than he might have expected. "I'm glad, Logan." Then she looked back to the fire station for a minute before saying, "Don't get mad at me for asking this again, but don't you miss it— just a little?"

And the question made him feel for a second like he couldn't quite breathe—yet then he exhaled, inhaled, felt normal again. Physically anyway. But he didn't answer her.

"Just be real with me, Logan. I mean, this is me, this is us. You know you can tell me anything."

And okay, yeah, he did know that. He'd found that out the other night. So he thought it through for a minute— and was real with her, as real as he could be. "Sure, I miss it. I miss the easy days of hanging out and laughing with the guys, I miss the sound of the dispatch radio, I miss the volunteer stuff we've always done. Hell, this will sound weird, but I even miss the smell of my equipment. And I didn't even realize it *had* a smell until I was walking past the firehouse one day when the doors were open and caught a whiff of it."

"Do you . . . miss knowing you were doing something truly worthwhile?" she asked then.

And damn it, it made his chest burn. Why wouldn't she let this go? "Who's to say what's worthwhile, Amy?" he asked, his whole body tensing. "There's nothing wrong with serving people drinks."

Still angled across his lap, she let out a sigh, looking like she'd been yelled at. And maybe he *had* snapped at her—but he was tired of her harping on this.

"Of course there's not," she said. "It's just that . . . you've always wanted more than that, Logan. Always. From the time we were kids. You always wanted to be a fireman."

"So what? Maybe that was just me looking up to my dad."

"Well, there's nothing wrong with that, either," she pointed out. "Because it led you to a good place, the place you were meant to be."

He drew in his breath. And told her exactly what he was thinking. "I'm not sure I believe in things like that anymore, that anything is meant to be. Was that fire meant to be? Was it meant to be that the Knights died? Was it meant to be that their daughter was left without parents?" It all echoed their conversation by the creek, so clearly he hadn't completely recovered yet. But he'd been doing better. And maybe he'd finally get there if Amy would stop pushing him on this.

"I believe . . . *everything* is meant to be," she told him. "Even if we don't know why. And maybe we're not always *supposed* to know why. But I know with all my heart that you're meant to keep doing the job you've always done, because it's where *your* heart is, and because you won't be truly happy or fulfilled unless you're doing it. And I'm only telling you this because I'm worried about you."

"There's nothing to worry about," he told her tightly.

"And maybe I shouldn't say this, but . . . well, you were afraid you'd have disappointed your dad at that fire, yet the truth is, if anything would have disappointed him, it's this—you quitting."

Whoa. Logan's heart sank to his stomach with a resounding thud he could hear in his head. Had she really just said that? Really just told him he was letting down his father, the best man he'd ever known? Really just said the thing she'd surely realized would hurt him most? And damn, it *had* hurt. The very idea, along with the fact that it had come from Amy, who he trusted in so deeply to always be there for him, to always lift him up and support him.

He found himself pushing her legs off of his—he didn't want to be cuddled up with her anymore. "I thought you cared about me," he said.

"I do care about you. More than . . ." She stopped, sighed, and sounded a little vulnerable as she said, "More than just about anyone, Logan, if you want to know the truth. That's why I'm telling you this—because I have to."

But that didn't help. Because everything inside him stung. His muscles felt heavy, and the area behind his eyes hurt. "If you cared about me, you'd let this go. It's like . . . you care about who I was, not who I am. Like you just won't accept me the way I am now, like you're hell-bent on changing me, controlling me."

"That's not fair," she said.

"What's not fair is to keep going on and on about this when you know it upsets me!"

He was so angry now that he just barely saw the sad, wounded look on her face. It was almost enough to make him feel bad, like he was the one being mean. But he wasn't. She'd pushed him too far.

And he knew even as he spoke that he probably hadn't spent enough time weighing his next words, but they came out anyway. "And if you want me to be real, Amy, here's something real for ya. Maybe you and me . . . maybe we just have too much between us for this to work."

"What . . . do you mean?"

He didn't look at her any longer—he kept his eyes on the rosebushes and gazebo. "It's just . . . not easy being with you right now."

"Oh." The word came out soft and short, and he knew he'd stunned her—and he was sorry, but he couldn't stop at this point. He needed to say this.

"Maybe we know each other too well. If we didn't—if we'd just met—you wouldn't think you know what's best for me, and we wouldn't have a history to complicate things, or a long friendship to worry about ruining." He glanced at her briefly again, but found he couldn't—it was too difficult knowing he was hurting her. What he was saying hurt him, too. But it was the truth and he thought they needed to face it. "Amy, maybe we need to cool things down between us before we *do* ruin our friendship."

Next to him, she let out a breath, then said, "What if our friendship is *already* ruined?"

That made him look at her. "Don't say that."

"Why not? I think it's true."

The words took his breath away, and he was still trying to get his head around them when she stood up.

He tilted his head back to stare at her. "Where are you going?"

"Look, if you think I'm trying to upset you, and if you don't want to hear the truth from me . . . well, then maybe you belong with Anna, somebody you don't have a past with. I'm sure she's much easier to be with than I am. And you're right about one thing—maybe it *would* be easier if we'd just met. If that were the case, I'm sure we'd *both* be a lot more careful with each other's feelings."

And then she walked away, those pretty, bare feet of hers taking off into the soft grass as he watched from behind. And he wanted to call her name, stop her, but the truth was—he didn't have the strength at the moment. He had no idea what he really wanted or which one of them was making sense here. Maybe both of them. Maybe neither.

But whatever the answer, he just sat on the park bench beneath the stars and let her go.

She felt it at her heart.

Jane Austen, from *Emma*

Sixteen

"I so wish you guys could have seen the Cinque Terre," Rachel said, her hands wrapped around a huge coffee cup. Amy sat with her and Tessa in the easy chairs in Under the Covers, listening as Rachel regaled them with tales of Italy. Right now, she was telling them about the five quaint seaside towns that comprised the area known as the Cinque Terre, one of which Mike's grandpa had originally come from. "It was so cool to meet Mike's relatives that still live there—even though they spoke very little English and we had a hell of a time understanding each other. And if you could have seen his great aunt hanging out clothes on a line between two houses— they really do that! And, oh, the lasagna she made for dinner—it's even better than Grandma Romo's! But don't tell her I said that, or I'll be dead to her."

Tessa and Amy both asked lots of questions about the

trip, which sounded amazing, and which made Amy realize just how little she'd traveled—how little she'd really *lived*—and how, mostly, for better or worse, it felt as if the town of Destiny held her entire existence. And the whole time they talked, she stayed naggingly aware that the chair she sat in was the same where she'd ridden Logan to orgasm just over a week ago. A week during which she hadn't heard from him, and she hadn't contacted him, either. She'd passed him on the road once, and they'd both lifted a hand to wave, but that was it.

Refocusing on her newly wedded friend, Amy couldn't help but notice how happy and glowy Rachel still looked, and she also couldn't keep herself from envying Rachel's relationship with Mike. Officer Romo wasn't Amy's personal cup of tea—he was just too moody and brusque for her taste—but he was certainly good-looking, and he treated Rachel like a queen, and . . . well, maybe moody and brusque wouldn't seem so bad if everything else was wonderful, and if someone ever made *her* look the way Rachel did right now.

"I'm actually happy to be home, though," Rachel informed them, stopping to take a big sip of her coffee. "Because I'm exhausted. Sightseeing all day, sex all night." She rolled her eyes. "I've barely slept since the wedding."

"That's why Lucky and I are going to Hawaii on our honeymoon," Tessa said smartly. "Much easier to save up lots of energy for sex while lying on the beach."

And for a very brief moment Amy wanted to throttle them both. For suggesting in even the slightest of ways that sex with the men they loved was any sort of hardship. She understood, of course, that Rachel's complaints made sense and were only practical—but she knew that if she had one-tenth of the joy Rachel shared with Mike, she would never do anything but walk around smiling. And if all-night sex made her tired the next day . . . well, she'd just yawn a little while basking in the hot memories.

"So," Rachel said, looking to Tessa, "wedding plans under control?" Tessa's wedding was coming up in just another few weeks, and though it would be a smaller affair than Rachel's, there was still lots to do. And this time around, Amy was the maid of honor, which meant even more of it fell to her.

"Everything's right on target," Tessa said. "Oh, and I arranged a fitting at the dress shop this Wednesday at five." The girls were wearing pale yellow and carrying Tessa's favorite flowers, daisies. The bridesmaids' dresses were similar in style to Tessa's—simple and flowy, like most of Tessa's fashion choices—which couldn't have been more different than Rachel's ornate but classic taste when it came to bridal wear. Amy thought the look would fit the natural, woodsy setting next to Whisper Falls perfectly.

"Okay then," Rachel said, "what else have I missed?"

And Amy and Tessa just looked at each other.

"Well?" Rachel glanced back and forth between them.

"Amy?" Tessa said, prodding her.

And Amy just sighed. Because, sure, right after the wedding, she would have loved telling Rachel this story. But now it had gotten a lot longer, and a lot less fun. The part that had been so wonderful had become totally overshadowed by the ending.

"Well, I had sex with Logan," she said, trying for a matter-of-fact tone. "Twice. Once after your wedding. And once in the very chair in which I'm sitting, and also on that coffee table." She pointed to where coffee cups now resided with the magazines and newspapers. "But it's over now. And I may never be happy again. But life goes on, right? And at least I have Tessa's wedding to focus on for a while." *Even though I'm always a brides-maid, never a bride. Even though I'm always the match-maker, never part of the match. Even though I'm going to eventually be seen by all of Destiny as the old maid cat lady who runs that nice little bookstore in town.*

She stayed lost in her own morbid thoughts for a moment before noticing the look of shock on Rachel's face. "So I go away for a week and a half and I missed your entire relationship?"

Amy let out another sigh. "That pretty much sums it up. Short and sweet. Well, short and sweet, and then . . . bitter." Amy bit her lip, drew her gaze from Rachel, and focused on the table in front of her. The table where Logan had made hot, delectable love to her. She kind of wanted to cry. *But don't. Get hold of yourself. You can cry later, when you're alone.* That was pretty much how her days had gone since her argument with Logan—she spent the daylight hours being her normal perky self in the bookstore—and then she went upstairs and hugged Mr. Knightley and cried all night. Over all she'd never have.

Yet . . . no, it was more than that now. Now she was also crying over all she'd *almost* had. Or it had felt within her reach anyway—truly possible. She'd felt so close to Logan on those two nights they'd been together. Except for the part with Anna at the carnival, which had sucked, she'd felt like her life was *finally, finally* going the way it was supposed to. Like she would finally get to be the happy, in-love one.

But now she was only the in-love one. Lonely. Heart-broken. In fact, she was almost desolate inside. Nothing made her happy anymore. Everything that had once meant so much to her now simply left her feeling . . . empty.

She knew she had plenty to be thankful for—her mother, her friends, her bookstore, her cat. The fact that her life was relatively easy—God knew there were plenty of people who were much worse off than her, and she hated feeling as if she took all the good things in her life for granted. And she really hated thinking it was because of a man, that the loss of a man—the loss of a man who she'd never even really completely had, no less—was ruling her happiness.

But it was more complicated than that. It was as if . . . as if she'd been somehow holding back her passion her whole life, as if she'd never been brave enough to admit to herself what she really wanted, maybe because she was afraid she could never have it. A hot guy. A wonderful guy. Great, fun sex. Wild, hungry desires—fulfilled.

And now that she'd let it all out, now that she knew with her whole soul just how desperately she longed to have all that—and also had gotten just that tiny taste of it—it hurt so much worse than if she'd never admitted it to herself at all. It hurt worse than never having had that taste.

It was then that Amy realized a tear was rolling down her cheek, and she was still staring blindly at the latest copy of the *Destiny Gazette* in front of her on the table, and Rachel and Tessa were watching silently, not knowing what to do or say because she never got emotional like this. She was always the hand-holder, the one assuring her friends everything would be okay.

Finally, Rachel reached out and squeezed her hand. "Ames, I'm so sorry."

She just nodded, unable to speak.

"Maybe . . . maybe if you tell me the whole story, I can help," she offered.

Amy knew, though, that Rachel couldn't do anything for her. She'd already discussed it ad nauseam with Tessa, and even her recent partner in romantic crime had lacked any real, usable suggestions at this juncture, concluding, "Maybe Logan just isn't in the right place in his life right now for this relationship. But maybe he will be someday." And that had sounded like cold comfort. Because the word someday had once bespoke a fairytale future, a time to look forward to. But at thirty-four, in the same small town where she'd been born and would surely die, someday sounded very, very far away, and a whole lot like never.

Yet despite all that, Amy pulled herself together and told Rachel the story—the amazing highs and the heart-rending lows. Just because maybe it was healthy to share it all with her friends. Maybe sharing would somehow help purge it from her soul. A little anyway. Just like Logan telling her about the fire.

Before, she'd accepted who she was—the shy, sweet girl who everyone loved but who just didn't get the guy. Yet now she could no longer accept that so easily. Recognizing that passionate part of herself had made her need more of what she'd had with Logan. She didn't know how to put those yearnings back in the box. She didn't know how to go back to being sweet, shy Amy who was so easily pleased and never minded being last in line.

When she was done talking, Rachel asked all the appropriate questions and said all the caring, hopeful things, along with the standard, "Well, if he's too stupid to realize how amazing you are, you don't want him anyway."

And sure, that always sounded logical—she'd said it to various friends herself many times. But the whole situation was far more complex than logic allowed for. And now she understood, even more than before they'd had sex, why unrequited love sucked so bad.

An hour after Amy had started telling her sad Logan tale, Rachel and Tessa stood to go—Tessa hadn't been working at the bookstore today, but had been running wedding-related errands when she'd bumped into Rachel and they'd decided to pop into Under the Covers. They both hugged Amy, and Rachel said, "Hang in there, Ames—things will get better." And Amy tried her hardest to believe that while knowing there just wasn't much else her friend could say.

A few minutes later, Amy sat with Austen in her lap, trying to thumb through a magazine and feel more normal, more like her old self. But it wasn't working—because her body now knew the need to be touched. And not touched by just anyone—but touched by the man she trusted and cared for. How did you get past that driving need when it felt . . . all-consuming?

When the door opened, the bell above jangling, it startled her a bit to look up and see Lucky Romo stepping in off the sun-drenched sidewalk. With his muscular frame and long, dark hair, Lucky wasn't her usual customer at the bookstore—and in fact, she wasn't sure he'd ever been in Under the Covers before now.

"Hey Amy," he said—and she instantly thought he looked a little uncomfortable. Lucky was motorcycles and chrome, not books and Tiffany lamps.

Experiencing the familiar need to put him at ease, she set Austen in the chair beside her, put down her magazine, and stood up with a smile. "Hi Lucky. What can I do for you?"

"Well, since you're Tessa's maid of honor, I wanted to ask your opinion on something."

Okay, this was wedding-related—that made sense, and put *her* at ease, too. She liked Lucky and thought he was a perfect even if unlikely fit for Tessa, but she'd never spent much time with him one-on-one. "Sure," she said. "Fire away."

"I was thinking about the honeymoon, and about Tessa's food issues." Tessa suffered from Crohn's disease, which severely limited her diet, and Amy knew that when Tessa ate at unfamiliar places, her digestion was a concern and that she disliked having to grill waiters about every ingredient of a menu item or exactly how it was prepared. "I thought maybe I could arrange a special oceanside dinner at our hotel one night—for just the two of us," Lucky said, "and have them serve things I know she can eat, just the way they need to be cooked, without her having to explain it to someone first. Do you think she'd like something like that?"

Amy could only sigh. She knew Tessa well and replied, "She would *love* that, Lucky. And it's so sweet of you to think of it, and to want to do something special like that for her."

He only shrugged, looking a little uncomfortable again—this time, Amy assumed, because of the way she'd gushed over his idea. "Well, I just thought it would be one night of her life when she wouldn't have to deal with her condition, you know? One night when she could feel normal. And . . . well, special."

Amy nodded. "It's perfect. I can't think of a better gift you could give her." Because though it sounded small, Amy knew exactly how much it would mean to her friend. And to her near shame, she found herself standing there truly envying Tessa for having a man who was thoughtful of her needs, who on his very own had come up with the notion of giving her one very special night. She thought it impossibly romantic.

And Tessa *deserved* romance, and *love*—she'd gone through hell dealing with her health. So Amy suffered a small pang of guilt for the bolt of jealousy that had shot through her. She only wished she could have someone who treasured her even half as much.

She'd truly thought having sex would solve all her problems. She'd thought being with Logan in a romantic way—even just once—would solve everything, would fulfill all the yearnings inside her. But now the problem was . . . it hadn't lasted. And maybe she was better off than she'd been before, but it wasn't enough. It just wasn't. She'd ended up heartbroken all over again, only for new, more complicated reasons now.

And added to all that, she feared that in addition to losing their burgeoning romance that maybe she'd truly lost Logan's friendship, too. She didn't know the answer to that. She didn't know the answer to *much* lately. And when she got right down to it, all she really knew for sure was that her heart hurt whenever he came to mind.

Which was . . . *always* now.

Logan sat on the ground in the Destiny Cemetery, just outside town, next to his father's grave, knees bent, forearms balanced atop them. The marker was typical—gray granite, about waist-high, the name Whitaker

across it in bold capital letters. There was a spot for his
mom on one side, the year of death not yet filled in, but
his dad's side had been completed now for far too long
for his liking.

He'd come to grips with his dad's death, but he'd
been thinking about him a lot lately. Ever since the fire.
Ever since he'd quit the DFD. Was Amy right? Would
his father be disappointed in him for giving up the job
they'd both loved?

"I don't want to let you down—I don't want to let *anybody* down—but I'm just afraid . . . afraid to let anybody
else die."

Aw shit. Since when did he sit talking to graves?
Never. Even when his dad had first passed away, he
hadn't had imaginary conversations with him. He was
more of a realist. Usually, anyway.

And yet, to his surprise, something about talking to
his father for the first time in a long while felt instantly
. . . easy, and almost even a little comforting. So he
thought—what the hell? He was the only person here
after all, on this bright, hot summer day, so no one else
would know anyway.

"Something changed in me that night, Dad. Something that . . . well, even though I'm doing better, starting
to pull myself together—something that isn't changing
back. It's like I lost some part of myself that night, like
. . . letting Ken and Doreen die made a part of *me* die,
too."

And then something hit Logan—hard. God, how had
he not remembered this before now? Maybe because
he'd been young when it happened, but . . .

When he'd been around six or seven, his father had
gone through a whole summer barely speaking, in a

dark humor, hardly paying Logan any attention at all. It had hurt and confused him at the time—it had felt . . . like his dad had just stopped loving him or something. He'd wondered what he'd done wrong. And as an only child, close to his dad, he'd felt . . . abandoned.

And then one night while his mother tucked him into bed, she'd told him, "Daddy is just sad right now, Logan. But don't worry, he'll feel better soon, and things'll get back to normal."

"What's he sad about?" Logan had asked in the shadowy light of his bedroom.

His mother had hesitated, and then lowered her voice as she replied. "You remember that fire last month? The bad one over in Crestview?" It had been an apartment building.

He'd nodded, having no idea where this was leading—because his dad was . . . his dad. Strong. Tough. Capable. He took care of them. He took care of lots of people.

"Well, honey," his mom had told him, "some people died. In the fire. And . . . it's just rough on your father right now, that's all."

The idea of death had been fairly new to Logan at that age, but he'd simply accepted it for what it was—an explanation, a reason. And he'd quit feeling so bad. He'd even gone out of his way to be nice to his dad. And soon enough, his father had bounced back and become the same fun, loving father he'd always been. And Logan had mostly forgotten about that time. Until now. This very second.

He swallowed back the lump that rose to his throat upon realizing that his dad had gone through this, too, or at least through something similarly painful. The people in that fire hadn't been personal friends the way the

Knights were, but . . . Logan didn't know how many had died there, either, and suddenly he had the suspicion that it might have been more than just a couple. And what if there had been children involved?

And yet his dad had quietly battled those demons, and then he'd gone back to work doing what he did, fighting fires.

"I wonder if you ever thought of quitting," Logan mused to the headstone. "I wonder if you were ever scared after that. Of it happening again."

In a way, it was hard to think of his dad being afraid—but in this moment he was forced to realize, perhaps more than ever before, that his father had only been a man, like him. Surely he'd been afraid. Who wouldn't after something like that? And yet his dad had gone back to work.

And he'd never discouraged Logan from following in his footsteps, either. "You must have thought I could handle it, whatever happened," Logan said. Then, struck with fresh emotion, he drew in a deep breath and blew it back out. "I'm sorry you were wrong about that, Dad. I did my best, though, I promise. I really did."

A lump rose in Logan's throat then, but he swallowed past it. His dad would understand that he'd needed to quit. He would tell Logan to do whatever he felt was best. And sure, his dad might not think being a lousy bartender was the right path to follow, but that was only temporary—soon he'd find something else that felt fulfilling, something that would have made his dad proud of him all over again.

"I love ya, Dad," he said softly, looking to the grass, the earth, below him. It was hard to believe his dad was in there somewhere. Then he shifted his gaze to the vase of silk flowers at the base of the gravestone—currently filled with yellow roses, which he knew were among his mom's favorites because they were so bright and sunny and cheerful. And he tried to let them—and the love and support his parents had always given him—make him feel a little happy inside.

As he got up to walk away, heading back through the maze of headstones to his car, he caught sight in his peripheral vision of a large mound of dirt off to the right in the cemetery. Not far from his dad's resting place, it was in a newly opened section with only a few markers so far, and this pile of dirt didn't yet have one. Because—he knew from experience with his dad's grave—they were waiting for the ground to settle thoroughly before they placed it. But two large sprays of dead flowers lay across it.

A lump rose back to his throat when he realized he couldn't quite keep walking, couldn't get in his car and drive away, before he went over. Ken and Doreen were buried there.

It was hard as hell to approach the graves, but he knew he had to. Just had to.

As he drew near, the dead flowers accentuated his sadness. And then he dropped to his knees—not because he ever made the conscious choice to do so, but because his legs gave out beneath him.

"I'm so sorry," he heard himself whisper. "I'm so damn sorry."

And he was struck by the stark silence all around him, and the blistering heat of the day—or it suddenly *seemed* blistering anyway—and everything inside him began to feel . . . a little bit futile again, and he wondered how he would ever, ever get over this.

But then a bird twittered in a tree somewhere nearby, and maybe it reminded him that life went on. Somehow, it went on.

And the truth was, he'd felt a lot better about the fire since talking to Amy that night by the creek—it really *had* helped. He hadn't had any nightmares since.

And maybe . . . maybe coming here would help a little more. And maybe he'd find more and more things that helped. Until eventually he could quit hurting so bad over it. And maybe what he needed to do right now— corny as it sounded, even corny as it felt—was to tell Ken and Doreen the things he couldn't the night their house caught on fire.

"If there was anything I could have done, I would have. Anything at all. And . . . I think you both know that. I think you both know I tried my best. But it was just too much. Nobody could have saved you. Nobody. Not even my dad." And wow—he wasn't sure where that thought had come from, but it was true. He'd spent most of his life thinking his dad could do anything, but every man had his limits, even Ron Whitaker.

"I wish I could have gotten there five minutes sooner. Hell—I wish the damn fire had never even started. But it did." He stopped, swallowed. "They say things happen for a reason, and we're supposed to just go through life believing that—but I've had a damn hard time with it lately." He shook his head then, at a loss. "And I don't know the answers, that's for sure. But the thing is . . . I did my best. And it wasn't good enough. And there's just . . . nothing more I can do except . . . go on, the best I can.

"I think you'd forgive me if you could. So . . . I think I need to start forgiving myself now, too. I think that's what you'd both want me to do."

He rested there on his knees for a few more minutes, quiet, listening for more birdsongs, heartened when they came. And when he finally got up and headed back toward his car, he felt . . . well, a little more at peace inside. Far from healed, far from over it—but every little bit of peace helped.

Part of Logan wanted to just head home, veg out on the dock with Cocoa a while, rest up for work at the Dew Drop in a few hours. But another part of him was in the mood to be around people—he couldn't deny that had really helped his mood ever since he'd broken out of that initial dark place. So he decided to head into town. Maybe he'd stop by the police department and see if Mike was around, and if not, he'd drive by Becker Landscaping and look for Adam's truck.

As he parked on town square, though, he couldn't help noticing Under the Covers across the way, looking quaint and tidy and as cheerful as usual. And it reminded him that he missed Amy. He tried not to think about her, tried not to think about all that had gone down between them these past couple of weeks, but he couldn't stop missing her, damn it.

And he missed her not only in the way you miss a friend, but also in the way you miss . . . a lover. *So Amy became my lover, and I ended up losing my friend. Wow, you sure are batting a thousand lately, Whitaker.*

And for a second he considered forgetting about Mike, walking over, peeking inside the wide front window, seeing if she was alone. Maybe if they just talked a little they could find a way to put all this behind them and move on.

But he wasn't sure *how* to put their troubles behind him. It still hurt that she kept trying to get him to do something he didn't want to, and something that was so painful to him right now, too. He knew she meant well, but . . . he needed support at the moment, not someone pushing him in a direction that no longer felt right.

And yeah, that night he'd found her in the bookstore and given her the stuffed cat, he'd really started thinking that maybe he could have something with her that went far beyond friendship. Being with her in that way had felt damn good, and discovering Amy's sexy side . . . well, seldom in his life had he ever thought anything more amazing or beautiful. And there was no denying that the two times they'd been intimate together were the two nights when . . . well, when he'd ended up the happiest—and the most at peace inside— since the fire.

Yet as he stood on the edge of the square, just staring across at the bookstore, he let out a sigh and felt a little deflated. Because that happiness sure hadn't lasted long. And even as much as he cared about her, even as good as it had begun to seem—how could it really be *that* good, *that* right, if she could hurt him like that and feel totally justified doing it?

There's always Anna.

He almost hated the little voice inside that had just reminded him of that. Because he still didn't know how he felt about her. Had that kiss on the ferris wheel felt wrong because they didn't belong together, or was it only because he'd been with Amy that night? And if he turned to Anna now, would that be running away from the heavy stuff? Or just doing something easy and fun that didn't hurt anyone?

Aw hell. Maybe you should just forget about women for the time being.

And with that thought in mind, he turned toward the

police department, ready to look for Mike, like he'd come here to do in the first place.

"Hey, Logan! Logan Whitaker!"

Uh-oh. He knew that pretty voice. And he turned to see none other than Anna Romo on the sidewalk just outside the bookstore. As always, she looked gorgeous, today wearing a stylish top with white shorts that showed off her long, tan legs. And when she waved and crossed the street toward the square, he really had no choice but to walk toward her. Even if something about the moment suddenly felt very wrong.

"Hi," she said when he finally reached her. Her infectious smile told him any hard feelings left over from the carnival had passed. "What's up?"

He attempted a smile, but wasn't sure it quite reached his eyes. "Not much. Just looking for your brother. Know if he's working today?"

"Mike?" Her mood soured at the mere mention of his name, and it made Logan's heart break a little for his best friend. "No idea."

He couldn't help giving her a chiding look, even though he spoke gently. "Go easy on him, Anna."

She just shrugged.

And he felt compelled to go on, for Mike's sake. "I kinda thought you two might make a fresh start now that he's back from the honeymoon. I talked to him yesterday and he seemed happy as a clam—which isn't like Mike," he added with a wink. "So you might want to take advantage of that while it lasts."

At this, though, she gave her head a saucy tilt, and said, "Want to see how long it lasts? Then go out with me. Just you and me, someplace private. Let's forget about Mike's overprotective streak and just act like two normal adults who want to go out and have some fun. And if he can take *that,* then sure, fresh start all the way."

Logan felt put on the spot. Did she want to be with him, or was this just a test for Mike? Or both? And should he go or turn her down? What did he really want to do? If you took Mike completely out of the equation, did he really want to be alone, someplace private, possibly intimate, with Anna?

The truth was—a month ago, yeah. A month ago, he'd been fascinated by her, drawn to her.

But now . . . something held him back. Same as on the ferris wheel.

And that was when he caught a glimpse of movement from the corner of his eye and glanced over to see Amy. She held a cat-shaped watering can and had just stepped outside to water the petunias in her flower boxes. And he could feel her pain at unexpectedly seeing him with Anna as keenly as any touch. Damn it. That was why running into Anna had felt so wrong just now.

He made eye contact with Amy for only a brief, hurtful second before she looked away, focusing on her flowers.

But it drew Anna's eyes to her, as well. Turning back to Logan, she lowered her voice. "You and Amy—how's that going?"

He swallowed past the small lump rising in his throat. "Not very well."

Anna bit her lip uncertainly, tilted her head, appeared sympathetic. "I'm sorry," she said, sounding sincere. "But maybe her loss is my gain. So what do you say, Logan? Want to get together?"

But he could barely even begin to weigh the idea of

going out with Anna in this moment. Because even if it kept sounding like the easy answer, like a fun escape from everything else going on, deep down he just . . . didn't want to. Just like the idea of confiding in her—it turned out his heart simply wasn't in it.

But his bigger problem at the moment was the way his stomach still clenched at knowing the very sight of them together had upset Amy. And even if she'd hurt him in ways, too, well . . . hurting her back crushed him. Hell, maybe he never should have made love to her in the first place. Maybe friends weren't meant to be lovers.

What a mess he'd made . . . of everything.

"He could not see her in a situation of such danger without trying to preserve her. It was his duty."

Jane Austen, from *Emma*

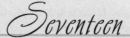
Seventeen

ell?" Anna asked.

Shit. Why did he always end up feeling stuck between these two women lately? How had his life gotten so complicated?

"I, uh . . . I'm sorry, Anna, I don't think I can. I really like you, but I'm just . . . not in a place where I should be dating anybody right now."

Her soft scowl managed to hold a hint of playfulness. "I'm not asking for your letterman jacket or anything, you know. Just getting together, having some fun." She tilted her head in the other direction. "I don't really know what's going on with you, but seems to me like you could probably *use* some fun."

And yeah, that was probably true, but at this point in

time, fun with Anna Romo just seemed wrong on *lots* of levels. "You might be right—but I'll have to pass, okay?"

She gave a teasing eye roll that made him thankful she could be so understanding. Especially since he was beginning to feel like he'd accidentally led her on. "Your loss, Whitaker," she said.

"Probably so," he told her. But Logan was learning there were many different kinds of losses, and some mattered a lot more than others.

Anna sat on the couch at Mike and Rachel's place, Mike at her side showing her pictures from Italy on his laptop computer. "That's Dona Romo and her oldest daughter, Elisabetta," he explained of their distant relatives. Then he went on to explain the twisting branches of the Romo family tree.

And the pictures were wonderful, she couldn't deny. And Logan was right—Mike was in a great mood since coming home. But she still felt smothered. She'd felt smothered when he'd called her at Lucky's place, inviting her over for dinner and pictures, just the two of them tonight because Rachel was doing some pre-wedding activity with Tessa. She'd felt smothered even as she'd agreed to come. She'd felt smothered as he'd grilled two steaks on the back porch, all the while talking about family, family, family, and how he wanted to host a big Romo reunion once Lucky got back from his honeymoon. And now she felt smothered as Mike told her all about their Italian heritage.

It wasn't that she didn't care—she did. It was that it was . . . just too much. Too much too soon. Ever since she'd shown up in this town, it had been heaped upon her in a way she couldn't have envisioned.

She'd come here, she'd sought out her family, she'd asked for all of this. And yet . . . the only real problem lay with Mike. Yes, she could feel Lucky's quieter and maybe slightly more awkward affection all around her, and her parents called her every other day to talk for a little while—but they just didn't make her feel suffocated in the way Mike did.

She found herself remembering a phone call with her friend, Julie, back in Indy, this morning. She'd been complaining to Julie about all of this, and then admitting that she sometimes felt like she was being a shrew, when Julie had said, "I just think you're so courageous to be there at all. And you could be running away from it, but you're not. I'm not sure I could be half as brave in your situation."

The words had heartened her, reminded her. She *was* courageous. Life with her mother had forced her to be. And it was nice to know someone besides her realized what a strange situation she'd put herself into here.

"Rachel and I are already talking about going back, maybe next year, and I was thinking you could come with us," Mike was saying now.

And at any other moment of her life, she'd have leaped on an invitation to go to Italy. But all she could say at the moment was, "Um . . . I don't know. Who knows what I'll be doing by then."

He just cast her a perplexed look. Which she supposed she could understand. After all, who turned down a trip to Italy?

"You know, before I went, I was thinking mainly about the sightseeing—but when I met the family still there, it was pretty freaking amazing. Just . . . to see somebody on the other side of the world that looks like you, and has your name, but leads a totally different kind of life. It's an incredible way to reconnect with the family's past, Anna."

And that was when something in Anna snapped. "I don't *want* to reconnect, Mike—I've reconnected enough already."

He drew back, clearly stunned. "Huh?"

Suddenly, she could barely breathe, and she knew she should probably measure her next words carefully—but she just didn't want to. "I'm tired, Mike. I'm tired of learning the name of every Romo relative in a thirty-mile radius, and now even the ones in Italy. I'm tired of being the main attraction of every event in this town. I'm tired of trying my damnedest to stay happy and upbeat and be my real, normal self while you keep trying to turn me into some angel who doesn't exist anymore." She stopped, took a breath, her heart beating too fast. "I'm just . . . tired of all of this. And I'm still not sure it's working out."

He'd sat staring at her, mouth open, the entire time, and now he blinked. "Not working out? What do you mean? We're your family."

"And you're smothering me. Not the whole family, though—only you. And I know you mean well—everyone tells me that all the time. But knowing you mean well doesn't make me feel any less suffocated. My God, I can't even go on a date in this town!"

"What do you mean?"

It frustrated her to see him look so baffled. "What do I mean? That the one guy in this town who I really liked, who I felt comfortable with and drawn to, you drove away."

He blinked again, leaned forward slightly. "Who, Logan?"

"Yes, Logan—who else?" The man exasperated her.

"He's so loyal to you and so worried about upsetting you that he doesn't want anything to do with me now. I've practically thrown myself at him because of it—because I just wanted to have some fun, some normal fun with someone whose last name isn't Romo—but you've managed to send him running in the complete opposite direction."

Now, she noticed, Mike looked tired, too. And despite herself, maybe she felt a little guilty for yelling at him, for appearing thankless for how much he cared about her. "Anna . . . Logan has kind of a lot going on right now. So, even if part of it is about me . . . it might be some other stuff, too."

"Amy, you mean?"

She watched as he drew in his breath. "Yeah, he told me about that a couple days ago. So I'm sure that's part of it. But there's more, too—stuff I can't really share. I'm just saying . . . it might not all be my fault."

Okay, she supposed she'd figured out there was more to Logan than met the eye. The fact that he'd given up being a fireman in exchange for a job as a bartender created questions. And maybe she was in a place in her life where she hadn't really been ready to *ask* those questions—she was dealing with enough fresh answers of her own. But it still stung to find out Logan's waning interest might be based on anything besides Mike's attitude. Because Mike's attitude, that was something they could get past. But she didn't know if she was ready to deal with anything deeper. Damn it, she'd just wanted to find one fun, uncomplicated ray of light in the maze of cobwebs her life had become—and she'd wanted that ray of light to be Logan.

She had no idea if her jumbled emotions showed on

her face, and she didn't really care, either. She was still in no mood to mince words. "Logan aside," she said softly, "I just don't know if I can keep on like this, Mike, being a part of this family in the way you want me to be." Yes, Julie had made her feel courageous this morning, but maybe at the same time, her friend's words had somehow given her permission to . . . stop. Stop being brave. Stop trying to fit a square peg into a round hole.

And with that, she got up and headed toward the stairs, trying now to speak evenly, calmly. "I'm going to get the rest of my clothes, then head back to Lucky's." Though she'd moved from Mike and Rachel's guest room upstairs, she'd later realized she'd left behind some dirty laundry in the hamper and hadn't been back to get it before now. "And Rachel promised to lend me a couple of books," she went on as she climbed the steps. "She said they were somewhere upstairs, but I don't think she got around to looking for them."

She sensed Mike following her up the staircase, and then heard him behind her. "Wait, Anna—at least let me help you."

That was fine—he could help if he wanted. But she remained overwrought, feeling like she did want to run away now. And not just from Mike and this house, but also from this town. And maybe even this entire existence she'd found here. She'd wanted to know where she came from; she'd wanted to find the people who'd lost her. But she just hadn't expected it to be so . . . pervasive, to take over her entire life.

"Do you know where Rachel keeps books?" she called over her shoulder as she reached the second floor, still tense and a bit rushed, even though she was trying to hide it a little more. She looked to the right, toward closed doors she'd never had the need to enter. "Maybe in the storage room?" That was how Mike had once identified one of the closed doors when she'd asked.

And as she reached down to turn the doorknob, she heard Mike say, "Anna, wait, don't."

But it was too late. She was already inside the room.

And she knew exactly what it was the moment she saw it. It was *her* room. From when she was little. Left the same, all these years. "My God," she whispered. To think she'd slept right down the hall for weeks without knowing this was here.

"I'm sorry," Mike said behind her, his voice smaller than usual. "I never meant for you to see this."

"You lied," she said softly. But the lying part didn't really matter. What mattered was that someone would leave a child's room like this for twenty-five years after she was taken. Colored pillows and stuffed animals covered the pink canopy bed, and a pink ballerina border circled the room. A little white dressing table still held a small child's brush and hand mirror.

"I didn't want you to know," he said even more quietly now. "That we never changed it. I didn't want you to think . . . we were crazy."

She looked up at him, looked deeper than usual—into his eyes. And she wasn't sure why, but somehow, standing in that perfect pink little girl's room, she understood more. She felt more. Mike's loss. To find out that first their parents had kept the room this way—and then even after the home became Mike's, he'd kept it the same, too. "I don't think you're crazy," she whispered.

"We . . . we started out leaving it like this so it would be the same when you came home. And then, later, no one ever talked about it or suggested making changes—

because it was like . . . to change it would be to stop hoping. And I never stopped hoping. Even when people told me I *was* crazy, I never stopped."

Anna stood there, looking around the space, feeling almost as overcome with emotion as she had in the beginning, upon first meeting Mike and her family. Only this time she hadn't expected it. She hadn't expected to see this room. She hadn't expected to *feel* this room, to sense that she'd once *known* this room. "I always wanted a pink canopy bed," she said gently, drawn back into her childhood in a way that tightened her chest and stole her breath. "Now I know why."

And most of all, she hadn't expected to suddenly really *feel*—truly grasp—Mike's pain over losing her. Even more than when she'd seen all the pictures of her in the house, in the albums. Even more than when she'd heard all the stories from the past. Somehow, now, standing in this "room that time forgot," she finally, really got it.

And without even thinking about it, she turned and put her arms around his neck, hugging him warm and tight. Her big brother. Her big brother who loved her. She felt that more than in any other moment before, gut deep. And she realized that, despite everything, she loved him, too. "I love you, Mike," she whispered against his chest.

"I love you, too, Anna," he said, enfolding her in his embrace.

And they stood there like that for a long moment in which she tried her damnedest not to cry. Until finally she got hold of herself . . . enough that she could draw back and tell him the rest, the rest of what she had to say, even if he wasn't going to like it.

"I love you, but . . . I'm just not sure what I want to do

now. It's . . . been a lot to take in, coming here to Destiny, trying to be a part of a family I don't remember. And I feel like . . . like it's sort of stolen my life, stolen me, the me who I was before I got here.

"I've never been part of a big family, never had siblings—nothing. I only had one woman who needed my care. And you know, I'm not even sure you really know me at all yet—the real, usual me—because you've never seen me in even remotely normal circumstances.

"I know everything you've done is out of caring about me, and I . . . actually treasure that more than I knew until this moment, Mike. But I'm not sure I can stay here long-term. I'm not sure of anything right now. So I just need to take some time to think, to figure things out. Without any pressure from you or anyone else.

"I'll stay at least until Lucky's wedding. And I feel blessed that I came back here in time to see you both marry the women you love. I'll always feel blessed to have found you all."

Logan and Mike sat at the Whippy Dip, the local ice cream parlor, after a softball game in Creekside Park. They'd kicked the other team's ass, which had lifted Logan's mood from where it had been the last week or so. And though their games usually came complete with a cheering section consisting of Amy, Rachel, and Sue Ann—and sometimes more—not many people had shown up in the stands tonight due to dreary weather, and despite the win, Logan was kind of glad they hadn't ended up out with a group afterward.

"My sister thinks you don't like her," Mike said, shoveling the last bite of a sundae in his mouth.

Sitting across from him at a picnic table outside, Logan could only blink. "I thought you didn't *want* me to like her."

"I didn't, at first. But now, if you wanted to, I'm thinking maybe it would be okay."

Logan just rolled his eyes. "You are fucking impossible, man."

"I know," Mike said, surprising him. "I flip-flop a lot with her because . . . it's so strange having her back suddenly. Great, but strange." And from there, he went on to tell Logan about his dinner with Anna a couple of nights earlier and how unhappy she'd seemed—about everything. And that, in the end, they'd made some peace—again, but that she still wasn't sure she wanted to stay in Destiny. "Which is killing me. But . . ." Mike shook his head. "At this point, there's not much I can do except try to back off and let her do her own thing. So . . . if you want to go out with her, you have my blessing."

Logan wasn't quite sure what to do with such shocking information. And he didn't know if Mike would be happy or pissed when he looked up from his own ice cream to say, "What if I don't want to go out with her? What if I'm not sure?"

"Well, under different circumstances, I might accuse you of leading her on. But I know I played a role in that. And I know you're still trying to get a lot of stuff sorted out in your head."

"Thanks," Logan said shortly, appreciative that Mike wasn't going to come down on him right now. Then he let out a short laugh at the thought that had suddenly hit him. "You know, some days it was easier just drinking beer and lying on the couch."

"But that's the problem with life in general," Mike

pointed out. "You can't just drink beer and lie on the couch. You have to deal with it."

Logan only sighed. "I don't quite know how, but I've ended up making a lot of messes lately, and I'm not sure how to clean 'em up. I've hurt Amy. I've offended Anna. I don't know what I want out of life, a job, a relationship—anything."

"Maybe you should have a party," Mike suggested.

And Logan just blinked his disbelief. That was Mike's solution? "You think a party is going to fix all this?"

His best friend simply shrugged. "It would just be a normal thing to do. Have some people over for swimming and grilling out, like you used to."

Hmm, true enough. Last summer he'd had the whole gang over a few times to enjoy his place on Blue Valley Lake, as well as once this spring, and they had been good, easy times. And he'd had some guys over prior to Mike's wedding, too. So maybe trying to recreate that kind of feeling wasn't a bad idea, after all. Hell, a get-together almost even sounded fun to him.

"All right then," he said. "What the hell. I'll have a party."

Amy was stressed out. And as someone who hadn't spent much of life in that particular state, she didn't like it.

She didn't know *what* to think about this picnic at Logan's house. When he'd called to invite her, he'd just said, "Things have been weird lately, and I thought it would be nice to do something . . . fun, and easy. That maybe it would help things get back to normal, you know?"

"I guess," she'd told him uncertainly. Because she kind of thought it was going to take more than a picnic to accomplish that.

And then he'd said, so sweetly that it had practically curled her toes, "I miss you, freckles. I miss hanging out, talking. It'll be good to see you."

"Yeah, I miss seeing you, too," she'd replied, her stomach fluttering. But after they'd hung up, she'd realized how many questions had been left hanging in the air. Were they back to being just friends now? Or more? And when he'd said he was inviting "everybody," who exactly did that include? Anna? Surely it included Anna. And what did *that* mean? Were *they* just friends? Or *more?*

"I don't even want to go," she told Tessa from her bedroom, putting on her bathing suit and speaking loud enough to be heard in the next room. The appointed day for the party had arrived, and the two of them had met for lunch at Dolly's before stopping by Amy's apartment to change. It was Saturday, and next weekend was Tessa and Lucky's wedding, so even though this sounded like a great opportunity to do what Logan had told her on the phone—see all their friends, have fun—she couldn't quite believe it would be that easy. "I'm too freaked out."

The fact was, as days had passed, she'd finally begun to accept that maybe everything with Logan was over, including their friendship. And though she'd kept right on going through the motions of her life—opening the bookstore every day, feeding the cats (both the upstairs cat and the downstairs one)—it was killing her. And while she'd, up to now, managed to keep a plastic smile pasted on her face, it was getting hard to hide her sorrow. Her mother kept asking if she was feeling okay, and just yesterday Caroline Meeks commented that she didn't seem like her usual, perky self.

And then this invitation had come along, somehow feeling both wonderful and awful at the same time. He wanted to reconnect! Yay! But she wasn't sure in what way. Ugh! She'd get to see him again! Yippee! But Anna would probably be there, too. Sigh.

"And I'd be looking forward to this a lot more if Anna wasn't coming," she confessed to Tessa now, who had indeed confirmed that Anna was on the guest list.

"Look," Tessa said, "just go into this open-minded. Try to have fun." Though as Amy stepped into the living room, swim bag in hand, Tessa's jaw dropped. "But you can't wear that swimsuit."

Amy just blinked. "What's wrong with my swimsuit?" The navy blue one-piece had served her well for many years, even if the Lycra was a little frayed around some edges.

Tessa simply blew out a big, tired-sounding breath. "What's *not?* Change back into your shorts. We have to run by the Daisy Dress Shop on the way and get you a new bikini."

Amy let her eyes open wider. "A bikini? I've never worn a bikini in my life."

"Then it's high time you did, girlfriend," Tessa informed her.

And . . . hmm, maybe that was true. But Amy hardly saw the use. "Tessa, it doesn't matter *what* I wear—I can't hold a candle to Anna."

But Tessa gave her head a pointed tilt to say, "Look, we don't really want him to be into you strictly for your body anyway—it's your personality and *you* that he really cares about. But at the same time, we've been over this before, Ames, and you at least have to look like you're . . . a girl. And *that* thing—" she motioned to the navy one-piece "—isn't doing anything for your feminine wiles. Now come on—let's go."

A little while later, Tessa had talked her into a simple

yellow flowered two-piece suit that . . . well, even if she wasn't completely comfortable revealing that much of her body, she did agree that it looked good. And she couldn't deny that all her friends had always comfortably worn swimsuits like this and that it was just a matter of getting used to it and . . . liking her body, being confident. And maybe, if nothing else, the intimacies she'd shared with Logan had indeed helped her feel more self-assured in that way.

"But I still don't stand a chance against Anna," she said, standing in front of a dressing room mirror, Tessa looking over her shoulder.

"Doesn't matter," Tessa told her, "because that's not what this is about. This is about you being a pretty, confident, together chick and letting it show a little. You're not in competition with anyone today, Amy. Today, just concentrate on being . . . you. And everything will be fine."

Amy loved Tessa for everything she'd just said. And as she stood looking in the mirror, she even . . . began to feel those things a little more: pretty, confident. And even an awareness that . . . she didn't actually want to *be* Anna Romo—she liked who she was just fine. And she was glad Tessa had helped her realize all that.

But at the same time, she couldn't help thinking her friend was making the day ahead sound far simpler than it was likely to be.

She was vexed beyond what could have been expressed—
almost beyond what she could conceal.

Jane Austen, from *Emma*

Eighteen

*W*hen Amy and Tessa pulled up, Logan's driveway
was filled with cars and Amy could see a small crowd
on the dock over Blue Valley Lake. Sue Ann's little girl,
Sophie, and Adam's twins, Jacob and Joey, ran around
the yard, apparently chasing butterflies if the net Sophie
held was any indication. The sun shone down from a
deep blue sky dotted with only a few puffy white clouds,
she could smell burgers on the grill, and there was no
denying that it appeared to be an almost idyllic Destiny
day.

Still, she had the sense that she should be ready for
anything, anything at all.

As she got out of Tessa's car, the first person she saw
was Logan himself. Coming out his front door and look-

ing downright . . . well, the word scrumptious came to mind, in a pair of red swim trunks, he gave her a gorgeous smile. "Hey, you're here. I was starting to think you stood me up."

She smiled, instantly liking the sound of that. That he'd noticed. That he'd cared. That his choice of words almost implied coupledom, even if only in a very loose, open-to-interpretation way. "Hey," she said. "We just . . . ran a little late, that's all." *Buying me a bikini so I could try to look hot for you.* And at the moment, he seemed so happy to see her that it warmed her heart and really made her feel a little silly about the bikini.

Until, that is, he approached, giving her a quick once over, to say, "You look great, freckles." Though she wore shorts over her bikini bottoms, it was clear that he appreciated her new swim look, and that, okay, maybe Tessa had been right on the mark.

She felt the compliment echoing through her breasts as she said, "Thanks," the word coming out breathier than intended.

That was when Logan leaned in, gave her a warm, lingering hug, and a sweet kiss on the cheek that—oh my—she felt all the way to her toes. And in other places, too. In fact, she hadn't felt anything move so profoundly and pleasurably through her body since . . . the last time Logan had touched her.

Amazing. She'd have guessed that after sex, something like a mere kiss on the cheek would have barely registered—and yet, she felt it so, so much. And it was in that precise moment when she heard Huey Lewis singing "The Power of Love," on a radio down on the dock, and she understood it—the power of love—more than ever before.

And she knew: *No matter what happens now, this is going to stay with me, forever. I will always love him. I will never not.* And she knew other people got over lost loves—she'd watched friends go through it, believing it would never happen, that they'd never feel better, and then finally, one day, they did. But Amy just couldn't imagine a time when she wouldn't feel completely consumed by Logan's presence, when she wouldn't yearn for him, when seeing him wouldn't cause a million different overwhelming emotions to erupt inside her.

"I'm grilling with Mike in the backyard," he told her then. "Why don't you guys join everybody else down on the dock and we'll be down with the food when it's ready."

"Sounds good," she replied.

And he said, "It's nice to see you, freckles," just before disappearing around the corner of the house, and her heartbeat sped up all over again.

"There, you see," Tessa told her, wide-eyed but quietly. "Everything's going to go great. This is going to be a wonderful day."

They grabbed stuff from the trunk then—a small cooler, a couple of camp chairs, and swim bags—and headed to the bustling dock, which was currently flanked by the pontoon boat Amy knew Logan had borrowed from a neighbor for use at the party. Lucky and Mick sat talking nearby, beer cans in hand as they watched Lucky's son, Johnny, who was eleven, tossing a tennis ball in the water for Cocoa to dive in after. She also spotted Adam and Sue Ann in the water—Sue Ann floated on an air mattress on her stomach while Adam perched near her face, his forearms balanced on the mattress's pillow. Near the dock's edge, Jenny and Rachel sat sunning on towels—along with Anna.

Anna, as predicted, looked stunning as usual, in a white bikini that made Amy feel downright drab on sight. She was pretty sure there wasn't even the tiniest bump, bruise, or flaw of any kind on her entire body.

But when Rachel looked up with a smile to say, "Hey, girls, about time," Amy pasted on her obligatory happy look and greeted everyone. Though she immediately discovered that she had trouble making eye contact with Anna today. Maybe so much had happened now in regards to them both vying for Logan's attention that it was going to be more difficult to hide her resentment. Ugh.

"Spread out your towels and soak up the sun," Rachel went on.

And Jenny said, "Amy, you look amazing. I love you in a two-piece."

Amy felt the warmth of a blush climb her cheeks as she said, "Oh—um, thanks."

Tessa and Amy both helped themselves to beverages—and though Amy seldom drank, she decided to go with the flow and reached for a wine cooler when Rachel pointed to the cooler containing them. After that, the girls chatted—about Rachel's wedding just past and Tessa's upcoming one, about what a gorgeous day it was, about the orchard, and Tessa's interior design business, and how hungry they were getting waiting on Logan and Mike, who Rachel dubbed "the two grill masters." Though Anna seemed quiet and mostly lay stretched out, eyes closed, looking intimidatingly gorgeous.

When Adam and Sue Ann got out of the water, Sue Ann looked Amy over, giving her a thumb's up and a knowing nod. She moved her lips to say a silent, *Hot!*, which made Amy smile.

And yet, despite herself, Amy just didn't quite feel

at ease here today. She knew she should. These people were her friends, the gang she'd hung out with her entire life. And this was hardly the first swim party she'd been to with them given that Logan had hosted such get-togethers before and that Jenny had lived on the lake growing up, and again for the last few years ever since meeting Mick.

The only new factor she could think of was . . . well, Anna. And her love for Logan. And the fact that Anna had a thing for him, too. When she put all that together, she found herself suddenly scrunching up her nose— Logan had really thought a swim party with both her and Anna there had seemed like a good idea? He'd really thought it would put things back to normal?

Just then, Jenny looked to Anna, who sat, lean and tan, on her towel, staring across the lake as if in deep thought. "Anna, you seem quiet. Is everything okay?"

And Amy's stomach pinched a little. Why was every-one always so concerned about Anna? No one seemed to notice that *she* might not be her usual, cheerful self. *But then again, Anna lets it show more than I do.* Amy couldn't help starting to think that maybe Anna was something of a drama queen.

"Sure—just tired I guess," Anna replied after a lengthy, theatrical pause.

And Amy couldn't help wondering—tired from doing what? *What does she even do all day?*

When Jenny looked perplexed, pleasing Amy, Rachel chimed in to say, "I think it might be a little exhausting to become a full-fledged Romo without much warning. At least *I* knew what I was getting into."

Everyone laughed lightly, just as Amy knew Rachel had intended, but Jenny turned things more serious again, still addressing Anna. "I'm sure it must still be hard for you, all this change."

"And I'm sure Mike isn't the easiest big brother to have," Sue Ann added, having joined them while Adam went to check on the kids.

"You can say that again," Anna replied, and everyone laughed. And Amy couldn't help feeling still more annoyed. Maybe it made her some kind of ogre, but hadn't Anna gotten enough attention by now? And sure, Amy knew that what had happened to her was tragic, but she never acted the least bit upset—she just pulled that quiet, brooding act that made her seem all sexy and aloof. Either that or she was Miss Outgoing, like the night she'd pulled Logan literally out of Amy's grasp.

"So, Amy," Tessa said, "any luck finding a home for Austen yet?" Of course, Tessa already knew the answer; she was clearly just trying to turn talk to something more lighthearted, which Amy appreciated.

"Not yet. And I still wonder if maybe I should keep her, but I'm still not sure if Knightley is up for a roommate. And I don't think I'd feel good about having a permanent bookstore cat, either—because I thought of that, but I already feel bad leaving her there all alone at night. She needs a real home, not just a store to live in."

"Everybody here is so into cats," Anna observed then as if that were bizarre or something.

So Amy replied, with just a touch of pride, "I guess my love of cats has sort of worn off on friends."

"I've never really seen the appeal of a cat," Anna said.

And Amy gasped as everyone else fell silent, all looking a little horrified. You just didn't diss cats around Amy and all of Destiny knew it.

"Did I say something wrong?" Anna asked, eyebrows lifting slightly.

When no one answered right away, Rachel said, "I was never a cat person either, until I moved back here. But now . . . yeah, we kind of love our cats."

Well, Amy certainly knew who Austen *wouldn't* be going to live with. Anna Romo.

All in all, it was a welcome respite from the tension when Logan and Mike suddenly appeared, descending Logan's yard and crossing Blue Valley Road toward the dock. "Dinner is served," Mike said, carrying a platter of hotdogs and hamburgers. Logan toted a casserole dish of baked beans between two pot holders.

"About time," Lucky said teasingly, but Amy couldn't agree more.

Everything else necessary for the meal had already been assembled on two card tables on the large dock, so within moments everyone was up and preparing their plates, grabbing napkins or plastic utensils, forking burgers onto buns. Everyone, Amy noticed, except for Anna, who she assumed preferred to wait for everyone else to finish.

"How's your chicken look?" Logan asked Tessa, and she informed him it was perfect, thanking him for making something special to fit her dietary needs. Meanwhile, Amy spooned relish onto a hotdog and scooped some baked beans onto her plate.

"Anna, you want a burger or a dog?" Mike called to her.

"I'll get something in a few minutes when everyone else is done," she replied from her towel.

But Mike only repeated the question. "Burger or dog? I'm already over here—I can get it for you."

And Amy felt sort of sick when Anna's okay-you-win smile made her look even more breathtaking than usual. "All right, I'll take a burger. You know what I like on it."

Oh brother, Amy thought. Mike already knew how Anna fixed her hamburgers? But then again, she guessed she shouldn't be surprised, given how much attention he paid her.

"Baked beans?" Logan asked then in her direction. "Chips?"

And as Anna answered him, Amy thought, *Really? It takes two of you to fix her plate?* Maybe Mike wasn't the only one who treated her like she was still a little girl who couldn't fend for herself. And Amy couldn't even be mad at Anna for it. She could be jealous, though, and she supposed that was indeed the particular sting that vibrated through her chest at the moment. Logan had seemed so glad to see her—but right now, he didn't seem to know she was alive.

A minute later, as Logan walked to where Anna sat, handing her the paper plate he and Mike had put together for her, he asked, "Need anything else?"

And Mike added, "Something to drink?"

Anna just laughed and said, "You guys are sweet, but I'm fine. I have a whole cooler full of drinks right here next to me."

Amy was thinking *she* might need another one of those drinks, her wine cooler bottle almost empty now as she took her seat back on her towel, plate in hand, when Mike added, "Well, if you need anything else, just let me know."

And Amy heard herself say, "Sheesh," the sound coming out of her completely unbidden.

"What?" Logan asked her.

Amy blinked, caught off guard, by both her reaction and his. "Well, I'm just sure Anna is capable of taking care of herself," she told him. "It's not like she's an invalid."

And she'd hoped someone might laugh, or chime in their agreement—but no one did. Instead, Logan only said, "I'm just being nice, Amy."

And her stomach pinched even more now. Because she'd just sounded like a jerk. For maybe the first time in her life. She wasn't quite sure how that had happened. "Of course. I didn't mean anything. I just thought maybe it would bug Anna."

Though clearly it didn't.

Conversation through dinner stayed light yet felt awkward and a little forced, and Amy wondered if that was her fault. And rather than ask Anna to pass her another wine cooler, even though the cooler containing them was indeed right next to her, she got up, walked over, and fetched one herself.

"Another wine cooler, huh?" Tessa asked.

"They're good," Amy said, feeling a little defensive. Everyone else could drink, but the moment she chose to without being prodded, even her good friends felt the need to question her on it?

After the meal, though, the mood finally seemed to lighten for real. Which was a relief, to say the least. The guys offered to clean up, and the girls decided to go swimming. Well, all the girls except for Anna. Not that it was a big deal. But Amy thought that Anna just never seemed to want to do what the rest of them were doing.

"After cleanup," Logan announced, "we'll take the pontoon out before it gets dark. Maybe watch the sunset from out on the lake."

The smaller kids cheered at this, whereas Lucky's boy, Johnny, seemed much more interested in the here and now, calling out, "Hey, watch this!" and then running to do a cannonball off the end of the dock and into the water with a loud splash.

"Can you keep an eye on him, babe?" Lucky called to Tessa as he scooped up some empty serving plates and platters, ready to head toward the cottage.

Fortunately, once she was in the water with the girls, Amy finally got her mind off Anna and ugly things like jealousy. She angled her body crossways on one of the blow-up mattresses, sharing it with Sue Ann's daughter, and they kicked their legs beneath the surface to propel themselves around.

Meanwhile, Sue Ann kept a close watch on Adam's twins, who floated on colored swim noodles—when they weren't using them to hit each other. And Rachel and Johnny threw a Nerf football back and forth as Tessa and Jenny talked weddings and about life changes in general.

"Lucky's officially moving in to my cabin, and we might add a room or two on the back," Tessa explained. "And we'll eventually transition his house into offices for both our businesses." Lucky already ran a lucrative custom motorcycle painting business out of his garage, and Tessa's interior design business was expanding all the time. In fact, Amy knew that soon Tessa would probably quit working at the bookstore and Amy would need to find someone else to take her part-time hours. And she was thrilled that Tessa's work—and her life in general—was going so well, but she would miss the easy camaraderie she felt having Tessa in the bookshop with her.

Changes. So many changes in the lives of all her friends the past few years. And changes for her, too, lately. Which she'd decided she wanted, needed. But they just didn't seem to be going her way. Sure, all of her friends had encountered big problems and conflicts on their paths to true love, but none of them had ever had to deal with another woman in the picture, let alone a figure so equally tragic and beautiful as Anna Romo.

"You quit kicking," Sophie accused her then.

Amy flinched, having gotten lost in thought. "Oh, sorry."

Sophie tilted her head. "I can't kick hard enough by myself to keep us going,"

But Amy just teased her. "Oh, I bet you could if you tried."

And things got easier, happier again. And Amy realized that . . . well, she had plenty of great things and people in her life, regardless of what happened with Logan. *So I just won't think about him that way for the rest of the day.* Maybe he was right, maybe a get-together with their friends *could* make things feel a little bit normal again. As long as she focused on the positive anyway.

"Well, Soph, I think my kicking legs are about exhausted—I'm ready to get out. How about you?"

"Yeah, mine are worn out, too," Sophie agreed, so together, they swam their mattress toward the dock's ladder.

"Up you go," Amy said, watching as Sophie maneuvered her way onto the dock in an adorable pink and white polka dot swimsuit. Sophie took the blow-up mattress from Amy, pulling it up onto the dock, dripping, and Amy followed, climbing the ladder herself.

And the first thing she saw was—dear God—Anna

and Logan sitting on the dock alone together, looking downright cozy as Anna said to him, "Do my back?" She then passed him a bottle of sunscreen. In response, he obediently scooted his way behind her, squirting lotion into his palm as she held her long hair out of the way.

They talked quietly, both smiling, and Amy couldn't hear the rest of what they were saying, but she didn't have to. Her blood boiled anyway. And worse than that, her heart hurt. And maybe even worse still, she felt . . . stupid. To instantly realize she was the obvious loser in this love triangle she'd unwittingly gotten herself into. And after she'd actually felt a little hope upon getting here, getting that sweet kiss on the cheek from Logan. It felt . . . cruel suddenly, to be invited here only to watch the guy she loved flirting with another girl. Even touching her now.

As quickly as she could, though, she yanked her eyes away and back onto Sophie, so that if one or both of them noticed her, she wouldn't be caught staring, or appearing the least bit concerned with them whatsoever.

"Something to drink, Soph?" she asked softly—and soon enough, she sensed in her peripheral vision that Logan did look up as he finished the sunscreen application.

But Amy just kept talking, focusing on Sophie and on the soft drink she'd just gotten for her from one of the coolers, pretending for all she was worth that Logan and Anna were the last things on her mind.

Even though what she'd seen still stung like crazy.

Even though she wanted nothing more than to run away, from the dock, from the lake, from him, from all her friends, from all of this.

She wanted to run away to some imaginary place where some great guy might actually think she was a really great girl, and might actually fall in love with her. Was it so bad to want, just once in her life, to know what it was to be truly and deeply loved?

Something inside her was breaking. She could feel it, cracking, snapping. But as usual, she kept smiling as she talked more with Sophie, chatting about her cat, Dickens; she kept smiling as the others then began piling out of the water, laughing, talking, stretching out on towels to dry—just as the rest of the guys returned from the cottage, as well.

"When do we get to ride in the boat?" Adam's son, Joey, asked eagerly as Adam tossed each boy a towel.

"We can leave in a few minutes, as soon as everybody dries off," Logan said. "We should get going before the sun goes behind the woods." Indeed, the sun had begun to dip toward the horizon, and a glance up reminded Amy that sunset came earlier on the lake due to the trees and hilly landscape.

"So, Anna," Adam said, "you getting settled here in Destiny?"

And it was all Amy could do not to roll her eyes. She knew Adam was just being nice, making conversation, but still . . . when had her life turned into *The Anna Romo Show*?

"I guess," Anna replied with a noncommittal shrug. "Not quite sure of my plans yet. Whether I'm going to stay or go."

"Oh Anna, you just got home, you can't leave," Sue Ann said as if the loss would kill them all.

And Jenny added, "Everyone's been so happy to have you back."

Hmm, not *everyone*.

"Well, coming here is a big change from the city," Jenny's husband, Mick, pointed out.

And Anna agreed with him, saying, "Definitely. A much slower pace."

And just like earlier, Amy heard herself begin to speak without quite having weighed the decision. "You don't seem as if you like it here much."

And the moment the words left her mouth, she felt the air around them all thicken.

But Anna gave an easy reply. "Some things I like, some I don't." Though her smile, cast in Amy's direction, looked a bit forced.

And then Amy heard herself talking yet again, not quite able to control herself. "I'm just saying, you shouldn't stay if you don't want to. I'm sure you don't feel like you fit in very well."

The silence that fell over the dock was heavy, intense. Amy felt people staring at her. But maybe the wine coolers had affected her more than she'd realized or something, because suddenly she didn't care. She didn't care what anyone thought. They didn't know what she'd been going through. Even Tessa and Rachel, though they knew the story, couldn't feel what it was like to be inside her, wanting so badly to just have what everyone else had. They couldn't know what it was like to feel Anna was somehow stealing it from her.

Finally, Anna said, "Um, it's a process, I guess. But . . . you've all made me feel welcome."

"Well, it's hard when all of us have been friends our whole lives," Amy said. And part of her knew it really was time to shut up now—but some other part, some part she didn't know very well, kept right on going. "I mean . . . you might *never* fit in. You'd probably be happier back in the city. You seem more like that type of person."

"What type of person?" Anna asked quietly. Her voice struck Amy as smaller than usual, and this strange, new, mean part of Amy she'd never encountered in herself before . . . liked that.

"A city person," Amy said. "You know, just not as friendly, not as worried about other people. No offense."

Anna's answer came out dry. "Um, sure."

And it was then that the stark silence and stares struck Amy once more. And even as Anna wordlessly stood up, slipped her feet into a pair of sparkly white flip flops, grabbed up her towel, and walked away, off the dock, Amy wanted to feel justified. She wanted to feel like she'd had every right to do what she'd just done. And she kept trying to cling to that belief, that need, even as Mike flashed her a look of utter astonishment and followed after his sister. Even as Rachel did the same, murmuring, "I should go with Mike."

Lucky followed after them, and Tessa's expression finally told Amy exactly how badly she'd just screwed up.

"Amy," Jenny began critically from where she sat next to her, "what were you thinking? It's not like you to be mean."

"I . . ." *Have no answer.*

That was when Logan stood up, walked over to where she sat, and glared down at her. In all the years she'd known him, she'd never seen him look so disappointed in her. "Who *are* you, Amy? I don't even know you right now. How could you say something so awful to someone who's been through so much and is just struggling to figure out her life here? That was just wrong. Wrong, and mean. Badly done, Amy. Badly done."

If the tension before had been heavy, now it was downright stifling. Amy felt as if she could barely breathe.

Sue Ann mumbled something about leaving "since it seems like maybe you two need to talk or something."

And as she and Adam quickly grabbed up all the kids' stuff, Tessa said, "I should probably take Johnny and go with Lucky, too. Will you be okay?" She touched Amy's shoulder.

Feeling a little numb, Amy just nodded. Tessa had brought her here, and God knew she wanted to run away more than ever now, but at the same time, she didn't feel she had a choice. She and Logan probably did need to talk, like it or not. She just didn't really know how she was going to defend herself, how she was possibly going to make him understand. Since she didn't completely understand herself.

Once the dock was empty of everyone but him and Amy, Logan walked onto the pontoon and sat down in the captain's seat. He suddenly needed to get out of the sun. What had just happened here? He barely knew. He'd never, in his whole life, seen Amy act cruelly. To anyone.

And now the whole party had ended, in about two minutes flat.

So when Amy stepped onto the boat a minute later, silently taking a seat on the padded bench that ran along the side, he quietly got up, unlashed the pontoon's rope ties from the dock, and then came back to his seat to turn the key, already in the ignition. The boat's motor rumbled to life.

"Um, what are we doing?" Amy asked.

"Going for a ride. Because Sue Ann's right, you and I need to have a talk."

"We couldn't do that here? And besides, you're gonna have to drive me home anyway."

"I just want . . . no distractions for this. I don't want either one of us to be able to walk away from it until we get some stuff settled."

As he steered the pontoon out into the open water of the lake, he glanced over to see her heavy sigh. She looked . . . regretful. As she should. At least they were in sync on that much. But at the moment he wasn't sure they were going to be very like-minded on much else.

They didn't speak as he drove—he wanted his full attention on this conversation once it started—and since the silence was beginning to be deafening, he reached down and turned on the built-in radio. The retro station whose signal was the only one to reach Destiny came on.

"God, I wish we could get some decent music around here," he muttered.

"I like this station," she said quietly. Reminding him how agreeable Amy usually was, how easy to please and how naturally happy. This was the Amy he knew. He wasn't sure *who* that had been on the dock a few minutes ago.

"*This* song's good," he said, pacified. About the music anyway. "Baby Blue" by Bad Finger filled the air with something both pleasing and a little melancholy at the same time. "I just wish there was more variety."

"Hmm," she said, sounding a little terse. "Yeah, I guess I didn't realize until recently just how much you like variety."

Oh boy. Had she really just said that? He couldn't keep

himself from tossing her a look—but he still held his tongue, for now.

When the slow-moving boat had puttered to what Logan decided was just about the center of Blue Valley Lake, he turned off the engine, then got up, walked to the back, and dropped the anchor over the side. The sun had dropped behind the trees now, bringing cooler air as the July day turned to night, along with streaks of pink and blue across the western sky. This wasn't exactly like he'd imagined the pontoon ride going, but it was time to face the matter at hand.

Walking back to where Amy sat, he lowered himself down onto the bench beside her. "So," he said quietly, "you want to tell me what that was about back there?"

She sat silent for a long moment, and he could sense her thinking through what she wanted to say, maybe gearing up for it. He didn't rush her—he wanted them to be totally straight with each other.

And finally she said, "Did it ever occur to you that if you wanted things to feel normal today that maybe inviting both Anna and me was going to make that difficult?"

"Yeah, sure it did. But I couldn't exactly leave either one of you out. And to be honest, I expected you both to be big enough to rise above the awkwardness of the situation and act like adults. I thought it would *create* some normalcy."

Next to him, she only sighed, looking unmoved by what he'd thought was a pretty rational, reasonable statement. "Well then, did it occur to you that if you wanted things to feel normal that maybe rubbing sunscreen on her back while the two of you whisper and giggle might not be the best idea? Unless you only wanted to make it normal for everyone but me. And me you wanted to make feel like an idiot."

Logan just blinked. And suffered a little guilt. Even if he didn't understand the idiot part. "I . . . couldn't really say no, could I? And the timing was bad—I had no idea you were about to come back up on the dock. But I'm sorry. Sorry you saw that."

"Well, I'm sorry *you're* so inconsiderate."

Damn, this felt like yet another new side of Amy. Not mean, but . . . not so soft and sweet, either. And *had* he been inconsiderate? He hadn't *meant* to, but . . . aw hell, he hadn't known how to handle any of this from the beginning and he obviously still didn't.

"Or . . . or maybe you don't realize how I feel, Logan," she went on. "I mean, I thought I'd made it clear enough without having to come right out and say it. But maybe I was wrong about that. So fine, I'll spell things out.

"The night you let her pull you away from me at the carnival, that about ripped my heart out. And just now, to find you rubbing her back that way—it hurt me more than I can say to see . . . that apparently she wins and I lose. And the reason it hurts so bad is because I love you, Logan. And not just like a friend anymore. I love you with everything in me, with all that I am. And I'm afraid I always will. So there. Now you know."

"I will tell you truths while I can."

Jane Austen, from *Emma*

Nineteen

Logan just sat there, dumbfounded, as her words hit him like a brick. Because . . . yeah, he knew Amy had serious feelings for him—he knew instinctively that Amy would *have* to have serious feelings about anyone before she'd sleep with them. But . . . love? Like being *in* love? With all that she was? That was a mental leap he hadn't quite made. And it caught him off guard, big time.

"Please say something," she said, her voice gone soft, sweet. Back to being the docile girl he knew.

"No, I didn't quite realize you felt that way," he said, still trying to wrap his brain around it.

She looked up at him, clearly stumped. "Didn't you read the notes? Back when I was your stupid secret admirer?"

The reminder took him back to how it had felt to find out it was her. How it had been shocking and yet . . . had made him happy. "First of all, you weren't stupid. You were sweet as hell. And yeah, of course I read them, but . . . I guess I thought they were exaggerated, for effect. Or something."

Next to him, she peered down toward her bare feet, crossed at the ankles. "No. No exaggeration. They embarrassed me, but everything in them was . . . completely true, completely real. And now I'm humiliated."

Logan still felt like he'd somehow walked into this relationship in the middle of it, like he didn't know things he was supposed to. "I don't get that part. Why are you humiliated? Why would you feel like an idiot?"

She let out a sigh he felt in his gut and said, "Because you want her, not me."

He just blinked, then crossed his arms, still trying to understand where she was getting this stuff. "What on earth gave you *that* idea?"

Which was when Amy lifted her gaze to his, now looking incredulous. "How about the rubbing of her back?"

He let his eyes go wide, realizing what a leap in thought she'd made from what was real to what she was imagining. "She asked me to," he explained, feeling defensive.

"Did she ask you to whisper and flirt, too?"

Now it was Logan who let out a breath. He suddenly felt a little less defensible. "Okay, yeah, I was whispering. And flirting." Only he knew he had to explain better. He just wasn't used to this, to owing anyone answers for how he behaved with members of the opposite sex. "But you know what? That's all it was. Whispering. And flirting. It . . . it means less than you probably imagine." The fact was, those moments with Anna had been easy, because that had become the prevailing nature of his relationship with her—flirting. And it was something he knew how to do, something he was good at. This more serious stuff going on with Amy—hell, *that* he was new at and didn't know how to pull off.

"It does?" she asked, peeking up cautiously. Her eyes struck him as wide, pretty, in the dusky light that had fallen over the lake.

"Yeah," he said, his voice coming out a little softer than planned. It was something about the way she was looking at him. Maybe . . . maybe now that he knew she loved him, really loved him, maybe he felt it coming through her eyes. And maybe he felt it sinking down inside him to someplace warm and comfortable.

"Wh-what does it mean then?"

Logan stopped, sighed, tried to think how to explain. "Maybe just that I'm better at flirting with a girl than . . . being real with her. You know I haven't had many serious relationships."

She nodded.

"And on the flip side, I'm good at being real with you. About most things anyway. But I'm not sure I'm very good at being real with you about . . . love. I don't even know if I've ever *been* in love, freckles."

"Then you haven't," she said without hesitation. "Because when you're in it, you know it."

"What does it feel like?"

"It's . . . the best, most awful feeling in the world. It fills you up. But it also owns you. Makes you feel a little helpless against it."

"Wow," he said, thinking it actually sounded pretty scary and was something he'd much rather push from his mind than explore.

"So, with Anna . . . what you feel for her isn't serious?"

He shook his head. "I wanted it to be. But . . . there's just something missing."

"Oh. Well, I'm sorry . . . sorry I was so awful to her." She hung her head, looking appropriately guilty. "I don't know what got into me."

He gave his head a tilt, tried for a smile. "I think I do. It's called jealousy. And I'm sorry I was . . . careless and inconsiderate. I didn't mean to make you feel at odds with her, and when I invited you both, I guess I didn't think through it very clearly. I tried to think it was simple, would be easy and fun. But I guess, no matter how you slice it, it's more complicated than that."

She nodded, and he knew without either of them saying it that they both forgave each other. For what had happened today. And maybe for a lot of things.

"I'll find her tomorrow and apologize," she said. Then she sighed. "And I'll need to apologize to Mike, too, and . . . well, pretty much everyone. I'm sorry I ruined your party, Logan."

But he just shook his head. "Like I said, I didn't think through it enough, so part of it was definitely my fault, too."

They stayed quiet for a few minutes, simply soaking in the night, he supposed, or maybe trying to figure out what was next between them, when Amy said, "You know, if you really want to create some normalcy, for yourself and this whole town, you could just go back to work at—"

"Don't say it, freckles," he cut her off. "I already have a job."

"You're a horrible bartender."

He could only sigh. "I know. But I'm getting better."

"Says who?"

"Anita. Sometimes." He stared out over the water, rethinking a recent conversation he'd had with his new boss on the topic. "But maybe she's just being nice," he concluded honestly. "She says I cut people off too early, that I'm too worried about them driving drunk."

"That's a good thing," Amy pointed out.

Logan had thought so, too. He guessed it was just in his blood to try to protect people a little. "Not if you're a bar owner, I guess."

"Well, we both know what you *should* be doing."

He just slanted her yet another look. "Amy. Don't go there."

"Fine, I won't. But we both know."

Damn it, she just wouldn't quit on that. But he held his tongue, not wanting to fight with her anymore—and this time he cast a look of warning that at least shut her up on the subject.

But she rolled her eyes at him anyway.

A few minutes later, Amy looked past him to the western sky, and said, "So pretty."

He turned to see it, too, and took in the deepening pinks and purples above the jagged silhouette of hills and trees surrounding the lake. "Yeah," he agreed.

They observed the dramatic sunset in silence for a minute until an old song by the Climax Blues Band came on the radio, the first line about a guy who hadn't had a care when he was a younger man. Logan thought it could very well describe *him*. There'd been a time—a long time—when he hadn't *needed* to have a care. But now . . . hell, he did. He'd seen people die. He wasn't sure what he wanted to do with the rest of his life and he needed to figure it out. His mother was getting older. His friends were all starting new phases of their lives—

while he was flailing around in an old one that suddenly felt . . . stale, used up.

And one of his best friends for his whole life was in love with him. And she was the sweetest person he'd ever known, even if she'd made a mistake a little while ago. And she looked so damn pretty sitting here next to him, pretty and . . . kissable.

As the romantic song went on, about love changing the guy's life, Logan reached out and took Amy's hand in his.

It made her shift her eyes to his, and his gaze dropped to her lips, which appeared darker in color to him than usual, maybe from the dim lighting, or maybe they'd been pinkened by the sun today, same as her cheeks. But the main thing he noticed about her lips just now was that he wanted to kiss them—and so he didn't hesitate. He bent toward her and pressed his mouth to hers. And when she kissed him back . . . damn, maybe he kept forgetting—maybe even choosing to forget—how good it felt, how easy it was to kiss her. Yeah, it had been a little awkward at first, all things considered, but not anymore.

He didn't even have to think as one kiss melted into another, and another—it was that easy. He just let his urges guide him. And before he knew it, they were quietly, wordlessly, sinking onto the floor of the boat together.

The move landed them out from under the pontoon's awning, which covered only the rear half of the boat, and lying on her back beneath him, Amy peered up past him to whisper, "The stars are already coming out. Nights are so beautiful here."

And it reminded him of being on that ferris wheel

with Anna, how he'd mentioned the stars to her—and
he realized all the more that he should have been riding
it with Amy. And how Amy loved Destiny as much as
him. And how intertwined their lives were in so many
ways that he'd just never even thought about before.

"*You're* beautiful," he told her. Pushing a lock of
hair from her face, he realized how true that was. And
it wasn't about makeup—because she wasn't wearing
any—or the bikini she had on. She was just beautiful in
ways he'd never noticed until very recently.

The way her green eyes sparkled when she laughed,
and how in awe she looked right now of something as
simple as the sky. Her mouth, which he'd discovered
was perfect for kissing, and the freckles that dotted
her cheeks and cute little nose. The smile that always
showed in her eyes. The *love* that shone in her eyes as
she gazed up at him right now.

He kissed her again, caressing her slender neck, letting his fingertips drift downward onto her chest.

"I wish I'd ridden the ferris wheel with you, Amy," he
told her. "I'm sorry about that."

"You already apologized, and it's okay. And besides,
right now, I'd rather think about what's right between us
than what's gone wrong."

The thought brought a small smile to his face as he
told her, "Good idea."

And as his cock hardened in his swim trunks—from
everything about her in this moment—he knew he
wanted her again, right here, right now, under the stars
in the middle of Blue Valley Lake. He didn't know how
things were going to end up between them, but that didn't
matter—suddenly all that mattered was reconnecting
with her in a deeper way than mere words allowed.

Fueled by fresh desire, he didn't hesitate to slide his palm down over her breast through her bikini top in a tender caress that he felt as profoundly as he hoped she did. The soft moan that erupted from her throat pleased him, stiffening his erection a little more. Yeah, there were still times when it surprised him to realize he and Amy were like this now, but it escalated his excitement, too. To know her in this way no one else did. To see a side of her she'd kept hidden. To know he was the one who brought it out of her.

When her nipple jutted into his palm, a low groan escaped his throat, and he needed more, now. Suddenly thankful she wore so little, he reached deftly up behind her neck and pulled the yellow string there, loosening the top enough that he could easily slip his hand inside. She let out a sexy breath as his touch closed over her bared breast—and God, it made him impatient, made him want to rush.

But stop, slow down. Take your time. Enjoy this. Enjoy her. Enjoy how fresh and special and good this new connection between you is.

So he took a deep breath and kissed her some more as he fondled the soft mound of flesh in his hand, as he ran his thumb over the beaded tip. Her arms circled his neck, tightening as she kissed him without reserve, and he knew she was indeed as excited as him. "How did I never notice," he heard himself whisper near her lips, "how hot you are?"

He liked how pleased she looked, and how confident, as she murmured back, "Some guys are just slow to catch on, I guess."

He grinned, thinking every guy in Destiny had been slow to catch on about Amy and feeling damn lucky he was the first to have smartened up. With her help, of course. "Thank God you sent me those notes, honey," he told her. And then he bent to lower his mouth over the same breast he'd been caressing at the exact second he moved his touch south, easing it boldly into her bikini bottoms.

Her light gasp was like sweet music to his ears, just before she said, her voice hot and breathy, "Yeah, thank God."

"You feel so good," he told her, his fingers sinking into the moist crevice between her legs.

She was breathing so hard now that it seemed difficult for her to get words out. "You . . . too." And then— wow—Amy got aggressive. Reaching down, she closed her hand over his ass and pulled him closer, and he was realizing how he must feel against her thigh when she managed to say, "So hard."

"Just for you," he told her.

She bit her lip, looking sweet and sexy at once. "I like that."

And he suffered a new sense of guilt over the whole situation with Anna. He'd been . . . damn, he'd just been selfish all this time. He'd been so wrapped up in his own troubles, his own confusion, that he'd never really stopped to think how Amy must feel knowing he was also interested in Anna. And somehow, what she'd just said had brought home to him how much she deserved his care and attention.

"I want to make you feel *so* good," he told her.

"You are, you do," she whispered, her voice as soft as the night that seemed to cradle them now, the sky gone as dark as black velvet.

And, then his Amy did something that surprised him

even more than any other aggressive move she'd made
with him so far—she eased her hand around from his
butt, over his hip, and in between their bodies. He
tensed with surprise at what was coming, but nothing
could describe the shock of pleasure that shot through
him when her hand closed over his erection through his
swim trunks.

A low growl escaped him, and he rasped in her ear,
"Damn, freckles, I want you. I want to be inside you.
Now."

Her lips trembled when she replied, "Oh God, I want
you, too. Please. Hurry. Get these off me," and the next
thing he knew, she was struggling to get out of her bikini
bottoms, and he was doing his best to help. After she
finally kicked them off, they both pushed at his trunks
until those were gone, too, and other than the undone
top that lay loose around her midsection now, they were
naked together on the boat.

Which was when Logan realized something downright awful. "Aw shit. I don't have a condom."

Unlike her earlier gasps, this one was more fraught
with alarm than excitement. "You don't have a condom?"

He let his eyes go wide on her. "I don't exactly tote
them around in my swim trunks. I mean, I wasn't
expecting this."

Her sigh seemed to say she understood—but they still
had a problem.

And he was feeling pretty desperate. Desperate
enough to say, "I'm always careful, Amy."

"I know," she said. Obviously not getting what he was
hinting at.

So he'd have to be clearer. "I'm always careful, so . . .
it would be okay if I wasn't that way tonight, with you."

She drew in her breath, looking uncertain, and he felt the need to say more.

"I mean it when I say I've always, always used protection. You gotta know that I would never risk endangering you of all people. And besides," he said, lowering his voice as he leaned his forehead over to touch hers, his need threatening to get the best of him, "if there's anybody in the world I should be that close to, flesh to flesh, nothing in between, shouldn't it be you?"

Amy could barely breathe under the weight of Logan's words. And sure, she knew she could insist on a condom and that they could take the pontoon back to his cottage and then resume their passion there. But she trusted him. And the bond she was experiencing with him right now felt so incredibly powerful, and right, that she knew a need unlike any she'd ever known to join her body with his before even another minute passed. She knew in her very soul that what happened between them tonight had the power to make or break them, their burgeoning romantic relationship, and her heart told her not to wait.

"Yes," she told him. "Yes, it should definitely be me."

"Aw, honey, I'm so glad you feel that way," he said.

And wanting no further ado, Amy drew her body to his beneath the stars.

When he entered her, they both let out soft sounds of pleasure, and she'd never felt closer to him. Oddly, despite the earlier strife, this somehow felt easier than the previous times they'd had sex—maybe she was starting to get used to it, but this time, rather than thinking about anything she was doing, she simply let herself feel, and she followed her instincts.

As he moved inside her, she arched her body to meet his. It felt so good that she clenched her teeth, sighed,

moaned, and worried about hiding nothing. Being made
love to by Logan was perfect, the most perfect thing
she'd ever experienced. It made her remember why she'd
gone through all this tension and heartbreak over him,
and it also gave her a glimpse of how truly, deeply amazing things could be with him in the future.

When, after a few blissful minutes, he pulled out of
her, she missed his presence inside her immediately and
protested. "Wait—why are you . . . ?"

His breath came warm, sexy on her ear. "Because,
like I told you, I want to make you feel good."

And with that, her lover—oh, she liked the sound of
that, of having a lover—began to kiss his way down her
body. Ohhh.

Slowing things down now, he kissed her breasts as he
ran his hands smoothly, tenderly over her skin. "Got a
little tan line going this afternoon," he whispered, smiling up at her as he moved between one breast and the
other.

"Uh-huh," she replied absently, watching, amazed to
be watching, amazed that this was *her,* virginal Amy
Bright, a virgin no more.

Her body practically hummed as Logan rained kisses
across her stomach, and then lower, lower, and the spot
between her thighs wept with want and joy before he
even got there. And when he got there—oh, she couldn't
hold in her sobs of pleasure.

It struck her then that maybe she was still feeling the
effects of the wine coolers, that maybe that was why she
was more able to let herself go this time, even more than
last, and just soak up every delicious sensation Logan
delivered. But she thought the truth was more because
they'd now gotten past the hardest part, the transition

from pure, platonic friendship to romance, and that maybe that meant the rest would be as easy as this had suddenly become, too.

As Logan's ministrations grew more passionate, the pleasure inside her grew, escalated, higher, higher, and she recognized the nearing orgasm before it broke over her, wild and intense and as deep as the night sky. And again, she didn't hold back—she cried out her pleasure, again, again, again, until finally the jagged pulses of feeling subsided, leaving her happy but spent as she relaxed and closed her eyes.

Until—mmm, yes—she sensed Logan crawling back up beside her again. And she let a sated smile steal over her, thinking at any moment he'd be lowering his body atop hers once more, easing his way back inside—so it surprised her when he whispered very close to her ear, "Why don't you turn over, on your hands and knees."

Amy just looked at him. "Huh?"

He cracked a small grin. "Too kinky too soon?"

She bit her lip. She didn't know if it was too kinky too soon—because she'd never really thought about that kind of thing before. She was so new at this, after all. But then she remembered that so far tonight her inhibitions had completely fled the scene, and that she kind of liked that. And that this was Logan, and she was so comfortable with him, even sexually now. So, despite fearing she probably looked a bit shy when she said it, she told him, "No. Not too kinky too soon."

And his smiled widened. "You're amazing, freckles," he said, making her thankful he'd transformed her into a more adventurous soul as she sat up and began to turn over, facing away from him. As a cool breeze passed over her just then, she *felt* amazing. Amazing and wild and sexy and fun. *I can have what all my other friends have. I can have exciting fun, and I can have the love that makes everything feel so easy, too. I can have it all!*

Sweet anticipation stole over her as Logan's hands closed over her hips, and her whole body ached with wanting him back where he belonged. And it truly felt that way to her now—that he belonged there, his body united with hers.

And then he was pushing his way inside her and she cried out, feeling him deeper this way, tantalizingly deeper, her body now fuller with him than ever before.

"Aw, Amy," he rasped behind her, "you're so tight, so wet."

"Just for you," she told him, the same as he'd said to her a little while ago. "Just for you, Logan."

And when he began to drive into her—oh Lord, she'd never felt anything like it! She found herself again gritting her teeth against the harsh pleasure, but happy to take it, to absorb each intense thrust he delivered. He'd never moved in her this way before—so hard, almost brutal. And she couldn't have imagined how good that would feel, how—more than ever before—it wiped away all thought or decision and left her room only to bask in the physical delights it brought. She didn't bother to hold in her moans—they came with each and every rough stroke. And she wanted it go on forever, even as she grew aware that her arms were quickly getting tired and her knees weak.

She peered out into the darkness at small lights along the shore that marked the homes and cottages there. And she felt like she harbored some wonderful, naughty secret from the people in those houses, the people who would never dream Amy from the bookstore could possibly be out on a boat in the middle of their lake having hot, wild sex right now. Nor could they know the deep, resounding joy it sent pounding through her veins to feel so feminine, to feel so womanly, to feel so daring, and to be experiencing it all with—and because of—the man she was in love with.

Finally, Logan's hot drives into her sensitive flesh grew even rougher, more demanding, his fingers now digging into the flesh at her hips, and behind her, he said, "Aw, Amy baby—I'm gonna come. I'm gonna come inside your sweet body. Now."

The thrusts that followed nearly stole her breath, but she loved them just the same because she loved having taken Logan there, having excited him so much. She loved the raw, unrefined intimacy passing between them, something that went far beyond that which they'd previously shared.

I love you, I love you, I love you. Like before, the words ached to flow from her lips—but still, something held her back. Pride, maybe? Maybe she just wanted to hear him say it first? She didn't know, and was too spent to examine it, yet she hoped maybe he could feel that love echoing from her anyway. She'd never felt closer to another human being than she did to Logan in that moment.

They lay quietly, his body collapsed gently upon hers, until he whispered, "You okay?"

"Perfect," she said, turning her head to look at him. Their faces were but a few inches apart.

"Good," he replied with a smile. Then, "Amy, that was . . . incredible."

She absorbed the compliment with her whole being, returning the grin. "For me, too."

Then watched as he rolled over on his back, his smile fading just a little as he peered up into the dark night with a sigh. And something about it made her stomach churn.

"Something wrong?"

"I just wish things were different, that's all."

And then her stomach sank. Because . . . oh God, she'd read this all wrong, hadn't she?

Somehow, as they'd made love, she'd made the huge assumption that now things *would* be different—that they'd be . . . a couple. Just like Rachel and Mike. And Tessa and Lucky. Why on earth had she thought that? Because he'd told her he didn't have real feelings for Anna? Because she felt so comfortable with him sexually? Because he'd seemed so into her? Despite all that, she supposed it had been foolish to somehow just assume everything would be the way she wanted now. Still, she heard herself saying, "They could be. Maybe they *will* be. If we just let them."

And it crushed something inside her when he gave no answer at all, simply lying there and staring upward, his expression so serious it was almost grim. If sex had left Amy feeling a bit spent . . . well, somehow *this* depleted any energy she had left. She rolled onto her back, too, now. And she tried to fight off tears. But they came anyway.

Oh God, stop. Stop crying. He can't see you like this. You're going to ruin everything.

But then again, what was there to ruin? If, after what they'd just shared, Logan was already so unyielding about their relationship, then maybe it hadn't been nearly as special as she'd thought.

"Amy? Freckles, what's wrong? Why are you crying?"

Oh Lord. Ugh. She'd hoped against hope that she could keep her weeping quiet and maybe somehow stop before he noticed, but it was not to be. And now he hovered over her, touching her face, wiping away tears—and despite having that feeling from earlier, of wanting to run away, there was definitely nowhere to run. She was trapped in the middle of the lake with him.

"I . . . I just . . ."

"What, honey? What's wrong?"

She had no choice but to be honest—to let go, give up, and tell him what burned in her heart right now. "Like I told you earlier . . . I love you. And . . . and I guess I thought that . . . what we just did felt so right that . . ." *That maybe it meant you loved me, too.* But she couldn't say *that,* couldn't be *that* honest. And that made her cry a little more.

"Oh God, I just wish I *didn't* love you, because it's screwed things up for both of us in so many ways. And I have no idea how you feel about me in return, and that hurts. And I've become a jealous shrew. And I barely even know myself anymore. And . . ." She crushed her eyes shut, still trying to quell the tears. "And I can't even believe I'm telling you all this!"

"Amy—Amy, come here, let me hold you," he said, pulling her into his embrace. "It's okay, baby, everything's okay. Because . . . that's the thing with us. You can tell me anything, even stuff like this. We can be real with each other—no stupid games or holding back because we already know each other so well."

"But maybe it would be better if we didn't, remember?" she asked.

"Yeah," he said softly. "You wouldn't be so damn pushy about what I should do with my life."

She sucked in her breath, almost offended. "I'll never stop doing or saying what I feel is best for you, Logan—that simple. And it's because I care for you."

"I know, I know," he said. "I was only kidding. Sort of."

"And maybe if we didn't know each other so well," she went on, "you'd be . . . more considerate of my feelings."

He looked remorseful. "You're right. I'm really sorry I've been careless that way, with Anna. I guess she's like . . . the path of least resistance."

I wish I was the path of least resistance. "I . . . I wish I could be as cool and confident and casual as Anna," she admitted then. "But that's . . . not who I am, how I'm put together. Things matter to me. *You* matter to me." And then she cried a little more, into his bare chest now, and she couldn't believe they were lying naked on a boat in the middle of Blue Valley Lake and that she was in tears and everything felt so uncertain. Still. Or again. Depending upon how she looked at it.

"You shouldn't want to be like Anna," he told her. "You're you, Amy, and you happen to be pretty great the way you are, okay?"

"For your information, I actually *don't* really want to be like Anna. I like myself just fine."

"Good," he said. "Because so do I."

Hmm. That sounded nice, and it almost lifted her spirits, but the truth was . . . what she'd said a minute ago he still hadn't answered—after all this, she didn't know how he felt, where she stood. So instead of replying to what he'd just said, she decided this was as good a time as any to make into the moment of truth. So she lifted her head from his chest, tried to wipe the wetness there away, embarrassed—and he pulled her hand away, murmuring, "Don't worry about that, silly"—and then she asked him what she ached to know.

"Logan, if we're so real with each other—you and I—how do you feel? About me, about us?" She peered down at him, and somehow already knew the answer couldn't be a good one, wouldn't be the right one. Or else she wouldn't even have to ask.

And when he hesitated, she had no patience. Not anymore. "Just say it, Logan, whatever it is. Just tell me."

He darted his eyes to hers, clearly a bit taken aback, but she didn't care, wouldn't apologize.

"I keep thinking things could be great between us, *should* be great," he said, "but it seems like everything is just too screwed up right now, in so many ways. You're so special to me, Amy, and I care about you so much . . ."

"But?" she whispered.

He drew his gaze away, back to the darkness above, and her heart sank a little further. "I care about you more than I've ever cared about any other girl, and I love being with you in this new way, but . . . well, you know I haven't had too many real, lasting relationships. And I'm just not sure if moving forward into something serious is a good idea for us right now."

In response, Amy sighed and rolled to her back, not sure she wanted to be snuggled up with him anymore. Yeah, she'd known already that he wasn't going to tell her what she wished for—*Yes, Amy, I love you, the same way you love me, and nothing will stand in our way any longer*—but getting confirmation hurt just the same.

"I can't do this anymore, Logan," she heard herself say as she realized her *own* truth.

"Do what?" he asked.

"Have sex with you. Without it leading somewhere. I thought I could do it without promises, but each time, it gets harder. I feel closer to you and want more of you, and I'm not sure I'm ever gonna get it. And I just can't keep torturing myself that way." The words stole her breath even as she said them. Because she was giving up the most amazing connection with him she'd ever had— but she couldn't see any other way at this point.

Next to her, he turned on his side to face her again, and gently cupped her cheek in his hand. "I understand—I get it. I know this isn't fair to you, and I promise I'll figure it out soon. I'll figure out what to do. About us."

An hour later, Amy sat next to Logan as he drove her home. It wasn't yet midnight, but it felt much later, as if the sun should be coming up soon. She supposed it had just felt like a long night—full of more emotional ups and downs than she could even process at the moment.

They stayed mostly quiet on the drive, in a way far more comfortable than awkward, because they'd known each other for so long and so well, and it hit her again what a nice perk that would be to their romantic relationship—if only they had one. Bonnie Raitt sang, "I Can't Make You Love Me" on the radio.

Her thoughts traveled back to that moment in time when he'd said he'd figure out what he wanted to do about them soon. The same way he often said he'd figure out his career path soon. How long would it take? And how much would it hurt if it didn't go her way? And was she supposed to just sit around waiting until then, watching as he flirted with other girls because he was better at flirting than deciding?

And as the rural outlying Destiny roads led them

closer to town, a lump rose in Amy's throat. Along with a realization. She was behaving like a doormat. She wasn't sure when that had happened—and God knew she had very little experience at relationships, so she was instantly inclined to forgive herself—but she didn't like the feeling.

She'd wanted to be honest, put her true emotions out there. But she hadn't quite made the leap in thought to the result—that it somehow automatically seemed to leave the decision, the outcome, entirely in his hands.

And . . . and . . . if Logan was so unsure, so iffy about their romance . . . why did she even want this, want him? She blew out a breath because that was a tough thought to swallow—and yet it was so true. It hit her like a ton of bricks that even if he chose to be with her now, the relationship would never be what she wanted it to be. Up to now she'd thought she'd take him however she could have him, take whatever bit of him he was willing to give her, but now she realized—part of him would never be enough. And she was worth so much more.

She'd told him love made you helpless, and that was the one thing she really hated about it. But . . . was she really helpless? No. Did she really have to sit around waiting for someone else to decide if she was worthy of them? No. She might still feel just as desperate inside, and she might feel empty when this maddening love affair was over, but . . . she did have a choice here. She had a choice to hold on to her dignity.

And what she was about to do would be hard as hell, but . . . at least she wouldn't leave him tonight still feeling as helpless as she had since falling in love with him.

So as Logan's car pulled onto town square, Amy took

a deep breath, girded herself, and asked herself: *Are you
sure you really want to do this?* But the simple answer
she'd just figured out was that she really had no choice,
not if she wanted to hang onto . . . her self, her self-
respect.

So when the car pulled to the curb outside the bookstore, she reached for the door handle, and—without
looking at him, because that would just be too difficult—
spoke in a clear, sure voice around that lump still resid-
ing in her throat. "Logan, what you said about figuring
out what you want to do about us—you don't have to
figure it out. Because . . . I already did. I don't think I'm
interested anymore."

She could feel his surprise, even without glancing his
way. "Interested in what?"

"You. Us. That way. Romantically." She opened the
door now, preparing to go.

But his shock was so great that it practically filled the
car, even if she saw his eyes widen on her with only her
peripheral vision. "What do you mean?"

"The thing is," she began, "if it's such a hard decision . . . well, I'd rather be with somebody who doesn't
have to decide, who just knows. Who knows I'm amazing. Who knows I'm the best thing that ever happened
to him. Who takes me with my faults. That's what I
deserve. And if you're not that guy—then a relationship
with you would never be enough for me."

And with that, she got out of the car in her bikini and
sarong, said, "Thanks for the ride. Goodnight," then
shut the door and walked away.

She saw it all with a clearness that had never blessed her before.

Jane Austen, from *Emma*

Twenty

The truth was, Amy shed a few tears in bed that night. Because she thought about how good it could be if Logan were in her bed with her. *But Logan doesn't know what he wants, and that's not good enough*. And despite her sorrow, she slept soundly and awoke the next day feeling stronger and more in control, even if not fully happy about the situation.

The first thing she did that day was drive to Tessa's to find Anna. And she didn't have to look far. When she pulled into Tessa's driveway, all was quiet, no one stirring, but she immediately spotted Anna sitting on Lucky's deck—his house being situated just above Tessa's cabin on hilly Whisper Falls Road. Anna looked as gorgeous as usual, even wearing simple shorts and a tank top, her hair pulled back in a ponytail. Seated in a lawn chair, her feet were propped on the deck railing, her head tilted back with eyes shut to drink in the sun.

Amy didn't hesitate to head up the small hill between the two homes. "Anna," she said as she approached the deck.

When Anna opened her eyes to see Amy, she looked understandably surprised and maybe a little worried. But Amy didn't want to waste even another second before clearing the air.

"I want to apologize to you," she said. "For yesterday. I don't know what got in to me, but I know I was very out of line and I'm sorry."

"Wow," Anna said, lowering her bare feet to the deck and sitting up a little straighter. "That's really big of you, Amy. And I appreciate it. Though . . . I guess, having thought through it now, I can understand how it happened."

Amy blinked, stunned. "You can?"

"Sure," Anna said with an easy shrug. "It's been like we're in a fight over Logan and it was your turn to swing, that's all. And . . . I know you have a much longer history with him than I do, so I probably should have backed off before now."

"Well," Amy said, not having expected this level of bluntness, "for what it's worth, I'm done swinging. It hit me last night that I shouldn't have to work so hard for someone's affections. That if he doesn't give them to me willingly that they're probably not worth having."

It caught her off guard yet again when Anna let out a short laugh—until she explained. "Funny, I was just sitting here coming to the same conclusion. And realizing that . . . well, maybe I've been pursuing Logan for the wrong reasons. He's been a nice distraction from everything else I'm dealing with right now, and I really *wanted* a nice distraction, but . . . if he's not into it, maybe it's God's way of telling me to quit looking for distractions and get to dealing with the stuff I need to deal with."

Amy tilted her head, struck by the depth of Anna's insight. Apparently, she wasn't the only one having revelations right now. And she wondered if Anna's hurt as much as hers, deciding that they surely did, even if in a very different way.

"I really regret seeing you as a rival, Anna. I feel like, under other circumstances, we could have been friends."

Anna offered up a small smile, then said, "Maybe it's not too late for that."

Wow. Amy hadn't expected Anna to be so receptive to her apology, but she was happy to say, "You're right, maybe it's not."

The following day, Monday, was the Fourth of July, and though normally Amy would have hooked up with her girlfriends and headed to Ed and Betty Fisher's farm for their annual picnic and fireworks display, this year was different. This year her friends had husbands, or almost-husbands, other people they went places with and were now responsible to. So Amy called her mom and asked if she'd like to be her date for the fireworks this year. The fact was, she'd probably been neglecting her mother some lately and it was time to remedy that. And maybe the picnic wouldn't be quite the same for her as usual, but times changed, life changed, and rather than whining about it, Amy knew it was time to act like the mature woman she was and simply roll with the punches.

Logan's mother decided to go with them to the event, as well, so Amy picked up both women and headed to Ed and Betty's picturesque place outside town. And though the Fourth of July celebration was one of Destiny's biggest social occasions of the year, even once Amy got there and helped her mom and Logan's mom settle in a nice spot under a shade tree, she kept a low profile. She was still licking her wounds a little, still trying to adjust to changes—both outward and inward—and for today, she felt perfectly content to hang out with her mom and Mrs. Whitaker.

She did, of course, run into various friends throughout the day, and each time she did, she found a moment to pull them aside and apologize for the way she'd messed up Logan's party. All were understanding, even Mike Romo, who said, "I know you've been going through a lot lately, with Logan. And believe it or not, I've occasionally been known to speak a harsh word or two myself when I shouldn't." And then he even winked at her! Mike Romo, of all people! After which he told her he knew she'd made the effort to talk to Anna yesterday, and that he admired that.

When darkness fell and the fireworks began, Amy sat on a blanket near the chairs occupied by her and Logan's mothers, quietly taking it all in. *Everything will be okay. Everything will be fine, and you will be happy again.* She had to keep telling herself that, had to keep believing it. And even though she remained pretty far from happy, she still felt tougher and more in control of her own destiny than she had a few days earlier.

When someone plopped down on the blanket beside her, she looked up with a start to find Tessa, who immediately locked arms with her and leaned in to say, "How are you?"

The answer was complicated at best, so Amy tried to give the short version of what had transpired at Logan's after everyone had left. And when she was done, Tessa said, "I'm really sorry you're hurting over this, Ames. But I'm really proud of you, too. You know, Logan never *has* been into serious relationships with girls, and maybe he never will be. But that has nothing to do with you. You're fabulous. And someday an equally fabulous man is going to walk into your life and recognize that the instant he meets you. It'll be like . . ."

"Destiny?" Amy asked, a little sad, but appreciating everything Tessa was saying.

Her friend nodded, then bit her lip, and in the glow beneath the fireworks overhead leaned closer to say, "I'm really glad you're my maid of honor, Amy. I love Rachel so much—you know that—but ever since I came home to Destiny, you've been there for me, and it's meant more to me than I can say."

Tessa's arm remained locked with Amy's, so now Amy reached out to squeeze the hand that clutched at her elbow. "Me, too. To all of it," she said.

And in one way the sweet sentiments made her want to cry—again, for all these changes, all that was getting away from her that she'd never get back. But on the other hand, it also reminded her to be grateful. For all her friends. For other things she loved—like her mom, and her bookshop, and her cat, and this town. Life went on and she would go on with it.

By Tuesday, Amy had discovered that the key to success in not pining over Logan was staying busy. So she managed to arrange a last-minute dinner at Dolly's with Sue Ann after she got off work at Destiny Properties. Sophie was with Sue Ann's ex until later that evening, so it worked out well for her, too.

And since Sue Ann didn't know about her romance

with Logan—and it had been harder to explain her actions on Saturday to her friends who didn't know the whole story, but she'd just blamed general stress— Amy found the dinner even more relaxing than she'd expected. It was nice to talk about Tessa's wedding, and Sophie, and Sue Ann's work, all without discussion of her ill-fated love life making it onto the scene.

When they said goodbye outside the café around eight, the heat of the July day had waned, bringing on pleasant night air, and as Amy meandered back up the street to her building, she thought she might fetch one of her Jane Austen novels and sit on the quiet town square for a bit while it remained light out.

Which was when she heard a fast-moving vehicle and looked over her shoulder to see Logan's car come barreling around the corner of the square, screeching to a halt beside her. She flinched as he hurriedly got out, pointing toward her second-floor apartment above the store.

"What are you—?"

"Smoke," he said. "Coming from your apartment. Spotted it coming out the window from across the square when I was driving by."

Amy let out a small shriek as she spun to look herself. She hadn't seen it before, just hadn't bothered looking up, but—oh God—he was right!

"Don't panic, freckles," he instructed firmly. "Just called the DFD on my cell—they'll be here soon."

But Amy knew that soon was a relative term. While the fire department set literally a stone's throw away across the square, it was after hours, and before a fire truck could come, the firemen would have to drive here from their homes, and that could take a while. Which led to one thought. "I have to get Mr. Knightley!"

She headed toward the outside stairs leading to the apartment, but she'd taken only a few brisk steps when Logan's hand landed on her shoulder, pulling her back. "No way, Amy. We have no idea what's happening up there—you're staying on the ground with *me*. Got it?"

She just looked up into Logan's eyes, because he knew how much she loved her cat. "But Logan, it's Knightley. I have to get him. I have to!" Yes, the thought of losing everything she owned was on the verge of paralyzing her right now, but Knightley was . . . Knightley!

"Damn it, Amy," Logan bit off under his breath, but when their eyes locked again, his softened just slightly, until he said, "Aw hell"—and then he took off toward the staircase.

Oh God. "Be careful!" she called. *And hurry up, fire department!*

Her next thought: Oh Lord, Austen! Because the smoke came from upstairs, but that didn't mean everything downstairs was necessarily fine. So even as she watched Logan head to her apartment, she dug her keys from her purse and scurried to the front door of Under the Covers. When she unlocked it, she feared she'd find smoke billowing through the store, but thankfully, no—things seemed okay down here, at least so far.

Even so, she called, "Here kitty kitty," pleased when Austen came trotting from between two tall bookshelves to greet her. Scooping the cat up in her arms, she nervously rushed back outside, praying silently. *Please let everything be okay. Please keep Logan safe. Please let him get Knightley out. Please, please, please.*

Her heart beat a mile a minute, waiting, trying not to advance into full-fledged panic. Logan had told her not to panic, and he knew about these things, so she should trust him.

Finally, after what seemed like a long few minutes, the apartment door opened and Logan emerged—with Mr. K in his arms!

Without even thinking, Amy lowered Austen to the sidewalk and rushed forward toward the stairs Logan now descended.

"It's gonna be okay," Logan called as he neared her. "No bad damage, only smoke."

She tossed a glance skyward. *Thank you, God!* Then returned her gaze to the man and cat making their way toward her.

When they met, Logan automatically handed Mr. Knightley off into her arms, saying, "He seems a little scared, but I think he's okay. Should probably run him to the vet tomorrow, though, to make sure."

Amy hugged the cat to her, ignoring the smell of smoke on him and now on Logan, too, just so, so thankful to have her beloved kitty alive and well!

"Looked like you left a curling iron on, and that maybe this guy bumped it and knocked it onto the carpet. There's a good size burn, but otherwise, just smoke—it never fully ignited."

"Oh, thank God!" Amy said, trying to take it all in.

"You'll need to wash your curtains and take steps to deodorize upholstery. And I'll borrow a couple of big fans from the firehouse—we'll open the windows and set them up and the place will smell a lot better by morning. You'll want to sleep someplace else tonight, though."

Amy nodded, more relieved than she could say. In fact, she could find few words at all. Only, "Thank you, Logan. So, so much."

Just then, sirens could be heard as several of the Destiny firefighters arrived at the firehouse at almost the same time, portable red swirling lights placed on the dashboards of pickup trucks and on the roofs of cars. As one of the big metal doors on the fire station lifted, revealing a red fire engine inside, Logan said, "I should go let them know it's not an emergency. But I'll get those fans, and bring a couple of the guys over just to double check and make sure I'm not missing anything. It's standard procedure."

But as he started to go, Amy said, "Wait," and then freed one arm from the cat to wrap it around Logan's neck and give him a hug she felt all the way to her toes. "Thank you again. I couldn't have faced it if I'd lost Mr. K."

"I know," he told her quietly, his arms closing warmly around her waist. "That's why I went in. I never want you to hurt, Amy."

She drew back just enough to look into his eyes. "I know that. And same here."

Their gazes met and held for a long, sad moment that threatened to paralyze Amy as much as the fear of fire had a few minutes earlier. Until finally Logan said, "Well, I should, uh . . ." And he withdrew one hand from her, pointing toward where sirens still sounded.

"Of course. Right," she said, then watched him go jogging across town square.

While Logan was gone, Amy put both Mr. K and Austen inside the bookstore. As both cats stood at her feet, peering up at her, she said, "Okay, it's like this. You two are going to have to spend the night together here, so be nice to each other. Use the time to work out your differences. Or at least don't scratch each other's eyes out before morning." In a way, Amy hated forcing that on them, and she hoped being in a strange place with another cat wouldn't freak Knightley out too bad, especially given that he'd already been through something stressful, but it was the only logical place for him tonight.

By the time Amy had locked the store back up, a flurry of activity was descending. Two Destiny firemen, already in full uniform, came to check out her apartment with Logan more thoroughly. And once the all-clear was given, as promised, Logan set up two large fans. She went inside with him, to open windows and pack an overnight bag—but she hurried when she realized how quickly the pungent smoke began to burn her eyes and throat.

"Don't worry," Logan told her, "that'll be much better by tomorrow, and once you do some deodorizing you won't even notice it. And by the way, you can come stay at my place tonight if you want."

Hmm. For some reason she hadn't seen that coming. And though she appreciated the offer, it seemed a lot more dangerous to her than a little smoke. "Um, thanks, but no," she said as she grabbed up her purse and overnight bag and they stepped outside.

Though she often left her apartment unlocked—a habit she'd gotten into from living in the middle of a small town, and on the second floor—Logan took her keys from her hand and locked the door since her hands were full. "Why not?" he asked. "Gotta stay somewhere."

"I'll go to my mom's," Amy told him. "Or Sue Ann's."

As they started down the steps, he said, "But why bother *them* when you're already with *me?*"

And, descending in front of him, Amy let out a sigh.

The truth was, Logan was now her only real friend who was both single and childless, which made him an obvious choice—if only circumstances were different. If only they were still just friends. So as they reached the ground and walked side by side toward the front of the building, she decided to simply tell him what she was thinking. "Because if I do that, we might end up . . . you know, in bed together. And that would be a bad idea."

When he responded by giving his head a cute tilt and flashing a flirtatious grin, it nearly buried her. "Maybe not *that* bad of an idea."

She let out a breath, feeling his words all through her body, most notably in her breasts and in the spot between her thighs. Oh boy. It would be so easy to just say yes. So nice, so sweet, so hot. And Amy had had few opportunities in life to feel so deliciously tempted.

But you have to be strong here. Because you know what you need to be happy and Logan isn't giving it to you. And one more night of heart-stopping sex, no matter how great, isn't going to change that. So she blew out another breath, hoping her duress wasn't obvious. "Like I said the other night, Logan, I'm just not . . . interested in that kind of relationship with you anymore."

They stood on the sidewalk in front of Under the Covers now, darkness having fallen over the town during the time it had taken for the firemen to come and go. Logan gazed down at her, appearing slightly perplexed. "Still? Because . . . ever since you said that, I've been thinking about you and—"

"Yes, still," she cut him off. To make sure he got the message. If he hadn't gotten it the last time she'd said it, maybe it was time to be more rigid about it. And sure, she wondered what he would have said if she'd let him finish—but she'd decided if he didn't insist on telling her that it must not be very important.

Just then, Sue Ann's car pulled up beside them on the street and her window went down. "What's going on? I just got back from picking up Sophie and I saw the lights." Even though it was quiet at the bookstore now, the firehouse remained lit up and open.

"I had a little mishap with a curling iron," Amy said, then explained the situation. "And since I can't spend the night here, any chance I could bunk with you and Sophie tonight?"

"Of course. You know Sophie's always happy to see you. Come on over and we'll make a slumber party of it."

As Amy gave her thanks, she heard a small, "Yay," from Sophie in the backseat and felt relieved that was settled.

"So," Logan began as Sue Ann drove away, "looks like you're all set for the night." But if she wasn't mistaken, he sounded a little let down.

Though she didn't let it sway her, replying only with a short, "Yep, looks like."

After which he leaned over and gave her a kiss on the cheek, which—as usual—vibrated all through her. "Goodnight, freckles."

"Goodnight," she whispered. And she couldn't deny feeling a little sad, but it wasn't about her decision to turn him down tonight—it was about the reason why. She loved him and truly always would, but she wouldn't settle for someone who didn't love her with the same passion.

"So," he said then, shifting his weight from one foot onto the other, "aren't you gonna say it?"

She blinked. "Say what?"

"How obvious it is that I'm supposed to be a fireman, that I was born to do this, yadda yadda yadda."

She tilted her head, thankful for the gentle evening breeze that blew past. "I don't have to," she answered softly. "You just did."

When she started her car a minute later, Pearl Jam was on the radio, singing "The Woman Behind the Counter," about someone who . . . could be her. Someone whose small town predicted her fate. Maybe she would always *be* the woman behind the counter in the bookshop who never quite got the things she most wanted in life. But as she'd reminded herself earlier, she still had so much to be grateful for, and one of those things was knowing that she hadn't sold herself short and never would.

. . . and the day was concluding in peace and comfort to all . . .

Jane Austen, from *Emma*

Twenty-one

"If you need anything, Christy, anything at all, just let me know, okay?" Logan said into the phone. After the girl on the other end agreed, he added, "Take care," and hung up.

Then he let out a heavy breath, ran his hand back through his hair, and leaned his head back onto the top of the couch as he tried to process the conversation he'd just had.

He'd known for a while now that there was one more thing he had to do before he could mentally move on from Ken and Doreen's deaths—and it was to talk to their daughter, Christy. She'd been away at college in Cincinnati when the fire had happened, and she was still there now, staying with friends, because this summer there hadn't been anything or anyplace to come home to.

Christy was an only child and knowing she'd lost both her parents had been just one more source of torture for him through all this.

He could tell she was still going through a rough time, understandably, but she'd been amazingly kind to him, even appreciative that he'd gone to the trouble to call and check on her. But the thing that had affected him most deeply about the phone call was how utterly shocked she'd been to find out he harbored guilt about the way they'd died. "I see it completely differently than you," she'd told him. "I take a lot of comfort in knowing the last person they had contact with was you, someone they knew and cared about."

And—wow—he'd just never thought about it that way before. Because the whole scene had been so nightmarish, he'd never before found even one glimmer of anything positive in it at all. And, of course, Christy hadn't been there—she might have a softer picture in her head of what it was like than how it really was. But still, what if she was right? What if Ken and Doreen also took a little comfort in the fact that it was him, not someone else? And at the very least, to know it brought Christy some comfort counted for a lot. It . . . it almost made him *glad* it had been him and not anyone else in the department.

Finally, he got up, called for Cocoa, grabbed her tennis ball, and walked outside with the chocolate lab on his heels. It was a hot day out, but he wanted to feel the sun on his face. Funny, he'd dreaded making that phone call—he'd refused to let himself think about it, he'd put it off, he'd completely avoided it—and he'd had no idea that he'd hang up with Christy feeling . . . better.

Reaching the dock, he sat down in his usual chair and

gave the yellow tennis ball a toss into the water. "Go get it, girl," he told the dog as she went splashing in. And damn, it felt good to have yet a little bit more of that ugly weight lifting off him.

Of course, a little lifted weight hardly turned his life simple. He still had concerns of different kinds to deal with.

Most notably, Amy. Who weighed on his mind almost constantly lately.

Plain and simple, he missed her. Worse yet, it had only been a couple days since he'd seen her!

And he couldn't deny that it wasn't just her friendship he missed—it was being close to her, holding her, kissing her, being inside her. Part of him still couldn't believe how quickly that change in their relationship had come, but come it had, and he was realizing now that . . . well, it had affected him more deeply than he'd known.

He was still surprised how much it had wounded him when she'd refused to come back to his place the other night after her apartment filled with smoke. And she'd seemed so . . . sure about it, not even tempted. Was she over him that quickly? Was everything between them really finished, done?

He understood her point about wanting a guy who was crazy about her—but she'd hardly given him a chance to even figure out whether or not he was that guy. And now . . . now it seemed like she didn't even care. And that hurt. Hell, it hurt more than he might have anticipated.

As Cocoa shoved the tennis ball into his hand and he flung it back out into the lake, he found himself flooded with recent memories. That moment at Mike's wedding when she'd told him she was his secret admirer—how sweet and frightened and hopeful she'd looked, and how much he'd just wanted to . . . protect her or something. Waking up with her in his arms by Sugar Creek the next morning had felt like some kind of dream, but definitely a nice one. And on the boat—well, they'd connected the other times they'd had sex, but that time, wow. Just wow.

And every time he found himself looking back over the various aspects of their new romance, he was amazed all the more to remember that beyond all these new parts of her he'd seen recently, she was still Amy, still his freckles. He'd just never known, never dreamed, that Amy could be . . . so brave, so adventurous, so passionate, so sexy. And also so . . . tough.

Because God knew he had some regrets about how he'd dealt with all this—and in the end, Amy had handled it like an incredibly strong woman. And maybe that part shouldn't surprise him, but it did. He'd known Amy was a lot of good things before this had started, but he never would have thought she was strong. And that, he realized now, was dead wrong.

Of course, for all her professions of romance and love, she sure had given up on him fast. A thought that kind of depressed him.

But on the other hand, he supposed a girl had a right to want to be pursued. And he supposed a girl had a right to want what she wanted, and Amy certainly knew what she wanted. And a part of him wanted to keep trying with her—but the fact was, he was afraid. Afraid of being in a real, honest relationship—he'd never been in one and he didn't know how. And afraid of ruining what remained of their friendship—maybe forever this time. The last few months had been a jumble for him and he was just beginning to make his way through all the muck and mire in his head, but for now, the one thing he knew for sure was that he missed her. He missed her friendship. He missed her kisses. He missed all of her.

After chucking the ball back into the water one more time for Cocoa, he checked his watch. His shift at the Dew Drop tonight didn't start 'til eight and he didn't have much to do until then. The thought of a long, empty day ahead made him sigh. He was discovering he didn't particularly love working at night, and that he missed coming and going from the firehouse during sunny days when Destiny was bustling—well, as much as Destiny ever bustled. And hell . . . maybe he missed feeling valuable, doing a job he was good at, where he felt qualified.

When Amy's place had nearly caught fire, he'd experienced the instant compulsion to rush in and help. Though it had been stupid of him to go in without equipment, on his own without any backup, taking care of that situation had actually been the most satisfying thing he'd done in a long time. Except maybe for making love to Amy.

Either way, he knew now that he had still more changes to make. Amy was right—he had to pull himself together, get over his fears, and return to the work he was born to do.

As Mike pulled his squad car into a parking spot on town square near Dolly's Main Street Café, he spotted his sister across the way, talking to Logan in front of the firehouse. It was good to see his buddy out and about, and hmm . . . at the fire station, too. He could only hope Logan was doing what they all knew Logan needed to do.

And as for Anna . . . damn, his heart pinched up all over again every single time he saw her. Emotionally, he'd been through hell and back over her and now that he had her in his life again . . . hell, he guessed he'd been holding onto the idea of her so closely for so long that now he just didn't quite know how to ease up.

But as he stood leaning against his cruiser, watching her—stopping only to spare a warning glance to a teenager who went driving by slightly too fast for the square—it hit him that . . . she was an adult now. Not that this was news, but . . . well, maybe the new part was the sudden, clear understanding that he simply had to accept her as that, as an adult. She wasn't his to train or discipline or mold or even to teach. She was already grown up, had already made all the big, important decisions about who she was going to be.

And for a strange, brief moment he saw her, once more, as a little girl again—as the little girl in that white Easter dress in his favorite picture of her. She was so far from being that same little girl now, and yet he loved her with exactly the same ferocity.

The fact was, he knew how to be a big brother to a little girl, but he didn't know how to be one to a grown up woman. And he had a lot to learn. About holding on even while you let go.

He waited as she parted ways with Logan and strode toward him across the square, looking as tall and sleek and beautiful as always, today heightened even more with a pair of the summery high heels she liked to wear. She was dangerously gorgeous, which made him want to beat guys off her with a stick—*but you can't do that. You can't. She keeps telling you she can take care of herself and you have to let her.*

"Thanks for meeting me," she said with a bright smile.

It made him flinch since, when she'd called him to arrange lunch today, he'd been afraid to find out why.

For all he'd known, he'd done something else she found offensive in him as a brother and was going to tell him off or announce she was leaving town.

"Always glad to," he told her, following her to the café's front door, then holding it open for her to step inside.

A few minutes later, after they'd ordered, she plopped the laminated menu back in its holder at the edge of the table and said, "Don't you want to know why I called you?"

Mike tilted his head, gave her a small grin. "So it's not just because you were dying to see your big brother, huh?"

She rewarded him with another pretty smile of her own. "It's actually because I have some big news."

The statement tightened Mike's chest. Especially when it hit him that just because she was smiling didn't mean he was going to like what she had to say. "What's the news?" he asked, wanting to cut to the chase.

"Here's the deal," she said. "A few days ago, I decided to leave. To just pack my suitcase, go home to Indy, and move on with my old life. And I even did it. I didn't tell anybody—I just took off, heading home."

Of course, with every word out of her mouth, Mike's heart crumbled a little more, but he did his damnedest to just sit there and listen and not let his reaction show on his face.

"But something made me turn back," she went on— and he started breathing again. Though he really wanted her to get to the point now.

"And it was realizing that I actually really love you guys now—even you," she said playfully, "and that I'm actually even starting to like this town."

Mike resisted the urge to reach out across the table and squeeze her hand—Rachel had told him she thought Anna found his affection overwhelming—and instead just said, "Well, that's the best news I've heard all day."

"But here's the thing, big brother," she continued, now sounding very take-charge. "I'm staying in Destiny, but I refuse to be under anyone's thumb, especially yours. And I'm getting my own place, doing my own thing."

"Your own thing?" he asked.

"You know my other mom left me some money, and so far, all I've done with it is take time off work and buy the Mustang. But now I've bought something else, too. Do you know that old Victorian house on the hill that overlooks Blue Valley Lake?"

Mike had to think for a minute, but then he realized the place she was talking about. It had been vacant and on the market for years now, and he was pretty sure it was in a serious state of disrepair. But he had no idea where she was going with this. "Um, yeah."

"Well, I bought it. And I'm going to restore it and make it an inn. This town *needs* something like that. And *I* need something like that. And I'll be *good* at something like that. So what do you think?"

It was all Mike could do not to bound across the table and give her the biggest hug of her life. But again, he restrained himself and said, "I think *that's* the best news I've heard all day."

Her response? To narrow her eyes, point at him with one long, tapered finger, and say, "You just stay out of my business unless you're invited into it. Got it?"

"Got it," he said.

* * *

It was Thursday evening by the time Amy got everything back into place in her apartment. As she stood on a step stool, rehanging the freshly laundered curtains in the front window, she breathed in deeply, pleased that everything smelled nice again.

And she felt happy inside because it was a good day in Destiny. Tessa and Lucky were getting married in two days, and when she'd talked to Tessa earlier, she'd sounded on top of the world. She knew from Tessa that Lucky, Mike, and Anna were all picking up their parents at the airport this evening, and she also knew that Anna had bought the old house on the hill above the lake with plans to make it an inn—and she was signing the papers with Sue Ann at Destiny Properties tomorrow morning. She was glad she'd made peace with Anna, and even glad Anna was staying and finding her place in Destiny.

And there was still one more thing creating Amy's happy mood, too. When she'd returned to Under the Covers the morning after the curling iron incident, she'd found her two favorite cats actually curled up in a ball together sleeping! They'd been friendly to one another ever since! And now she'd even moved Austen into the apartment, bringing her up when she closed the shop tonight. She'd fed the cats dinner in two separate bowls, but placed them closely side by side, and a few minutes later had spied them companionably sharing the same water dish. And now, from her spot on the stool, she glanced over to the couch to see Austen and Mr. K curled up there together again—and the sight warmed her heart.

Mr. Knightley had a girlfriend! Could anything in the world be sweeter? She didn't think so.

And then she actually laughed out loud, realizing

that she was an even better matchmaker than she'd ever realized before. *I can even make two persnickety kitties learn to love each other.*

Yet then the first hint of sadness she'd felt all afternoon snuck in. Even cats can work out their differences, but she and Logan couldn't?

Only then she was forced to remind herself—*it's not just differences. It's that he just doesn't love you that way. You've faced it. You're trying to accept it. And now it's time to try to move on.*

And since distractions had been such a big help to her this week, it seemed particularly fortuitous that Tessa's wedding was only the day after tomorrow.

"Oh! the best nature in the world—a wedding."

Jane Austen, from *Emma*

Twenty-two

The sun had just dipped behind the trees next to Whisper Falls as Amy made her way up the white runner that currently stretched down the center of Tessa's deck, soft music from a guitar accompanying her movements. She carried daisies tied with a lace ribbon and felt pretty in the pale yellow sundress Tessa had selected for her bridesmaids. And this time—as compared to Rachel's wedding just a few weeks ago—she really *enjoyed* feeling pretty, embraced it. Maybe she'd always thought that to think one's self pretty was arrogant, but now she understood that sometimes it was just . . . confidence. And if nothing else, her recent experiences had given her more of that than she'd ever had before.

Ahead of her, she caught sight of Jenny and Rachel standing alongside Tessa, and on Lucky's side of the small aisle were Mick, Mike, and Duke. It had made perfect sense that Mick and Jenny got to walk together, and the same was true, of course, for Rachel and Mike. So in comparison, Amy and Duke were a bit of a mismatch, but just like at previous events this summer, she'd found Duke surprisingly friendly and a little flirtatious. And at the moment, she couldn't deny that he looked pretty handsome, too—the man cleaned up well.

Reaching Tessa, who looked beautiful and perfect in an off-the-shoulder summery dress of white eyelet, she gave her friend a heartfelt smile as she took her place beside her. Being Tessa's maid of honor truly *was* an honor for her.

Though even as Amy watched the touching exchange of vows between Tessa and Lucky, she couldn't help being aware of other things around her—or people around her. To her delight, Caroline Meeks and Dan Lindley had arrived together and taken seats in the back row. Anna sat with her parents in the front on Lucky's side. And Logan sat three rows back, with his mother, looking as handsome as ever in a pair of brown pants and a white shirt, open at the collar.

And, of course, she still loved him. And seeing him made her heart beat harder, her palms sweat. Everything inside her felt a little electrified just by virtue of his nearness. And a familiar yearning coursed through her.

But just like every time that happened, she had to remind herself that he didn't feel the same way. She knew he loved her as a friend, and he was even attracted to her as a woman, but if he didn't feel that same electricity vibrating through his veins when she was near, then . . . well, it just wasn't enough.

That was when she caught Duke flashing her a quick wink across the way. The warmth of a blush automatically climbed her cheeks as she bit her lower lip, glanced down. But then . . . then she decided to be brave and raise her eyes back to his. Their gazes met, held. She smiled, just a little.

There was no real electricity there, but life was short, and even though Duke felt dangerous in some ways, in others, he felt bizarrely . . . safe. *Because you know in your heart you could never feel for him what you feel for Logan. So there's no risk involved. No pain waiting on the other side.*

If life were perfect, she would be here with Logan; she would be his date tonight. Later they would dance, and kiss, and make love, and she wouldn't have to worry about what would or wouldn't happen between them tomorrow. There would be no Anna. There would be only her. But life wasn't perfect. So even if being at the same wedding with Logan without *being with* Logan was killing her inside . . . well, didn't she keep telling herself to move on? Maybe tonight Duke brought that opportunity.

Logan couldn't deny it. He felt better than he had in months. Well, not about everything—but some things. One thing in particular.

Now that the ceremony was over, people milled about and he was busy mingling and socializing. But he kept his eye on Amy. Because he hadn't gotten to say hi to her yet. And because she looked amazing in yellow. And because her eyes looked bigger and greener to him than usual for some reason and he thought they pretty much lit up the whole event. He wasn't sure why, but everywhere he went, at every moment, he stayed aware of where she was, what she was doing.

When a trill of pretty laughter sliced through the air, he recognized it as hers, even with his back turned as he spoke with Adam and Sue Ann. When he looked over his shoulder, he saw her with Mike and Rachel, drinking champagne, then reaching to straighten the cake topper on the wedding cake, which sported a bride and groom on a motorcycle. Why did it suddenly make him feel so . . . weirdly left out just to be over here when she was over there?

"Hey, Logan."

He spun his head back around to find Anna, looking like a knockout as usual in another red dress.

"Hi," he said, and they made small talk about the wedding, her parents' visit, and her plans to open an inn. He'd already heard about that since news traveled fast in Destiny, but he acted surprised anyway, and he told her he hoped it would be exactly what she needed to be happy here.

Then he heard himself saying, "I have some news, too." He hadn't particularly planned to tell her, but *she'd* just shared news with *him*, and given that they *had* built a friendship these past weeks and spent plenty of time together, it made sense. And the truth was, he was excited. And wanted to share it with someone. "I got my old job back. I'm working at the Destiny Fire Department again."

Her smile widened as she said, "Really? That's great. Why the change?"

Why the change? The words sank down inside him like a stone. And then it hit him—she didn't know. For all the time they'd spent together since her return home, she didn't know all the crazy, weird, horrible stuff he'd been going through. She didn't know how nutty it seemed to the whole town that he'd left his job to become a bartender. She didn't know about the Knights or the fire that killed them. She didn't know about his dad or that firefighting ran in the family and was in his blood. She didn't know that Amy had been right all along and he just hadn't been ready to accept that. She didn't know him at all.

And it wasn't her fault. He just . . . hadn't chosen to share. Because he hadn't wanted to burden her. But he also hadn't wanted to burden himself. He'd only wanted to run. From things that mattered. Important things. Things that needed to be dealt with. Worked through. And then embraced.

And that was when he realized he was telling the wrong person about his return to work.

And God knew he didn't want to be rude to Anna—but he reached out, gave her hand a small squeeze, and said, "I'm sorry, Anna, but I just realized something urgent I need to do. Do you mind if we finish this conversation later?"

She was gracious, smiling kindly as she said, "Sure, no problem."

Turning back toward where Amy still stood talking with their other friends, he made a beeline toward her, approaching so fast that she, Rachel, and Mike all looked up with a start as he practically skidded to a stop beside them.

"You okay?" Mike asked, a look of dry amusement on his face.

"Never better," he said. And that might have been a slight exaggeration, but all things considered lately, he still felt it was a fair answer.

"Well, I'm damn glad to hear it," Mike said with a grin.

Then Logan switched his glance briefly to Amy—

God, she was just beautiful today—before looking back to Mike and Rachel once more to say, "Would you guys mind if I talk to Amy alone for a minute?"

And even as Rachel said, "Of course not," Logan was already placing his hand at the back of Amy's elbow, ushering her a few steps away.

"Hey, what's up?" she asked sweetly once they were off by themselves. "Everything okay?"

For the first time it occurred to him that maybe he should be a little embarrassed, given how hard he'd fought her on this and how angry he'd gotten in certain moments—but with someone as close to him as Amy, he knew he didn't have to worry about that. "More than okay, freckles," he told her. "I wanted to let you know I worked my last shift at the Dew Drop last night—and I'm pretty sure Anita wanted to weep with joy when I told her. And yesterday afternoon I saw the doctor in Crestview, the one I needed to get clearance from to go back on the job again. I'll be resuming my old duties at the DFD first thing Monday morning."

A light, lovely gasp left her as her eyes widened in gorgeous delight. "Oh Logan," she said. "You have no idea how happy that makes me."

He tilted his head. "Actually, I think I do. That's why it seemed important to tell you before I go spreading the word all over town."

Her vibrant smile was the last thing he saw before she threw her arms around his neck for a hug. And damn, it felt good—right—to have her lithe little body pressed against his, good to close his arms around her waist, good to just soak up all the warmth and tingly sensations it delivered.

But then, that quickly, she was pulling back, ending

the hug. Still smiling, still clearly elated for him—but the hug was over. And he missed it already.

Just then, Jenny came up, touching Amy's arm. "Time for pictures in the yard," she said.

"I'll be right there," Amy told her, then looked back to Logan. "I couldn't be more thrilled, Logan. It's like . . . the world is right again. You know?"

"Yeah—I know," he told her softly. Because he knew exactly what she meant. He'd been trying damn hard to feel right about not being a fireman, but now that he'd relented and gone back to where he belonged, he realized how off-kilter everything had been all this time.

From there, Logan drifted back into mingling—he talked to his mom and Amy's mom for a while, and he got them pieces of cake when it was cut. He spoke to John and Nancy Romo for a few minutes, and then he tracked down Mike and shared the news he'd just told Amy.

"About damn time," Mike said, slapping him on the back, and Logan just laughed because that simple sentiment was so true.

He listened to all the toasts, and picked up on the fact that the only damper on the day for Tessa was that her brother, still serving in Afghanistan, wasn't here to share her special day. But the mood was lightened again when the party was moved to the portable dance floor set up in the yard and Tessa shared the first dance with Lucky in a pretty unusual way—moving to "You Never Can Tell" by Chuck Berry, they recreated the dance John Travolta and Uma Thurman did in *Pulp Fiction*. Logan laughed along with the crowd, amazed Tessa had managed to talk Lucky Romo into such a thing.

As the dancing continued, though, as one song blended

into another and Logan watched various friends and Destiny-ites take the dance floor, something inside him slowly went a little bit melancholy. He couldn't put his finger on why. He danced with his mother once, and also with Amy's, to make sure they were having a good time. And he knew he could be asking any number of girls to dance to keep himself entertained if he so desired. But instead he found himself slouched at a table, watching everyone else have fun, stuffing his face with more wedding cake than he really wanted to eat.

It made no sense to him that one moment he was on top of the world, telling Amy about his return to work, feeling more clearheaded about that particular topic than he had since before the fire at the Knights' house— and the next he was feeling oddly . . . disconnected from this party and a little bit down.

And he no longer thought it was about the fire, or the Knights. He'd finally begun to make peace with what had happened. This was about something else.

But he only understood what it was about—with a startling and almost dumbfounding clarity—when he saw Duke Dawson walk up to Amy and ask her to dance. And when he watched her smile and take the biker's hand.

When that had happened at Mike's wedding, he'd instantly worried for her because . . . well, Duke was just so wrong for her, and potentially dangerous. But this, what he suddenly felt now, went way beyond anything like worry. It was a red-hot coal burning in his gut. It was the muscles in his chest stretching so tight he thought they might snap. It was . . . searing, blinding, heartbreaking jealousy.

And it came . . . with fear. But not a fear of being in

a relationship—nope, this fear was brand new. It was fear that it was too late. That he'd messed up too much. That she really was already over him, over what they'd shared. It was fear that he'd been so mired in his own troubles when she'd expressed her new feelings for him that he just hadn't fully been able to feel it, respond, until now.

But now that he'd come to grips with the Knights' death, now that he'd gotten his job back and knew once more what he was supposed to do with his life . . . damn, now he knew one more thing, too. One more big, huge, life-changing, life-fixing thing. It was the next, last thing he was supposed to do that would make everything the way it was meant to be. And it was . . . loving Amy.

And not just a little. But . . . for keeps. To grow old with.

It suddenly made so much sense.

Amy's description of being in love on the pontoon boat came back to him. *It fills you up. But it also owns you. Makes you feel a little helpless against it.*

And he knew he'd been a fool for not seeing it until now.

And as he sat there watching her smile and flirt with Duke Dawson, who continued to spin her around the dance floor—he realized he had to do something, *this very minute*. He'd already waited too long, after all. And with every passing second, damn, he was letting her get further and further away from him.

So he didn't hesitate. He stood up and walked onto the dance floor. And like once before, he touched Duke on the shoulder to say, "Can I cut in?"

Unfortunately, this time Duke looked even more irritated than he had at Mike and Rachel's wedding. "You're starting to make a habit of this, dude."

"I know. And I'm sorry. I don't mean to be a jerk. But it's . . . important."

Duke just gave his head a doubtful tilt and said with some sarcasm, "Well, hell, if it's important, be my guest." Then he stepped aside.

And Logan and Amy were facing one another. And oh God, he was struck all over again by how amazingly pretty she was. And he heard himself saying, "You're so beautiful, Amy."

She blinked, looking a little taken aback and adorably sweet. "Um, thanks."

But that wasn't what he'd come out here to say. What he'd come out here to say, among other things, was, "I need to thank you. For pushing me to be the best man I can be."

Another soft, gorgeous round of blinking from her—so he just went on.

"You kept pushing me even when I didn't want to be pushed, and without that, I'm not sure I would have figured out where I needed to be—back at the firehouse."

"You would have," she said quietly, surely.

"Maybe," he told her, "but it would have taken a lot longer."

She just shrugged.

And he saw no reason not to barrel forward with the other stuff he had to say. "You're the one, Amy."

He'd never seen her eyes go bigger, rounder, as when her jaw dropped and she said, "Huh?"

"You're the one. The one I want to be with. The one I want to grow old with. The one I love."

"But, but, but . . ." Amy stopped, swallowed past the lump in her throat. Was this real? Could it be happening? She'd had some champagne, so maybe she wasn't understanding him correctly. "I've been so awful, Logan. At least in ways. I was jealous. And mean to Anna. And no matter how many times you asked me to shut up about the fire department, I didn't. I haven't been myself lately. And I still don't know how I could have done some of that stuff."

"I do," he said simply. "It's because you love me. And because I guess sometimes love makes people a little crazy."

She just nodded. Because it was so true. "It just . . . sent me into a dark place at times. It made me feel desperate. It made me feel ways I've never felt and I just didn't know how to handle it."

"I don't care about any of that, freckles—it's in the past. What I care about is . . . do you still feel that way? Do you still love me? Is there any chance you can forgive me for being an idiot and taking so long to figure this out? That we belong together? Is there any chance for us at all?"

Amy could barely speak because she could barely breathe. Because this *was* real. Logan loved her. *Logan loved her.*

"Yes," she whispered. "Of course I still love you. More than anything."

And that was when Logan made the most shocking move of all. He dropped to one knee, right there on the dance floor.

She sucked in her breath as someone stopped the music. Every eye at the wedding was on them. But hers were on Logan. And his gaze was so clear and blue and beautiful even in the dim, dusky light as he took her hands in his that she could see nothing else.

"I know this might seem fast. Hell, I haven't even taken you on a proper date yet—which I regret. But in

another way, it's not fast at all—it's been slowly coming
our whole lives. All along, the girl who used to try to fix
me up with every other girl in town . . . was the one I'm
supposed to be with.

"You've been in my life forever, Amy Bright, and that's
exactly where I want you—but in a whole new way now.
You're sweet, you're beautiful, you're loving—and even
though this might surprise a few people, you're sexy as
hell, freckles. You're everything I could ever want, and
the only thing I don't understand is how it took me this
long to see it.

"But wait—yes I do. It's because I was afraid. I let
myself down in ways in that fire, and I don't know much
about successful relationships and I was afraid I'd let
myself down there, too—that I'd let down both of us.
But now that I'm not afraid anymore, now that I know
I love you, I promise I'll never stop. I'll never give you
another reason to cry, Amy, I swear. I love you. I love
you with my whole heart. I belong with you, and you
belong with me. Marry me, Amy. Marry me."

Amy couldn't speak. She could only nod. So that was
what she did. Nodded profusely. And then finally found
one very important word inside her, which she managed
to force out on a soft breath. "Yes. *Yes.*"

And then as the crowd began to applaud, Logan was
on his feet, hugging her, holding her, and she thought
briefly of all her friends watching this, sharing this
supreme and impossible moment of joy with her even
though she couldn't see them right now. Because right
now she could still see nothing but Logan—she had no
desire to see anything else, and even as they hugged, she
shut her eyes tight, wanting to feel only him.

Soon he began to sway with her, just slightly, dancing

with her a little—until she found herself laughing, and whispering to him, "There's no music playing."

Yet, in her ear, he began softly singing the same song they'd danced to at Rachel's wedding, "You're In My Heart." He sang to her that she was his lover and his best friend. That she'd be his breath when he grew old. That she was in his soul.

As he was in hers.

So many thoughts raced through her head just then. How happy this was going to make so many people. That she would finally be a bride instead of just a bridesmaid. That all her pain and desperation had been so unnecessary, and that she could have seen that if she'd only been more patient and given their relationship a chance to unfold. And that now nothing but happiness lay before them as they began to make a new life—together—in Destiny.

"It is such a happiness when good people get together—
and they always do."

Jane Austen, from *Emma*

Epilogue

*M*eow."

Amy stood next to the trunk of the big weeping willow
in Logan's front yard. Well, her front yard now, too. But
she was still trying to get used to that. "Knightley, come
down from there," she said, fists on her hip as she peered
upward into the branches, making eye contact with the
gray-and-white feline. "You, too, Austen," she said,
switching her glance to the black-striped ball of fur one
branch over. "You two are going to get me into so much
trouble."

A few minutes later, a fire engine from the DFD
rounded the bend on Blue Valley Road that led to the
lakeshore cottage. When it pulled up, Logan stood on one
side of the truck decked out in his full fireman regalia.

"Really, freckles?" he said when their eyes met. "You called the fire department for me to get cats out of a tree again? And at my own house this time?"

She cringed slightly as he stepped down from the truck. "Sorry. But you know how these two are." She pointed upward. "They have minds of their own." The fact was, the two cats had become the best of friends—and where one went now, the other followed. "Knightley got out while I was carrying in boxes, and Austen was right on his tail before I could stop her."

Just then, Cocoa came bounding toward the base of the tree, barking repeatedly as she looked up at the cats as well.

"Oh good, *this* will help," Logan said dryly, peering down at the dog.

Amy gritted her teeth slightly. "Guess *she* got out, too." And actually, since Amy had moved in a couple of days ago, the cats and dog had gotten along fine, other than Cocoa standing around looking perplexed at the sight of new animals, especially ones that seemed unduly fascinated with her tennis ball. "And really, this is your own fault," she pointed out to the man she loved.

He flinched, looking surprised. "It is?"

She crossed her arms. "You're the one who insisted I move in *now* instead of waiting 'til after the wedding next spring."

He just shrugged. "Well, the wedding's a long time away. And I like waking up with you."

The sentiment eased her stance and drew a heartfelt smile from her, even as it made her feel kind of warm and gooey inside. "I like waking up with you, too." Then she pressed her hands to his shoulders through his gear and raised on her tiptoes to give him a kiss.

Someone inside the truck cleared their throat then, however, reminding them both of the matter at hand. "Cats," she said, pointing treeward again.

"Yeah," he said, but his tone of voice told her his mind was still on that kiss.

"We're just in an adjustment period," she told him. Same as she'd told him when he'd complained that she had too many books and movies and suggested she leave them at her old apartment above the bookstore, and she'd refused, explaining that she liked having the things she loved close to her. "But once we get through it, everything from here on out is going to be smooth sailing. I can feel it."

And she really did. God knew they'd traveled a bit of a rocky road to get here, but the hard part was behind them now and Amy finally had everything she'd ever wanted. Before falling in love with Logan, she'd had many things she loved in her life—but he made it complete.

And falling for Logan had brought about another big change in her life, too—since then, she'd given up her hobby of matchmaking. It hadn't been a conscious decision—she'd just lost the verve for it. Even if she *had* made some good matches over the years, she'd finally realized that in every match she'd ever tried to make, she'd really, actually just been wishing for a love of her own.

And now she had one. With her best friend.

Over the past few years, Amy had watched dreams come true for all of her close girlfriends—now hers had come true, as well. And just like the characters in her Jane Austen novels, they were all going to live happily ever after.

Next month, don't miss these exciting new
love stories only from
Avon Books

Lessons from a Scandalous Bride by Sophie Jordan
Miss Cleopatra Hadley goes from poverty to plenty virtually
overnight: her true father is willing to share his wealth *if* she
marries into high society. Wary of marriage, Cleo avoids Lord
Logan McKinney's advances until their attraction proves too
powerful, and her worries dissolve with one passionate kiss . . .

Return of the Viscount by Gayle Callen
Desperation drove Cecilia Mallory to seek union with a stranger,
one who would wed her sight unseen. Bracing herself for an
older, undesirable husband, Cecilia is shocked to find her fiancé
to be quite the opposite—Viscount Michael Blackthorne is
young and devastatingly attractive. What could such a man
really be after?

Night Forbidden by Joss Ware
Bruno emerges from hiding after the apocalypse to find the
world run by the malevolent Strangers. Scouring the savaged
landscape for answers, Bruno stumbles upon Ana, an
Amazonian ocean-dweller. Ana and Bruno are tempted in ways
they never knew possible . . . there's only one problem: Ana
holds a secret that could mean Bruno's undoing.

The Warrior Laird by Margo Maguire
When Lady Maura Duncanson steals Dugan MacMillan's
treasure map, he has no choice but to hold her hostage. After
one look at the handsome laird, Lady Maura has no intention of
returning to her dreadful fiancé, and Dugan finds that the more
time they spend together, the less he is willing to surrender her
to any man . . .

REL 0712